FLIGHT

Also by this author:

Non-Fiction:
Holocaust's Child

Fiction:
The Dead Side
Something About Kate

FLIGHT

THE DEAD SIDE

W.R. BLOCHER

FLIGHT
THE DEAD SIDE

iUniverse books may be ordered through booksellers or by contacting:

iUniverse
1663 Liberty Drive
Bloomington, IN 47403
www.iuniverse.com
844-349-9409

Because of the dynamic nature of the Internet, any web addresses or links contained in this book may have changed since publication and may no longer be valid. The views expressed in this work are solely those of the author and do not necessarily reflect the views of the publisher, and the publisher hereby disclaims any responsibility for them.

Any people depicted in stock imagery provided by Getty Images are models, and such images are being used for illustrative purposes only. Certain stock imagery © Getty Images.

ISBN: 978-1-6632-4851-0 (sc)
ISBN: 978-1-6632-4850-3 (e)

Library of Congress Control Number: 2022922437

Print information available on the last page.

iUniverse rev. date: 12/27/2022

To David B., whose voice inside my head
kept telling me to keep it real.

CHAPTER ONE

They're coming! They're coming!" Debbie screams nearly out of breath as she runs down the path coming out of the forest into the encampment near the sea. Lynne, more than a head taller, is trotting by her side, his long legs easily matching her pace as they covered the nearly twenty-six kilometers back to camp nearly nonstop.

Her screaming grabs the attention of the three sitting in camp chairs around a small fire set in the middle of the seven wood cabins they'd built in a clearing by the river. The forest is on the other sides, a trail leading east to the nearby ocean shore and west back inland.

"What!?" Sam calls back as he and Sarah spring to their feet swiveling toward the pair.

"Where!? When!?" Sarah simultaneously calls out.

George looks terrified as he slowly stands up.

"We caught 'em on top of the mountain last night," Lynne says calmly, as if the race back to camp was nothing. Debbie collapses on the ground, trying to regain her breath and her composure.

"How many?" Sarah and Sam ask simultaneously.

"Two Sergeants, six privates," Lynne says, as a panting Debbie waves a hand in agreement.

"Did you get them all?" Sam asks.

"Far as I know," Lynne replies.

"What does that mean?" Sarah challenges him.

"We killed all we saw. Don't know if there were others we didn't see."

"Did you hide the bodies?" Sam asks.

"Yeah, as well as we could," responds Debbie, pushing her blonde hair off her face.

1

"Couldn't bury 'em," Lynne adds. "No shovel and didn't know if those other fuckers were near. Stuck 'em in a hollow and covered 'em up with leaves and such. Should be good 'til they start to stink."

Sam just nods, suspecting that probably only gives them just a couple of days at best.

"George," Sarah says to the group's cook who is still standing rooted to the ground, his body shaking marginally less than at first. "George!" The sharpness of her voice cuts through his haze.

George just looks at her, fear and despair mixing on his face as memories surface of The Enemy's brutality that most of them had been subjected to after they had been forced into army training camps and the repeated attempts to hunt them down and kill them after they fled.

"Go get the others," she says, gently. He continues to just look at her. "George, go," she says sternly. "Go get the others. Now!"

George nods speechlessly. Turning, he runs toward the beach.

Sarah turns back to the others, picking up her fourteen-month-old daughter who was playing at her feet but has been frightened by the commotion, holding her off to the side of her pregnant belly. "What are you talking about?" Sarah quizzes the others who are in quiet conversation.

"We have to set guards and get out of here as fast as we can," Sam says.

"We need the guards far enough out so that we will have enough warning," Debbie adds, who has regained her breath and stood up.

Lynne nods in agreement. "Can't get trucks over that ridge very easy."

"What about the old logging road?" Sam asks.

"That's overgrown now," Debbie replies. "They'll have to cut down trees and regrade it before they can get any vehicles over on it."

"Good," Sarah says, shifting Judy from her right side to her left, kissing the child's head as she moves her. "It will be alright," she whispers to the little girl who is resting her head on her mother's shoulder, holding onto Sarah's long black hair.

"Okay," Sam says, "we need …"

"What the hell is going on?" Josh yells as he comes striding up, followed closely by Becky and Mary, who is carrying her three-year-old son, Adam. George brings up the rear, his legs wobbly.

"Didn't George tell you?" his sister, Debbie, asks. The siblings had grown up on the Live Side and rescued the others from certain death at the hands of The Enemy just more than three years ago.

"All we could get out of him was The Enemy is coming and we needed to get back here," Josh responds.

"Lynne and I killed eight of them, including two Sergeants," Debbie tells him as the others come up, explaining the size of the patrol they ambushed. "They were on top of the ridge last night. They had no problem coming up from the Dead Side."

"Shit! Did you get all the fuckers?" Josh exclaims, angry but not surprised the barrier had evaporated between the Dead Side where The Enemy operated without opposition and the Live Side which was free of that danger. They all suspected it would happen sooner or later. All were hoping for later.

"Got all we saw," Lynne replies, taking his M-1 rifle off his shoulder, resting the butt on the ground. He was among the original group that fled a camp, stealing weapons and ammunition when they left.

"So," Josh says, looking hard at him, "others may have gotten away." It wasn't a question.

Lynne just nods yes in reply.

"Are the spare sails ready?" Sam asks Mary.

"Almost."

"What does that mean?" He challenges her about the work she has been overseeing that is to provide wind power to move the small ship they have been building during the nearly two years they've been near the shore.

"Another day, maybe two," she replies. "Remember we have to sew pieces of canvas together so they won't by pulled apart in a strong wind. That is hard to do by hand. It takes time."

Sam nods, saying, "Make it one day," provoking a sour look from Mary. Then he turns to Josh. "You're finished with the ship, right?"

"Yeah," he replies, cautiously, "but we haven't taken it out for sea trials yet. We don't know how it will do at sea."

"But it floats, right?" Sarah says, understanding where Sam is going.

"Well, yes …" Josh starts to say.

"And no leaks?"

"None that haven't been patched, but …"

"Then we need to get all the food and water we can on board, and get the hell out of here," Sam says.

"We can't do that!" Josh protests. "If we run into bad weather, we have no idea how the ship will handle. We could all drown!"

"And if we stay here, we'll all be dead, including the kids," Sam says, waving at his daughter who is clinging tightly to her mother, frightened again by the loud, angry, scared adults. "Their rifle fire," he says waving at Lynne and Debbie, "will have alerted the others to trouble. They'll come looking. At least, we have to work on that assumption."

"It's too …" Josh begins to protest.

"We'll stay within sight of land," Sarah says, cutting him off. "We don't know how long it will take those animals to get over the mountain in force."

Josh digests that for a moment. "Okay," he says reluctantly, giving into the force of their logic and the danger they all face. "What happens if The Enemy is there when we go ashore? What then?" he asks, resuming his protest.

"That's just a chance we'll have to take," she replies. "Better that risk than the death we know we'll face if we stay here."

Josh just nods his head, admitting defeat.

"Right," Sam says, "Lynne, Debbie, Becky, Josh, George and I will form two-man" … "Person," Becky interjects – "person," Sam corrects himself, "teams to guard the edge of the woods this side of the house."

"Wait a damn minute!" Sarah objects. "I'm standing guard, too!"

"No," Sam says firmly.

"Why not?" she challenges him, shifting their daughter back to her right side and getting about four centimeters from Sam's face, raising on her toes so they are nose to nose, her dark eyes blazing. "Because of Judy? Adam only has Mary, but Judy has both of us!"

Sam looks at her quizzically. "Ah, are you forgetting something?"

"What?" she demands.

"You're pregnant," he states matter-of-factly.

A look of revelation crosses her face. "Oh," Sarah says as she steps back. "That."

"Yes, that," a little sarcasm creeping into his voice, as he reaches down and gently touches the bulge of her belly. "Are we good?"

"No, but I'll buy the argument. For now," Sarah responds, leaning over and giving him a quick kiss.

"George," Sam says, shaking the small man out of his frozen state, "how are we set for food?"

George thinks for a moment. "George?" Sam pushes him, not being sure his question has gotten through the fog.

George licks his lips, looking around at the faces of what has become his family. "We have enough canned stuff for about a month and dried meat for, say, a bit longer, if we're careful. We can probably harvest a couple of weeks of fresh stuff tomorrow," he says, his voice gaining strength as he talks, getting lost in his recounting of their provisions, "but I wouldn't count on it staying good for very long."

"Okay, good," Sam says. "How about water?" he says turning to Josh.

"We probably have enough containers to carry four weeks or so, but no one will be able to bathe or wash," he announces.

"Wash in salt water," Lynne comments.

"Yuck," Mary says. "That water is cold."

"It's better than stinking each other out," Becky says, smiling. The others chuckle at the thought.

"I know where there are a few more barrels. Could give us two more weeks. Have to wash 'em out, though," Lynne says.

"Good," Sam says, "do that." Turning to Sarah, who has an uncanny ability to gauge time, he asks, "How much daylight left?"

"Four hours."

"Not too late to get some sort of start today," Sam says, thinking. "We should get our own stuff together tonight and start loading the boat tomorrow. George," he says, turning to the other man, "you and I will take the watch tonight."

"All night?" he asks.

"We have to. It's too far to rotate watches."

"When do we sleep?"

"We'll take turns," Sam says. "Get something together we can have for dinner, and we'll head out."

"Okay," George says reluctantly, as he turns to get some food. "Can I bring a blanket?" he asks turning back.

"Of course, you can, silly," Sarah says, cutting Sam off before he can say something sarcastic.

Sam just shakes his head and goes to fill some canteens from the river that flows past their campsite to the sea.

"Who's going to fix supper?" Lynne asks as he realizes George won't there.

"I will," Mary volunteers, "if you'll watch Adam."

"Me?" Lynne says, a look of fear crossing the face of the big man, who has stood up against the worst The Enemy could throw at them without flinching.

"Yes, you," Mary fires back.

"Don't worry," Debbie says, "I'll help you."

"Thanks," Lynne says, looking relieved.

CHAPTER TWO

Why don't we sleep in the house?" George asks as Sam picks out a spot at the edge of the forest for their cold camp, about ten kilometers from the cabins. George is standing just inside the tree line from where he can see the back of the home they all shared about a kilometer away until it was decided the Dead Side could someday come over the mountain that stood between life and death.

Why The Enemy couldn't come over, they have never been able to discover. But the possibility of it happening one day is why they moved closer to the sea and set about building a small sailing ship to escape quickly when the time came.

That time has come.

"Why not the house?" George repeats, turning back toward Sam.

"It may not be safe," Sam says, not looking up as he works to put up the small tent they brought to provide some cover in case of rain. "Now, help me set up."

George sighs and goes to help so they don't have to work in the dark, which is rapidly approaching as the sun slips behind the ridge on the far side of the valley that had provided them with a safe haven. Since moving to the coast, they occasionally used the house when some of them came up to plant, tend and harvest vegetables, wheat or corn, hunt the deer and rabbits that abound in the area, or fish in the nearby lake that flows over a waterfall, forming the river that runs to the sea.

Soon after moving, they built crude but solid cabins for themselves, furnishing them with beds, tables, and chairs scavenged from the deserted houses in and around the abandoned town at the bottom of the waterfall. The town's people had fled or died. Only Josh and Debbie McFarland remained of the people who originally took shelter in the valley. None of them know where The Enemy came from or why they are so intent on killing every living thing. And only the McFarland siblings have memories of their childhood, or even know their last names. The others have no memories from before they were forced to join The Enemy's army.

The only real problem they had building the cabins were the fireplaces they needed for the winter. Their first attempt ended with the cabin burning down. Fortunately, they tested it before moving anything inside. They figured out the problem—mainly Sarah, who apparently was a civil engineer in her previous life, did—and their next attempt was successful.

Eventually, they built seven cabins grouped around a central meeting area with a large fire pit where most of the cooking is done during nice weather. A protected cooking area was built in the late fall of their first year there so George could keep turning out meals.

Sam and Sarah shared a cabin. When their daughter was born, they named her Judy after a member of their squad who was mortally wounded fighting The Enemy. The siblings, Debbie and Josh, started out sharing a cabin, but Debbie moved in with Lynne after a couple of months. Having a woman around softened the big man, making him more approachable and less gruff. Josh and Becky never moved in together, but they frequently spend nights in one of their cabins. George was the only one still living alone. Mary lives with her son, Adam, whom she named for his father who died fighting The Enemy, buying time for the rest of them to escape.

Sam and George had climbed the path by the waterfall and moved to the edge of the small forest that formed the boundary of the open fields which stretched more than fifteen kilometers to the ridge that until now had separated them from The Enemy.

"Why isn't it safe?" George asks about the house as they finish putting up the tent.

Sam stops working and looks at the house, which is rapidly being swallowed by the growing darkness. The house, as well as the barn and a couple of smaller outbuildings, is showing the effects of neglect over the past two years. The house is still in reasonably good shape, although some shingles are missing from the roof and it could use a coat of paint. The barn's roof is beginning to sag, and one of the outbuildings is developing a definite lean.

"I doubt The Enemy is there, but it will be the first place they look when they do come. And if we're there, we'll be caught in the open trying to escape."

"But it will be dark," George protests. "They'll never see us."

"And if we don't see them coming? They could be on top of us before we have a chance to react."

"Oh," was the only response the crestfallen George could muster. "How about a fire to cheer us up?" he asks, brightening up at the idea.

Sam looks at him crossly. "Are all great cooks this stupid or just you?"

"I don't know," comes the plaintive reply. "I don't know any others."

"Me either," Sam spits out. "We can't have a fire," he continues, forcing himself to be calm. "It could be seen for miles. It would be an arrow pointing directly at us."

"Oh." Another crestfallen reply.

"Look," Sam says to George, "we are all scared."

"You, too?" George asks a bit surprised because Sam always seems so confident.

"Especially me," Sam says with a short laugh. "We're all family now. We all support each other. We also depend on each other, especially now. If we are going to survive, we all have to pull together, to get over our fears."

"I don't know if I can," George says dejectedly, looking at the ground. "I'm a coward."

"No, you are not!" Sam says sharply. Then making his voice gentle, "You just have more trouble getting over your fear than some of the rest of us. We'll help you. And we all know you want to help us. In an emergency, we may sound nasty, especially Lynne"—that draws a look of worry from George—"because we may not have time to be nice, but never ever forget that you are family and we will stick by you just like we all stick together."

George just nods, and sighs deeply.

After eating a cold supper, Sam says he'll take the first watch and tells George to get some sleep. George doesn't need any more encouragement for that. He is soon sleeping on the soft bed of leaves they'd gathered under the tent.

Sam looks at him, then stares out into the night, trying to pierce the darkness. Most of his watching is with his ears, trying to sort out anything that is not one of the usual night sounds. After about half an hour of not hearing anything he shouldn't, he relaxes a bit. And that is when his mind wanders back to what he now thinks of as The Beginning—memories he would rather not recall but can't avoid.

The memories start in that graveyard where he came to awareness, not knowing who he was or where he was or how he got there. He can see himself as if he's an outside observer. He sees himself push off the headstone he's leaning against. He loses his footing when he tries to walk, rolling down the hill onto the side of the road. He's lying there, bewildered, when he hears them coming—hundreds of marching feet. The columns of four come swinging around the bend in the road.

One of the Sergeants nearly trips over him. Sam is brutally driven to his feet and thrust into a line with only three marchers. They march for days, are fed just bread and water, and forced to sleep in open fields even when it's raining, maintaining their marching order. All he can ever remember is his first name. Where he came from, who his family was, whether he had a girlfriend or a boyfriend, if he was ever married or had children, and what he did for a living are all lost to him. It is a memory black hole shared by the other draftees, which is how Sam thinks of them all.

Sam's head comes up with a start, as he intently listens to the night. He thinks he heard something. He's not sure of what. He sees a shape moving carefully across the meadow from right to left. He fingers his rifle, ready to fire. Finally the full moon comes out from behind a cloud. It's a deer. Just a deer.

Sam relaxes again. And the movie in his head starts to play again. Finally, the group is marched into a field, and formed into squads of eight. Each squad is given a tent, and each member a cot and bedding. He's in a tent with Sarah, Lynne, George, Judy, Frank, Mary and Adam. They endure a brutal training regime of forced marches and exercises, overseen by the Sergeants, all of whom are male. Sam and the others never see any officers, just the Sergeants. The slightest misstep, especially on the rifle range, brings a savage beating or death at their hands. Desertion meant a slow painful death, not just for the deserter, but for everyone in the squad.

None of them wanted to be there, but none of them was willing to risk an escape attempt. It's all of them or none of them. And while some, himself, and he thought Lynne, Adam, and Sarah, would be willing to try, he had doubts about the others, especially Mary and George.

Things stayed that way, until—Sam's head swivels to the left as he catches a shadow moving across the meadow out of the corner of his eye. He stares intently, listening even more intently. Nothing. Either his imagination is overactive or whatever caused the shadow is gone. He decides it must have been an animal of some kind. His body relaxes again, and he realizes that his watch must be over. It's been at least four hours, probably more.

Sam goes to the shelter half and gently nudges the bottom of George's foot. Nothing. He nudges harder. George grunts and rolls over.

"George!" he hisses.

No response.

"George!" he hisses a bit louder, giving George's foot a light kick.

"What?!" comes the irritated response. "Go away! I'm sleeping! It's a beautiful dream."

"George! Get up! It's your watch!"

"Not now!"

Sam is irritated now. He kicks George's foot hard. "Get the fuck up! It's your watch!"

"That hurt!" George protests. "Did you have to kick me?"

"Get up! I wouldn't have to kick you so hard if you didn't sleep so soundly." The irritation in Sam's voice is obvious, even though he knows George is a sound sleeper who is always hard to wake up.

"Okay, okay," the resignation in George's voice just as obvious. "Any problems?" he asks as he gets to his feet.

"No. It's been quiet, outside of the usual night sounds."

"The usual night sounds?" George's voice has an edge to it.

"Yeah, like the deer."

"Oh, okay," he responds, relieved, as he picks up his rifle to assume his watch at the edge of the woods.

"Leave the rifle," Sam orders.

"What? Why!? You had yours!"

"Yeah, but I'm not likely to start shooting at shadows."

"And I am?" George sounds offended.

"Let's just say we aren't taking any chances," Sam says kindly. "If you hear or see anything, come and get me. Okay?"

"Okay," comes the resentful reply as George puts down his weapon and moves to the edge of the woods.

Sam watches him go. After George has settled down at his post, Sam crawls into the shelter and closes his eyes. His mind, however, is still racing—back to the movie in his mind.

The breaking point came when six Sergeants grabbed Mary when she went into the woods everyone used as a toilet. They dragged her into a field on the other side of the trees to rape her. Raping the women in the camp had become a common event. George, who was sent to protect Mary, came running back to tell Sam what happened. The two of them went through the woods. Crouching behind a large boulder on the other side, they can see the attack's beginning. But they have no weapons and are outnumbered three to one. They were frozen in inaction. Until Sarah came along.

Without hesitation, she went to attack the Sergeants. Unwilling to let her fight alone, Sam followed. George trailed behind, not wanting to fight but not wanting to stay behind. The suddenness and ferocity of the attack caught the six Sergeants by surprise and the trio killed all of them. Realizing that they had no choice now but to desert, Sam gets most of the others from the camp, while Lynne, who came looking for them, and Sarah raid the armory, collecting all the weapons and ammunition they could carry.

While the others were waiting for Lynne and Sarah to return, some Sergeants came out of the woods. Firing semi-automatic rifles, they killed Frank and mortally wounded Judy, who died several days later as they fled. Sam and George returned fire with the pistols taken off the Sergeants they killed, but the volume of return fire from the Sergeants was overwhelming. They were saved when Lynne and Sarah came in on the Sergeants' left flank, ending the threat.

"Sam!" George hisses, kneeling next to him.

"What?" comes the irritated reply.

"I think something is out there."

"Something? Okay, show me," Sam says, rolling to his feet.

The two men creep to the edge of the woods. Crouching down next to a large tree, George points out into the meadow. "There."

"Where?" Sam can't see or hear anything.

"Right there," comes the insistent hiss in response.

"I don't see it."

"It's right there! Halfway to the house, but a bit to the right," George says, his voice rising.

"Shhhh," Sam says, as he stares at the area George has indicated.

"Stay here," Sam orders, as he moves toward the area George is worried about. His rifle at the ready, Sam moves cautiously in a crouch. Finally, he spots the dark shape that spooked George. He kneels and takes his rifle off safety. He doesn't see movement or hear anything. If it's one of The Enemy, he must be asleep. As he eases forward, the shape sudden moves, growls at him and lumbers off. The bear breaks into a trot as it heads away. Sam lets out his breath. He stands, putting his rifle back on safety and goes back to the woods.

"It's a bear," he says to George. "Didn't you see it come into the meadow?"

"I ... I ... I must have been looking in the other direction," he pleads.

"Keep your head on a swivel, if you want to stay alive," Sam orders him, his voice calm but firm.

"Yes. Okay."

Sam grumbles, telling George to get him if he sees anything else, and heads back to the tent to try to get some more sleep. He mostly fails at that, just lightly dosing. The movie resumes.

With Lynne carrying Judy, they flee into the woods, staying off the roads to avoid the search parties they're sure the Sergeants will send out. They find food and some bottled water in abandoned houses that are falling apart from neglect. They also get water from streams. When Judy dies, she is buried in an unmarked grave in the woods to keep from alerting any searchers they had been there.

Eventually, a pickup loaded with Sergeants and soldiers catches up to them, but they are able to ambush it, killing all but one. Becky eventually wins their trust, bringing their number to seven. In a series of running fights, Adam is mortally wounded but lives long enough to hold off the attackers to give the others, including his lover, the pregnant Mary, time to escape. But once he is overrun and killed, the Enemy comes on fast.

They are saved by Debbie, who leads the group to the top of the ridge separating the Dead Side from the Live Side. Josh joined them on top of the ridge where they camped for the night. The next morning all nine headed down further into safety and the siblings' homestead some fifteen kilometers from the ridge. Not knowing whether that would ever change, they eventually picked up and moved near the seashore and built a ship so they could escape.

Sam sighs. Of all the memories he has, the years in the valley and near the shore are the best. Idyllic. He and Sarah became a couple, and she gave birth to their daughter. Now they are expecting a second child.

But The Enemy is threatening them again.

And they have to flee.

Again.

The thought drives away all possibility of sleep. Sam gets up and quietly goes over to George. He's awake but barely—and never hears Sam coming.

"What the ..! Where'd you come from?" the startled man hisses.

"Can't sleep."

"Can I?"

"Yeah. Go ahead," Sam says. George doesn't need to be told twice. Sam soon hears him snoring. 'Good grief,' Sam thinks. 'Does he have to advertise our presence?' Then he chuckles to himself, realizing the snoring is actually quite soft. He settles down to keep watch the rest of the night.

Josh is their savior. He learned enough about boat building from his father to construct the small one-mast sailing ship—fifty-two meters long with a twelve-meter beam, the widest point. The small library in the abandoned town had plenty of fiction books, now fragile with age, but not much else, including nothing on ship building.

Josh was able to find enough oak wood at an abandoned lumber yard to build the hull, teaching the others how to treat the wood so it would bend properly to form the curved bow. The two decks were built with pine, not ideal he told them, but the best he could do. The top deck, the weather deck, is where they will sail the ship and where most of the cooking will be done. The lower deck, protected from the elements by the weather deck, is where they will sleep, and store their personal property and their food and water. Josh found elm trees they cut down and turned into a mast and a boom to create a schooner sail and a bow sprint so they could use a jib sail raised between the main mast and the bow sprint. It was Sarah who devised a kind of crane to lift and mount the mast while their ship sat in the mouth of the river. Steering's done with a tiller.

They have taken out The Hope—Mary came up with that name—just a short distance in tests. Becky found some white paint to put the name across the stern. They had painted the hull black to cover up the tar they used to waterproof the ship. The sea was calm, and they found a few leaks which were quickly patched. But they have no idea how The Hope will handle in rough seas. And they have no idea how rough the seas can get.

All they have is hope.

And desperation.

CHAPTER THREE

Darkness is slowly dispelled as dawn's light filters through the trees, turning the deep black lighter and eventually into grey. Sam starts using his eyes more than his ears. He can see well past the house now as he sweeps from right to left, looking for anything out of the norm.

He swivels around quickly, his rifle at the ready, at the sound of a twig breaking behind him.

"Easy there," Lynne's voice comes out from among the trees. Sam relaxes, and Lynne and Debbie step out from behind the trees. "Thought we shouldn't come up on you without warnin'."

Sam just nods. "Wake sleeping beauty, will you?" he says, motioning toward George.

Lynne looks down at the sleeping man, then kicks his foot hard enough to jolt him awake.

"What the hell!?" George exclaims, sitting upright.

"Rise and shine," Debbie says lightly, smiling down at George, who is looking none too happy.

"How are things going?" Sam asks the two, looking down at the bags Lynne drops to the ground.

"Good," Debbie says. "The spare sails should be ready when you get back."

"Got more water drums ready to fill," Lynne adds.

"We started loading the food and water," Debbie says.

"And the bags?" Sam asks.

"Sacks," Lynne corrects him.

"What?" Sam asks, confused.

"Those are sacks, not bags."

"What?"

"Sacks are bigger than bags."

"Whatever," Sam responds, only a little less confused.

"We thought we'd get what we can from the garden before we go," Debbie says.

"Why don't we do that now?" Sam suggests. "George and I can take it back with us. And if we can't carry it all, you can bring the rest when you come in the morning."

"Sounds good," Lynne says, reaching down for the sacks.

The four of them walk out of the woods and cross the meadow, reaching the four-acre garden Debbie oversees.

As they walk, they all keep a wary eye toward the ridge, listening as well for any signs of The Enemy's approach, such as gunfire.

"We'll need to post a guard far enough out to provide enough warning," Sam says as they reach the garden. "Lynne …"

"No!" Debbie says forcefully. "Sam, you stand guard."

"What? Why me?"

"Sam," she says with gentle quietness, resting a hand on his left shoulder as she looks the slightly taller man in the eye, "you have many fine qualities, but there is a reason we keep you away from the garden."

"You do?" he responds, confused. "I never …"

"Of course, you didn't," she says, stepping back with a big smile spreading across her face. "Sarah and Josh were in charge of keeping you otherwise occupied. And we never ask you for help here. You are the worst gardener I have ever seen."

"You haven't seen many," he protests.

"That may be, but you are more of a danger than a help with growing plants. So, just be a good boy and go keep us safe. You and Lynne are the two best at that. And he knows what and how to harvest."

Sam looks at her and then over at Lynne, who is grinning from ear to ear, then back at Debbie. A broad smile slowly creeps across George's face.

"Fine. I'll be over that way," Sam waves toward the west. He turns and heads out a couple of hundred meters. He looks back at the other three who have begun to work, and then takes a knee in the tall grass, watching and listening intently, but he can't help but be amused by the revelation of the plot to keep him out of the garden.

As time passes, Sam sits down, still keeping a careful watch. His head jerks to the right. Was that a rifle shot? He sweeps the area with binoculars but sees nothing. He closes his eyes, concentrating on his hearing. Silence. Then a fusillade comes from that direction, driving him to his feet, clutching his weapon. As if in answer, more shots come from the center right.

He doesn't need to hear anymore. He turns and runs toward the others. Lynne is staring off to the right, his rifle at the ready. The other two are finishing filling the sacks in their hands.

"Time to go!" Sam announces as he reaches them.

Lynne just nods.

"How close are they?" Debbie asks, as she closes the sack.

"By the ridge," Lynne says, staring intently in that direction.

"He's right," Sam adds.

"What are they shooting at?" George says, almost in a wail. "There are no people out there, are there?"

"You ever wonder why we never saw any animals?" Sam asks.

"Oh," comes George's flat reply. "When they see this garden, they'll know we're here. They'll come after us."

"That can't be helped," Debbie tells him.

"We'll be long gone by then," Lynne says. "Got to scoot."

"But …" George starts to say.

"They won't know where we are or when we were here," Sam assures him. "And we'll be at sea by the time they reach the coast, as long as we don't stay around here worrying about them coming."

George just nods, trying to look confident, but failing miserably.

Ten of the twelve sacks are full. Lynne reaches down, and taking four, throws them over his shoulder. The others each take two.

"Lynne, take point," Sam orders. "I'll bring up the rear."

Lynne nods and sets off at a fast pace. Debbie keeps up easily, but George struggles to manage the pace with a sack over each shoulder. When the others are about forty meters ahead, Sam takes a last look behind him as the gunfire continues and heads off after them.

He hopes what he just told George is right. They would never survive a fight with their backs to the sea.

CHAPTER FOUR

S omething's wrong!" Mary, who has been watching the children, calls to the others when she sees all four guards coming quickly toward them.

Sarah, Becky and Josh pause loading the ship at her cry. Frozen in place for a moment, they quickly recover and head toward the approaching quartet. Passing Mary, Sarah scoops up her daughter. Mary picks up her son and follows.

"Enemy's comin' over in force," Lynne says matter-of-factly as the two groups converge.

"What's wrong with him?" Sarah asks, waving her free hand toward George who has dropped his sacks and slumped to the ground, his head hanging between his knees, his breathing labored.

Debbie glances at him. "Oh, he's just a bit out of breath. We came down pretty fast and didn't take any breaks. You okay, George?" she asks kindly, turning toward him and leaning down.

George just waves a hand in response without looking up.

"See?" Debbie announces.

"How's the loading going?" Sam asks as he comes up, stepping around George and his sacks.

"We're nearly done," Josh says. "Maybe a couple more hours. Maybe less with all of us here. Do we have the time?"

"We should," Sam says, "they don't seem to be coming on quickly, and they'll probably take some time at the house. But let's not push it."

"We should wait for the morning," Josh says, "so we can get help getting out to sea from the land breeze and the morning tide."

"Can we wait that long?" Becky asks, the worry obvious in her voice.

Josh just shrugs. "I don't know, but sailing any sooner may prove difficult, if not impossible."

Sam looks at the ship, tied up next to the riverbank, planks of wood running from shore to the main deck. "What if we finish loading and move The Hope to the mouth of the river. We'll be a kilometer further from The Enemy and it will be easier to sail in an emergency. We can use the sweeps and the rowboat if we have to." They had built four sweeps, kind of like giant oars, which could be affixed to the sides of the hull to row the ship if the wind failed. It would not move fast, but it would move.

"I don't like it, but okay," Debbie says.

"Let's get to work," Josh announces, and then doles out tasks to each of the others, except Mary, who continues entertaining the kids and keeping them calm.

In little more than an hour and a half, the ship is loaded. With Josh, Mary, and George on board, the bow and stern lines are cast off from shore. The Hope is allowed to drift down stream toward the river's mouth.

The rest of them walk along the shore, their attention more on trying to hear gunfire or other signs of the approaching Enemy than anything else.

"What's the name of this river?" Sarah asks, as she walks besides Sam, who has Judy happily planted on his shoulders, alternately pulling his hair and drumming on his head.

"What?" he responds.

"The river," she says. "It has to have a name. What is it?"

"I don't know. You want to know now? After two years living next to it? Maybe Josh or Debbie knows," he replies, rather flummoxed.

"No. I asked them."

Sam thinks for a moment. "Escape River."

"I thought you said you didn't know its name?"

"I just gave it one," he says. "You want the river to have a name, well, there it is. And it is as good as any."

"Why?"

"Because it's given us a way to get the hell out of here!"

Sarah barks a little laugh, then reaches out to put her arm through one of Sam's as he holds their daughter.

"Here, catch the rope!" Josh calls as he throws the bow line to Lynne. The rope's end is weighted with a piece of scrap metal so it will carry to shore. Lynne grabs it; then Sam, Sarah, Becky, and Debbie join him in hauling the bow as close to the bank as possible and then tying the line to a tree. As Lynne secures it, Sam heads to the stern where Josh is ready to throw another line. Except the current has pushed the stern away from shore so it takes several tries before Josh can get the line close enough so Sam can wade out to retrieve it.

Climbing back onto the bank, he's joined by the other four to haul the stern in. The problem is the rope is not long enough to reach any of the trees. They try using the tree the bow line is secured to but come up just short. In frustration, they just look at each other in bewilderment.

"Is there a problem?" Josh calls from the ship.

"Yeah," Sam calls back, sarcasm dripping from his voice, "you could say that."

"You know," Lynne opines, a big smile spreading across his face, "we could just stay here all night."

"That's your great solution?" Sarah says, as she releases the line to go rein in her daughter who is heading for the riverbank.

Lynne just shrugs, a big grin on his face.

As the remaining four stand there, straining to keep the stern from swinging away from the bank, Josh comes up. He used the rowboat to bring a one-and-a-half-meter straight piece of metal and a sledgehammer. "We can use this," he says quietly.

"Where did that come from?" Sam says, a bit surprised by the scrap metal.

"I brought it along. You never know when you'll need a piece of junk," Josh says, handing the sledgehammer to Lynne while he holds the metal vertically to the ground. "Don't miss," he orders Lynne.

Lynne grins as he releases the stern line. The sudden pull catches Sam, Becky and Debbie by surprise. They pull back harder, but the ship's weight and the force of the current, start to pull them toward the river. They dig in their heels to slow the drag, but that's all they can do—slow it.

"Hurry up!" Debbie pleads through gritted teeth.

"Don't rush him!" Josh counters, closing his eyes as he holds the spike in two hands.

"Now, y'all just be quiet," Lynne says calmly, as he rests the sledge on top of the spike and then swings with all his might, driving the spike deep into the ground. "You can let go now," he tells Josh. "Help the others while I get this done."

Josh doesn't need to be told twice. He quickly releases the spike and grabs a piece of the line. His added strength is enough to stop the ship's swing.

Lynne drives the spike a meter into the ground, and then, using the sledgehammer, bends to the very top at a 90-degree angle away from the bank. With his help, the stern is pulled into shore and the rope secured around the spike.

When it's done, they all look relieved.

"That was easy," is all Sam has to say. They all turn and walk toward the ship—and the next problem. How to get onboard? In his rush to get the ship secured, Josh had neglected to secure the boat, which has now drifted from shore and is resting against the ship's stern.

"The planks aren't long enough," Josh observes, talking about the planks they had used further upstream to get onboard.

"We need the boat," Debbie observers. "You get it," she tells her brother.

"Why me?"

"Because it's your fault it's out there," she responds. The others are trying to suppress a laugh, but none of them are willing to get involved in this sibling spat.

"Shit," Josh says, looking around at the others and finding no help. "Shit," he says again, stripping off his shirt, shoes and pants. He plunges into the chilly river in nothing but underwear, swims out to the two-meter-long rowboat he built and swims back to shore, hauling it in with the rope over his shoulder. When he gets to the bank, Lynne reaches down, takes the rope and pulls the boat next to the shore, securing it to the same spike the ship is tied to.

"I don't suppose anyone has a towel?" Josh asks, pulling himself onto the bank. No one responds, or even looks at him as they all try to suppress laughter. He looks like a drowned rat, his slim body shivering from the cold water, with his long dark hair hanging down over his face. His brown beard dripping wet. "Didn't think so," he says, resignation in his voice as he retrieves his clothes and dresses, soaking them in the process.

"Everyone needs to get on board, and we need to rig the sweeps in case we have to leave in a hurry," Josh says through chattering teeth.

"And you need dry clothes," Becky says, unable to suppress her mirth any longer. Josh just gives her a dirty look—the result being that all of them laugh harder.

"Aw, shut up," he says, starting to laugh himself.

As the laughter dies down, Lynne turns serious. "Need to post a guard way up stream."

Everyone just stops and turns toward him. "You know, he's right," Sam says.

"Yeah," Sarah joins in.

"Why?" Debbie asks.

"Because if The Enemy comes down before we cast off, we'll need all the warning we can get," Sam says, still looking at Lynne.

"Me and you," Lynne says, indicating Sam.

"No!" Debbie says emphatically.

"Why not?" Lynne challenges her.

"Because …" her voice trails off. She doesn't have a good reason, just that she doesn't want him to be at risk of not escaping.

"Because you will be needed on the sweeps if it comes to that," Sam jumps in. "You are by far the strongest. You can do the most good here."

"Well, you can't go alone," Lynne protests.

"Right. Becky will come with me."

"Why her?" Josh protests.

"There's no one else. George and Mary are no good for this. You," he says to Josh, "are needed to sail the ship, no one else can even try to do that. We've already eliminated Lynne. Debbie is the best at handling food rationing, and knows more about sailing than anyone but Josh," he says looking around the group. "That just leaves Becky."

"But …" Josh starts.

"I'm going," Sarah says firmly.

"No!" Sam says just as firmly.

"Why?" she challenges, standing with their noses nearly touching. "Because I'm pregnant?"

"That, and because of the baby," Sam responds, quietly.

"One, I'm not that far along. Two, if they get by you and surprise us, we're all dead. Including Judy. I'm going."

"And if we both are killed? And the rest escape? Judy is an orphan. Do you want that?"

"They'll take care of her," she says of the others. "I won't lose you. I'm going. End of discussion."

"But..." Sam starts.

"End of discussion!"

They stare at each other for a long moment. Sam finally breaks eye contact, admitting defeat. He takes Judy from Sarah, kisses their daughter, and hands her to Debbie. "You take care of her, understand? Keep her safe."

"I will," Debbie answers, taking the little girl, who is looking worried.

"We need some more ammunition, and some food and water," Sam says, exasperation still in his voice.

They use the boat to get everyone else on board the ship, then Sam and Sarah get the supplies they need.

"Be back before dawn," Josh tells them. "We can put to sea then."

The couple acknowledge the warning. Back on shore, they tie the boat to the spike and shoulder their gear. Sam turns, just staring at the ship.

"She'll be fine," Sarah tells him gently. "And so will we."

Sam just gives her a worried look.

"Come on," she tells him, "let's go."

They turn and head upriver.

CHAPTER FIVE

After walking for more than an hour, Sarah and Sam stop at the edge of the abandoned town at the bottom of the waterfall, its buildings in various stages of collapse. Its stores had been the source of most of the supplies they needed to build their cabins and The Hope.

They also found clothes—including baby and children's clothes—shoes, socks, warm weather gear, and other necessities that made life easier.

In the years they have spent together the group has become family, depending on each other's strengths, compensating for each other's weaknesses, and tolerating each other's idiosyncrasies.

"This is a good spot," Sam opines about the wooded area they stop in, heavy trees around them casting deep shadows.

"Why not go into town?" Sarah asks.

"If, no, when," Sam corrects himself, "they come down," he waves toward the path leading down next to the waterfall, "they'll search the town, and we'll probably hear them before they even start down. We can bug out without risking being seen."

"Okay," Sarah says, putting down her load. "Do you really expect them tonight?"

"No, you know they never like moving after dark. But if they reach the house and realize that it's been used recently, they may come on fast. Remember, we just harvested the garden."

"Better to be cautious."

"Exactly," Sam says. "Josh wants us back before dawn. So, I guess it's up to you when we go."

"I got it," says Sarah, who has the uncanny ability to know how much time has passed despite having no watch or clock.

"Why don't you sit down and rest," Sam says. "You need to preserve your energy."

"Don't baby me!" she barks at him.

"Well, excuse me for loving you," he says defensively.

"You do?"

"Yeah, you don't know that?"

"I assumed it, but you've never really said it."

"I haven't?"

"No!" she says sharply.

"I thought I had."

"You haven't!"

"I'm sorry," he says sheepishly. "I do love you. And our children. And all I want to do is protect all of you."

Sarah just stares at him for a moment. "I love you and the kids, too," she says patting her stomach. "But I'm not an invalid and Becky says I'm just about seven months along. I'm good to go. I can hold my own. When I'm as big as a balloon, then you can pamper me. Okay?"

"I guess," Sam says, staring at her stomach and remembering how big she got with Judy near the end. "Why don't you get set up here. I'll take a look over the top," he says, gesturing toward the path leading up by the waterfall.

"Why don't we both go?" she challenges him.

"Because," Sam says with a sigh, "if I run into trouble, I will need covering fire if I have to bug out."

"Alright. But I don't like it."

"Noted," he says, slinging his rifle over his right shoulder and heading off on the disintegrating road toward the town. After about twenty meters, he glances over his shoulder and sees Sarah staring after him. She gives him a wave, and he waves back, then resumes his patrol. What he didn't tell her was that it was possible, however unlikely, The Enemy was already in town. If that was the case, he wanted her safe. Besides, someone had to get back to the others with a warning.

He walks as quietly as he can, his rifle at the ready, down one side of the main street, as close to the buildings as he can get. If The Enemy is on this side, they would see each other at about the same time. If they were on the other side of the street, it's a longer shot so there's a greater chance they'd miss. He pauses at each corner, peering cautiously down the side streets before crossing. When he gets to the other end of town, he breathes a sigh of relief. Relaxing a bit, he climbs the path to the top of the waterfall.

At the top, he kneels just below the brow of the hill, and carefully peers over the top. He doesn't hear any gun fire, but in the direction of the homestead he sees what looks like the glow of a large fire, or fires. Hidden by trees, it is hard to see if there is more than one fire, and the massive column of smoke doesn't help.

"Shit," he says under his breath, as if making any noise would bring The Enemy down on top of him. He starts to push on to get a better idea of what is going on but stops at the edge of the woods. About a kilometer separates him from the house. Too much open space to risk it.

He pulls out his binoculars to scan the area in front of him trying to find the source of the fire. Sweeping from left to right, he completes nearly two-thirds of the arc when he freezes. He wipes his eyes and looks again. About two kilometers away, a group of The Enemy—he estimates about a hundred or more—are marching in his direction. They're expecting trouble. They have two point soldiers out, and flankers.

"Crap!" It comes out louder this time, all thought of finding the source of the smoke gone. "Maybe they'll turn. Or stop to camp." It's more hope than certainty. He watches for another five minutes or so.

Convinced they are going to keep coming, he grabs his rifle and heads back to Sarah at the run. He nearly loses his footing going down the path. At the bottom, he sprints as fast as he can.

Seeing him coming, Sarah realizes something is wrong. She is standing, her gear already on, when he comes up. She just looks at him, waiting for the bad news.

"A hundred or more," he says through his heavy breathing, "coming this way. Maybe an hour, maybe less."

"We better go," she says matter-of-factly, looking past him toward the waterfall.

"Right," he says, grabbing his gear. He's moving before he has it on, Sarah at his side, moving quickly despite her advancing pregnancy. The trip back takes them about half the time it took to get to the town.

"They're coming, a hundred or more, about an hour behind us unless they stop at the town," Sam tells Lynne, Becky, Debbie and Josh who are standing on the shore, discussing the best way to get The Hope moving in a hurry if they have to.

"We didn't hang around to find out what they're going to do," Sarah explains, "because if they don't stop, they'll be right behind us."

"This is bad," Josh says. "The tide is coming in and the wind is blowing in from the sea. Everything is against us."

"Don't matter anyhow," Lynne observes. "We got to go."

"The big man's right," Sam says. "Josh, you and everyone get on board, except," he pauses a moment to think, "Debbie. We'll form a rearguard to delay them as much as we can."

"And how will you get to the ship?" Josh asks.

"The boat. Leave the rowboat. We'll take that."

"Why Debbie?" Sarah asks, a challenge in her voice.

"Lynne has to help with the sweeps to get the ship moving. So that leaves her. She's a good shot."

"Bullshit!" Sarah spits out the word. "After you and Lynne, I'm the best shot here. And I have combat experience. She doesn't."

"Look…"

"Discussion's over!" Sarah declares. "I'm staying and you can't make me get on that ship without you. We either live together or die together."

"No, I won't…"

The big hand on Sam's shoulder stops him. "Bro, you lost this fight," Lynne says quietly.

"And we don't have time to argue," Sarah adds.

"Shit! Shit! Shit! Okay. Everyone get moving. Shit!" he orders. Sarah's laughter draws Sam's attention. "What's so fucking funny?" he asks in exasperation.

"You," she says, stifling her laugh.

"Shit."

"Okay, general," she says, a twinkle in her eye, "what do we do now?"

"Pray."

"Besides that."

"We go up the road about a couple of klicks and set up an ambush. When the shooting starts, we leapfrog each other back here. When we're about a hundred meters or so from the boat, we hightail it here, and row like hell. Hopefully, The Hope will be far enough out to sea to be safe, and they'll be so busy waiting for the next ambush that they won't rush out here and catch us."

"That's your plan?"

"You got a better one?"

"Do we get to go to Valhalla or is that just a Viking thing?"

"Just the Vikings," Sam says, catching her light mood.

"Too bad," she says as they head back up the path. "I heard it's a fun place."

CHAPTER SIX

This is the spot," Sam announces after they come around a sharp curve in the path through the forest. "We can see a good distance down the trail even in the dark, and with this bend they won't get a clear shot when we pull out."

"Sounds good," Sarah says. "I'll take the right."

"That's the most exposed," Sam protests.

"Yeah, it is." Her flat response gives no room for argument.

"Okay, but you pull out first," Sam says as he picks a tree on the left to use as cover while still giving him a clear shot down the trail.

"Fine." Sarah almost spits out the word.

"How much daylight do you think we have left?" Sam asks.

"Three hours or a bit more," Sarah says, looking at the way the sun is streaming in among the trees. She finds it difficult to find a position that will be comfortable, finally settling on her left side so she can fire from the right side of the fat oak tree she is behind.

"Enough time for them to reach us if they don't stop at the town for too long," Sam says, contemplatively. "But we'll at least have some darkness to fall back in." Silence descends as the couple each gets lost in their own thoughts. "Let me know when it's an hour after full darkness," he tells Sarah. "If we don't see them by then, they've probably stopped for the night. And even if they haven't, they won't be coming on fast."

"Sounds good. I'm going to get some rest."

"I'll watch," Sam says.

After a while, he looks across the trail. Sarah is sleeping, her breathing slow and regular. He thinks about her beauty, their daughter, their unborn child, and wonders where they will be able to live in peace and safety, if there is such a place. "We're crazy to bring children into a world like this," he says quietly to himself as he resumes his watch on the trail. "What kind of life will they have?" Sarah has told him that having children is a sign of hope, of belief that things can get better, that life is worthwhile. He would like to believe that, but …

The sound of steps behind him, breaks into his reverie. He flips around, his rifle pointed at the curve, ready to fire on whoever is coming around.

He relaxes as Becky appears, freezing as she sees the rifle pointed at her.

"Don't shoot!" she exclaims, her voice waking Sarah, who instinctively raises her weapon as well.

"What the hell are you doing here?" Sam nearly yells at her, both in surprised and relief.

"I thought you could use another rifle," Becky explains. "I'm not the greatest shot in the world, but I can shoot down that road good enough to hit The Enemy."

"Sam," Sarah says quietly as Sam opens his mouth to speak, knowing he is about to tell Becky to go back.

"What?" The exasperation is clear in his voice.

"We could use the help. Let her stay."

Sam is quiet for a moment. "Is the ship moving?" he asks Becky.

"Yeah. Lynne is on one sweep, and Josh is on another on the other side. Debbie and George are on the third next to Josh. Mary is steering."

"Wait a minute!" Sam says, concerned. "With one sweep on one side and two on the other, that's going to push The Hope to one side, unless Mary can keep it going straight, and she's not very strong."

"No worries," Becky says. "The last I saw the others were having trouble keeping up with Lynne."

"Oh," was all Sam could say.

"What about the kids?" Sarah asks. "Who's watching them?"

"Did you know Josh built a big playpen for them on the lower deck?"

"He did?" comes from both Sarah and Sam.

"Yep. Mary put the kids in there with some toys. So, they're safe and playing happily."

"Good," Sarah says. Sam just nods, a bit amused at Josh's foresight.

"Where do you want me?" Becky asks.

"Next to Sarah," Sam says, explaining the plan to leapfrog back if The Enemy comes. "Sarah pulls out first, then you."

"And you?" Sarah challenges.

"Don't worry. I'll be close behind," he assures her.

Becky finds cover behind a tree next to Sarah, and the trio settle down to watch.

"They're coming," Sarah says quietly.

Sam listens intently. "How do you know? I don't hear anything," he says in a stage whisper.

"Exactly. No birds. No little furry critters scurrying around. It's too quiet," she says, recalling the complete lack of animal life on the Dead Side.

"Shit," Sam mutters, peering into the deepening shadows, hoping not to see anything.

"It's late," Becky opines. "Maybe they'll camp for the night."

No sooner has she spoken than a number of bodies emerge from the gloom down the trail.

"No such luck," Sam says in a low voice. "Get ready. Hold your fire until I open up."

"Yes, general," Sarah answers, humor and sarcasm mixed in her voice. Sam just looks at her, a bit bemused, and sees her smiling at him. Then he returns his attention to the approaching figures.

About a hundred meters up the trail, six figures can be seen. Two are walking in front, their firearms at the ready. The others are more relaxed, walking casually behind. One is carrying a canister-fed machine gun. When Sam sees that, he decides that somehow they are going to claim it. The firepower could save them.

The question is how to get it.

He decides to let them get to within ten meters. With three of them firing, even if one is Becky, they should be able to kill all of them quickly. They've already settled on him taking the guys on the left, and the other two taking those on the right. The one with the machine gun is in the middle, with three behind him. 'Guess he'll get a double dose,' Sam thinks.

Sam decides to take the machine-gunner out first. As The Enemy Soldiers approach, he takes careful aim at that one, who looks like he's a Sergeant anyway. Two birds with one stone, Sam decides. 'Where did that saying come from?' Sam shakes his head to clear his mind and concentrates on his target.

When the first two are about ten meters away, Sam opens fire. The machine-gunner drops, the bullet striking him square in the chest. Sam quickly shifts to the front guy on the left who hasn't had time to really react, bringing him down. By then, the others are also down. Sam brings the last one down, rising to a knee to shoot her in the back as she tries to flee. None of The Enemy had a chance to return fire.

The trio quickly emerge from their hiding places, finishing off the four who aren't quite dead yet. They strip all of them of their ammunition. Sam retrieves the machine gun and the two spare canisters, and yes, that was a Sergeant.

"Do we stay here? Get some more when they come?" Becky asks.

"No," Sarah says, "they'll expect us to be here."

"They'll probably try to outflank this position," Sam adds. "Surprise! No one will be here. But that will slow them down. And they won't know where we've set up further down the road."

"What if they just push on through, like they did at the bridge?" Becky asks, recalling the battle they fought as they were fleeing when the Sergeants pushed the soldiers over the bridge spanning a deep ravine, regardless of casualties, and even killing those who tried to retreat.

"They could overrun us easily," Sam says, contemplating the problem.

"We wouldn't stand a chance in this terrain," Sarah points out.

"It's time we bug out," Sam announces.

"How long before they come to find out what happened?" Debbie asks.

"Depends on how far away they are and how curious they are. That Sergeant didn't have a radio, so they'd have to send out another patrol, but this one will come heavy," Sam replies, analyzing the situation for his own benefit as much as answering the question. "Let's not find out. Sarah, take point. I'll be rear guard. Let's move and move fast."

"They'll come fast," Sarah predicts as she sets a fast pace back to where the rowboat has been left. Sam periodically stops and listens, relieved to hear nothing but their own boots crunching on the debris scattered across what had once been a road.

It is fully dark when the two women emerge into the clearing where the boat is tied up. Sam is trailing about fifty meters behind. He stops to listen for anyone following. This time, he hears feet. And they're coming fast.

"Damn, she was right," he says out loud about Sarah's prediction. He turns and runs toward where Sarah has pulled the boat into shore. Becky is already in and the oars are in their locks.

"They're right behind me," Sam tells Sarah in a low voice.

She glances past him and then, without a word, gets into the boat.

Getting in right behind her, he tells her to cast off the line tied to the bow. "You two row, I'll guard the rear," he says, relieved to have the power of a machine gun, not just a rifle.

The oars are not muffled. The noise they make as the boat is rowed sounds incredibly loud to all three of them.

"I hope the ship is out of the river by now," Sarah says, as she pulls hard on her oar. It takes a few strokes for the two women to get in sync so the boat will go straight, but they sort themselves out and are soon making good speed down the river.

They haven't gotten far when the sound of rifle fire and the sight of muzzle flashes pointing in their direction erupt from shore.

"They're firing blind," Sam says. "They can hear these damn oars but don't know where we are for sure." He gets the machine gun ready, bracing the tripod on the boat's side. The Enemy hasn't reached the riverbank yet. As long as they are further back, their fire will be high since the river is half a meter below the edge of the bank.

Sam keeps a close watch on the bank, looking for the silhouettes that will be his targets. If he has trouble seeing them against the dark background, their muzzle flashes will give them away. The trouble is, when he opens fire, he'll give their position away. He decides to wait until The Enemy fixes their position.

While he's thinking about this, he realizes the oars aren't making any noise. He turns to look at Sarah. She and Becky have stopped rowing, just using the oars to steer.

"The tide is going out," Sarah says quietly. "Between that and the current, we are making pretty good speed. No noise."

Sam just nods and goes back to watching the bank. The firing has stopped. In the darkness, The Enemy can't find a dark boat on dark water.

He lets out the breath he has been holding, but keeps his concentration focused on the shore. He worries they can be seen even in the dark, and The Enemy is laying a trap for them down river. He glances at Sarah, who is also studying the bank intently.

The voices a bit down river from them draw all three's attention.

"Sergeant! What's that?" a voice calls out about one hundred meters down river.

"Where, worm?" comes the reply from a voice out of the dark.

"There! Near the end of the river!"

Silence for a moment.

"All you worms, on me!" The sound of running feet head down stream.

"Fuck!" Sam says, as he looks down river where he can dimly see The Hope nearing the river's mouth. They won't be safe until they are out to sea, out of rifle range.

"We have to help them!" Sarah says, the intensity clear in her voice. "Start rowing! Row hard!" she tells Becky. Immediately, the boat jumps forward propelled by the two women, kept in sync by Sarah's cadence. Sam checks the machine gun. He can't start firing until he has targets—and he won't have targets until The Enemy starts firing. Or until he hears sounds from the bank, then he can just spray the area.

All three of them know there is no one on The Hope who can really return fire, so if they are to survive, the trio in the boat have to become the target. Sam just hopes they are past The Enemy when the firing begins so Sarah isn't directly in the line of return fire. At least The Enemy hasn't changed, Sam realizes from the way the Sergeant talked. That means the Soldiers are motivated by fear. And that means they won't be as enthusiastic when they come under fire from a machine gun.

He hopes.

The minutes drag by, seeming like forever. Sam glances down river. They are closing on The Hope which is just about to emerge from the river. Just then the left bank down close to and on the beach erupts in rifle fire.

A target.

Sam shifts so that his weapon is pointed down river at the muzzle flashes, and opens fire, spraying bullets in an arc. The firing abruptly stops amid screams of pain and fear.

Sam also stops firing.

"Why'd you stop?" Sarah pants between strokes.

"Don't stop!" Becky says at the same time.

"I'm hoping that they haven't pinpointed us. Keep rowing hard! Our only chance now is to get out of here as fast as we can!" He feels the boat jump forward as the oars are worked even harder, none of them caring about the noise they make now. Sam is counting on having created enough commotion on the shore to distract The Enemy from the noise.

He hears shouting from the shore but can't really make out what is being said among the screams and sounds of panic. Then a spattering of firing resumes—behind them toward the opposite shore.

"They must think we're over there," he says under his breath, relieved the firing is wide of the mark.

More firing breaks out, this time in the direction of The Hope. Sam aims and lets off a long burst at those muzzle flashes, realizing he is giving away their position. He sweeps the bank with suppressing fire, knowing from the reaction that he has scored at least some hits. 'Those fuckers are still sloppy,' he thinks with satisfaction.

The firing at the opposite bank stops amid some shouted commands, and then resumes in their direction, mostly high but some coming uncomfortably close. Sam swings the machine gun in that direction and opens fire with a series of short bursts at the muzzle flashes. Some of the flashes stop, but others keep spitting out bullets. Then The Enemy downstream starts firing in their direction, again most of the rounds going wild, but a few close enough for Sam to hear them flying by.

"Uhhhh!" Sarah cries as the boat jerks to the left.

"Sarah!" Sam cries as he stops firing and starts moving in her direction.

"Keep firing!" she orders him, as she resumes pulling hard on the oar. "It's only a scratch! I'm fine! Now shoot the bastards!"

Sam hesitates for moment, and then resumes firing at the muzzle flashes that stretch for about two hundred meters up the river from the ocean. He fires in short bursts up and down The Enemy's firing line, praying his muzzle flashes don't improve their accuracy.

As they near the river's mouth, The Enemy's fire starts to become more accurate. Sam figures that they won't make it the last few meters to the sea when rifle fire erupts from the stern of The Hope, which has cleared the river. It's accurate and fast. 'Lynne and Debbie. It has to be,' Sam thinks. Their fire draws some of the attack away from the boat.

The boat passes the river's mouth. Sam sweeps the shore where the attackers are closest, but also maintains some fire further upriver. As they reach The Hope, they pull along the port side, still in the line of fire from the beach, but it allows Sam to keep up his suppressing fire.

"Sarah's hit!" Becky yells.

"How bad?" Josh says.

"Not bad at all," Sarah replies matter-of-factly. "Just a flesh wound."

Josh throws a line down to secure the boat to the ship. Lynne has gone back to the port sweep, and with two others on one of the starboard sweeps, The Hope begins to pick up some speed, helped by the outgoing tide and freshening wind, which catches the partially raised main sail.

First Debbie, then Sarah climbs up the rope ladder that's thrown down to them, while Sam keeps firing short bursts at the shore in answer to the rifle fire coming at them. When the women are up, Sam swarms up the ladder to the deck, turns around quickly, and resumes firing.

"Might as well stop," Josh tells him. "We're far enough out now. Their fire isn't even close anymore."

Just then a bullet whizzes between them.

They look at each other a moment. "Better keep your head down," Sam opines.

"Do you think they'll come out after us?" Debbie asks.

"Where's Sarah?" Sam says, a bit of panic in his voice. "How bad is it?" He looks around. Seeing her and Becky, the group's medic, on the far side of the deck, he strides over to them. "How bad?" he demands.

"Just a flesh wound," Becky says as she finishes bandaging Sarah's right arm.

"You sure?"

"Yes, she's sure," Sarah snaps, watching as Becky finishes bandaging her. "It just took some meat off. Didn't hit the bone or any arteries, so I'm good. How's Judy?" she says, directing that question to Mary who's come up onto the deck. She'd gone below to check on the children after George took over tiller duties from her.

"The kiddies are fine," Mary replies. "They're playing happily below. They couldn't really hear the gunfire so they didn't get scared."

"Good," Sarah says, standing up. "Guess I'll need a new shirt," she says, fingering the torn, bloody sleeve.

"Come on," Josh says, "the wind is picking up. We can hoist the sails."

"You stay put," Sam tells Sarah. "You can't help with that arm."

"Yes, I can," she replies. "See?" she says, demonstrating by rotating her arm—the pain stopping her midway. "Okay, I'll steer. I can do that with one arm."

"What about a new shirt?" Sam asks.

"It can wait," she says, taking the tiller from George, telling him to help with the sails.

The sweeps are secured and soon the main sail is fully up. It catches the wind, propelling the ship at about ten knots instead of the two or three it had been moving at. When the jib goes up, it billows out, adding five knots to their speed, heeling the ship over a bit to starboard.

Josh takes over the tiller from Sarah, who's in obvious pain trying to control the ship, which she wasn't sure how to do anyway.

Ducking under the main boom, which is a meter and a half off the deck, Sarah goes to Sam. Looking back at Josh, she says, "We have some OJT ahead of us."

"You've got that right," Sam says about the 'on the job training' they all need on sailing the ship, while trying to study her wound in the dark gloom of night. "Will you go below and rest now?"

"Okay," she says as she heads toward the ladder leading down.

CHAPTER SEVEN

They all are gathered on the fantail at the stern of The Hope in the early morning light, watching the land that had been their home disappear in the distance. The green haze to port is the only indication of where the sea ends. Sarah has changed her shirt and is holding Judy with her good arm. Adam's playing at his mother's feet.

"So, now what?" Becky asks, watching the land slip away.

"We never really talked about that, did we?" Debbie says, absentmindedly.

"No," Sam says, just as absentmindedly.

"Guess we better," Lynne opines.

"Does anyone know how to sail this thing?" Sarah asks, almost as an afterthought. "Outside of Josh," she adds quickly, forestalling any objection.

"I'm not that good at it," he says, watching the sails and tacking the ship to keep them filled.

"That's comforting," Sam says.

"He's better than he lets on," his sister asserts.

"That's good," Sarah says, "since none of the rest of us have a clue."

"I don't know how to navigate," Josh says defensively. "And even if I did, we don't have the equipment we would need."

"What do they call it? Dead reckoning?" Sam says.

"I don't like the word 'dead'," George quips.

"Well," Sam answers, "we're not dead, yet. The question is where do we go from here. Any suggestions?"

Silence.

Everyone just looks at each other. No one has a clue.

"Well," Sam says, sighing, "since we don't know how to navigate and we have no clue what's out there," he says waving toward the ocean to starboard, "or how big it is, we probably ought to stay within sight of land."

"What about The Enemy?" Debbie asks.

"Yes, what about The Enemy," Sam says. It's a statement, not a question.

"We don't really know, do we?" Sarah says. "Are they everywhere? Or just where we left?"

"We can't stay at sea forever," Josh points out. "Sooner or later, we'll have to go ashore for water and food."

"We can help that by fishin'," Lynne says.

"True," Sam says, "but Josh is right. Sooner or later, we'll have to go ashore. And we have no idea what we'll find."

"Will we ever be able to find a home?" Mary says, starting to cry, tears rolling down her face. She snatches up Adam and holds him closely, making the little boy squirm.

"We'll find a place," Sarah tells her reassuringly. "We have to. For the kids' sake."

"Promise?"

"Promise."

"For right now," Sam says, "let's just keep heading north. Can we," he says, turning to Josh, "get out of sight of land and still find our way back?"

"We should," he says, "we have a compass. Why do you want to?"

"In case we're being tracked from shore," Sam says, scanning the green haze on the port side.

"Gotcha," Josh says, understanding where Sam is going with this thought. "Why don't we turn south for a bit, then head out to sea, before turning back north?"

"Do it," Sam says.

"Right," Josh says, "let's bring the jib down for now." When that sail is down—the work is sloppy and halting, but it gets done—the ship slows noticeably but keeps plowing through the water.

"By the way," Debbie says, "why are we headed north?"

The others just look at each other.

Finally Josh replies, "We have to be headed in some direction and that just happened to be the way we got the best speed with the wind behind us."

"Oh," Debbie replies. The rest just accept the explanation because no one really has another answer.

Josh pushes the tiller over, bringing The Hope around onto a southerly course. He holds that for about an hour, then heads out to sea. When the land has disappeared over the horizon, he reverses course, to a northerly heading.

While he is doing this, Josh is explaining to the others how to sail the ship—how to handle the tiller, how the sails interact with the wind, how to turn the ship so the sails stay full, to watch out for the boom on the main sail so as not to get hit when it swings across the deck, and when the jib can be used. Once they are back heading north, he gives each one a turn at the tiller, explaining how to use it and how to stay on course.

"Josh," Sam says, "you're the captain of this vessel. You get us organized."

"Okay," he says, pausing for a moment. "Someone needs to be on the tiller twenty-four/seven." He pauses again. "There're eight of us. We'll divide into four watches, two to a watch. That way, one person can be on the tiller and get a break from the other. And if something happens, the second person can get the rest of us."

"How long is each watch?" Becky asks.

"Ohhh, let's say, four hours?" Josh says.

"Is that a question or a statement?" Sarah asks, almost laughing.

"A statement. It's a statement," Josh replies, regaining his composure.

"Why four hours? That's a long time," George says.

"That's a fair question," Sam says. "Why four hours?"

"Ummm, two's too short. Six is too long," Josh says with a shrug.

"There's your answer," Sam says, turning to George.

"If you have the night watch, when do you sleep?" George asks.

"When you get off watch," Josh says, a bit perplexed by the question with an obvious, to him, answer.

"Oh, okay," George says, somewhat mollified but feeling completely out of his depth on a ship.

"I think we can run the jib back up," Josh says. "Want to try it without me?"

"Got it," Lynne says, heading forward, with Sam close behind. Debbie and Becky follow him. After hesitating for a moment, Sarah hands Judy to Mary, and follows the others, telling George to come along. He reluctantly follows.

"You know I can't swim," he unhappily tells Sarah's back.

"Then don't fall overboard," she says. "But if you do, we'll fish you out."

As they reach the others, Lynne and Sam are hauling up the jib under Debbie's directions. Becky's body language says she's anxious to help, but since she can't find an entry point, she has to content herself with watching. Sarah and George arrive too late to help.

With the jib up, they head back to the stern, proud of their success.

"Good job," Josh says. Then he divides them into watches, putting Lynne with Mary and Sam with George. He sees Mary and George as the two weak links. Sarah and Debbie are paired, while Josh puts Becky on his watch.

"I could say something, big brother, about how you divided up the watches," Debbie says. "But I won't."

"What are you talking about?" Josh replies, perplexed. He looks around at the others, most of whom are trying to hide smiles, except for George, who just looks confused. "No! Being together has nothing to do with it," he protests. "I'm just trying to balance the watches; match the strong with the weak."

"And which am I?" Becky asks, her eyebrows raised, a small smile on her lips.

"You?" Josh replies, realizing he has just walked into a trap of his own making. "Sam, George, take the first watch," he orders, turning bright red.

"Sure," Sam says, laughing as he heads for the tiller. Then he stops, and turns to George, "Take the tiller, George."

"Why me?"

"You need the practice."

George accepts that logic, replacing Josh, who gives him another quick lesson on how to watch the sails, and to make sure the wind stays in them.

"Any questions?" he asks when he's done.

"Yes," comes George's tentative reply. "What if I screw up? I can't swim."

Josh just laughs. "We'll give you swimming lessons first chance we get. And don't worry about screwing up, the worst that can happen is you lose the wind. And that we can fix real easily. Just watch the compass," he says, tapping the instrument affixed to a wooden stand in front of the tiller. Just keep the needle pointing in the general direction of north. Understand?"

"Yes. How will I know when my watch is finished?"

"Good question," Josh says, perplexed himself, turning to Sam who has been watching the whole time.

"Sarah will let us know," he says. Then turning forward he yells, "Sarah, let us know when four hours are up."

"Will do," she says, waving back from the railing where she is holding her daughter, talking to her about the sea. Judy is just starring wide-eyed at the small waves flowing by.

The day passes quietly but busily as Josh repeatedly runs the members of his crew through drills for raising and lowering sails, and tacking against a northerly wind so they can keep traveling in the direction they want to go.

As night falls, everyone but Sam and George, who are back on watch, goes below to sleep. The jib has been taken down for the night as a precaution against strong winds coming up so everyone one can sleep.

Well into the watch, George asks Sam if their four hours is up.

"I don't know," comes the reply from Sam, who is handling the tiller. The wind has shifted to the northeast, which means the novice helmsman has to put his full attention on tacking the ship so they stay reasonably on course.

"What about now?" George asks a few minutes later. "I'm tired."

"What?" comes the distracted reply.

"What about now? Is our watch finished?"

"How the hell am I supposed to know! Do I look like a timekeeper? Do I have a watch?" As soon as the words are out of his mouth, Sam knows he has made a mistake. In the gloom, he sees George's shadowy figure disappear to the deck below. "Shit," Sam says out loud, realizing what is about to happen. "I'm dead. Or he is. Or both of us."

Stumbling around in the dark below deck, George trips over a prone form.

"What the fuck?!" comes Becky's irritated cry.

"Sorry," George whispers, as he nearly falls over the sleeping form of Lynne. Fortunately for him, Lynne is a deep sleeper. All the minor collision does is prompt the big man to mumble something and roll over.

Without further mishap, George finally reaches the play pen area where the two mothers are sleeping with their children. He kneels down beside one figure, and gently shakes her shoulder.

"Hmmm? What?" comes the sleep reply from Mary.

"Oh, sorry, go back to sleep," George says hurriedly.

"Hmmmn."

He scoots over to the other form. In the dark, he can't tell head from feet because Sarah is completely covered by the blanket as her body is wrapped around her daughter.

Finally working up his courage, George goes for a spot about mid-point on the theory, and fervent hope, that he will either be touching her knee or shoulder. Anything in between could prove dangerous.

It turns out to be Sarah's knee.

"Sarah," he whispers.

No response.

"Sarah," he says just a bit louder.

"Go away," comes the irritated reply.

"Is it four hours yet?"

"Go away!"

"Is it time to change watches?"

No response.

"Sarah?"

No response.

"Sarah?" comes the increasingly desperate question.

"If you like living, you'll leave. Now!"

George swallows hard. Carefully retracing his steps, this time without tripping over anyone, he heads back up to the main deck.

"Well?" Sam asks, amusement in his voice.

"She wouldn't tell me," comes the dejected response.

"She did let you live. That's something," Sam says, unable to suppress a laugh.

"But how are we supposed to know when our watch is finished?" George says. "I'm exhausted."

"Don't worry about it. The watches will change when they change. It's all guess work for us. And I'm tired, too."

George walks forward, grumbling and yawning at the same time.

Sometime later, at the first hint of dawn, Lynne and Mary come up on deck to assume the watch.

CHAPTER EIGHT

L and! Land! We see land!"

Debbie's call brings everyone onto the weather deck in the morning light. The sun is just over the horizon to their east. To the west, they can see forest along a shore.

Sarah has the tiller and is staring at the compass which is still pointing generally north. "I'm not sure what's going on," she said. "We've been headed north the whole time."

"Don't worry about it," Josh assures her. "Either the current pushed us west or the land juts out east here. Or both."

"What do you want to do?" Lynne asks no one in particular.

Sam says, "It's been, what, five days since we sailed?"

"Are you saying we should go ashore?" Becky asks.

"Not all of us," he replies. "We can sail close to the beach and two or three of us can scout the area. Try to figure out if it's safe. Maybe find some fresh water or fresh meat."

"Who's going?" Josh asks.

"Me, Lynne," Sam says, pausing a moment, "and Debbie. We're the best shots."

"I'm a better shot," Sarah protests.

"You're staying, and I'm not going to argue with you this time," Sam says, almost harshly. "You're carrying our future. You can't be risked."

"That's bullshit! Yes, I'm pregnant, but that doesn't mean I can't still do my part for our survival."

Sam shrugs. "You're not going."

Sarah accepts defeat, this time, but she scowls at Sam, and he knows he is in trouble.

"Put the tiller over," he tells her, "and gets us near shore."

Glowering, Sarah steers The Hope toward the beach. As they near the shore, they pull the jib down, then crowd the forward railing, scanning for any trouble. Sam slowly pans along the shore with the binoculars looking for signs of life. He doesn't see any.

"I don't like it," Mary says. "I don't even see any birds. Shouldn't we be seeing birds? I don't think you should go. Let's get away from here."

"You might be right," Sam says, lowering the binoculars. "But it's early. Maybe the birds aren't up yet."

"You better be careful," Josh says.

"We will be," Debbie says.

"Let's do this," Josh suggests. "I'll go in with you. Someone will stay with the boat just off the shore. That way if there's trouble, we can make a fast getaway."

"Good idea," Sam says, "but George will go instead.'"

"Why?" the question comes simultaneously from George and Josh.

"Because Josh is needed to handle the ship. He's not expendable," comes the matter-of-fact reply.

"And I am?" George asks.

"Not any more than me, Lynne and Debbie," Sam says with a snort. "Josh is just less expendable than the rest of us."

"Pull the boat in," Josh tells George, who unhappily accepts the logic. He goes to the stern and starts to pull in the rope tied to the bow of the rowboat, which has been towed behind the ship. The others are transfixed by the approaching shore, searching for clues about whether it's safe.

"It's in. What do you want me to do with it?" George asks.

Josh looks at him. "Get it on the port side. We'll put the ladder down to it."

"Okay," he says. As he starts to move, he stops. "Which is the port side?"

"That one, left of the bow," Josh says, pointing to the left side of the ship facing the front.

"Right," George says, starting to pull the boat around again. As he walks it forward, he watches the shore along with the others, wondering what dangers lurk out of sight. "I don't like this."

"I don't either," Sam says. The response makes George realize he had spoken out loud.

"Then why are we doing it?" George asks.

"To find out if The Enemy is this far north," Sam replies.

"Perhaps they started here," Mary observes, cutting Sam off before he can finish his thought.

"Perhaps they did," Debbie agrees. "But it doesn't really matter where they started, just where they are now."

"We should also try to get some more fresh water," Sam says, as if he was just continuing his comment. "If we can't stay here, and I don't think we can, we don't know how long we'll be at sea. We don't want to run out of water and be forced to land where The Enemy is thick."

"If they aren't here, why can't we stay?" Mary asks. "I like being on land where the floor isn't moving." That comment provokes a communal laugh.

"The problem," Sam says, still chuckling, "is that even if The Enemy isn't here, we don't know if and when they might show up. We need to try to find a place where we can be safe for a long time."

"Like an island?" Becky asks.

"Like an island," Sam agrees.

"Get ready to lower the main sail," Josh says. "We can run in the rest of the way with the tide."

They all now know what to do. Each goes to the area they have been assigned, and soon the sail is smoothly lowered, and tied to the boom.

"Sarah," Josh says, "bring us to starboard, parallel to the shore."

"Gotcha," she says, pulling the tiller over so the ship is now broadside to the beach.

"Can you keep this distance from shore?" Sam asks Josh. "We can't afford to run aground, and I sure as hell want you here when we get ready to return."

"We'll use the sweeps," Josh says. "The current is weak, so it shouldn't be a problem."

"Good," Sam says. "Sarah, have the machine gun ready. If we have to come back in a hurry, I don't want to get shot."

She looks at him sideways for a moment. "I'll miss the others," she says dryly.

Sam glances at her and smiles. "You do that."

"I will," she says, motioning to Mary, who has already put the children in their playpen, to take the tiller.

"Let's go," he says to the other three who are going ashore.

Josh throws the ladder down to the boat. The first one down is Sam, who swings over the side and then, holding onto the rope sides, carefully descends on the wood slats. When he is down, he steadies the boat next to the ship as the other three clamber down.

After they are all in, Lynne breaks out the oars and starts rowing by himself. His powerful strokes quickly propel them toward shore. Sam and Debbie are in the bow, staring intently at the shore. Sam glances behind him. Josh has broken out two of the sweeps. He is on the port side with one, while Becky is on the starboard side. Mary has the tiller. Sarah is standing by the railing, watching the shore through the binoculars, the machine gun is leaning against the railing next to her.

Sam turns his attention back to the shore.

"No signs of life," Debbie says, a bit apprehensively.

"Yeah," Sam agrees. "Not a good sign. We'd better be careful."

The surf is less than a meter, waves lapping gently on the sand, so the boat glides smoothly up to the beach, but when the bow hits the sand, the sudden stop jolts all four of them.

"You guys stay here," Sam orders in a low voice. "Let me scout ahead."

They all just nod as he jumps into the shallow water and quickly runs up the beach and into the trees. Behind him, the others have gotten out of the boat. Lynne and Debbie come just past the surf. Kneeling, their rifles at the ready, they watch Sam disappear into the forest. George takes the bow rope and comes up behind them, his rifle slung across his back.

Sam works his way into the woods made up mostly of pine trees rooted in the sandy soil. He stops every few meters and listens.

And hears nothing.

No birds.

No insects.

'Right now,' he thinks to himself, 'I would welcome a mosquito bite.'

He pushes forward as quietly as he can, watching his steps to avoid stepping on dried twigs that would make a noise. He doesn't think The

Enemy would set ambushes just for the sake of setting an ambush. But what if they were spotted coming ashore? He can't discount that possibility.

Nearly half a kilometer from the beach, he comes across a small stream of clear quickly flowing water. He tastes it, and discovers sweet, cool liquid. He scans the forest on the other side. Seeing and hearing nothing, he crosses the stream, deciding to go in another half kilometer.

Another hundred meters, and he freezes mid-step. He hears yelling, faint but distinct. Slowly he puts his right foot down. He goes into a crouch as he creeps forward.

Another two hundred meters brings him near to the edge of the forest. Before him is a huge open area, partially covered with tents in orderly rows. Off to one side is a clear area filled with people in uniforms drilling. Sergeants are walking up and down, screaming, threatening, and delivering blows and kicks to their captive soldiers.

Sam scans the area. A few Sergeants are in the tent area. None are looking his way. There is no indication he and the others, or The Hope, have been seen. Swallowing hard, he slowly creeps backwards, watching the camp carefully.

As he turns to go, he freezes again. Two figures, a man and woman, enter the woods a few meters from him. Sam slowly drops to the ground, so as not to draw attention to himself. He watches as the man, wearing Sergeant chevrons, shoves the obviously terrified woman in front of him. She's begging him to leave her alone. He's just laughing.

Sam has seen this before.

The Sergeant slaps his victim hard across the face, nearly knocking her to the ground, and orders her to take off her pants if she wants to live. The woman is crying, but with trembling hands starts fumbling with her belt buckle.

"Hurry it up, bitch! I ain't got all day!" the Sergeant, who towers above the tiny, slim woman, harshly orders.

The woman is too terrified to speak, as she finally gets her belt undone. Slowly, she starts to take down the pants.

"I said, hurry …" The Sergeant's order is cut short as Sam's left hand yanks his chin up, shutting his mouth, while the blade of his knife slits the Sergeant's throat, severing his arteries and windpipe. Sam eases the body to the ground to minimize noise. The woman freezes in shock and surprise. Sam wipes his knife clean on the Sergeant's uniform, and then, just for good measure, uses his rifle butt to smash in the Sergeant's head, splitting open his skull, letting the brains and blood spill out.

"Pull up you pants and let's get out of here," Sam quietly tells the woman, who is frozen with fear. "Don't just stand there! We have to move if you want to live!"

The woman just stares at him, and at the smashed head at her feet.

"I…I…"

"Lady, we have to move!" he says, keeping his voice low as he stresses urgency.

"But they'll kill me if I run!"

"They're going to kill you now anyway when they find this mess," Sam says, gesturing at the body.

She swallows hard. "Where…"

"To safety. I have a way out of here. But we have to move. Now!"

The woman swallows hard and nods. She pulls her pants back up and fastens the belt, then looks at Sam for direction.

"Who are you?" she asks quietly.

Sam, who has been looking in the direction of the camp for any sign of danger, looks back at her. "We'll talk about that later. Right now we have to go."

She just nods.

"Walk as quietly as you can. Understand?"

She nods.

Sam starts off, almost soundlessly. His new companion, however, steps on dried leaves and small branches, making a crunching sound that seems as loud as a siren to Sam, who winces. He turns to her, looks down at her feet, then back at her.

"Quietly!" he orders in a low voice.

She nods. Watching her steps now, she manages to reduce the noise a bit. Not enough to please Sam, but he realizes it's the best she is going to do. He stops at the stream, the woman almost running into him because she is looking down as she walks. He puts a finger across his lips to indicate silence. Then he listens intently for any indication they are being followed or the Sergeants are searching for them. Satisfied, he motions her to follow him as he crosses the stream.

About half-way back to where Sam had left the others, Lynne and Debbie suddenly rise out of the underbrush, rifles at the ready.

"What are you doing out here?" Sam asks quietly.

"Thought we heard a herd of elephants comin'" Lynne says.

"Who's she?" Debbie asks, pointing at the woman who is trying her best to hide behind Sam.

"A stray I found," Sam says, "There's a whole camp back there. Sergeants all over the place. We have to get out of here fast."

The other two just nod. Sam starts forward, the woman staying as close to Sam as possible, looking at Lynne and Debbie with fear and uncertainty. Debbie falls in behind her. Lynne watches the trail for a moment, and then turns to bring up the rear.

"Who's that?" George asks as Sam emerges from the trees with the woman right behind him.

"We've got to get out of here," Sam says, ignoring the question. "The Enemy has a big camp about a kilometer back."

He doesn't need to tell George twice; he quickly pulls the boat as close to the beach as he can get it.

The woman freezes again at the sight of George, and then she sees the ship off the beach.

"Who? What?" she stutters.

"Later," Sam says. "When we're safe. Now get into the boat!"

The woman doesn't move, just staring at things. Debbie takes her by the arm, "Come on, sister. Time to go." Nearly pulling the woman into the surf, she shoves her onto the boat.

Sam turns to watch the tree line as Lynne emerges. Sam just nods toward the boat with his head. Lynne nods back, gets into the boat and readies the oars. Giving one last look into the trees, Sam slings his rifle, and with George's help, pushes the boat out into the surf far enough for Lynne to propel it out to sea. George and then Sam jumps aboard.

Joining Debbie in the stern, Sam unslings his rifle as the two of them watch the rapidly receding shore.

"Who is she?" Debbie asks, not taking her eyes off the tree line.

"A Sergeant was about to rape her," Sam says matter-of-factly.

"You couldn't just leave?"

"If Sarah found out I did that, she'd kick my ass," Sam says, smiling a little as he swaps glances with Debbie.

"Right," she says dryly, remembering their story about how they fled their camp after stopping Sergeants from raping Mary, and how it was Sarah who acted first.

CHAPTER NINE

When they reach The Hope, George throws the line up to Josh who is standing by the railing. As he ties off the boat, Sarah calls down, "Where did you pick her up?"

"Can we come aboard first?" Sam calls back.

"If you must." Sarah is still put out with Sam.

"We must," he says, as Debbie climbs the ladder, followed by the woman, then George and Lynne. When Sam gets on deck, Josh moves the rowboat back to the stern, tying it off.

"We have to get out of here," Sam says. "There's a large Enemy camp about a kilometer in, and sooner or later they are going to come looking after they find the dead Sergeant."

"The dead what?" George says.

"You didn't know?" Sarah asks him.

"Uh, no. I was on the beach, holding the boat…."

"We have to get out of here. Now!" Sam says. "Let's get the sail up. Then we can talk."

Josh gets everyone moving to raise the main sail and the jib. The Hope is soon moving at more than ten knots, away from the shore. Sam scans the beach. Still no sign of activity. He wonders if this group uses boats. He doesn't know, and he doesn't want to find out. He finally relaxes as the land slips under the horizon with no sign of pursuit.

Becky is on the tiller as the group gathers around her.

"Who is she and why is she here?" Sarah says, eyeing their new addition.

"I don't know her name," Sam admits. "We didn't have time for formal introductions. I came across an Enemy camp at least as large as the one we were in. As I was pulling back, I saw this Sergeant shoving her into the woods. He was going to rape her."

"How do you know?" Josh asks.

"That's what they do," Becky spits out in disgust and anger.

"He was forcing her to take off her pants, saying something about doing it if she wanted to live," Sam adds as explanation.

"You killed him," Lynne says, making a statement.

Sam nods. "Cut his throat and clubbed him with my rifle. Shooting him would have made a bit too much noise."

"That was kind of overkill, wasn't it?" Sarah says.

Sam raises his eyebrows. "It felt right. Anyway, I couldn't leave her there."

"Why not?" Debbie asks.

"They would have killed her in a very unpleasant way," Sarah says. "In our camp, they stripped people and put them up on crosses. They just let them die slowly after beating them to a pulp. Except with women, sometimes they raped them first."

"They raped one to death. Then they hung her up anyway for all to see," Mary says, tears flowing down her face at the memory.

"Oh," was all Debbie could say, shuddering at the thought.

"What's your name?" Sarah says gently, turning to the woman, who is standing inside the semi-circle they have formed, her eyes fixed on the deck. "Hey, honey, you're safe with us. No one is going to hurt you here. And you're welcome to come with us."

No response. No movement.

Sarah walks slowly up to her, wrapping her in a protective embrace. She feels the quiet sobs coming from the woman, feels her shirt becoming wet with her tears. After a little, she pulls back a bit from the woman. Gently raising her chin, she asks, "Are you hungry?"

The question elicits a weak, "Yes" and a shallow nod.

"George," Sarah says quietly, "will you get our guest something to eat?"

"Oh, yes, sure," he says, heading below.

"Now," Sarah says. "Can you tell me your name?"

"Jessica," she says in a whisper.

"Jessica," Sarah says, a bit louder so the others can hear. "We know what you've been through. Most of us escaped from a camp like yours."

"You did?"

"Yes. There were eight of us," Sarah says.

"A whole squad?" Jessica looks at her, amazed.

"Yes. Three of us died fighting them. They kept coming after us. Debbie and Josh saved us when The Enemy was about to catch up," Sarah says, indicating the sister and brother.

"The Enemy?"

"That's what we call them," Sarah responds.

"Here," George says as he comes up with plate of dried meat and fruit, along with a cup of water.

"Sit down and eat," Sarah says. "We can talk later."

"Thanks," Jessica says, taking the plate and cup. Quickly sitting on the deck, she starts eating hungrily.

"Let her alone to eat," Sarah says, looking down at her.

As Jessica eats, the rest go to the stern, gathering around Becky who has the tiller.

"Can we trust her?" Debbie asks in a low voice, staring at Jessica's back.

"Yes, I think so," Becky says definitively.

"What makes you say that?" Josh asks.

"Because I was like her, only worse," she replies.

"What?" Debbie asks.

"She was part of a squad the Sergeants brought along when they were searching for us," Sarah says.

"She was the only survivor of the ambush we set for them," Sam adds.

"I thought we should kill her," Lynne says. "Didn't trust her."

"Why didn't you?" Debbie asks, "Kill her, that is."

"They wouldn't let me," he answers, indicating Sarah and Sam. "Turns out, they were right."

"She proved herself to us," Sarah says. "And she's been part of our family ever since."

"The Sergeants rule through terror and fear," Becky says. "None of the soldiers have any loyalty to them. Hell, none of us," she says, sweeping her arm around the group, "even knew what we were supposed to be fighting for."

"Now we're just fightin' them," Lynne says, a fierceness in his voice.

"She's like we were," Mary says, looking at Jessica, "brutalized and scared. It will take her time to heal, but once she really understands she is safe with us, she'll become one of us."

"You sure?" Josh asks. "Are you willing to risk our lives on that?"

"Yes!" Sarah and Sam say simultaneously.

"Look," Sarah says, "you trusted us when you didn't have to, and we came out of the same shit she did."

"We saw you fighting The Enemy," Debbie says. "That's why we trusted you."

"If you're worried about her," Sam offers, "we'll keep a close eye on her until we are all comfortable with her."

"Just let's not tie her up," Becky says. "That is really nasty."

"Tie her up?" Josh asks.

"We sort of tied Becky up every night until she showed us she could be trusted," Sarah says.

"To a tree. In the rain. In the cold. It was miserable," Becky says, shivering at the memory.

"It wasn't that bad, was it?" Lynne asks, mischievously.

"Bastard!" Becky says, smacking him on the arm.

"That hurt," Lynne says, smiling while rubbing his arm.

"Good!" Becky says, though she knows he didn't really feel it.

"You hit like a girl," he observes.

"I am a girl, or haven't you noticed?"

Lynne just grins down at her in response.

"Well, if we're finished with the fun and games," Sarah says, "I'm going to talk to our guest."

"I think the rest of us should stay away," Sam says. "We'll just intimidate her."

The others agree and scatter around the ship to do their chores or just relax. Lynne, Josh and Debbie get fishing gear to see if they can catch dinner. Mary goes below to check on the children, while George just stares out to sea. Sam sits on a deck chair, watching Sarah go to Jessica, not sure whether they can really trust their new passenger, and, if they can, whether she will be an asset or a burden to their group. 'I guess we'll just have to find out,' he thinks as Sarah sits down next to their new addition.

Sarah sits quietly next to Jessica, who is about finished eating, having hungrily gulped down the meat and fruit on her plate. She glances at Sarah, but quickly turns her attention back to her plate. When it's empty, she puts it on the deck in front of her, and scooping up the cup of water, drains it quickly. She puts it down, next to the plate, and keeps staring down at the deck.

"Jessica?" Sarah says gently, then waits for a response.

"Yes?" comes the weak reply after nearly a minute.

"You're safe now. You don't have to fear the Sergeants anymore. We will protect you."

"Okay," she says, still staring at the deck.

"Do you believe me?"

The question is greeted with a shrug.

"Right," Sarah says, still in a quiet, calm, soothing voice. "Tell me, where did you wake up?"

The question elicits a shudder from Jessica, who finally looks up at her companion, fear and wonder in her eyes. "How…how do you know about that?"

"Because it happened to me. And Sam. And Lynne. And Mary. And Becky. And George."

"Not the others?"

"No," Sarah says, shaking her head. "Their parents found a safe place. They were born there."

Jessica's eyes go wide. "Why did you leave?"

Sarah looks out toward the sea for a moment, before looking back at Jessica. "The Enemy was coming."

"The Enemy?"

"The Sergeants and their soldiers. Like we were once. Like you were."

"Oh."

"They would have killed us. We decided two years ago to build this ship in case they ever came," she said, pausing. "And one day, they did."

"Were you in a camp?"

"Yes."

"How did you decide to run away?" Jessica asks, now looking at Sarah and speaking in a stronger voice, her curiosity pushing her fear down.

Sarah sighs. "Some Sergeants were raping Mary. Me, Sam and George stopped them."

"How?" wonder and bewilderment mixed in the question.

"We killed them," she says, a hint of pride in her voice.

"But didn't they have guns?"

"They never saw us coming. They were too busy attacking Mary."

"Oh. And then?"

"And then we had no choice. They would have tortured us to death. So, we took their guns, raided the armory while they weren't looking, and took off. Frank was killed in the gunfight we had before we could escape," Sarah says, sadness creeping into her voice as she relived the memory. "Judy was badly wounded. She died later. We buried her in the forest." Sarah swallows hard, collecting herself. "We managed to find food and water along the way. We fought The Enemy several times when they were hunting us down. Adam died giving us time to escape. He had been badly wounded and couldn't run anymore. He bought us time. Becky, we picked up along the way," Sarah says, skipping that story. "She was like the rest of us. Like you."

"And the other two?"

"Josh and Debbie are brother and sister. Debbie found us as The Enemy was closing in. She led us to safety," Sarah says, her voice regaining its certitude. "Where there is life, there is no Enemy. She took us over a ridge where there were animals, deer, rabbits, bears, fish in the streams, birds, insects. Even getting bitten by a mosquito was kind of nice because we were safe."

"But they came over anyway?"

"Eventually. That's when we sailed off on The Hope. Josh's father had taught him how to build boats, and he was able to use that experience to build this ship," she said, omitting the trial and error that they went through during the initial attempts. "Now, what about you? Where did you wake up?"

"In a classroom."

"Really?"

"Yes," Jessica says, nodding. "You?"

"On the lawn of a college campus."

"Oh. What does that mean? Where we woke up?"

"I have no idea," Sarah says, laughing a bit. "Sam thinks it has something to do with our past, but that is just a guess. He really doesn't know," she says, conspiratorially. "He woke up in a graveyard, so what does that mean?"

Jessica laughs a bit in return, finally beginning to relax.

"But he may be right," Sarah says with a shrug. "We just don't really know. What kind of a classroom?"

"It looked like an elementary school."

"Okay, then what happened?"

"I went outside and one of those Sergeants grabbed me. When I tried to pull away, he beat me and beat me, knocking me to the ground, then he kicked me, all the while calling me names and threatening to kill me and rape me. I was terrified." Jessica stops talking, her eyes beginning to fill with tears.

Sarah reaches out and takes her hand, reassuring her. "Let me guess: You were put into a marching column, where you had to walk for days, sleeping in formation at night. Every morning, they gave you a loaf of bread and a bottle of water that had to last the day."

"How did you know?"

"Same thing happened to us. We eventually were taken into a big field where we were formed into squads and had to put up tents and all that."

"Yes. Yes." Jessica responds, brightening a bit.

"The training was brutal. The Sergeants beat anyone who did anything wrong. They were always cussing us and yelling at us. Anyone who tried to escape was tortured to death." Then changing the subject, Sarah asks, "Did you get any weapons training?"

"We just finished that. Anyone who pointed a rifle in the wrong direction was killed. They were starting to teach us how to make attacks."

"Good. That could come in handy."

"Where are we going?" Jessica asks.

Sarah takes a deep breath, then lets it out. "We don't know. We are looking for a safe place to live and raise our children."

"Children?" Jessica says, brightening up.

"Yeah, Sam and I have a daughter, and Mary has a son. Adam was the father. And I'm nearly eight months' pregnant," she says, patting her stomach.

"Children," Jessica says, wonder in her voice. "May I see them?"

"Soon," she says, then changes the subject again. "What do you remember about before you woke up in that classroom?"

"Nothing, not a thing."

"Just like the rest of us," Sarah says. "Any idea what you're good at?"

"Good at?"

"Yeah, like I'm good at engineering, Sam's good at military stuff, so is Lynne. George is a great cook. Mary is great with the kids. Becky is our medic. Debbie is our gardener, although there isn't much for her to do now. And Josh is our captain. He's the one in charge of running this ship. So, what are you good at?"

Jessica shrugs. "I don't know. How can I find out?"

Sarah gives a short laugh. "Give it time. You'll figure it out."

Jessica just nods.

"For now, why don't you roam around the ship so you know where things are and get to know everyone. Lynne's a bit gruff, but he'll come around eventually."

"Okay," Jessica says as the two women get to their feet. "Isn't Lynne a girl's name?" she asks innocently.

"I wouldn't bring that up with him or anywhere near him," Sarah responds, lowering her voice. "It will hurt his feelings because he doesn't see it that way."

"Oh, okay," comes the answer from the somewhat bewildered newcomer.

Sarah watches her go toward the group who are fishing, then she glances around, and finding Sam, picks up the plate and cup and heads to him.

"What do you think?" Sam asks, glancing up at Sarah before returning to watch Jessica.

"She'll be alright. She's still in shock. You turned her world upside down and she has to adjust to not being in danger every minute of every day. But she's alright."

"Good," is all Sam says, getting up from the chair to hold Sarah's hand.

CHAPTER TEN

After walking around the main deck, and talking to everyone there, except Lynne who just looks at her and walks away, Jessica goes below. The light is dim, just coming from what filters down through the hatch and a grate set in the deck above. She stands at the bottom of what Josh has told her is a ladder, although to her it is a steep stairway, letting her eyes adjust to the light.

In the middle of the room, she sees what appears to be a playpen—about three-meters square with slatted railings rising to about a meter from the floor. A gate is cut in the middle. Inside are two small children. Mary's playing with them, using wooden toys and blocks.

"Hi," Jessica says shyly as she walks up to the gate, which comes up more than halfway up her chest.

"Hello," Mary responds, looking in her direction. The two children stop playing to look at her as well. The boy gets up, and walks to the railing, with the younger girl coming behind him. They stand holding the bars, looking up at her in curiosity.

"May I come in?" Jessica asks.

"Sure," Mary says.

As she enters, the little girl runs to her, wrapping her arms around Jessica's right leg, and looking up at her. The little boy runs to Mary, standing next to her.

"Judy is the one hanging onto your leg," Mary says, smiling broadly. "And this is my son, Adam," she says as she pulls him to her front and hugs him. "Judy is Sarah and Sam's daughter."

Jessica nods and looks quizzically at Mary, who loses her smile.

"Adam's father is dead. He died before Adam was born fighting The Enemy. His name was Adam, too."

"I'm sorry," Jessica says.

"Thanks."

"You take care of them both?"

"Only when Sam and Sarah are working. Josh built this playpen to keep them safe when we are all busy. He also made the toys for them. He's really good with his hands. If it weren't for him, we wouldn't have this ship and we would all have been killed when The Enemy came over the ridge."

"Why are they in here now?" Jessica asks.

"They actually enjoy it because this is where their toys are," Mary responds. "And it's big and safe. They are both curious. We don't want one of them falling off the ship."

"That makes sense."

"Want to play with them?"

"I'd love to," Jessica says, sitting down next to Mary.

"It's alright," Mary tells Adam. "Go ahead and play."

Judy has already disentangled herself from Jessica and gone back to building with the set of blocks scattered in the middle of the pen. Adam keeps a wary eye on Jessica as he goes to help Judy.

"He'll warm up to you," Mary tells Jessica. "You're the first new person he's ever met."

"He's shy, unlike Judy who seems to be fearless," Jessica observes.

"Yes," Mary agrees. "They are each like their mothers."

"I see," she says, watching the children. "Hey, do you want to learn a song?" she asks them. Then quickly turning to Mary, she asks, "Is that okay?"

"Sure," Mary says, intrigued and more than a little pleased to have someone else to help with the children.

Judy comes right over, while Adam hangs back a bit.

"Mary had a little lamb, little lamb," Jessica begins to sing, using her hands in a pantomime of what the song is saying.

Judy is enthralled, coming right up to Jessica, and despite himself, Adam inches over, drawn by the music.

Jessica soon has both children singing along with her after a fashion.

Mary listens for a bit and then joins in as well.

64

When that song is done, they roll into another and then another.

Finally, Jessica turns to Mary to ask, "Have they been introduced to the alphabet?"

"They're kind of young for that."

"Not really. They won't really learn it, but when it comes time for them to, they will have some memory of the letters, which will make it easier for them. And we can do 'Do-Re-Me' which will help them learn music, which it appears they both like.

Mary thinks for a moment. "It can't hurt," she finally says.

"Good," Jessica says, turning back to the children. "We're going to sing an alphabet song, okay?"

Both nod enthusiastically, Adam having lost all fear of this new adult.

"What do you think?" Sam asks Sarah as she comes back up on the main deck. After bringing the plate and cup down, she'd watched from the bottom of the stairs as Jessica interacted with the children.

"I think she was a teacher, an elementary school teacher."

"What makes you say that?"

"She's teaching the children songs and wants to introduce them to the alphabet and music."

"Aren't they too young for that?"

"That's what Mary said. But Jessica says going over it now will help them later when they actually have to learn it."

"So she's good?"

"Yeah. Maybe better than good if she can help our kids like that."

Sam nods, and glances at the compass to make sure he is still steering north, having just started his watch on the tiller. He glances to his left to make sure that there is no sign of land.

"Hey, Josh!" he calls.

"What?" comes the reply as Josh comes aft.

"Do you think we should go to the left …"

"You mean port."

"Right, port, until we can see land. Maybe steer off that."

Josh thinks for a moment. "How sure are we that The Enemy is not using boats? If they have power boats, there is no way we can outrun them."

"We haven't seen any evidence of that. I think if they had them, they would have come after us. You know that camp I saw looked just like the one we left. Outside of pickup trucks, we never saw any evidence of them having big trucks or cars, or planes for that matter."

Josh thinks for bit, staring off in the direction of the land. "Okay, if you think it's safe."

"I do," Sam says, pushing the tiller over until the faint blue outline of the land can be seen a couple of hours later, then he steadies up on north again, keeping the shore in sight just at the horizon.

The Hope heads north that way during the next two days as they fall back into their routine of taking turns on watches and helping to sail the ship. The land slants to the east, so The Hope is steered a bit east of north to keep the land a blue haze on the western horizon.

Jessica becomes increasingly involved with the children, teaching them and playing with them. Mary is learning from her. And while Sarah and Sam stay involved with Judy, especially when they are not on watch, they make space for Jessica to work with their daughter.

As they use up the fresh food, George is able to concoct recipes that, while not exactly up to his previous standards, are at least palatable.

CHAPTER ELEVEN

H ey, George!" Josh calls.

"What?" comes the reply. George is sitting on the deck watching the sea slip by in the early morning light.

"Take the tiller, will you," calls Josh, who is steering the ship.

George stares at him a moment. "But it isn't my watch," comes the weak protest. "And I have to get breakfast going," comes the stronger protest. "And isn't Becky on watch with you? Shouldn't she be the one to take the tiller?"

"Oh, just come over and take the tiller for a damn moment, will you? Breakfast will have to wait," comes the irritated reply.

"Oh, okay," he says, getting up and walking to the stern. "What's going on?"

"I'm not sure."

"Then why …?"

"I'll let you know in a bit. Just keep us on course."

"Right."

After the exchange, Josh walks to the starboard side, and stares toward the east, and the newly risen sun and blood red sky.

"Get the others," he says absentmindedly to Becky who has just come back on deck from checking on the others below.

"Right now? Not everyone is awake yet," she protests.

"Mary and, what's her nose, Jessica, don't have to come up," he says, finally looking at her. "But the others do."

"Is there a problem?" Becky sounds worried.

"There could be," he says, turning back to fading red sky in the east.

"Oh," she says, glancing toward the east but not understanding what Josh is worried about.

"Go get them, please," he says.

She nods and disappears below. In the next fifteen minutes, first Lynne, followed by Debbie, Sam and Sarah come up on the weather deck. Then Mary wanders up, yawning. Sarah looks questioningly at Mary.

"Jess has the kids. They'll be fine," Mary assures her.

Sarah just nods and turns her attention back to the group that is forming around Josh. He is still staring out to the east. None of the others are really awake yet, so he's not getting any questions.

"The sky was red at sunrise," he comments quietly, gesturing to the east, his gaze fixed in that direction.

The other's just exchange quizzical glances.

"And?" Sarah finally asks.

"Dad had this phrase he used to say: Red in the morning, sailors take warning; red at night, sailors delight."

"What does that mean?" Sam says, sounding confused.

"He said, if the sky's red at sunrise, it might mean a storm's heading this way."

"And at night?" Becky asks.

"The storm's heading away."

"So we're in for a storm?" Sarah asks.

After a long pause, Josh turns to the group. "I'm not sure. We could be. We better be prepared."

"How do we do that?" Lynne asks.

"We need to make sure everything is tied down, on this deck and below. If we hit rough seas we don't want things flying around."

"Okay," Sam says. "Anything else?"

"We need to get the rowboat in and lash it to the deck."

"Is that why you had us put in those O-rings?" Becky asks.

"Partly. But also, if the seas get rough enough, everyone on this deck needs to be tied with a rope."

"Why?" comes non-swimmer George's nervous question.

"In case one of us gets washed overboard," Josh says matter-of-factly. "We can pull that one back on board. It's just a precaution," he says to the circle of worried faces. "As the wind picks up, we'll have to take down the jib and maybe shorten the main sail."

"Why's that?" Sam asks.

"If I'm right, if the wind gets too strong it can shred the sails or pull down the mast. And if we are going too fast, we could lose control of the ship. I've never done this before, so I'm just working off what Dad said."

"Then let's get busy," Sarah says. "Who does what?"

"Mary," Josh says, "will you take the tiller?"

"Sure," she says, replacing George.

"Good," Josh says. "Umm, Lynne, Sam, help me get the boat on board." The two men nod in affirmation. "Sarah, break out the rope. We'll need two-meter lengths for the boat and, umm, probably five- or seven-meter lengths for each of us."

"Okay," she said, heading below for the ropes they had brought with them.

"You others go below and make sure everything is tied down. George you better have food prepared for several days in case you can't cook."

"Okay," he replies.

"Debbie," Josh says, turning to his sister, "check for any leaks we can stop up. We have some buckets, don't we?"

"Yes, we do."

"Get them out and secured in easy to reach places in case we have to bail water out."

"Right," she answers

"Let's go," Josh says with a wave of his arms.

They all scatter to get things done. Lynne pulls the rowboat, which has been trailing the ship, alongside using the rope that has tethered it to The Hope.

"Why bring the boat onboard?" Sam asks.

"If the sea gets rough enough, the line could break, and we'd lose the boat. Or waves could hurl it onto the deck. And if it hits one ..."

"Enough said," Sam says quickly. "You've made your point."

Josh just nods, watching Lynne work.

"What now?" Lynne asks as he brings the boat alongside where they put the ladder down.

Josh looks down at the boat for moment. "Just a minute," he says, turning and heading below. He quickly comes back with rope and an O-ring. He climbs into the boat, and sitting in the stern, fastens the O-ring into the stern. One is already in the bow. Then he ties a rope to the stern O-ring.

"Here," he calls, throwing the rope up to Lynne, who snags it. Josh then hands the oars up to Sam before climbing back on board.

"I have this end," Lynne says, nodding for the other two to take over the bow line.

With him pulling up the stern and the other two the bow, the boat is soon on deck. Sarah has come back on deck with the rope. As she ties long lengths to the O-rings scattered around the deck, Josh ties the oars to the boat's seats.

"Okay, let's turn it over," he says as he gets out of the boat.

The three men flip the boat over between the rings Josh had arranged on the deck. They lash it securely to the deck.

"Okay," Josh says. "Sarah, make sure we have two ropes around the tiller so whoever is on it won't get knocked around."

"Got it," she says.

"I'm going below to check on things," he says. Sam and Lynne follow him down. While Josh checks the supply cupboards, Sam and Lynne help George finish lashing down the water and food barrels using the O-rings in the bulkheads and deck. Lynne grumbles about how lose some of the lines are, redoing some of the work others have already done.

"Well," Josh finally says, "I think we've done just about all we can do to get ready."

"What about the kids?" Jessica asks."

"The kids?" Josh asks, sounding a bit confused.

"We don't want them thrown around, do we?"

"Are you saying we should tie them down, too?" Sam asks, humor in his voice.

"No, not exactly," she responds. "But we have to do something to protect them."

"Well," Josh says, scratching his head, and looking at Sam, who just shrugs. "Why don't we put blankets around along the sides of the playpen.

Then you," he says to Jessica, "and Mary can tie yourselves inside and hold the kids. Does that sound good?"

"Yes, excellent," she says.

"Okay then, why don't you and George take care of that."

"Will do," she says, leaving the children in the playpen and going to get the blankets.

Josh gives one more look around; satisfied with what he sees, he heads back up to the weather deck, followed by Sam and Lynne.

The sky is bright blue, but the sea has become a bit rougher. The waves have grown to nearly a meter and a half.

"The sky is clear," Sam says, scanning the horizon.

"Let's hope it stays that way," Josh says, looking at the ocean.

CHAPTER TWELVE

L ooks like the storm isn't coming," Sam comments almost laconically as he and Josh are standing to one side of the mast.

"Looks like," Josh replies. They watch the sky all day, and until mid-afternoon, it's clear.

Then, just as they are beginning to relax, clouds start racing by as the wind and seas pick up, the waves growing to nearly two meters.

"Let's take the jib down," Josh says.

"What I don't understand is why is the storm moving in from the northwest if it started in the east?" Sam comments, sounding perplexed.

"I have no idea," Josh admits. "I'm just going by what Dad said."

"Right," Sam says, accepting the explanation. "Let's go."

"Lynne!" Josh calls as the two head forward to pull in the jib. "We need your help! Sarah! Debbie! Becky! Give us a hand!"

As the crew gathers, Josh hands out assignments. "Sarah, double-check the ropes and make sure we have enough of them scattered around the deck. Debbie, make sure everything is secure below. Becky, Lynne, help us lower the jib, and we should shorten the main sail."

As they scatter to get things done, George, who is on the tiller, yells out. "I'm having trouble keeping us heading north!" As he tacks the ship to keep it on course, the beam goes broadside to the waves, making The Hope roll more than usual.

"Be right back," Josh tells the others as he heads aft. Lynne, Sam and Becky go forward to get the jib down.

As Josh reaches the stern, a three-meter wave rolls the small vessel twenty degrees.

"Turn the ship around," Josh tells George.

"What?" comes the confused response.

"Turn the ship away from the wind," Josh repeats. "We need to head away from the wind so we don't roll the ship."

"But we won't be heading north," George protests.

"True, but we won't drown either."

That was all George needs to hear. Without comment, he puts the tiller over until the wind is behind the ship, pushing The Hope to the southeast.

When Josh goes back forward, the jib is down, and they are working on shortening the main sail. He helps them finish.

As they work, Sarah ties George to three O-rings. He resists until she points out it's better than drowning. Then she goes forward, reaching the other four as they finish with the sail.

"Who's on watch?" Josh asks.

"Me and George," Sam says.

"Do you think he can handle the tiller if the weather gets worse?" Josh asks.

"If he can't, I'll help him."

"Okay, but I think we need more than two on deck in case something happens."

"I'll stay," Sarah volunteers.

"Me too," Lynne says.

"Good," Josh says. "All three of you get tied to the deck. I don't want to lose anyone. The rest of us will be below. Debbie, Becky, and I will relieve you in a couple of hours or so."

"What if the weather gets really bad?" Sarah asks.

"In that case, you guys may have to stay on deck by yourselves," Josh says. "Or all of us will be up here trying to keep the ship together."

"Let's hope it doesn't come to that," Sam quips, drawing a variety of looks from the others. "But," he says, turning as serious as he can, "Sarah, go below if it gets any worse."

"I will not!" she protests.

"Yes, you will," Sam says in a tone that accepts no disagreement. "You are too pregnant to be tied around your waist and you can't risk being washed overboard."

"We'll see about that!" Sarah shoots back, equally adamant.

The two engage in a silent faceoff, which lasts several minutes, finally breaking it off by turning away from each other, leaving the dispute unresolved. Sam keeps a close eye on Sarah, who can't seem to find a good way to tie the rope around herself so she just holds onto it.

The weather doesn't turn worse, but the wind drives them southeast throughout the night. As the sky begins to lighten in the east, a faint change from black to grey comes through the heavy cloud cover; the wind lightens up and the sea begins to calm.

Everyone is tired. Watches change every two hours, but Lynne and Sam each take extra watches so three are on deck at all times.

Sleep is hard for even those below as the ship pitches and rolls in the seas. The children went from finding the rolling deck fun to terrifying then fun again depending on the size of the roll, keeping Mary and Jessica up throughout the night, and depriving Sarah of sleep when she's with her daughter.

As the sea calms, everyone below deck falls asleep finally. Josh and Becky are on watch as the waves first drop to one meter and then nearly disappear, while the wind becomes a soft breeze. Tying the tiller amidships, Josh and Becky hoist the main sail to its full height. They watch it billow as it catches the breeze, pushing The Hope along at about three knots.

Then the rain comes. The large cold drops fall in torrents, drenching the two on deck. Becky goes below to see if she can find their ponchos. Her rummaging around wakes Sam and Sarah.

"What's up?" a sleepy Sarah asks as Sam struggles to hold on to sleep, pulling her a bit closer to him. She lightly smacks the arm he has around her pregnant middle and he pulls back quickly.

"Nothing," comes the reply. "It's just pouring and we need something to keep dry. I know we have some ponchos somewhere."

"Raining? Did you say raining?" It was George who suddenly comes awake and starts to listen to the driving rain against the deck overhead.

"Yeah?" Becky says, turning to him, wondering why the sudden interest.

"Water! That's water! We need water!" he says, excitedly, throwing off his blanket. "Where are those buckets?"

"Over there," Becky says, gesturing to the port side where they are tied down.

"Right. Let's get them upstairs!" George says, an urgency and confidence they are not used to hearing from him.

"Okay," Sam says, springing up and heading for the buckets after pulling on his boots.

"Here they are!" Becky announces, holding up some ponchos. "Everyone who goes up needs one of these," she says, handing them out to the three who are moving, before donning one herself and then heading up to get one to Josh, and to tell him what's going on.

The other three are soon on deck with the buckets. They find a clear spot to put the buckets down to catch as much of the rain as possible.

"I have an idea!" George announces as he heads below. He is soon back with some tarps. "Here, let's rig these up so they catch the rain and funnel it into the buckets."

While they're doing that, Lynne comes on deck lugging a water barrel, drawing amused and approving glances from the others. He puts it next to the buckets and pries the top off the nearly empty barrel.

"I'll get another," he says, heading back down. He is soon back, struggling with a barrel that is half full, until Sam helps him put it in position. The others have created a makeshift funnel for the first barrel, but lacking another tarp, they move one from a bucket to the second barrel.

"How long do you think this rain will last?" Sam asks, looking at the sky.

"No clue," says Josh who has turned the tiller over to Becky and come forward to see what's going on. "This is a great idea."

"It's all George," Sam says.

"Except the barrels," Sarah adds. "That's Lynne."

"Boy, this is like standing in a shower," George observes.

"Oh my God, yes, it is," Sarah says, thinking. "Josh, get back on the tiller. Becky!" she calls as she waves for her to come forward.

"What's going on?" Josh asks.

"Showers!" Sarah responds.

"What?" Sam asks, perplexed.

"You'll see!" Sarah replies. "Go!" she orders Josh who hasn't moved, shooing him with her hands. He shakes his head and heads aft, taking the tiller from Becky.

"What's up?" Becky asks, as confused as the men.

"Come along!" Sarah orders, taking her hand and pulling her toward the ladder leading below. Becky looks at the others, all of them confused, but follows along.

In a few minutes, all five women are on deck, heading toward the bow.

"You guys can either go below or go to the stern. God help anyone who comes forward!" Sarah calls to them.

"What's going on?" Sam demands.

"Showers!" she announces.

It finally dawns on him what is happening. "Guys, we better do what she says. And don't look at them while their showering."

"Oh," George says, catching on to what is happening.

Lynne just chuckles. "We all will just keep watch on the barrels."

"Good idea," Sam says, unable to resist a glance toward the bow where the women are stripping down to nothing.

"It's cold!" Mary complains as she sheds first her poncho and then starts taking off her clothes.

"No worse than the camp," Sarah points out.

"Still, it's cold," Jessica adds.

"What camp?" Debbie wants to know.

"The one we got away from," Becky says.

"Oh, that camp," comes the reply.

The women are all soon naked and passing around the two bars of soap they have brought with them, shivering in the cold rain but enjoying their first chance to get clean in weeks. When they are done, they throw on their ponchos, grab their now soaked clothes, and head for the deck below to get warm and put on dry clothing.

"Here," Sarah says, handing the two bars of soap to Sam as she passes.

"What?" he says, taken by surprise.

"You guys stink! Time for you to get clean."

"But it's cold!" George complains.

"Suck it up, buttercup," Sarah asserts, with a touch of humor. "You either get clean or stay up here for the rest of the trip. Got it?"

"Alright," George replies, cowed.

As the women disappear below, Josh ties the tiller in the center position. Everyone but George quickly strips and starts to wash.

"Are you sure she won't let me below if I don't do this?" George asks, not wanting to take off his poncho, let alone his clothes.

"It would not be wise to test her," Sam assures him, smiling broadly.

George grumbles some more about the cold but strips along with the rest.

They are soon finished, and like the women, they throw on their ponchos, gather up their wet clothing and start to head below.

"Wait a minute," Sam says to Josh. "Who's steering the ship."

"It will be okay for a while. The sea is calm, and we have nearly no wind. Let's go get dressed."

As they head below, they pass Sarah, Becky, Debbie and Jessica coming on deck carrying clothes.

"Laundry," Sarah announces. "You guys bring yours up when you're dressed."

"You're doing laundry?" Sam asks hopefully.

"We are doing laundry."

"Thought so," he says, nearly laughing.

The laundry gets done, and the two water barrels are nearly full when the rain finally slacks off. A light rain falls for another two hours before the sky finally clears.

"Where do you think we are?" Sarah asks Josh as the group gathers on deck to watch a sunset full of color. Clothing has been hung all over the ship to dry.

"Not a clue."

"Should we head back north?" Debbie asks.

"Not a clue," Josh says again.

"What? Are you clueless?" Becky asks, laughing a bit.

"Not a clue," comes the reply, humor in his voice.

After a few minutes, Josh says, "We've been heading southeast for more than a day now. The wind is behind us. Why don't we keep heading this way tonight and figure it out in the morning. I think we could all use a good night's sleep."

No one argues with that.

CHAPTER THIRTEEN

"Good morning," George says as he comes on deck his arms loaded with a camp stove, a couple of pans, and a variety of cans. Debbie is sitting on the deck watching the ocean go by as The Hope stays on its southeasterly course.

"Morning," comes the reply as she glances at him and then back at the empty ocean. "I wonder if we'll see land?"

George just shrugs. "I have to get breakfast. They're starting to wake up down there."

"Good. I'm hungry."

"Me too!" calls Lynne who is on the tiller.

"It will be just a few," George says as he goes forward to near the bow, picking a spot out of the wind for his cooking. With the jib still down, he doesn't have to worry about the rigging.

As he cooks, the others straggle onto the deck. Sam carries Judy with Sarah right behind, beginning to feel a bit ungainly as her pregnancy advances. Jessica, Josh, and Becky come up yawning and stretching in the cool morning breeze. A few minutes later, Mary comes up with Adam in tow, helping him climb the steps.

"Adam! Stay away from the railing!" Mary orders her son as she releases his hand.

"That smells good, whatever it is," Josh says.

"You're just hungry," Becky responds, nudging him.

"It still smells good," he says, smiling.

Sam walks forward until he is at the bow, looking out at the ocean in front of them, wondering what is out there and where they are heading.

"Breakfast is ready!" George calls, breaking into his reverie.

Sam looks back at him, smiles, and then gets in line for the food George is dishing up. He takes two plates, one for himself and one for Sarah. She is holding their daughter and has a plate for her. Josh has brought up a bucket of water from below along with cups. Lynne ties the tiller and comes forward to join the others.

With everyone sitting on deck eating, George eats his breakfast directly from the pans he cooked in. Silence prevails as they all hungrily down the food. Adam is eating with his right hand, a spoon in his left. Sarah softens Judy's food in her mouth before giving it to her daughter who has trouble chewing hard food, the little girl reaching up to her mother's mouth for her bite.

When they're finished, Sarah hands Judy to Sam. It is her and Debbie's turn to clean up. They use a bucket tied to a rope to pull water from the ocean to wash the dishes, not wanting to use their precious supply of fresh water. Josh goes back to take his turn on the tiller as Becky checks the main sail and around the deck for any problems, a routine that has developed at the start of each watch. George heads below to put away the unused food and store the water bucket and camp stove.

Sam wanders aft, followed by Lynne, Mary with Adam, and finally Jessica, who still doesn't feel a full member of the group, so she stands back a bit from the others.

"So, what now?" Sam asks Josh, who is back on the tiller.

Josh thinks for a moment. "To tell the truth, I'm not sure. Do we turn back north or do we keep going this way to see what we find? You're guess is as good as mine." The exasperation in his voice is clear. "We can't stay at sea forever." He looks at Sam and then the others, his expression pleading for advice and wisdom.

He doesn't get any. The others just look at each other and away.

"Any ideas?" Josh prompts them.

"Well …" Sam starts to say.

"Hey! What's that?!" Debbie calls from the bow, drawing everyone's attention forward.

Sarah is standing as far forward as she can, shading her eyes from the sun, which is not far above the horizon.

Everyone heads for the bow, Mary scooping up Adam as she goes. Josh ties the tiller to join the crowd. As they reach the bow, they all gaze quizzically in the direction Sarah and Debbie are staring.

"What? Where?" Sam asks Sarah.

"There!" she says, pointing just to the right of the bow.

Sam stares for bit before he too perceives a faint blue haze on the horizon. "Land?"

"Think so," Lynne says, standing behind them. "Sure looks like it."

"I'm getting the binoculars," Sam announces, giving Judy to Sarah and working his way through the crowd that has formed at the bow. He runs below and is soon back. He trains the binoculars at the slowly growing blue haze.

"Well?" Sarah asks impatiently.

"Here," he says, handing the binoculars to Sarah. "What do you think?"

She studies the blue smudge for a moment. "Land. It's got to be land."

She starts to hand the binoculars to Josh but Lynne grabs them. Josh looks startled but accepts the move.

"Yep, land," Lynne pronounces, handing the binoculars to Josh, who quickly agrees.

"Let's check it out," Josh says.

"Do you think it's safe?" George asks, worry in his voice.

"I don't know, but it's not where we came from that's for sure," Josh says.

"We'll be careful," Sam says, "like we were the last time we went ashore. Maybe we can find some fresh food and more water, if nothing else."

"Let's get the jib up," Josh says. "We'll get there faster."

Sarah and Debbie hurriedly carry the dishes below, as Sam hands his daughter to Jessica, who heads toward the stern with Mary and Adam.

As the jib goes up, The Hope gathers speed, pushing through the calm sea at about twelve knots. Everyone—with the exception of Mary who has Adam near the stern, and Lynne, who has now taken the tiller—is crowded toward the bow watching as the blue smudge on the horizon slowly grows, finally starting to take shape, and then turning green and brown as vegetation and mountains come into view.

"Do you think it's an island or something larger?" Debbie asks Josh who is studying the land through the binoculars.

"It may be an island," he says. "I can see water on either side of the land, but," he says with a shrug, handing the binoculars to her, "I can't see if it's just a peninsula."

"We'll find out when we get closer," Sarah says, staring intently at the land as if she can will it to give up its secrets.

"When will we get there?" Jessica asks, trepidation in her voice. "And what if The Enemy is there?"

"Then we won't stay," Sam says, matter-of-factly. "Don't worry, we will be careful. None of us want to die. And we have the children to think of."

Jessica nods and swallows hard, still fearful of what lies ahead.

"At this speed," Josh says, "I think we'll be close in about four hours."

"That long?" Sarah asks, disappointment in her voice.

"We can always break out the sweeps and row," Sam jokingly offers.

"Not funny," she says flatly. "I want to get there."

"So do I, sweetie. So do I."

Silence descends as they all go back to watching the land growing larger.

"Here," Jessica finally says, "let me take Judy and Adam down to the playpen for a while."

"Okay," Sam says, handing his daughter to her. Jessica, with Mary's help, takes both children below.

The group finally breaks up, some doing chores, others just resting. George fixes a cold lunch for everyone, accompanied by the day's ration of canned orange juice that was salvaged from the deserted town at the foot of the waterfall along with the camp stove and the gas to run it.

Late in the afternoon, individual trees have become visible along the shore. Sam is in the bow with binoculars, most of the others gathered around him. Seagulls fly by, inspecting the ship.

"What do you see?!" an excited Sarah asks him, resisting the urge to rip the binoculars from his hands so she can take a look.

"Trees. White sand. Waves breaking on the shore."

"Any people? Any Animals?" Becky asks.

"No, not yet, but those birds are a good sign … wait a minute?" Sam says, fixing on one spot intently. "Holy shit!"

"What?!" comes the chorus around him.

"Holy shit!" he says again.

"Let me see!" Sarah says, grabbing the binoculars from him. "Where?"

"There!" he says, pointing to the spot.

"What the hell did you see?!" Josh demands.

"They …"

"Holy shit!" Sarah blurts out, cutting him off. "They have a cannon!"

"What?" Josh says, grabbing the binoculars. He adjusts the focus. "Holy crap!"

"You got that right," Sam says. "It looks like they just pulled it onto the beach. I didn't see it before, and then when I saw it, they were moving it."

"Are they going to shoot at us? Are they The Enemy?" Becky asks.

"I don't know but," Josh says, peering closer at the figures on the beach, "I don't think so? It's hard to tell, but they aren't in uniform, and I don't see anyone like the Sergeants. Looks like there's a woman in charge and she's working with the other…let's see…the other seven. No, I don't think it's them."

"That's a relief," Sam says.

"Maybe it's different over here. Maybe the women are in charge?" Becky offers.

"Could be," Josh says.

"I don't think so," says Sam, who has taken the binoculars. "They are all working together. The Sergeants never did that."

"So we can assume they are like us?" Sarah offers.

"We still have to be careful," Sam says.

"But why the artillery?" Josh asks.

The answer comes in the form of a loud boom from the direction of the beach, quickly followed by a large splash twenty meters in front of the ship.

"Fuck! They're shooting at us!" Sam says.

"Let's get out of here!" Josh says, running toward the stern, calling on Lynne to reverse course.

"I guess they don't want us to land," Sarah observes dryly.

"You think?" Sam says.

"I think, honey. I think."

Another boom and a shell hits the water even closer as The Hope begins a slow turn into the wind.

"Take the jib down!" Josh calls.

Sarah and Sam jump to pull that sail down, soon joined by Josh, Debbie and Becky.

A third shell hits the water a few meters away as the ship completes its turn.

"Alright, assholes, we're leaving!" Sarah yells in the direction of the beach.

As The Hope tacks away, Sam goes to the stern to take another look at the beach. "They're not firing anymore. I guess they figure we got the message."

"Assholes," Sarah says in a dejected voice, putting her arm around Sam's waist, resting her head on his shoulder. "They didn't even give us a chance."

"I guess they're scared, too," he says quietly.

"We're heading north again," Josh comments as he stands next to them.

"Good choice," Lynne comments dryly.

CHAPTER FOURTEEN

Josh wakes with a start. The Hope's movement has suddenly changed from the gentle roll of the last four days to deep dips and sharp rolls. He throws off his blanket, and scrambles through the dark to go up to the main deck.

He's greeted by waves running up to four meters high, driving the bow into the troughs and water over the bow. A driving rain nearly blinds him. The jib has been taken down as it is every night, but the ship leans over on its right side, the water almost reaching the deck.

Lynne is on the tiller. Mary is sitting on the deck, her arms wrapped around the compass stand.

Josh closes the hatch to below and heads over to them.

"When did this start?" he yells to Lynne as the wind picks up more.

"Just a bit ago."

"Keep heading into the sea," he tells Lynne. "Otherwise we could capsize."

"What?"

"Roll over."

Lynne nods his understanding as a wave crashes over the bow.

Josh bends down and hands Mary a rope to tie around her waist, then thinks better of it. "You better go below to be with Adam," he says in her ear. "He'll be frightened."

Mary nods but keeps a firm grip on the post.

"Here, let me help you," Josh says, taking her right arm and helping her get to her feet. She reluctantly releases her grip on the compass stand, and the two make their way across the pitching deck. They nearly collide with Sam, who is coming up on deck to see what is going on. Once below,

Mary goes to the playpen while Josh wakes George, Debbie, Becky, and Jessica, telling them they all need to be on deck to handle the sail.

"I'm coming, too," Sarah says, disentangling herself from the frightened Judy, who has wrapped her arms tightly around her mother's neck.

"No!" Josh orders.

"Yes!" Sarah answers.

"No!" he says again. "You need to be here for your kid. She's terrified. And you're pregnant. You're too off balance to be safe on the weather deck."

"I'll tie myself on."

"Where? Your stomach? That could kill your baby. Any higher up could kill you. Any lower down could slip off."

"And if the ship sinks because I wasn't on deck to help, my baby will be dead anyway, and my daughter," Sarah challenges him.

"You're staying put. That's final," Josh says. "If you want to do something, make sure everything down here is still secure. Then go take care of your daughter!"

Josh can feel Sarah glaring at him, but the lack of a response means acceptance, no matter how grudgingly.

He heads back on deck. Sam has tied ropes around Lynne to keep him in place, and he's now helping the others get secured.

"Better get one yourself!" Josh yells to him through the now howling wind.

Sam just nods. Both men find ropes which they tie around their waists. Josh sends Debbie to Lynne to help him with the tiller if the big man needs it, impressing on her the critical importance that they keep heading into the waves. He then gets the others to help him pull the main sail down so that only a small area is left to catch the wind, providing some steering control. The wind is coming out of the southeast and gaining strength.

"Make sure everything is tied down well," Josh yells to the others when they are done with the sail.

The waves grow to five meters, crashing over the bow as The Hope dips into each one before rising again, exposing the keel, before coming crashing down into the next trough.

"Everyone but Sam, go below," Josh bellows above the howling wind, the others barely able to hear him. As they turn to go, a rogue wave crashes over the port side, knocking everyone off their feet and washing them to the starboard railing. Sam grabs Becky's arm just as she's about to go over the side.

As the soaked crew scramble to their feet, Jessica lets out a scream. Pointing to the stern she gestures wildly at Lynne whose yells are blown away by the wind as he fights to keep the ship headed into the waves.

It takes a moment for the scene to register on the rest—Debbie is missing.

"Shit!" Josh yells, as he runs back to the stern, slipping on the wet, pitching deck, closely followed by the others. George crawls back on all fours, terrified about being washed overboard.

"The wave took her!" Lynne yells in Josh's ear when he gets back there.

Panic stricken about losing his sister, Josh stands frozen for a moment. When he turns around, he sees Sam, Jessica, and Becky pulling on the rope tied around Debbie's middle. Sam is in the back, having started to pull the line in. As more comes in, the others join him, the waves at times pulling them toward the stern. Josh grabs Jessica just as one particularly powerful wave nearly pulls her overboard.

"One overboard is enough!" Josh yells into her ear. Her response is just a nod as she gasps for breath. George stands slowly, uncertain about his footing. Then Josh takes the front position. With the four of them pulling, they manage to get a nearly drowned Debbie up to near the top of the stern. When Josh releases his grip on the rope to pull her aboard, the other three slide toward the stern, and Debbie goes back into the water.

Josh glances at Lynne, wanting the big man's help. "That won't work," Josh says out loud, realizing that if Lynne releases the tiller, the ship could capsize, and they all could drown. He glances back to see George, standing fearfully behind Sam, terrified of being washed overboard and drowning.

"George!" Josh yells, gesturing wildly at George. George says something that the wind blows away, but his gesture of pointing to himself conveys all the message Josh needs.

"Yes! You!" Josh yells, confident George can't hear him, but gesturing for him to come aft again.

With fear written on his face and in his movements, George works his way slowly toward Josh, who impatiently keeps gesturing to him to hurry up.

"Grab the rope and pull!" Josh yells in his ear when he arrives.

George's eyes go wide, but he manages to overcome his fear of the storm. He grabs the rope, joining the others in pulling Debbie back up.

As she nears the top, Josh lets go again. This time, with four people on the line, she stays up. Her brother reaches over, grabs one arm and hauls her back aboard. They collapse onto the deck, Debbie gasping for air. The others release the rope.

"Get below! All of you!" Sam yells to George and the women. With George in the lead, they all head below, taking off their ropes before going below deck.

Sam then turns to the two figures sprawled in the pitching deck. "Josh! Get your sister below! There's nothing more you can do up here! Lynne and I will handle the tiller! If we need help, I'll fetch you!"

Josh nods as he gets to his feet, Debbie still lying on the deck, gasping for air and coughing up water. He and Sam get her to stand. Both men walk her back to midship, where the entry to below deck is. The short journey seems as if it takes forever, with the men fighting the pitching deck, drenching rain, and howling wind as they help the nearly drowned woman. Sam unties the rope around her waist as Josh frees himself. Then Sam helps the siblings get started below. When they are near the bottom of the stairs, Sam closes the hatch.

Freeing one line from its O-ring, he makes his way back to the stern, where he ties the second rope to the compass post, making it short enough that he can't be washed overboard should another rogue wave hit. Then he moves into position to help Lynne, who is visibly tiring in his battle to keep the ship headed into the waves.

"Thanks!" Lynne grimly yells into Sam's ear.

CHAPTER FIFTEEN

Shortly after dawn, a dawn so grey the light barely makes it through the heavy cloud covering, the wind dies down, the sea subsides. The rain has become a light mist. The exhausted pair take turns on the tiller, one slumped on the deck to rest. Lynne and Sam are shivering from the cold drenching they have endured for hours. Neither is able to sleep.

Josh comes on deck, followed by George, carrying hot coffee in a pot and two cups. He used the last of their stash to make it.

"Glad to see you made it," Josh tells the two. Lynne just looks up at him from where he is sitting on the deck, his face drawn and grey. Sam just nods, too exhausted to speak, his body slumped over the tiller.

"I'll take over," Josh tells him.

Sam just nods. Releasing his grip, he slumps down beside Lynne.

"Here," George says, "I thought you'd need this." He pours a cup, offers it to Sam, who wraps his hands around it, enjoying the warmth, his nose nearly in the hot black liquid, the steam warming his face, the smell helping to revive him. Lynne takes the cup offered him, with a nod, and starts to sip it, sighing contentedly.

"Are you okay?" Sarah is kneeling next to Sam, a worried look on her face. He didn't even notice her coming up.

He nods. "Yeah. I'm just kind of tired. And cold. I think I could use some sleep."

"I think so, too," she agrees, kissing him on his forehead. "You too, big guy," she says, looking at Lynne. "Go below. Get dry. Get some sleep."

Lynne just nods as he finishes the coffee.

"Can't yet," Sam says.

"Why not?" Sarah demands.

"We've got problems."

"What problems?" Josh blurts out before Sarah can say anything.

"That thing on the front, what do you call it? The bow sprint?"

Josh quickly looks forward.

"It's gone," Sam says. "It must of broken off during the night."

"George!" Josh orders. "Take the tiller."

George puts down the pot, taking over from Josh, who heads forward.

What he finds is the broken bow sprint is being dragged along the side of the ship by the rigging connecting it to the main mast. He checks the mast—and finds cracks in it.

"Crap!" he exclaims. He heads below and soon returns with an axe. Cutting the rigging, he frees the bow sprint which washes away, taking the strain off the mast.

By this time, Sam and Lynne have come forward.

"What can we do?" Sam asks.

Josh looks at the two exhausted men. "Right now, you can get some sleep. You're no good to me like this. Besides, I need to figure out what to do. I'll get you when I need you."

"Fine," Sam says.

Lynne just nods.

As Sarah ushers them, the two men head below for dry clothes and rest. Josh starts examining the cracks in the mast, trying to figure out how to reinforce it with the few materials on board. He walks slowly around the mast, closely studying the cracks in the wood where the strain from the wind has damaged it. He knows he needs wood and some way to bind it to the mast. If that isn't done, the next storm will almost surely bring it down. And that would be catastrophic, probably ending in their deaths.

As he's contemplating the problem, trying to keep his mind focused on solutions instead of a future disaster, Sarah comes up behind him.

"What's the problem?" she asks, her voice making him jump in surprise. He wheels around to see her a few feet away holding Judy.

"How, how, how's Debbie?" he manages to stammer out.

"Sleeping. We got her in dry clothes and warmed her up. She ate some, and then just fell asleep," Sarah says, shifting Judy from her right hip to her left. "Now, what's the problem?"

"The problem?" Josh responds, his mind still locked into contemplating what to do not in discussing it.

"Yes. The problem!" she says a bit impatiently, gesturing at the mast.

"The mast?" It comes out as a distracted question. "Yes. The mast," Josh says, turning back to the tall wooden pole rising ten meters from the deck. "It's cracked at the base." Josh starts warming to his explanation. "If you look at it here," he says leaning over and indicating a section just above the deck, "you can see the cracks. A couple of them are pretty big, but most are small."

"What you're saying," Sarah says, straightening up from looking closely at the cracks, "is another storm could easily bring it down."

"That's about it," he responds resignedly, straightening up as well.

"What do we do about it?" Sarah asks, urgency entering her voice.

"To tell the truth, I haven't figured that out yet," he admits. "Any suggestions?" he says, looking hopefully at her.

Sarah thinks for a moment. "Wood," she says finally. "We need long pieces of thick, hard wood to stretch vertically from below the cracks to above them." She pauses for a moment. "We shouldn't nail them …"

"We don't have long enough nails," Josh interjects.

"We need," she says, nodding in recognition, "to find a way to bind the new wood onto the mast." She pauses again. "I know," she says, in triumph, "we can take one of the wooden food barrels and use the metal hoops."

"But that wood is not strong enough for this job," Josh protests.

"Yes," she says, thinking again. "The wood from the boat is," she says gesturing toward the boat tied to the deck.

Josh looks at it for a long moment, horrified by the suggestion.

"If we use the boat," he protests, "how will we get to shore?"

"If we lose the mast," she counters, "why would we need the boat?"

Josh nods in acceptance. "I still don't like it," he says in exasperation.

"Neither do I," Sarah agrees, "but what choice do we have?"

"Little to none. If we don't strengthen the mast, all we can do is hope we don't run into another storm."

"Are you willing to gamble our lives on that?"

"No," he replies, dejectedly, shaking his head. "I'll need Sam and Lynne's help."

"The women can't do it?" Sarah challenges him.

"Becky can," he says. "Debbie is in worse shape than Sam and Lynne. Becky alone won't do."

"And me?!" the outrage building in Sarah's voice.

Josh looks at her growing stomach. "Come on, Sarah," he says, looking back up at her. "You can tell us what to do. We need you to make sure we do it right. But, come on. You shouldn't be doing heavy work."

"How do you know that?" she protests. "Are you a doctor?"

"No, but one-third of our future is in there," he says, pointing at her stomach. "We have to protect that. So please, just supervise. Besides, I think Sam would throw a fit if you did heavy work."

"Sam doesn't own me!" she protests, her voice rising, startling Judy who looks up at her to see what is wrong. Sarah makes herself calm down. "It's alright, baby," she says, gently looking reassuringly at her daughter, holding her little hand, and kissing her lightly on her forehead.

"He does love you," Josh says. "That's been obvious since I first met you guys. And he seems to be really protective of you."

"That does not give him …"

"And you are really protective of him," Josh hurries on. "So, it cuts both ways."

Sarah snaps her mouth shut, strangling the protest that was about to come out, acknowledging the truth in what Josh says.

"We'll let them sleep until this afternoon," Josh says. "In the meantime, we can organize the tools and get the barrel on deck so we can get the iron rings off."

"I guess I have no choice," Sarah responds.

She gives Judy to Mary, who has brought Adam up on deck. Jessica is with her, so the two women take charge of the kids, no questions asked. The children are taken below to the playpen.

Sarah and Josh also go below, being as quiet as possible so as not to disturb the sleepers. They find a barrel half full of flour, and Sarah examines the metal hoops holding it together.

"What do you think?" Josh asks.

"I'm not sure this will be enough," Sarah says, contemplatively, "but it's a start. Perhaps we can use some rope as well." She straightens up, looking around at the other barrels. "There is one more with these hoops." She goes over and takes off the top, looking into it, she finds it's a quarter full of flour. "Is there another barrel we can put this flour in?"

"I don't know," Josh says as he checks other barrels. "Here, we can combine the flour in these two barrels in one. That would free this one up."

"Okay, let's get this barrel topside," Sarah says after they combine the two barrels.

They pick up the empty barrel and wrestle it up the stairs as quietly as they can. But not quietly enough, catching the attention of the children who stop their quiet play, Adam asking loudly what is going on. To keep from waking the sleeping trio, Mary and Jessica grab the kids and follow Josh and Sarah toward the ladder up to the main deck.

"Let me do that," Jessica tells Sarah, handing Judy to Mary.

"I got it!" Sarah protests.

"Not good for the baby," Jessica counters, grabbing part of the barrel with Sarah. Josh is on the front end, walking backward up the stairs, with Jessica, who despite her small size, manages to keep the barrel high enough to clear the steps. When they get the barrel on the deck, Josh rolls it over to the mast.

"What's going on?" demands George, who is still on the tiller.

"Construction work," Sarah calls back.

"Not with my barrel!" he protests, releasing the tiller and running forward. With no one holding the ship to the wind, The Hope quickly loses headway and slows.

"George!" Josh yells. "Back on the tiller! Now!"

"Not until you tell me what's going on!"

"I'll get it," Jessica offers as she heads for the stern.

"Thanks," Josh says distractedly. She soon has the ship tacking again with the wind.

"What are you doing with that barrel?" George demands again.

"We need the metal hoops to repair the mast," Sarah explains, studying the barrel for the best way to remove the three hoops holding the wood together.

"You can't do that!" George explodes. "We'll need it when we find new supplies!"

"If this mast comes down, we won't need new supplies," Josh tells him.

"Why not!?"

"Because," Sarah says, glancing up from her study of the rings on the barrel, "we'll all be dead."

Her matter-of-fact tone takes George back for a moment. "How, how do you know that?"

"If the mast breaks," Josh tells him, "the ship will not be able to move and it will be only a matter of time before we run out of food and water or the ship gets rolled over by a wave."

George is quiet for a few seconds, then says hopefully, "We still have the sweeps. We could use those."

"No," Josh says, shaking his head. "They're no good for anything but short distances in calm water."

"But my barrel!" George protests.

"Sorry, George," Sarah says soothingly, "but we don't have a choice."

George grumbles for a few moments, then heads back to take the tiller, needing something to do to keep his mind, and mouth, off a disaster he can't stop.

"Okay," Sarah says, finishing her examination of the barrel and the mast. "I think we can do it with these hoops and a lot of rope."

"You don't want to use the other barrel?" Josh asks.

"No," she replies, shaking her head, knowing they would have to put flour into an empty beef jerky barrel, a barrel that has no hoops. "I am just too nervous about spoiling the flour."

"Even if Becky says it's okay?"

"Even then. She's been great as our medic, mainly because she hasn't had to do too much. But she's not a chemist. At least I don't think she is. Any advice from her would be a best guess. And I'm not willing to risk our food supply on that. Besides," she says, emitting a little laugh, "I don't want to drive poor George stark raving mad by taking another of his precious barrels."

Josh snorts a laugh. "You got me there." Josh looks at the cabin hatch. "Let's get the guys and get to work."

"They haven't had enough sleep. It's only been a couple of hours," Sarah protests. "We'll let them sleep until this afternoon. At least four more hours."

Josh looks at her, amused.

"What's so funny?" she demands.

"You. You get your back up when we try to protect you, but you are like a mother hen with everyone else. Especially Sam."

Sarah just snorts and walks over to play with Judy.

Josh shakes his head in amusement, then heads below to get the tools and ropes they'll need.

CHAPTER SIXTEEN

"Good morning. What's for breakfast?" Sam says, stretching and yawning as he comes up on deck.

"You mean good afternoon," Sarah says, laughter in her voice.

"Afternoon?" Sam's confused.

"Yep," she says, "you guys slept for a long time."

"Guess we were tired."

"Guess so."

"What's to eat?" Lynne says as he wanders up.

"George!" Sarah calls to their cook who is gazing out to sea, oblivious to his surroundings.

"Yes?"

"Can you get these two some food?"

He looks around, and seeing Sam and Lynne, starts moving. "Give me a few minutes," he says as he heads below.

"How's Debbie?" Lynne asks.

"I'm just fine," she says, getting up off the deck where she was sitting. "Thanks for saving my ass."

"I kind of like your ass," Lynne says, a shy smile spreading across his face.

"I'm not going there," Sam declares, "but you're welcome."

Sam looks around the ship, checking out the cracks in the mast. Seeing the tools, ropes, and metal hoops on the deck, he asks, "What's going on here?"

"We have to strengthen the mast," Sarah says.

"With those metal hoops?"

"Well, not just those metal hoops," she replies a bit evasively, knowing what's coming.

"What else?" Sam sounds perplexed.

"Wood." It's a flat statement.

"Wood from where?"

"The boat."

"The boat?" He's really confused now.

"Yes, the boat."

"What boat?"

"That boat," she says, pointing at the boat tied to the deck.

"That boat?" Sam says, confused and a bit outraged, looking at the boat and then back at Sarah, pointing as well.

"It's the only boat we've got," she says matter-of-factly.

"That's right. It's the only boat we've got," Sam shoots back, his aggravation rising. "Josh!" he calls. "Do you know about this?"

Josh, who has been at the stern walks forward. "Yes," he says as he reaches the pair.

"And you're okay with this?" Sam challenges him.

"It depends on what you mean by 'okay'," comes the reply.

"What do you mean by that?"

"I don't like the idea, but we have no choice," Josh says.

"Why not?" Sam demands, looking back and forth at Josh and Sarah.

"We have to strengthen the mast or we could lose it," Sarah says, as patiently as she can. "We definitely will lose it in a storm if we don't do anything. To fix the mast, we need wood. And the only wood we have that is strong enough is the boat."

"But, but …," Sam starts to protest.

"I know," she says, resignation in her voice, as she puts her arms around Sam's neck and kisses his nose, "but we have no choice. If we lose the mast, we lose the ability to move, and we could capsize."

Sam just stares at the two of them, as he and Sarah untangle themselves. "You're saying this is the best of the bad choices."

"That's about the size of it," Josh says, sighing.

"Okay then," Sam says, after a pause. "Let's do it."

"Eat first," Sarah orders him. "You two," indicating Lynne, "need some food before we get to work."

Sam suddenly remembers how hungry he is. "Good idea. Where is George with that food?"

"Don't worry, he'll be up soon," Sarah says.

"Daddy!"

Sam looks down to see Judy holding up her arms. He swoops her up and hugs her. "How's it going, kiddo?"

"I hungry, too," the little girl says.

"Well, you can eat with me. Would you like that?" He gets a vigorous nod and a hug in response.

"Come and get it!" George announces, carrying two plates and some water onto the deck.

"What's this?" Sam asks, looking at a flat bread-like things with jerky on top.

"Pancakes," George announces.

"What? How?"

George shrugs. "They aren't great," he says as he hands a plate to Lynne, who drops to the deck and starts eating without worrying about what he's consuming. "Just flour and water. Oh, and a bit of that cinnamon I scored."

"Daddy, I'm hungry!" Judy protests, eyeing the food.

"Sure thing, Sweetie," he says, sitting down on the deck and settling her on his lap. "Start with this." He hands her a piece of the jerky.

"I want pancake!" she protests.

"Of course you do." He pops the jerky into his mouth and feeds his daughter a piece of the pancake, who starts happily chewing. "Here," he says, "chew slowly." When she swallows, he gives her a sip of water and then some more pancake.

When they have finished eating, the children are sent below with Mary and Jessica to keep them out of harm's way. George also goes below to clean up from cooking and to get ready for dinner later. Becky takes the tiller.

Josh takes one look at his sister and tells her to take it easy. "You still look pretty beaten up," he tells Debbie, looking just at the bruises and rope burns he can see, as well as the exhaustion on her face.

"I'm okay," she protests.

"Do what he says," Sarah orders her, the tone of her voice accepting no contradiction.

Debbie nods, and goes over to Becky, sitting on the deck next to her. Josh just looks at Sarah, and walks away, shaking his head. "Mother hen," he mutters under his breath.

With Sarah supervising and the men working, the rest of the afternoon and into early evening is taken up by dismantling the boat, taking care to not damage the wood, putting the pieces vertically from the deck to above the cracks, the curves on some pieces facing out, and then securing them with the hoops and rope. While this is going on, the sail is kept just high enough to provide steerage, and with the wind blowing from the southwest, Becky keeps The Hope heading northeast so the boom stays out of the way of the work. George comes back on deck, and helps as much as he can, eventually going below to make dinner.

"Do you think it will hold?" Sam asks, standing back to look at their work.

"I hope so," Sarah says.

"That's comforting," Sam says.

"No it ain't," Lynne says, drawing amused looks from Sam and Sarah.

"It's the best we can do," she says, folding her arms above her bulging stomach. "Only time will tell if it's enough."

"It'll work," Josh says. "It has to."

CHAPTER SEVENTEEN

Does anyone know where we are?"

They're all sitting around the stern eating a meager lunch, the two children playing after finishing their meals. It's been five days since the storm. The sea and the wind are calm, pushing The Hope along at about six knots.

The question comes from Becky, who gives voice to the worry they all have.

"You mean outside of being on the ocean?" Sam answers somewhat sarcastically.

"Yes," she shoots back, "outside of that!"

"No," Josh says, dejection in his voice. Sam studies the deck in front of him, not wanting to look at anyone. "We're out of sight of land," Josh continues. "We have no navigation tools. And even if we did, none of us know how to use them. All I can tell you for sure is that we are still heading north, sort of."

"Sort of?" Debbie interjects.

"Yeah, sort of. Sometimes we go west of north and sometimes east of north, depending on the wind and currents. We can't put too much pressure on the mast."

They had run into some foul weather since the mast was repaired, and to everyone's relief, it held. But for how long, they don't know. They live with the fear of the mast breaking, and not being able to replenish their dwindling supply of food and water. The canned vegetables and fruits are nearly gone. Any water used to turn the flour into something edible just means that much less to drink. Soon they would have nothing but some jerky. And that wouldn't last too much longer.

"What do we do?" Mary asks, the fear evident in her voice.

The question is met with silence.

"We need to find land," Sarah offers.

"But which way do we go?" Sam asks. "Do we keep heading north? Do we turn east or west? How do we know where to go?"

"And if we do find land," Lynne says, "will The Enemy be there?"

"And even if The Enemy isn't there, will we be able to find the food and water we need?" Sam adds. "Before we starve."

"But if we do nothing, we will certainly starve," Sarah asserts, her look challenging the two men who seem to her to be losing hope. "We are not going to give up!"

"You're right," Sam acknowledges, his spirits reviving. "Let's decide which way we go."

"How do we do that?" Debbie asks, looking around at the others before settling on her brother. "Josh, what do you think?"

"I think," he says hesitantly, "that I'm not sure."

"Let's vote," Becky suggests.

"Vote?" George asks.

"Yeah, vote. Since none of us know what we're doing, and we all agree we have to do something, let's vote on which way to go."

Silence descends on the group as everyone mulls the suggestion.

"Secret ballot or show of hands?" Sam finally asks.

"Secret ballot?" Sarah repeats, giving him a look that asks if he is an idiot.

Sam shrugs, smiling. "Just thought I'd ask."

"Secret ballot," she says sarcastically, shaking her head and letting out a little laugh.

"Well, then," Josh says, "show of hands it is. Everyone who wants to head north, raise your hand."

"Wait a minute," George interjects. "Which way is the closest land? We should go that way."

Everyone just stares at him in disbelief.

"Uh, George?" Sam finally says. "None of us know where the closest land is, or we would head in that direction without taking a vote."

"Oh," comes the dejected reply.

"Let's try this again," Josh says. "Everyone who wants to head north, raise your hand?"

No hands go up.

"Well, I guess north is out," he says. "West?"

Lynne, Mary and Becky raise their hands.

"Okay, that's three for west," Josh announces. "East?"

Sam, Sarah, Jessica, Debbie and Josh raise their hands.

"That's five for going east," Josh announces. "George, are you not voting?"

"I ... I haven't decided," he replies tentatively.

"Well, it's five-to-three, so your vote won't change the outcome," Josh says. "Are you guys okay with this?" he asks the trio who voted for heading west.

Lynne just nods.

"Yes," Mary says.

"Can anyone explain to me why they voted to head east?" Becky asks.

"Can you explain why you voted to go west?" Sam replies.

"It seemed like the right way to go."

"You just answered your question," he says, smiling. "None of us really know which is the right way to go, so it's just a guess."

Becky nods. "I guess so."

The next few days are spent on a generally easterly course, with everyone scanning the horizon for any sight of land. While they have some rain, the sea and wind do not turn violent. Josh rigs some fishing lines, using small pieces of jerky for bait. He manages to catch some fish, adding some fresh food to their diet.

Only the children are not worried, even though they pick up on the adults' anxiety. The adults don't talk about their impending starvation, or what will happen if they run into another major storm. They just exchange worried looks and do their work around the ship trying to keep busy and their minds occupied.

"Hey!" Becky calls after coming on deck one morning. "What's that?" She is standing on the starboard side of the ship, scanning the horizon with the binoculars.

Everyone crowds around, straining to see what she is looking at. All they can see is the sea.

"Here!" Sarah says. "Let me see."

As Becky hands her the binoculars, she points in the direction she's been looking. "Just there!"

Sarah follows her point, puts the binoculars to her eyes, and adjusts them.

"Oh my God!" she exclaims.

CHAPTER EIGHTEEN

O n deck!"
"Report!"
"Ship, sir! Off the starboard quarter!"

First Officer Horace Clark of the HMS Marianne scans the ocean with the powerful binoculars fixed to the bridge railing in the direction the lookout up in the crow's nest indicated. He quickly finds the ship coming out of the morning mist which the lookout spotted and studies it for a moment. Turning, he walks quickly through the bridge to the Captain's cabin just aft of it and knocks on the door.

"Enter!" the voice inside calls.

Clark enters the cabin to find Captain John Nichols at his desk, filling out the daily log from yesterday. He stops typing on the laptop and turns toward the door.

"What's doing?" he asks his second-in-command.

"Sir, we have an unidentified ship off to starboard."

"Unidentified?" Nichols asks, perplexed. "We don't have any other craft anywhere near here, do we?"

"No, sir. And sir, this is a sailing vessel."

"A sailing vessel?"

"Yes, sir. She's making her way under sail. There is no indication of an engine. And she appears to be built all of wood."

"All of wood, you say."

"Yes, sir. She's off the starboard quarter."

"Well, I guess we better go have a look, shall we."

"Yes, sir," Clark says, standing back to allow the Captain to go out the door and then follows him through the bridge onto the starboard flying bridge.

"The ship is there," Clark says, pointing out to sea.

The Captain looks until he sees the tiny image of a ship on the horizon. He swivels the mounted binoculars until he has it in his field of vision.

"You're quite right," he says to Clark as he stands up, thinking. Clark stays silent, waiting for Nichols to ask his opinion or to issue orders. "This is unacceptable. To have the radar down so we have to depend on our lookouts. We should have known about that vessel an hour ago. But I guess it can't be helped."

"No, sir," Clark responds.

"Mr. Clark," the usually relaxed Captain says in a formal way that makes his First Officer brace for whatever is coming. "Clear the ship for action."

"Aye, aye, sir," Clark responds forcefully, and then turns to issue orders.

"Ms. Thompson!" Nichols calls to the ship's Second Officer who has the bridge watch.

"Aye, sir!" replies Adele Thompson, who after hearing the orders given to Clark knows she will be getting some as well.

"Break out the small arms," the Captain says calmly. "Distribute them to the crew."

"Aye, aye, sir," she says smartly, then heads off below.

Nichols goes back to examining the strange ship. "Helm! I have the con," he calls to the sailor manning the helm inside the bridge cabin as he straightens up after taking another look at the other ship.

"Aye, sir!"

"Make three-quarters speed. Put us off the starboard side of that vessel. Pass her by the stern."

"Aye, aye, sir," Petty Officer Marsha Jackson replies. "Making turns for three-quarters speed," she says as she pushes the engine controls increasing the turn of the ship's twin screws and swinging the wheel to bring the ship toward the other vessel. "Sir! How close do you want us?"

"A hundred meters should do nicely," says Nichols, who has gone back to studying the other ship, wondering if it could be a trap. He feels his six hundred-meter armed fishing trawler pick up speed as the ship swings toward the west.

Across the ship, the fifteen crew members are busily stowing away the lose gear lying about the deck, uncovering the one-hundred-fifty-millimeter gun forward of the superstructure, and the six fifty-caliber machine guns, three on each side. Shells for the gun and ammunition for the machine guns are brought on deck and readied for use, with one shell loaded into the deck gun and belts of ammunition into the machine guns.

"Mr. Clark!" the Captain calls to the officer on the main deck who is directing all the activity.

"Aye, sir!" Clark says, looking up at the bridge three and a half meters over the deck.

"Make sure the crew stays covered. If this is a trap, I don't want any unnecessary casualties."

"Yes, sir."

"And Mr. Clark!"

"Sir?"

"Tell MacTavish not to try to sneak a peek. He'll get his fool head blown off that way."

"Yes, sir, I'll tell him," Clark responds, although his tone of voice carries a clear message: Such an order probably won't work, which the Captain knows as well. Able Seaman Sean MacTavish is the loader for the deck gun, which, like the machine guns, has a thick metal shield protecting the crew from fire coming directly from the front. MacTavish, though, has a distressing habit of wanting to see what's going on, even when such curiosity could prove fatal.

"Johnson!" the Captain calls up to the lookout.

"Aye, sir!"

"Keep a sharp watch. You see anything untoward, I want to know right off."

"Aye, aye, sir."

"Sir, the ship is cleared for action," Clark says after returning to the bridge.

"Very good, Mr. Clark." After studying the other ship for another moment, Nichols turns to the other officer. "Well, Mr. Clark, what do you think."

"It's strange, sir," Clark says after a moment's pause. "We've never encountered them at sea before. They've never tried crossing the channel. What would they be doing out here? It's just strange."

"That it is. But what if they are coming from America? Maybe that group has built ships and is now trying to cross."

"Frightfully strange way of doing it," Clark says, doubt in his voice. "That ship doesn't look very seaworthy to me."

"True," Nichols responds, "but we know they are not particularly technologically advanced."

"Yes, sir, that's true," Clark admits.

"Captain!" the lookout calls.

"Yes, what is it?" Nichols says looking up.

"Sir, I think there is baby on that ship."

"A baby? Are you sure?" Clark calls up.

"It looks like it, sir. A woman appears to be holding a baby."

"Helm," the Captain calls.

"Aye, sir."

"Full speed!" Nichols orders, wanting to close on the ship as quickly as possible, his curiosity piqued.

"Full speed, aye, sir."

"They've turned toward us!" Debbie says, worry in her voice.

"We need to get out of here!" Mary says, scooping Adam up in her arms.

"What's wrong, Mommy?" the little boy asks, picking up on her fear.

"Nothing, sweetheart," she says as calmly as she can. "Everything will be alright." Somewhat reassured, the little boy clings as closely as he can to his mother.

"We can't outrun them," Josh announces. "They have engines. We have a damaged mast. And even if it wasn't damaged, we couldn't outrun them."

"What are we supposed to do? Just wait for them to kill us?" George asks.

"Maybe they won't," Sam says, putting his arm around Sarah who is holding their daughter tightly. The little girl doesn't know what is going on but has picked up on her parents' anxiety and is clinging to her mother. "We don't know who they are. If they're The Enemy, we're dead. We can't escape. But if they're not, perhaps they'll help us. Or at least leave us alone."

"They must be The Enemy," Jessica says flatly, resignation in her voice.

"We don't know that," Sam responds sharply.

"Who else could they be?" she asks.

"We don't know that either. What we do know is that The Enemy hasn't gone to sea," he says, adding as an after-thought, "at least as far as we know."

"That's not particularly comforting," Debbie says.

"It's the best I can do," Sam says, resignation in his voice.

"I ain't giving up without a fight," Lynne says, his body tensing.

"Lynne, stand down!" Sam orders. "They have a cannon and machine guns. They're on a metal, motorized ship. They can blow us out of the water anytime they want."

"I ain't giving up without a fight," Lynne repeats with emphasis.

"Look, if they are not The Enemy, and they see us with weapons, they may shoot first and ask questions later," Sam says. "It's probably what we would do. Our only hope is that they are not The Enemy and will help us."

"So, we just sit here and wait?" Mary asks, the anguish in her voice clear as she holds her son more tightly.

"So we sit here and wait," Sarah says. "Sam's right. If they want to kill us, there's nothing we can do about it."

"What's that flag?" asks Jessica, who has been studying the other ship through the binoculars.

"What flag?" Josh asks.

"The one on its mast," she says, staring at it. "It's blue with a red-and-white cross and red-and-white X."

"Let me see," he says, taking the binoculars. After he looks, he passes them around, until everyone gets a look. "Any ideas?"

Josh's question is greeted by a chorus of "no's."

"It seems like I should know," Sam says, "but I don't."

Silence settles on the group as the opposing ship races toward them, quickly narrowing the distance.

"Sir," Clark says, standing up from the bridge binoculars, "take a look. If I'm right, two children are on that ship, and one of the women is pregnant."

"So you are," Nichols says after studying the people on the opposing ship. "We've never seen any pregnant women or children among them. On the other hand, we don't know what it's like on the other side of the pond."

"What do you want us to do, sir?"

"At the moment," the Captain says, thoughtfully, "nothing. We will approach with caution. Be ready to sink them if we see any hostile intent. But, if they are refugees, then perhaps we will have new recruits."

"Yes, sir."

"Just make sure the crew stays undercover until we know what's going on."

"Aye, aye, sir," Clark turns to go down on the main deck. "Especially MacTavish," he calls over his shoulder.

"Especially MacTavish," Nichols says quietly as he goes back to studying the people on the other ship.

As the distance closes, he can see them more clearly. The woman holding what appears to be a little girl looks quite pregnant. The man next to her has an arm protectively wrapped around her. 'Husband?' he thinks. The other woman with a child is not standing close to anyone else. 'She must be alone,' he thinks. The big man looks belligerent. One of the women is standing partially behind him. 'Must be together.' Another woman and man also appear to have paired off. The last man and woman don't seem to be with anyone else. 'So, three couples and three singles,' Nichols thinks, standing up from the binoculars and going into the bridge cabin to retrieve the megaphone he'll be needing soon. His confidence is growing that these people do not pose a threat to his crew. But he's not willing to let his guard down. Just in case.

"Mr. Clark!" the Captain calls down to his First Officer who is patrolling the deck, keeping the crew calm and under cover.

"Sir?"

"No firing unless I order it."

"Aye, aye, sir."

"Make sure everyone knows that. I don't want any unnecessary violence."

"Yes, sir."

The Marianne passes down the port side of The Hope, keeping about one hundred meters off, before turning and passing up the starboard side.

"Helm," the Captain calls.

"Aye, sir."

"Keeps us abreast of that ship."

"Aye, sir. Matching speed," Jackson says, slowing the Marianne to match the other ship's slower speed.

"On the other ship!" Nichols calls through the megaphone. "Who are you and where are you out of?"

His questions are greeted with apparent confusion, with the people looking at each other as if in search of an answer.

"Answer the question or I will be forced to fire on you!" he calls. "Mr. Clark," he calls down to the deck after taking down the megaphone. "Make sure no one fires without orders."

"Yes, sir," Clark responds, repeating the orders to stay under cover and hold fire.

"Sir," the man who had his arm around the woman with the little girl calls through cupped hands, stepping in front of them, "we are not sure where we are from. Two of us say America; the rest don't know for sure. We are fleeing The Enemy who tried to kill us. We are looking for some place safe, where our children will be safe."

Nichols stares at them for a bit, not sure what to make of the response. "How can you not know where you are from?" he calls across.

"It's a long story," the man calls back. "One we'd be happy to share with you if you can take us to safety."

'The Enemy?' Nichols thinks to himself. 'Who is he referring to? Could we have a common enemy?'

"What proof do you have about this?" Nichols calls back.

"None," comes the reply. "But why else would we be out here in the middle of the ocean on this rickety piece of crap?"

The reply elicits a quiet laugh from the Captain and members of the crew. Nichols is inclined to believe the man, but he is going to be cautious.

"Alright, then," he calls back, "we'll tow you into port. You can explain yourselves there."

"Thank you," the man calls.

"God bless you," calls the woman holding the little boy.

"We'll pass you a line," Nichols calls. "But be mindful of this: Anything happens that I don't like, we'll sink you. Understood?"

"Yes, sir," another man calls back.

Nichols studies them for a moment. "Mr. Clark," he calls down to the main deck.

"Sir?"

"Secure from general quarters, but have the crew retain their arms."

"Aye, sir."

"Ms. Thompson," Nichols calls.

"Sir."

"Pass a line to that ship and secure for towing."

"Aye, sir."

"Helm."

"Aye, sir."

"Dead slow. Put us ahead of them. Prepare for towing."

"Aye, sir, dead slow." Jackson maneuvers the Marianne in front of the other ship.

Using what looks like a shotgun, Thompson fires a metal weight attached to a thin line from the stern onto the other ship's bow. After it lands on deck, the people on that ship just look at it and then look at the ship in front of them, not sure what to do.

Finally, a big man picks up the line and looks at her, obviously seeking directions.

"Pull the line over!" Thompson calls, pantomiming the motion. "A larger line will follow!"

The big man nods and starts pulling.

"Twits," Thompson says quietly, but loud enough for the crew members around her to hear and laugh.

As the light line is pulled over, the heavy towing cable it is attached to follows.

When that is done, Thompson calls, "Secure the cable to something sturdy. Like the mast."

The big man waves at her, and with the help of two others, drags the cable to the mast. It's soon secured to the base, below where the cracks are.

"We're ready!" one of the men calls back.

Thompson waves in acknowledgement. Going forward, she calls up to the bridge. "Captain, it looks like the cable is secure."

"Looks like?" comes the dubious response.

"Well, sir, I don't think that lot," she says, waving toward the stern, "really know what they're doing."

"Very good, Ms. Thompson. We'll take it slow. Keep a close watch to make sure the bloody thing stays attached."

"Aye, sir."

"And Ms. Thompson."

"Sir?"

"I want an armed guard placed to keep a watch on those people."

"Aye, aye, sir."

"Helm."

"Aye, sir."

"Ahead slow."

"Ahead slow, sir."

Nichols and Clark stand together on the bridge watching as the cable tightens and starts pulling the other ship through the water. The Captain has the Marianne's speed slowly increase so the two vessels are soon moving through the water at fifteen knots. He would like to go faster, but he's not sure how much strain the other ship's mast can take.

"One of us will have to be on duty the whole time," Nichols tells Clark and Thompson, who has joined them on the bridge.

"Aye, sir. Good thing our hold is filled. I'd hate to go back without a full catch."

"Are we doing the right thing?" Nichols asks no one in particular.

"Do we have a choice, sir? Other than to let them die out here?"

"No, Mr. Clark. No, we don't."

CHAPTER NINETEEN

D o you think they'll kill us?" a fearful Mary asks as they are all gathered on the stern having breakfast. It's the second day since the Marianne took them under tow. They have been heading steadily east the whole time, but no sight of land yet.

"Naw," Lynne drawls, "they would have done it already if they were goin' to."

"Are you sure?" she asks, seeking reassurance.

"He's right," Sarah says. "They could have blown us out of the water when we met."

"Or just left us adrift," Sam adds.

"Where are they taking us?" Mary persists.

"The guy in charge said a port," Debbie answers.

"Where?"

"We'll find out when we get there, I suppose," Josh says.

"Mary," Sam says, "we are no longer in control of our own fate."

"If we ever were," Becky adds, somewhat bitterly. "I still wonder how all this happened to us."

"Maybe where we're going we'll get some answers," Sam says. "And then again, maybe not."

"You are so reassuring," Sarah admonishes him. "Now, help me get up."

Sam scrambles to his feet to help Sarah, who is ungainly this advanced into her pregnancy, get up. He then picks up Judy, and walking forward, scans the horizon with binoculars. "Here you want to take a look?" he asks his daughter, holding them to her eyes. She pulls away at first, then grabs them, or tries to. They are too heavy for her to hold on her own, so her father has to help. She studies them closely, feeling them, tasting them.

"No," Sam says gently, "you can't eat those."

Then, with his help, Judy holds them to her eyes, letting out a squeal of delight as she looks through them.

Sarah walks up beside them, her arms folded over her very large belly.

"Here," Sam says, offering her the binoculars.

"Thanks." She takes them and begins to scan the horizon. As she sweeps right, she freezes. "Sam,"

"Yes," he says absently, not noticing what she's doing as he plays a little game with Judy.

"Look," she says, handing him the binoculars. "Over there." She points to the right, just a bit off the bow.

"What?" he says, his attention drawn back to her. He takes the binoculars, and after running interference from Judy who is reaching for them, looks to where Sarah pointed.

"Is that what I think it is?" he asks, looking at her.

"I think so."

"Hey, Josh!" Sam calls.

"What?" comes the reply from near the stern.

"Come take a look at this," Sam calls.

Josh, followed by everyone but Jessica who is on the tiller, comes forward. Sam hands him the binoculars, and points to where he should look. Josh adjusts them, and stares across the water.

"Good God, is that what it looks like?" he asks.

"You tell us," Sarah says.

"What is it?" Debbie asks.

"Land," Josh says. "Land."

"It must be where they're taking us," Sam says.

"Land." Wonder and relief are in Debbie's voice. "I had just about given up ever seeing it again."

"You and me both, sister," Sarah says.

"How long before we get there?" Mary asks.

"Maybe three, four hours," Josh estimates. "Maybe longer. I'm just not sure how far that is. And I don't know if that is where they are taking us."

"Where else could they be taking us?" Mary says, fear growing in her voice again.

"I don't know," Josh says, handing the binoculars to his sister so Debbie can have a look. "There are all kind of questions we need answers to."

"Like," Sam says, "were they attacked by The Enemy? If they were, how did they stay alive? Is this another Live Side that could collapse? Do they fight The Enemy a lot? A little? How do they get their food? They obviously have at least some technology, so where'd they get it?"

"What kind of society are we being taken to?" Sarah says, picking up where Sam stopped. "How will we fit in? But at least they speak English like we do, sort of anyway."

"Is there anything else?" George asks.

"Daddy said there used to be all kinds of languages," Debbie says. "Maybe there still are."

"Oh," George says, letting the issue drop.

They are all transfixed by the approaching land, staying glued to the bow, watching as the blue haze rises higher from the ocean, eventually turning pale green. As they drew closer, the Marianne turns to the northeast, pulling The Hope behind.

"Where are we going?!" Mary says, growing hysterical.

"Take it easy, girl," Sarah says. "They're taking us to a port. Maybe there isn't one there," she says, indicating the land that is now passing to starboard as they turn north. "Or maybe, it isn't their port. Don't worry, we'll get there."

"Promise?"

"Promise," Sarah responds, hoping she sounds more convincing than she feels.

The group at the bow slowly breaks up as each one wanders back to amidships, watching the land to starboard slip by.

As evening falls, the two ships turn north.

"Is that a peninsula or an island?" George asks.

"Can't tell yet," Lynne says, studying the passing land.

"We'll soon find out," Debbie says, putting an arm around Lynne's waist. "We're starting to turn east."

The group falls silent for a bit.

"Well, I hope it's not too long," George opines. "We're nearly out of food and water. A day or two at most."

As the day passes, the two vessels round the headlands of what is either an island or peninsula, and then turn south, eventually heading southeast.

CHAPTER TWENTY

H ere you are, sir," Clark says, handing the Captain the megaphone. "Think they're awake yet?"

"If not, they soon will be," Nichols replies, making sure the bullhorn is on. The sun has just cleared the land to port, the long rays slanting in through low clouds, creating a profusion of colors. "I'll be happy to get rid of this lot."

"They've been no trouble, sir," Thompson says, coming up behind the two senior officers.

"True," Nichols acknowledges. "Still, I will be happy to let someone else take responsibility for them."

"Yes, sir," Thompson says.

"You on the ship!" Nichols calls through the megaphone. He waits a few seconds, then repeats the call. After a third call, three men and two women come to the bow. One of the men waves at him.

Nichols waves back, then holds the megaphone to his mouth again. "We will be entering the port of Liverpool in about an hour. When we enter, you will drop anchor in the bay, and await further instructions. Do you understand?"

The man who waved cups his hand and calls something out, but the wind blows away the words.

"What did he say?" Nichols asks.

"Don't know, sir," Clark answers.

"Say again," Nichols calls again.

Again the wind blows away the words.

"Ms. Thompson, go down and see if you can hear him," Nichols says.

"Aye, sir," Thompson says, quickly descending the bridge ladder and going to the stern. She yells something at the man on the other ship, who yells something back, shaking his head. Thompson nods she understands, and holds up a hand, indicating the man should wait. She comes back to the bridge ladder.

"Sir," she says, looking up at the bridge, "he says they have no anchor."

"No what?" the Captain says incredulously.

"No anchor, sir."

"How can they not have a bloody anchor?"

"Don't know, sir, but that's what he says."

"Oh, bollocks," the exasperated Captain says. He puts the megaphone to his mouth again. "Standby," he calls to the man, who waves assent.

Handing the megaphone to Clark, Nichols goes into the bridge. Picking up the radio microphone, he contacts the port. "Liverpool base. This is the Marianne."

"Liverpool base," comes the nearly immediate reply.

"These people we are towing have no anchor."

"Say again, Marianne."

"No anchor," the exasperation clear in his voice. "They have no anchor. What do you want us to do?"

"Standby."

Nichols stands there fuming for what seems hours but is only about five minutes.

"Marianne. Liverpool base."

"Go ahead, Liverpool."

"Drop your tow as you enter the harbor. They will be met and boarded. You are to proceed directly to your dock to unload."

"Roger. Out." Nichols holds the handpiece for minute, then putting it on the receiver, heads back to the aft portion of the bridge.

"Sir?" Clark says expectantly, handing the megaphone back to the Captain.

"Bollocks," he says. "We leave them adrift in the harbor and go to the wharf. Theoretically, someone will be out to take care of them."

"Yes, sir," Clark says, humor and doubt mixed in his voice. "Do you think they know where we're taking them?"

"I doubt it, Mr. Clark, I doubt it. It's all bollocks," Nichols says.

"Perhaps we should tell them?"

"Perhaps we should, though I seriously doubt they will have a clue of where Liverpool is," Nichols replies, glancing at Clark, then making sure the megaphone is on. "On the other ship," he calls.

The man with whom they've been communicating waves in acknowledgement. The pregnant woman comes to his side, handing him a little girl.

"When we enter Liverpool harbor, we will drop the tow. A boat will be out to meet you and tell you what to do. Do you understand?"

The man, now with a crowd gathered around him, waves back in acknowledgement.

"Good," Nichols says. "That's done," he says, handing the megaphone to Clark. "Now, let's go home. I want to get rid of this lot, and then see the missus and the kids."

"Yes, sir. I'd like to see my wife as well."

"When's she due?"

"In a couple of weeks, sir. I plan to take some shore leave when the baby arrives."

"Good for you." The Captain looks down to the main deck, and spotting his second officer, calls out: "Ms. Thompson."

"Sir."

"Make all preparations for entering port. We have to get Mr. Clark home so he can see his baby born."

"Aye, aye, sir," comes the reply from a grinning Thompson.

"Where is Liverpool?" Becky asks.

Everyone just looks at each other until Debbie speaks up. "England. I think."

"England?" Mary asks.

"It's an island," Josh adds. "It's off the coast of Europe." He looks at Debbie for confirmation, who nods her head.

"Europe?" Becky asks.

"I think I kind of remember that," Sam says.

"Me, too," Sarah says, thinking hard. "That means, I think, that we've crossed the Atlantic Ocean?"

"We must have," Debbie says, "because we've been heading east. That means we were in America."

"America? That sounds right," Sam says, concentrating hard. "I wonder why I forgot that?"

"We forgot everything, sweetheart," Sarah says. "How could we not forget that, too?" she adds enjoying the irony, since none of the original group remember anything but their first names.

Sam just looks at her and sighs.

"Well," Josh says, "it's a good thing our parents were around to teach us geography. And now we'll soon find out what's going to happen."

"What do you mean?" Mary says, fear rising in her voice.

"We'll find out what kind of reception we'll have," he answers.

"They're going to be suspicious," Sam says. "And I don't blame them."

"What do you mean?" Debbie asks.

"Given how that ship," he says, indicating the trawler towing them, "approached us, you have to think the folks on shore will be suspicious. My guess is they faced The Enemy at some point. Perhaps they still do."

"What do you think they'll do?" Becky asks.

"I really don't know," Sam says. "But I think we'll have to be careful about how we approach them." Turning to Lynne, he adds, "That means keep your cool."

A glowering Lynne just nods.

"Don't worry," Debbie says, putting her hand inside the big man's. "I'll keep him from exploding. Understand?" she says, looking up at him.

Lynne just nods, looking a bit sheepish now.

Sarah stifles a laugh, then turns to watch the approaching shore, along with the others.

As they enter the harbor, a city starts to take shape in front of them. Josh scans the waterfront with the binoculars.

"I can't make out people yet," he tells the others, "but there seems to be a lot of ships and boats. There are some cranes loading or unloading a ship. I can't tell for sure."

"Wait until we're closer," Sarah says. "Then we'll figure things out."

"On the ship!" comes the booming voice from the trawler.

Sam waves, indicating that he hears the call.

"Cast off the tow line!"

Sam waves in acknowledgement. He turns to go back to do that, but Lynne and Debbie beat him to it. They soon have the heavy cable untied. The Hope slows as the trawler moves away, pulling the cable over the deck and then into the water. The trawler's crew soon has the towing cable secure, and the ship starts picking up speed.

The group on The Hope watch it move off.

"Should we raise the sail?" Sam asks, not sure what to do now that they are adrift in the harbor.

"No!" Sarah says emphatically. "They could take that the wrong way."

"Good point," he says.

"Why don't we put up the sail?" Jessica asks, coming up to the bow where Sam and Sarah are still standing.

Sarah does a double take at her, while Sam starts to laugh.

"What's so funny about that?" Jessica asks.

"I…" Sarah starts to say, then her mouth just snaps shut.

"What she means to say," Sam says, squashing his laughter, "is that I just asked that same question. And she shot me down."

"Why?"

"Because," Sarah says, finding her voice again, "if we start sailing toward shore, they may take it wrong and fire at us."

"Oh," Jessica responds. "I hadn't thought of that."

"Don't feel bad," Sam interjects. "Neither did I."

"I have an idea," Becky says, walking up, "why don't we…"

"Stop! Stop right there!" Sarah orders as Sam's laughter rebounds, and Jessica first looks confused, then hides a giggle behind a hand. "If you are going to suggest raising the sail, don't! They may think we are going to attack or something and shoot at us."

"You make a good point," Becky says, "but I wasn't going to suggest that."

"Oh, sorry," Sarah says, a bit sheepishly. "What were you going to say?"

"I just thought we should pack up our clothes. Get ready to go, you know."

"That's … not … a … bad … idea," Sarah says slowly, recovering her composure. "Stop laughing!" she snaps, turning to Sam who is in danger of losing his balance as waves of laughter come rolling out.

"What's going on?" Josh says as he and George come up.

"Nothing!" Sarah snaps, bringing them up short while Sam just waves at them, trying to straighten up. "Becky thinks we should pack our things so we can be ready to go ashore," she says.

"Sounds good," Josh says, uncertain what he had just walked into.

"Let's go!" Sarah says, leading the group to the stairs below. "You," she says pointedly to Sam, "keep watch. I'll pack for all of us. And I'll take Judy, thank you very much." Sarah takes their daughter from Sam, who has wrapped his arms around her to keep her from falling as he laughs. He nods in acceptance as he manages to suppress his laughter and stand up straight. Judy readily goes to her mother after the awkward hold Sam had on her, the little girl trying to figure out what is going on with her parents, not sure if she should be smiling or frowning.

Sam follows the group aft, but as they go below, he heads for the stern where Lynne has the tiller.

"What's goin' on?" the big man asks.

"They're going to pack up," Sam responds.

"Good. I want off this thing," Lynne says as he manages the tiller to keep their vessel straight as The Hope glides further into the harbor.

"Don't we all."

The two fall silent as The Hope drifts on the incoming tide. Sam scans the docks with the binoculars, looking for signs of trouble and for what kind of society they are about to get involved with. After about five minutes, he lowers the glasses.

"You know, I don't see anything but people working, loading and unloading ships, moving cargo. No soldiers. No brutality. Just people working."

"That good," Lynne says. "What's that?"

"What's what?"

"Over yonder," he responds, pointing to three gunboats rapidly approaching from the shore. Sam takes a look through the binoculars, and what he sees inspires concern. He quickly walks to the stairs leading below.

"Everyone on deck!" Sam calls down. "We're about to have company!"

All those below come tumbling up the ladder, the two mothers carrying their children. Sarah is moving a lot slower than usual, as the child in her arms and the child in her womb make it harder for her to move.

"Over there," Sam says, pointing at the rapidly approaching boats, as he responds to everyone's questions.

"Who are they?" Debbie asks.

"Our reception committee," Sam says, trying to take Judy from Sarah's arms to lighten her burden.

"No!" she tells him brusquely, pushing his arm away and holding her daughter tighter.

"That's a lot of firepower," Josh comments, scanning the boats with the binoculars.

"Firepower?" Jessica asks, worried.

"Yeah," Sam acknowledges. "Heavy machine guns on all of them. It looks like one has a twenty-millimeter cannon."

"Shit!" Becky spits out.

"What do you think they're going to do?" a nervous George asks.

"We are about to find out," Sam says as the three boats slow as they near The Hope. One positions itself off the stern, while another takes position to starboard. The third swings slowly around the vessel, crossing the bow, and coming down the port side before circling around to halt alongside the one to starboard. All their weapons are pointed at The Hope. People on those two gunboats exchange words that can't be heard on The Hope.

"You, on the ship!" a male voice booms over a loudspeaker. Sam looks for who's talking but only sees men and women with weapons pointed at them. "Prepare to be boarded!"

Sam and the others exchange glances, some worried, some curious. Mary steps behind everyone, cradling Adam her arms.

"Be advised: Any resistance will be met with deadly force!" the booming voice warns.

That is just too much for Sarah. "Hey, asshole!" she yells at the top of her voice, startling Judy. "We have children!"

"Calm down," Sam says soothingly. "It's just a precaution on their part. Besides, I don't think he can hear you."

"Precaution my ass!" she shoots back. "They better not hurt Judy. Or Adam," she adds almost as an afterthought.

"No one is going to get hurt," he assures her.

"They won't hurt my daughter!"

"Or mine," he quips.

"Well," Debbie interjects to break the tension, "at least they speak English."

"They sound funny," Becky observes.

"It's the accent," Josh comments.

"But it sounds funny," she repeats.

They all stop talking as a small boat with seven armed sailors in blue uniforms leaves the gunboat from which the warning came and comes alongside The Hope. Sam steps forward slowly and puts the rope ladder over the side, then steps away.

A burly man nearly as big as Lynne comes swarming up the ladder. As soon as he's on deck, he unslings his semi-automatic rifle and stands a couple of meters away from the group, watching them suspiciously. He's quickly followed by a woman wearing an officer's uniform and armed with a sidearm, who is then followed by four other sailors, all carrying semi-automatic rifles. The seventh sailor stays in the boat, keeping it alongside.

"I am Leftenant Bailey-Jones," the officer announces. "Chief FitzGibbons," she says, turning to one of the sailors without waiting for a response from the group.

"Yes, ma'am."

"Conduct the search. Leave one here with me."

"Yes, ma'am," the Chief Petty Officer says, pointing at the burly sailor to remain and motioning the others to follow.

"Why are you searching our ship?" Sarah challenges the officer.

Bailey-Jones eyes her suspiciously, then relaxes, deciding a pregnant woman holding a child is not a threat. "To make sure you are not bringing anything dangerous with you."

"What do you mean dangerous?" Josh asks, stepping forward.

"Are you in charge here?" she asks him.

"Not really. Sort of," he corrects himself. "I'm kind of the captain of this ship, but none of us are really in charge."

"You're the sailing master." It comes as a statement, not a question.

Josh looks confused. "I'm not sure what that is."

"Never mind," Bailey-Jones says dismissively. "What brings you to our shores?"

"Survival," Sam responds.

"Excuse me?"

"Survival. We're escaping from The Enemy trying to kill us."

"On this?" she asks incredulously, looking around the battered vessel, her eyes coming to rest on the patched-up mast.

"It was this or death," Sam says matter-of-factly.

"I see. You lot must have been desperate," Bailey-Jones comments.

"Lady, if you had an army coming after you to kill you, you'd be desperate, too," a little sarcasm filtering into Sam's response.

"An army?" Bailey-Jones says doubtfully, looking at them with renewed suspicion.

"Yes, an army," Becky spits out.

"A brutal, vicious, murderous army that just wants to kill everything in sight," Sarah says sharply, pulling Judy in tighter. "We fought them, and we fled. We're looking for a safe place, a peaceful place to live and raise our kids. Do you know any place like that?"

Bailey-Jones looks at her with growing understanding but says nothing.

"Ma'am," the Chief says, coming back on deck followed by the other sailors.

"Report."

"They have small arms, but besides that just clothing, bedding, food and water. It seems the provisions are just about finished."

"Very good," she says. Then turning back to the group, says, "Why the weapons?"

"We fought The Enemy," Sam says. "That's why we're still alive."

"And where are you from?"

They all just look at each other.

"We're not really sure," Sam says at last.

"America. we think," Debbie offers. "My geography is not the best."

"I see," the officer says. "Standby."

"We're not going anywhere," Sam says, letting full sarcasm out now.

Bailey-Jones glances at him as she takes out the hand-held radio hooked to her belt. "Commander?"

"Yes," comes a male voice Sam recognizes from the speaker.

"It seems we have refugees."

"Nothing untoward?"

"No, sir. The ship has been searched. Nothing but small arms, which they explained are for self-defense."

"Standby."

"Yes, sir."

Silence descends on everyone on the ship for a few minutes as they await the verdict.

"Leftenant, we'll take them under tow. You and your party will remain on board until they land."

"Yes, sir." Bailey-Jones turns to FitzGibbons. "Chief, prepare to secure this vessel for tow."

"Ma'am," she replies, then takes two of the sailors to the bow. The Chief supervises as the two take the cable passed by the gunboat, securing it to the mast. The Hope then starts being towed toward shore.

"Where are you taking us?" Sarah asks Bailey-Jones.

"The Commander didn't say. But I should think we're going to the Customs Dock."

"Why there?"

"If you must know, it's where all arriving ships are cleared for unloading."

"Any people?"

Bailey-Jones looks at her for a moment. "You're the first."

"The first?" Sarah asks, a bit shocked and disappointed.

"Yes, you're the first lot. At least on this side of the island."

"Island?"

Bailey-Jones looks at her curiously, wondering about her lack of geographical knowledge. "This is Great Britain, you know. We are two big islands, Britain and Ireland, and a number of smaller ones. Ireland is to the west. You came around that. Britain is just over thirty-three kilometers from Europe."

Sarah doesn't say anything for a moment, digesting the information. Finally, she asks, "Is Europe like where we came from?"

"I dare say I don't know, since I don't know what it was like where you came from. But I can tell you the Continent is in bloody awful shape."

Sarah thinks about that a bit. "Anyone escape from there?"

"Some. They all landed on the east coast. I don't know how many. Now, if you'll excuse me, I have duties to attend to," Bailey-Jones says, walking off to where her sailors have congregated amidships. The Hope's passengers are all gathered around the stern. The sailors are watching them still and keeping their distance but are much more relaxed than before.

The refugees are nervous and hopeful, wondering what awaits them.

CHAPTER TWENTY-ONE

"Please move to the port railing," Bailey-Jones tells the refugees as they near the dock.

The gunboat slows down as they approach the dock, allowing The Hope to slow as well without colliding with the gunboat's stern. One of the sailors takes over at the tiller, steering The Hope as it nears the dock. The gunboat slowly turns to port now moving parallel to the dock on its starboard side with just enough speed to maintain steering.

Sam is studying the people who are lined up along the dock's edge. Their uniforms are a different shade of blue than the sailors'. Some have sidearms. Some are unarmed. None are behaving in a hostile manner.

"Our reception committee," Sam says quietly to Sarah as they move back.

"They don't look dangerous," she replies just as quietly. "Let's hope looks are not deceiving."

Sam just nods in agreement. Everyone is tense, worried about what the future holds.

As The Hope slows to nearly a stop, its starboard side next to the dock, the sailors cast off the towing cable and the gunboat picks up speed, heading off. Three of the police officers throw lines to the sailors still aboard The Hope, who then pull the ship against the dock, securing the tiny vessel. Several of the police officers slide a temporary gangway from the dock onto the deck.

"Alright," Bailey-Jones says, turning to the refugees, "you lot will disembark here and then be cleared in the Customs House. You can leave your belongings on board for now. You may retrieve them after processing."

"Processing?" Debbie asks.

"Yes, right, paperwork," she replies. "We must keep our bureaucrats happy, mustn't we?" She smiles a bit, then steps back, and sweeps her arm toward the gangway.

Sam takes Judy, and follows Sarah, who takes the lead to the dock.

"May I help you ma'am?" a sailor asks Sarah as she steps up on the gangway, reaching out take her arm.

She pulls away quickly, suspicion across her face, but her voice stays calm. "No, thanks. I can do this on my own."

"Yes, ma'am," the sailor says, retreating several steps.

As she steps onto the dock, a female police Sergeant greets her. "This way if you please, ma'am," the officer says indicating which way to walk, then leading the way. Sarah hesitates, seeing the three chevrons on the Sergeant's epaulettes on her shoulder.

"At least they're polite," Sam tells her quietly as he comes alongside of her, prompting Sarah to start walking again. "No, baby girl, stay with me," he tells Judy, who has reached out for her mother as soon as they were side by side. Sarah reaches out and touches her daughter's hand. The little girl relaxes back into her father's arms, her head swiveling around as she takes in the new sights and sounds surrounding them.

Lynne is the last off the ship. They walk in a cluster with six police officers on either side of them and three behind them. Lynne is tensed up, waiting for trouble. But the officers are relaxed, chatting among themselves. He overhears talk about evening plans, football games, children, spouses, and a bit of bitching about their bosses. None of them are paying much attention to the people they are guarding.

"Here we are," announces the Sergeant who is leading the procession. She opens the door into the building, stepping inside, and holds it open until they are all in, along with five other officers. Three officers take up position along the back wall, while the Sergeant and two others walk with the group into the room.

In front of them is a long, low counter with two men in identical dark business suits sitting behind it.

"At least their ties are different," Sarah whispers to Sam as they walk to the desk.

One of the men looks around the group to the officer who led them in. "Sergeant, is this the lot for processing?"

They all stiffen at the words "Sergeant" and "processing", which immediately puts the three officers on alert.

"Is there a problem?!" one of the men behind the counter demands.

"What do you mean 'processing'?" Sam asks.

"What?" comes the somewhat confused reply. "We have to fill out the documents you'll need if you are to stay here. Understand?"

"Yes, I think so," Sarah says.

"Well, then," the irritated bureaucrat says, "shall we get started? We'll start with you two." He motions Sam and Sarah to come forward, assuming they are together. "You lot may sit until it is your turn," he tells the others. They take seats in the chairs arranged in three rows two meters from the counter.

"Now," he says as Sarah and Sam sit in the two chairs in front of the counter—Sam has to pull over one of the chairs that was in front of the other man, who apparently is absorbed in some work on computer—"shall we start with you?" he asks Sarah, his hands poised over the keyboard in front of his monitor.

"Okay," she says.

"Right. Given name?"

"Excuse me?" she says, perplexed.

"Your given name. Your first name?"

"Sarah."

"Is that with an 'h'?"

"Ah, yes, I suppose. 'S-a-r-a-h'," she spells out.

"Very good," the man says crisply. "Middle name."

"What?" she says, confused.

"Your middle name," he demands.

"I don't know," she says, hesitantly. "I don't know if I have one."

"That's absurd. Everyone has a middle name."

She just shrugs in reply.

"Lovely," he says, his irritation growing. "What is your surname."

"My surname?"

The man heaves a sigh. "Your family name. Your last name, if you must."

Sarah shakes her head. "I don't know if I have one."

"What? Of course you do. Now what is it?" he now demands.

"I don't have one that I know of," comes the hesitant reply.

The other bureaucrat has stopped working, taking in the unfolding scene with curiosity.

"This is just simply absurd. What about you?" the man interviewing them says, turning to Sam. "I suppose you don't have a middle or surname either?"

"Sorry," Sam shrugs.

"I find this impossible to believe," the exasperated bureaucrat says, "that you refuse to divulge your surnames. What kind of game are you playing?"

"We're not playing any kind of game," Sarah says. "All we know are our first names."

"Unbelievable. Wait here," he says, getting up. "Sergeant!" he calls to the officer in the back. "Keep an eye on this lot."

"Yes, sir," she replies as the bureaucrat disappears through a door in the back wall. She and the other officers exchange amused glances, but don't move. All the refugees glance at them, and when they see the officers' reaction, they relax.

Sam and Sarah exchange looks, with concern and amusement mixed in—concern about what will happen now, and amusement over the bureaucrat's reaction.

After about ten minutes, the door in the back wall opens and a woman in a business-like blue dress which comes down well below her knees and up to her neck walks out quickly followed by the bureaucrat. When she reaches the counter, she leans her hands on it and looks at the two adults in front of her intensely for a few moments.

They return her stare.

"Am I to understand," she says, straightening up, "that you refuse to divulge your surnames?"

"No, ma'am," Sam says.

"Then why won't you give them to us?"

"Because we don't know them," Sarah says.

"How can you not know them?" the woman demands.

"That," Sarah says, "is a long story."

"A very long story," Sam adds, "and we don't even know if we have last names. Or if we did, why we don't remember them. We don't remember anything much of our past."

"What? How can that be?" she demands.

"That is another question we have no answer to," Sarah responds. "We'd love to know ourselves."

"Well, I never."

"Me either," Sam quips, not sure what she means by that expression, but unable to resist a response. Sarah smacks his leg under the counter, shooting him a look to behave. He just gives her a small smile in response.

"Do any of your mates know their surnames?" she demands.

"Well, ah, those two," Sarah says, turning around to indicate Debbie and Josh.

The woman looks at them. "Husband and wife?"

"Brother and sister," Sarah says.

"I see." She thinks for a moment. Then she waves Josh and Debbie to come over. Having heard the exchange, they approach tentatively.

"Mr. Franklin," the woman says, "you may process these two. The rest of this lot will be quarantined in the Dorset until this can be sorted."

"Yes, ma'am," Franklin responds.

"Sorted?" Sam asks.

"Yes, well," the woman says, "I will have to contact the Home Office to find out what to do. Never in my life have I confronted such an outlandish situation." At this point, the others have stood up and moved a couple of feet toward the counter to better hear what is going on.

"The Home Office?" Sam asks.

"Yes, yes," the woman says, distractedly. "The Home Office."

"What's the Home Office?" Sarah asks.

"What? You don't know what the Home Office is?"

"Not a clue," Sarah says.

"This is just unheard of," the woman says, her exasperation growing. "But never mind. You two," she says, pointing at Josh and Debbie, "come sit down and we'll process you."

"Excuse me?" Debbie says. "We'd rather wait for the others. We came here together, and we'd like to stay together."

The woman looks even more annoyed. "That goes for you as well?" she asks Josh.

"Yes. Yes, ma'am."

"Very well. Mr. Franklin and these officers will escort you to the Dorset …"

"What's that?" Becky asks.

"It is a hotel," she responds emphatically. "You do know what that is?" She hurries on, not giving anyone a chance to respond, "Now, if you don't mind, no more interruptions. Where was I? Yes, Mr. Franklin and these officers will escort you to the Dorset, where you will be given rooms. You will also take your meals there. You may not leave the hotel under any circumstances …"

"Even if it burns down?" Sam asks impishly.

The woman glares at him. Sarah smacks him on the arm.

"Under any circumstances," she resumes, "until this absurd situation is cleared up."

"How long will that take?" Sarah asks.

"I have no idea," she pronounces.

"And after we're processed?" Jessica asks.

"Then you are no longer my problem," the bureaucrat announces.

"Whose problem will we be?" Becky asks.

"Someone from the Home Office will come along and sort you."

"Before we go to the hotel," Sarah asks, provoking an irritated glare from the woman, "may we get our belongings from the ship?"

"Yes. Yes, of course, you may," comes the irritated reply. "Mr. Franklin, officers, see to this lot."

"Hold a minute!" Sam says sharply. "What happens when she goes into labor?" he says, indicating Sarah.

The woman looks at Sarah, perplexed, then down at her stomach. Her eyes widen. "Well, in that event, we shall summon an ambulance and she'll be taken to hospital." Having made that pronouncement, she abruptly turns around, disappearing through the door in the back wall.

"Nice lady," Sam says dryly.

Sarah nudges him and giggles.

"Alright, you lot, follow me," Franklin orders.

He leads them back outside, the officers falling in step with them, not bothering to keep their distance.

"Sorry about that," the Sergeant tells Sarah and Sam, loud enough for the others to hear.

"Not your fault," Sam says.

As they get their belongings from the ship, Josh takes a farewell tour of the vessel he designed and led in building. He doesn't expect to return to it ever again.

"Are we ready yet?" Franklin asks, impatiently.

"I think so," Sam says, having given Judy back to Sarah so he can carry all their belongings. Lynne takes some of the load from him.

"This way, then," Franklin announces.

He leads them past the Custom House, walking two blocks further to an older hotel. As they crowd through the double doors into the lobby, Franklin tells them to wait there, and then goes to the reception desk.

"We'll need rooms for," he turns around and counts, "nine adults. Two of them have small children."

"Wait a tic," Sam says stepping forward. "We're together," he says, indicating Sarah and himself.

"As you wish," Franklin says, turning back to the receptionist. "We'll need eight rooms…"

"Wait," Debbie says, "we're together." She puts her arm through Lynne's.

"As you say," Franklin says. "Anyone else?"

"Her and me," Josh says, indicating Becky.

"Very well. Is that all?"

No one says anything.

"Right. We'll need rooms for three couples and three single adults."

"And to whom shall we send the bill?" the clerk asks.

"The Home Office. They also will be taking their meals here."

"That may be a bit of a bother," the clerk says.

"Why is that?" Franklin demands, annoyed that this will take any longer.

"Our chef just left," the clerk says. "We only have a dishwasher and prep cook who doesn't know much."

"Oh, bollocks …"

"George can cook," Sarah says.

"Who?" Franklin turns around.

"George, him," she says pointing at George who is startled at hearing his name. "He's a great cook."

"We can't have that," Franklin says. "You are under quarantine."

"That just means we can't leave," Sam counters. "It doesn't mean he can't cook."

Franklin turns to the clerk for help.

"I'll ask the manager," the clerk says with a shrug. That response deflates Franklin.

"Oh, very well. Do as you wish. You lot," he says, "if you leave the premises, you will be put in jail. I promise you the accommodations there are much worse."

"Yes, my lord," Sam says, giving a mock bow, but not knowing where the "my lord" came from.

"I..." the exasperated bureaucrat says, walking quickly out followed by chuckles and laughter from the refugees and the officers.

"Listen," the Sergeant says after he's gone, "Mr. Franklin wasn't wrong. If you leave without permission, we'll be required to arrest you and put you in jail. So please, stay put. There is a fenced patio area at the back of the hotel that you can use to get some air. And I believe the rooftop is open," she says, looking at the clerk, who nods. "I am required to post officers at all the exits. They all have radios, so when your time comes," she tells Sarah, "just tell one of them, and we'll get you to hospital. The one we have here is quite good."

"Thank you," Sarah says, looking relieved.

"Can I go with her?" Sam asks, worried.

"That can be arranged. You'll have to have a police escort."

"As long as I can go."

"Don't worry. We'll see to it. I'll talk to the Chief Superintendent and make sure everyone knows."

"Thanks," Sam says.

"Now, I have to get things organized and you lot have to get settled," the Sergeant says, brushing a finger across Judy's cheek, making the little girl giggle.

"Sergeant?" Sarah asks.

"Yes?"

"Do we have to keep calling you 'Sergeant'?"

"Tiffany Anderson," she says, turning to go.

"Thank you, Tiffany," Sam says to the retreating form.

She waves in acknowledgement as she walks away.

Then they all crowd around the desk, getting their room assignments and finding out about eating arrangements and how to clean their clothes. They find out they'll have to settle for sandwiches and instant oatmeal until, as the clerk says, "cooking arrangements can be sorted."

Sam and Sarah find two queen beds in their room. What really sells them on the accommodations, though, is the shower which sprays hot water just by turning a knob. That and having plenty of soap. They quickly undress, and, taking Judy with them, get into the shower, luxuriating under the warm water.

CHAPTER TWENTY-TWO

George wakes up at dawn, the light filtering through his room's window. He lies in bed looking at the light fixture on the ceiling. He's disoriented, wondering where he is. Slowly, as he comes fully awake, he remembers the last couple of days.

'Hotel,' he thinks. 'We're safe in England?' He has to think that one through. 'Yes, England.'

He suddenly comes fully awake as panic sets in. "Breakfast. I have to get breakfast ready." He contemplates the problem as he sits up in bed: Where to get food? Where to cook it? Then he remembers being told the hotel has a restaurant. A restaurant means a kitchen. Kitchens have food. And given what he's been working with, George is sure he can make a good meal with whatever is in the kitchen.

He throws on his clothes and hurries downstairs. On the main floor, he looks around, orienting himself. The clerk behind the desk looks up at him, but before she can say anything, George spots the entrance to restaurant. Walking in, he looks around the large room, holding twenty square tables, each with four chairs. A dozen light fixtures hang from the ceiling. The beige walls are decorated with pictures of places he does not recognize.

He spots the swinging doors to what he assumes is the kitchen. He goes through, pushing the double doors open, making a grand entrance into the kitchen. The large rectangular room has two long metal tables running down the middle, each with a small raised shelf above the back of the main table. The shelves have warming lights hanging over them. The stoves and ovens are arranged down one wall. Sinks and a dishwashing station are on the other, along with two large refrigerator-type doors.

He takes a quick inventory: flour, yeast, baking soda, baking powder, potatoes, pasta, onions, garlic, tomatoes, cooking oil, salad olive oil, and a variety of vinegars and spices, as well as salt and pepper, several kinds of mustard, and other condiments. He can't recall when he's seen them, although he knows what they are and how to use them. Knives, cutting boards, bowls, cooking spoons, and other implements are arrayed around the kitchen. He finds serving trays, dishes, bowls, tableware, glasses and cups. A large variety of metal pots and pans. An industrial dishwasher. Two large sinks. He goes into the large, walk-in freezer. He finds beef, chicken, and pork, including bacon. In a walk-in cooler are a variety of fresh vegetables and cheeses. All kinds of cheeses. And eggs. Lots and lots of eggs. Milk. Butter.

As he walks out of the cooler, he rubs his hands together, more out of satisfaction than anything else. He feels at home at last. Confident and relaxed.

"Now, what do I make for breakfast?" he says to no one in particular. He thinks for a moment, then decides to make a variety of dishes. None of them have had really fresh food, a really well-cooked meal since they left the McFarlands'.

Finding an apron, he puts it on and starts setting up, putting eggs, bacon, bread, butter, cheese, flour, and other ingredients onto the prep table. Getting out bowls and whisks, he makes pancake batter and scrambles eggs for omelets or just scrambled eggs. He keeps some eggs off to the side in case anyone wants them over easy or sunny side up.

Then it hits him. "Crap." He heads out to the front desk, seeing the clerk, he asks, "Can you wake my friends up?"

"Excuse me?"

"My friends. Can you wake them up? I'm making breakfast."

"Breakfast?" she says, raising her eyebrows.

"Yes, breakfast. They'll be hungry." With that he turns on his heel and hurries back to the kitchen.

After he finishes prepping the food, he turns on the gas under the built-in grills. He decides to wait on the eggs so they are hot when he serves them.

"What the bloody devil is going on here?" The voice, heavy with a Northern British accent snaps George out of his zone.

He turns around to see a man in a suit staring at him, looking outraged.

"I'm making breakfast," George answers simply, turning back to the stove.

"I can see that!" the man protests, surveying all the food that is out. "Who gave you permission to use this kitchen? To use the hotel's food?"

"We were told," George says as he ladles some pancake batter on the grill, "we would eat here. Since I'm our cook and you don't have one," he turns to look at the man, "I decided I'd better fill in."

"And you can cook?"

"So I'm told," he says as he puts bacon on another part of the hot grill.

"What is your training and your experience? What are your references?" comes the stern demand.

"I have no idea what my training is," comes the deadpan reply as he pays attention to his work. "My experience is cooking for us since we fled The Enemy. My references," he says, flipping the six pancakes on the grill, "will be down for breakfast. Now, if you'll excuse me, I have a meal to make."

The man looks at him thoughtfully. "Will you make me some breakfast as well?"

"No prob. What would you like?"

The man surveys the prep table. "Three pancakes, a rasher of bacon, and a cheese omelet with scallions should do it."

"Coming right up," George says. "By the way, do you have any coffee?"

"Coffee? You must be mad! Beans are very hard to get and we haven't had a shipment in two months. It's all because of this bloody unpleasantness."

"Unpleasantness?" George says, pausing for moment to digest the word. "I guess that's one way to put it, as long as you know no one is trying to kill you."

"I see," the man says, calming down. "Hopefully, we will get a shipment of beans in a month. Trade is very spotty these days."

George just nods in acknowledgement as he quickly finishes making the omelet on the grill and slides it onto a plate with four slices of bacon. He puts the pancakes on a separate plate, putting some butter on the top one.

"You'll have to take this to your table. I don't have servers handy."

"I see."

"You'll have to get your own water as well. Milk is in the cooler. I didn't see any juice. Glasses are over there," he says, waving toward them.

As the man picks up his plates, he asks, "When will your mates be down?"

"My what?" George asks, as he puts more pancake batter and bacon on the grills.

"The people you are with?" the man says as if he's explaining the obvious to an idiot.

"Real soon, if that clerk of yours went to get them."

"I'll have to send her."

"You what?!" George turns around, a bit miffed.

"I could hardly send her before I knew what was going on, now could I?"

"Send her!" George orders.

"Straight away," the man says, not used to being talked to that way. He carries his plates out into the restaurant, returning two minutes later. "She's off," he says, getting some water.

"Good," George says without looking around.

Lynne and Debbie are the first to come down. They go into the restaurant, but only see a man in a suit sitting at a table eating.

"He's in there," the man says through a mouthful of pancake, gesturing toward the kitchen door.

"Thanks," Debbie says as she and Lynne head to the kitchen.

"What's going on?" Debbie asks, surveying the scene.

George turns around with a big grin on his face. "Breakfast!" he announces. "We have eggs, bacon, and pancakes. No coffee," he says apologetically. "It seems they've run out. Anyway," he says, brightening up, "what would you like? I can fix the eggs just about any way you like."

"Short stack, scrambled eggs, bacon, toast," Lynne says.

"Any you?" George asks Debbie.

"I don't know," she says, "umm, how about an omelet with, let's see, cheese, and toast."

"Coming right up. Glasses are over there," he says, waving at them, spatula in hand. "Napkins and tableware are over there," he says, waving in another direction them. "Go find a table. And, oh, can you take some salt and pepper shakers out for the tables?"

"Okay," Debbie says, surprised and pleased by the sudden change that has come over George.

She and Lynne find a table, and sitting down, they look around the room.

"He's different," Lynne says.

"Yes, he is," Debbie agrees. "I've never seen him like that. It's a nice change."

"Yup," Lynne agrees.

Becky, Josh, and Jessica walk into the restaurant. They ignore the man in the suit, and head directly for their friends.

"What's up?" Josh asks.

"George is making breakfast," Debbie says, nodding her head toward the kitchen door.

Josh licks his lips and leads the way into the kitchen. Seeing George working at a stove, they head toward him.

"Breakfast?" Jessica asks.

George looks up briefly. "Take those two plates out to Debbie and Lynne." It comes as an order to no one in particular.

"Yes, boss," Jessica says, more in humor than sarcasm. George doesn't notice.

"Now," he says to the other two. "What would you like?"

"Anything?" Josh asks.

"No," George says, almost offended, "something from what you see here." He waves at the food that is spread out.

Jessica returns as the other two are making up their minds. All three place their orders, and are told about the glasses, napkins, and tableware.

"Do you want me to wait for breakfast to be ready?" Jessica asks.

"Yes. That would be good," George says, not looking at her.

The other two head out into the restaurant as Jessica leans against the prep table marveling at the speed and efficiency at which George works.

As George cooks, Mary, and Sam and Sarah come into the kitchen with their children.

"You'll have to wait," George informs them, before they have a chance to say anything more than good morning. "I can only keep so many orders in my head."

"Here," Jessica says, "I'll write it down." Not finding a pen or paper, she goes to the front desk and quickly returns with both. While she's gone, George tells the late arrivals what's on the menu, and where to find the milk. Jessica writes down their orders. Then as George puts food on three plates, she gets a serving tray, loads it up, and disappears out into the restaurant.

The other three head out into the restaurant to find a table. As they leave the kitchen, Sarah spots a collection of highchairs in a corner, and tells Sam to grab two.

As they are walking out, the man in the suit comes back in. He puts his plate and glass next to the dish station.

"Excellent American breakfast," he says, watching George work.

"What's that?" George asks, glancing up.

"I am told on good authority that Americans like big breakfasts."

George just shrugs.

"We Brits prefer smaller breakfasts."

"Then you should have asked for one," he responds brusquely. "I'm no mind reader."

"No. You're not," he says, pausing a moment. "Would you mind awfully cooking for our other guests and staff?"

George stops and looks at him. "No. Not in the least."

"Lunch and dinner?"

"You supply the ingredients; I'll supply the meals." He starts to turn back to the stove, but then looks at the man again. "Who in the hell are you anyway?"

"I am Trevor Howard, the manager of this establishment," he announces. "And you are?"

"George."

"George what?"

"Just George," he says distractedly as he concentrates on his cooking.

"What is your surname?"

"My what?"

"Your family name?"

"Not a clue, bud."

That makes Howard pause. "How can you not know?"

George shrugs. "None of us know. Except Josh and Debbie. They know theirs."

"And you're from America?"

"Your guess is as good as mine," George says, putting food on plates. "Now, if you'll excuse me, I have to serve this." He and Jessica start to head for the door. "By the way, if you want me to cook," he says. "I'll need a kitchen crew."

"Yes, of course. I will have them fetched."

George isn't sure what that means, but he assumes it means they will be coming, "And I'm not going to stay here all day. Breakfast will be over at nine. Lunch from eleven thirty to two. Dinner from five to eight, no make it nine. I'll need the crew here half an hour before we open for service."

"It sounds like you have done this before," Howard observes.

"Couldn't tell you that," George says as he leaves. He and Jessica bring the food to the others, then George returns and makes his own breakfast.

After eating, the others disperse, going into the hotel's sitting room or onto the patio. Jessica takes the two children to work with them. George returns to the kitchen, where he feels at home. He runs the pans, plates, tableware and glasses through the dishwasher, cleans the grills and the food prep area, then sweeps and mops the floor. When he's done, he sits back and surveys his new domain.

"Now, if I only had a coffee," he says.

"Sorry, mate, but we're flat out of that. And no tea, neither."

The woman's voice startles George, who jumps and turns quickly around. "I didn't hear you come in," he says defensively to the blonde woman, a few centimeters shorter than he is. He finds her blue eyes piercing, as if they are drilling through him.

"I'm your prep cook, server, and all-around everything girl," she announces.

"Okay," he says, getting his breath back. "What's your name?"

"Tuppence O'Leary. I'm from Ireland." The last comes out almost as a challenge. "And you? What're you called? Mr. Howard says you only have a first name. Is that true?"

"George," he says, nodding.

"That's bloody weird."

He just shrugs. "It is what it is."

"If you say so, mate."

"Do we have menus?" he asks.

"We used to, but they are really not good anymore. A lot of the stuff we don't have the makings for yet. New shipments are supposed to be coming in any day. That means nobody really knows when they will arrive, especially things like tea, coffee, and pepper."

"Okay, then let's figure out menus. You have good handwriting?"

"The best!" she brags.

"Great. Get something to write with and we'll create one. You'll have to help me because I don't know what you people like to eat."

"Right," she says, heading out for a pad and pen.

When she returns, she finds George has pulled some chicken and pork from the freezer and has them in the sink with water running over them so they'll defrost.

"We have to keep it simple," he tells her, "until I get settled in."

"Brilliant."

They soon have a simple menu ready for lunch and dinner, including fish and chips, and shepherd's pie. Since George doesn't know what those are, Tuppence first describes them to him and then promises to find recipes he can use. George is open to that if he is allowed to make changes to them.

"Too bad we don't have any wine," George sighs.

"We have a lot of that," Tuppence says.

"Really. Where?"

"In the cellar."

"Where's that?"

"This way," she leads him to the back of the kitchen and through a door that leads down into a large cellar, filled with a few thousand bottles of wine.

"The problem is that when this lot is gone, we can't get anymore, not easily anyway," she says as he wanders between the racks.

He nods in return.

"But beer and whisky are no problem," she says. "We make both here."

"Here?" he asks, turning back to her.

"In Britain."

"But not wine?"

"Not good wine. That comes from the Continent. That's a no-go zone."

George just nods and heads up stairs. "Who are you?" he says as he enters the kitchen to find a young man lounging around.

"I'm your dishwasher and go-fer," he says.

"He's Michael Howard," Tuppence quietly tells George. "Mr. Howard's son."

"Okay," George says. "So, let's get organized for lunch. Miss, is it miss?"—she says yes—"Miss O'Leary, write up menus. Separate ones for lunch and dinner, and oh, yes, breakfast."

"Right. But call me Tup."

"Tup?"

"My nickname. I'm not calling you George and have you call me Miss O'Leary."

"Fair enough."

"What prices do I list?" she asks.

That stumps George, who looks at her blankly.

"Don't worry, Mr. Howard and I can work that out," she assures him. "Thanks."

George spends the next eight days, getting his kitchen—which is how he thinks about it now—organized. He talks Howard into getting him a police escort so he can go to the docks to buy fresh fish. He also learns how to make meat pies, which he discovers are popular here, especially for lunch. And when he can get fresh fruit he makes pies, and cakes when he can get the ingredients for that. But sugar is hard to come by. Howard and Tup convince him to offer teatime with its small sandwiches and biscuits in mid-afternoon and move dinner to seven to ten thirty in line with English habits.

"George," Howard says, coming out the cellar with a bottle of their precious wine, "may I have a word?"

"Yes, sir," he says. The restaurant has closed for the evening, so Howard takes a couple of wine glasses and a corkscrew, and leads the way into the dining room. He sits down and motions George to take a seat at the table. Howard opens the wine, pours two glasses, putting one in front of George, who swirls it a bit, smells it and then takes a sip.

"This is good," he says appreciably.

"Yes, yes 'tis," Howard says. "Look here, I would like to offer you a position."

"A what?"

"A job."

"As a cook?"

"As my chef."

"Sounds good," George says, all of sudden feeling happy.

"You'll be paid four hundred quid a week, and, of course, have a room here. Actually, a suite with a sitting room and a bedroom."

"Quid? What's a quid?" George asks, having fixated on that word, not really hearing the rest.

"A quid? Four hundred pounds a week," Howard says, who has now become accustomed to George not understanding many of the terms he uses. But he thinks George should at least know about money.

"Pounds of what?"

"Pounds of what? You must me joking."

George shakes his head.

"Right. It's money. Four hundred pounds a week. You're an excellent chef. Business is up in the restaurant. I think you are worth it."

"Okay, I guess. When do I start?"

"When do you start?" Howard says incredulously. "My boy, you've already started."

"I mean, when do I start getting paid?"

"This week. Every Friday. And you may move into your new quarters tonight."

George holds out his hand, which Howard takes.

"It's a deal," George says, overjoyed to have a kitchen of his own.

Later that day, he asks Jessica to move in with him. She has started helping Tup serve in the dining room when she's not working with the children, and then she and George hang out together, enjoying each other's company as they both overcome their shyness. She thinks about it for a couple of days and then joins him, adding a woman's touch to his austere rooms.

CHAPTER TWENTY-THREE

Y ou know," the impeccably dressed man sitting behind a table in the restaurant, tells Sarah and Sam, "we have already performed a backgrounder on you lot. We know you were found at sea in a wooden sailing vessel, which is very nineteenth century of you, by one of our fishing trawlers. We know that you were in danger of foundering and were brought here. That you apparently originated in America, from whence you were fleeing. Is that right so far?"

Sam and Sarah, who left Judy with Jessica, exchange glances. "It sounds about right," Sam says.

"Except we're not sure about the America part," Sarah says.

"Then from where did you depart?" the man asks.

"We don't really know for sure," Sam says.

"How can you not know?"

"There were a lot of trees and a river. We came through mountains," Sam offers.

"It's a long story," Sarah says.

"Well then, we'll leave that for a bit later," says the man, who introduced himself as Harold Wilson as a senior official coming directly from London. Earlier in the day, the group had been told to gather in the dining room after lunch and before tea to be interviewed by an official from the Home Office.

Wilson is accompanied by another man, who takes notes and digs up documents as needed. Sam guesses he's a clerk of some kind. Wilson and his clerk have set up shop in a corner of the dining room away from the kitchen. George is still in the kitchen, getting ready for dinner, but since he's so close, he is allowed to stay there. When the refugees—they have accepted the term as a description for them–have gathered, Wilson asks who would be first.

Sarah and Sam go up, leaving Judy with Jessica.

"Now," Wilson continues, "let's start off with the easy questions. Name?" he says, looking at Sam.

"Sam."

Wilson looks both irritated and perplexed. "Is that short for Samuel?"

Sam shrugs, "Don't know."

"Middle name, then?"

"Don't know."

"You don't know?" comes the incredulous replay.

"Yes, sir. I don't know."

"Surname?"

"Don't know that either."

"And what about you?" the exasperated bureaucrat asks, turning to Sarah.

"Sarah is all I know. Sorry."

"How can this be? Are you lying? Why are you hiding your names? Is there something nefarious going on?"

"No, sir," Sam assures him. "We really don't know our middle and last names."

"Or even if we have them," Sarah adds.

"What about the rest of your lot?"

"Well, Debbie and Josh know their names, but none of the rest of us do," Sam says.

"And why do they know their names and you don't?"

"Because they know who their parents are, who were there when they were born, and they grew up with them," Sarah says.

"And you didn't? Were you in care from birth?"

"Care?" Sarah asks.

"Wards of the state."

"I don't think so," Sam says.

"You don't think so? You don't know?" Wilson says, his exasperation growing.

"That's about it," Sam says.

"How can that be?"

"It's a long story," Sarah says.

"So you say. Well," Wilson says, looking at his clerk, "I think we need to call the minister to receive instructions."

"You call a minister for this?" Sam asks.

"Yes, of course, she's in charge of the Home Office."

"What kind of minister?" Sarah asks.

"What do you mean? She's a member of government, of course," comes the confused reply.

"You have clergy in your government?"

"Clergy? Heavens, no."

"But you just said a minister runs your agency," Sam says.

"Not that kind of minister!" comes the indignant reply. Wilson's clerk is doing his best to suppress a laugh, and failing miserably.

"Oh," Sarah says. "Then what kind?"

"Political, of course," he says, exasperated. "Now, if you will excuse us, we must get direction from our political minister." Wilson and his clerk standup. "We will resume these interviews at this time on the morrow," Wilson announces as he heads for the door, the clerk trailing behind.

"What did you do to him?" Becky asks, walking to where Sarah and Sam are still sitting, trying to figure out what exactly just happened.

"It seems," Sam says, "we confused him."

"How?" Jessica asks, handing Judy to Sam.

"We don't know our last names, and aren't sure where we came from," Sarah says.

"I guess that would do it," Mary says.

"We did tell him that you and Josh know your full names," Sarah tells Debbie, who has joined them along with the others. "But I don't think he knows what to do with the rest of us."

"He's going to ask his minister," Sam adds.

"His what?" Josh asks.

"His minister, but he didn't mean the religious kind," Sam explains. "I guess they have political ministers here who are part of the government."

"Oh," Becky says. "I don't understand."

"Neither do we," Sarah says, standing up. As she does, she looks down at her pants. "My water just broke."

"Your what!?" Sam says, looking up at her and then down. "Hospital. We have to get you to the hospital."

"I'll go find that lady cop," Debbie says.

"Tiffany Anderson," Sam says, handing Judy back to Jessica.

Debbie nods in acknowledgement as she heads off.

"Let's start toward the door," Sam tells Sarah, "nice and easy."

"I'm going into labor," she replies irritably, "I'm not crippled."

"I know, sweetie," he says, taking her arm to give her support.

"I can walk on my own just fine," she snaps, pulling her arm away.

"Okay, okay," he says in surrender.

"Don't baby me!"

"Okay," he responds meekly.

"I'll take care of Judy," Jessica says. The offer is greeted by nods from Sarah and Sam, both of whom are somewhat distracted.

As Sarah starts toward the door, she turns to Sam who is frozen in place, "Are you coming or what?"

"Coming. I'm coming," Sam says, catching up.

"You know, we've done this before," she says.

"I know," Sam says.

"Then act like it!" she orders.

"I'm trying. Trust me, I'm trying."

"Try harder," she orders.

"Yes, ma'am."

"Drop the sarcasm!"

"I ..." he starts to say.

"The ambo will be here directly," Anderson says, interrupting Sam as she comes up, much to his relief.

"Thanks," Sarah and Sam say simultaneously.

"Can I go with her?" Sam asks, worry in his voice.

"Yes," Anderson assures him, "I'm sending a constable with you. Sorry, but it's the rules."

"I don't care if you send the army, as long as I can go with her," he says.

When the ambulance pulls up, Sarah is helped in by an EMT and Sam climbs in after her, while a constable takes a seat next to the driver.

Anderson and their companions watch as the ambulance pulls away and turns a corner.

"Alright, you blokes," Anderson says, turning to the others, "back inside." She shoos them back in.

CHAPTER TWENTY-FOUR

G ood morning," the diminutive red-headed woman in an official looking dark dress tells the refugees gathered in the hotel's lounge two days after Sarah gave birth. "My name is Lady Ashley Channing. This is Mr. Michael Harrison," she said indicating the man standing a little behind her. "Thank you for joining me."

"Didn't know we had a choice," Lynne grumbles.

"Yes, right," Channing says, as the others try to hide smiles, "you don't really, but we must complete your paperwork if you are ever to get out of here and on with your lives."

Lynne just snorts as Debbie nudges him. Channing looks at him over her glasses, then goes on.

"I was told there would be nine of you, but I only see eight?"

"Sarah just gave birth. She'll be back from hospital tomorrow," Sam says.

"Right. Mother and child are doing well?"

"Yes, thanks. Both are healthy and resting," he says.

"Brilliant. Does the baby have a name yet?"

"Frank," Sam says. "He came in at seven pounds, four ounces, and twenty-one inches long."

"Lovely. Now, we can process the rest of you," Channing says, "so you have the proper papers and can be settled into new lives."

"Where's the guy who was here the other day?" Becky asks. "He said he would be back the next day but never showed."

"Mr. Wilson has been called away to other duties," Channing replies. "I am taking his place. Now an explanation first, since I have been given the impression you do not know anything about our government."

The statement is greeted with a variety of assents. "Great Britain is a constitutional monarchy. Our king is head of state, while the prime minister is the elected head of government. The monarch is hereditary, while the prime minister is typically the leader of the largest party in Parliament. The heads of each cabinet office, such as Home Office and Foreign Office, are members of government and report to the prime minister. They are technically servants of the crown but are elected by British subjects who are eligible to vote. Have I confused you?"

"I think we follow you," Josh says, a bit tentatively.

"Don't worry about that now. I think you get the general idea. You'll be able to have a better grasp on it later after you have a chance to learn. For now, let's get started with your paperwork." Everyone leans forward expectantly. "Now, as I understand it, none of you know your last names."

"We do," Debbie says, indicating herself and her brother, "but none of the others do."

"Right. Why don't you and your brother work with Mr. Harrison, since your cases should be straightforward. Mr. Harrison," Channing says, turning to her clerk, "please take these two into that corner," as she points to a table that has been set up, "and get started. If you run into any problems, I'll be right here."

"Yes, ma'am," he says, motioning to Debbie and Josh to join him as he moves to the table.

"Now," she says, turning to the others, "will you join me?" She motions to Sam.

He shakes his head, saying, "I'd rather wait for Sarah to get back, and do this tomorrow."

"You're the husband?" Channing says.

Sam gives her a funny look. "We have never had a formal ceremony." He starts getting defensive, worried about what the paperwork will do to them. "We don't need a ceremony or a piece of paper to know that we're family."

"I apologize," Channing says, a bit taken aback. "I did not mean to offend."

"Sorry," Sam apologizes. "This is all new to us, and I guess I'm defensive about my family, about everyone here."

"Understandable. I hear you have been through quite an ordeal. No need to be concerned. We will not separate those who wish to stay together."

"Really?" Becky says.

"Yes, really," Channing replies, realizing she is dealing with a group of people who are deeply suspicious of others. "I have no idea about the ordeal you have been through, but be assured the British government has no intention of forcing you to do anything you do not wish to do, and that includes whom you form relationships with. We do, however, expect you to become contributing members of our society."

"That we'll do," Sam says.

"A word if you please," Channing says to Sam, taking him to two chairs set in another corner. After they sit down, she leans toward him and says quietly to him, "I am given to understand that you are the leader of this group. Is that correct?"

Sam shrugs. "I'm not sure how accurate that is. They do what I ask because they want to, not because I have any authority to make them."

"You have moral authority, it seems, that everyone else respects."

"Except for Sarah," Sam says with a smile.

"Yes, I would not be surprised," Channing says, leaning back.

"Sarah is a force to be reckoned with," Sam says.

"And the mother of your children."

"Yes," he replies, blushing a bit.

"Right. We will do your paperwork tomorrow when she returns."

"Thank you," he says, relieved.

"What I would like from you now, however, is some help understanding you and the people in your group."

"In what way?"

"Well, a short history of your experience."

Sam thinks for a moment, sighs and decides to tell this woman with an aristocratic bearing everything. "Josh and Debbie are different. Their parents fled the initial attacks and ended up in a valley on the coast with other people. That's where they were born and grew up. They had some fights with The Enemy…"

"The Enemy?"

"That's what we call whoever the hell it is who forced the rest of us into the military. There were thousands of us. We each awoke, came to,

I don't how to describe it really, in different places. The one thing we all had in common was none of us remembered anything but our first names. Weird, right?"

"Yes, I would say so."

"Anyway, there were these Sergeants who grabbed each of us, shoved us into a marching formation and drove us on. Anyone who resisted was brutally beaten. After a while, we were marched into a huge field, formed into eight-member squads and put up tents. That's when the military training started. It was pretty rudimentary: marching, PT, eventually small-arms training. We never saw any heavy machine guns or artillery. And we never saw any officers, just the Sergeants. I have no idea how the command structure was set up and run."

"I see."

"Anyone who tried to escape was caught, stripped, beaten and put up on crosses to die, along with their entire squad. They just left them up there until thirst or the weather took them."

"Horrible."

"Yes, but it was an effective deterrent."

"So then, why did you escape?"

"The Sergeants started grabbing women and raping them. One day they took Mary," he says, indicating the woman with the young boy. "They had her in a field on the other side of some woods from the camp. George and I were behind a big rock deciding what to do. There were four armed Sergeants, and two of us. Along comes Sarah, who blows right past us. Didn't have much of a choice at that point, so we followed her. We managed to kill the Sergeants. It was a surprise attack, and they didn't expect any resistance from us."

"And the four of you escaped?"

"It wasn't that simple. If we had run off at that point, the other members of our squad would have been tortured to death," Sam says. "That's how those sons-of-bitches operated. We went back for them. Lynne, with Sarah's help, raided the armory so we had more than pistols. But while we were waiting for them to get back, some Sergeants attacked us. Frank was wasted right off. Judy was badly wounded. She died a few days later. We buried her in an unmarked grave in the woods."

"There were seven of you when you fled?"

Sam nods. "Six, after Judy died."

"And they were?

"Me, Sarah, Lynne, Mary, George, and Adam."

"I see."

"As we worked our away to what we hoped was safety, Mary and Adam hooked up…"

"Hooked up?" Sam just looks at Channing. "Oh, I see," she says, glancing over at the little boy.

"The Sergeants kept looking for us, and eventually a pickup truck full of Sergeants and Soldiers came rolling down the road we were on. We ambushed them, killing all of them but one. Becky. She joined us."

"I see. You recruited her."

"In a manner of speaking. They caught up with us a couple more times, but we were able to find good defensive positions behind rivers to fight them off. But Adam was belly shot in the last fight. We were in a mountain pass when they caught up with us again. Adam gave his life to hold them off so we could escape. Without a hospital, he was going to die," Sam says, his voice dropping low as sadness washes over him.

"We got a head start," he continues, "but not enough of one because Mary was pregnant and couldn't move that fast. They would have caught us, and killed us, but Debbie found us and led us over the mountain into their valley." Sam says. "For some reason, The Enemy couldn't cross the mountain. Don't ask me why, because we never figured that one out. All we knew is we felt safe.

"Anyway, we lived there for several years," he says. "Their father was the only one left alive from the original group, and Debbie and Josh were the only children who survived. The three of them lived together on a farm, and we did, too. After their father died, we decided to move to the coast and build a ship to escape on, just in case. Shortly after we finished work, The Enemy came over the mountain, so we set sail."

"And were does … ah … Jessica," Channing says, looking at sheet of paper she's been carrying, "fit in?"

"We stayed in sight of land at first, and after about a week, we decided to go ashore to see if we could find fresh water, and whether it was safe to land. I was scouting inland when I came across a Sergeant about to rape her. I killed the Sergeant and she joined us. That's about it," he says with a shrug.

"Except I understand that you ran into a storm that nearly wrecked your little vessel."

"True, but we managed to survive until the trawler picked us up and brought us here."

Channing thinks for a moment. "Do you know anything about what happened before?"

"No, but Debbie has a diary her mother wrote that tells her story about what happened," he answers."

"Really? Do you think she'll loan it to us?"

"You'll have to ask her."

"I certainly will," she says, pausing again. "Now, tell me what can each of you do?"

"Do?"

"What job. What work. I understand your George is quite the chef. In fact, I lunched here and am looking forward to dining this evening. His meals are superb. Did he know he was a chef?"

"No," Sam says, shaking his head. "But the funny thing is, we might not know about our past, but we seem to know what we're good at. My Sarah is an engineer…"

"What kind?"

"Ah, civil, I think. Becky is some kind of medical person," he goes on as Channing takes notes. "Jessica seems to have been a teacher. At least, she has a way of working with the little ones, teaching them. Lynne must have been a soldier. I haven't figured Mary out."

"And you?"

"A Marine."

"A soldier, as well," she responds.

"A Marine. We're better."

"Of course you are," she says, patronizingly.

Sam let's that pass.

"Excuse me," George says, coming up.

"Yes?" Channing asks.

"Can I do my stuff? It's getting late, and I'm behind on dinner prep."

"Right away," she says. "If you'll excuse us," she says to Sam.

"No prob," he replies. Since he's done until the next day, he finds Anderson and arranges an escort back to the hospital.

CHAPTER TWENTY-FIVE

G ood morning, I presume you are Sarah?" Channing asks Sarah, who has taken a seat next to Sam on the opposite side of the table from the British official.

"Yes," she says.

"It is so nice to meet you. I am Lady Ashley Channing. And this is?" she says, indicating the newborn Sarah is holding.

"Frank. Wait, 'lady'?"

"Ah, yes," Channing says with a bit of an ironic smile. "It is one of those archaic titles we English are still enamored of, though I assure you, I work for a living as a member of government. 'Frank' you say. Is that short for Francis?"

"We're not sure yet," Sam says.

"Not sure? Didn't you fill out a birth certificate at hospital?"

"They wouldn't let us," Sarah says, "since we don't have last names. They said without those we couldn't give the baby what they called 'a proper name.'"

"Quite right. Let's solve that problem right now, and in the process, we'll fill out a birth certificate for your Frank," Channing says kindly, opening her laptop and loading a form onto it. "Your husband has explained your history to me. So, we can just crack on. By the way, where is your daughter?"

"Judy is with Jessica," Sam says. "Does she have to be here?"

"No, not really. She is too young to provide information for herself. Now, who wants to go first?" she says, looking back and forth at the couple. Who look at each other.

"Uh, why don't you go first," Sarah tells Sam.

"You sure?"

"Yes. I'm going to have to feed the baby anyway, he's starting to wake up," she says, pulling a blanket up and over her left shoulder and across her chest.

"I guess I'm chosen," Sam says looking back at Channing who is fascinated by what is going on across the table.

"I do not think I have ever witnessed that before," she says.

"How did you feed your children?" Sarah asks looking up after getting Frank started.

"Well," Channing says, blushing heavily, "it was all done in private."

"That would be nice," Sarah responds, "but given the conditions we've been living in I didn't have that luxury."

"No, I guess you wouldn't," Channing says, composing herself. "Now," she says turning to Sam, "this matter of a surname. You must have one. That is how people are identified, along with their National Insurance number."

"The others all got last names?" he asks.

"Yes, they did."

"How did that work?"

"We discussed it, and eventually came up with a name each liked, or accepted, and was acceptable to government. Your friend George chose 'Cook' for a last name, while Jessica picked 'Child'."

"Some names are out of bounds?"

"Yes. There are rules. The name must not be profane or objectionable."

"What would make a name objectionable?"

"Oh, there is a whole list of rules, however, we don't need to go into detail on those. We'll find a name that will do, and if you come up with one that is not proper, I will let you know."

"You've done this before?"

"Not for quite some time, and never on this coast."

"This coast?"

"The west coast. In the early days, we had people coming over from the Continent who were in the same condition you find yourselves. That was the east coast, the Channel coast. That was, oh, I would say, the last of that lot reached us nine or ten years ago."

"And what did you do with them?"

"The same thing we are doing with you. We brought them into our society. We really had no choice since there was nowhere we could send them. So we kept them," she said, smiling. "Now the matter of a surname?"

"Yeah," Sam says, sighing, "I, we, haven't given it much thought. We were too busy staying alive to worry about it."

"But now you are safe, and it is time to give it some thought."

"Right," Sam says, raising his eyebrows. "Do you have any ideas?" he says, turning to Sarah.

Sarah thinks for a moment. "Hope?"

Sam sits back in his chair, a bit surprised.

"Hope?" Channing asks.

"It's our ship's name," Sam says, still looking at Sarah. "The one we escaped on."

"I see. Is that what you want to use?"

"Do we both have to use the same last name?" Sarah asks.

"No. I suppose not, but I thought you were husband and wife."

"Does that mean we have to use the same last name?"

"No, I don't suppose you do."

"Is that the way people do it here?" Sam asks, looking at Channing.

"It is most common that the wife takes the husband's name, although at times some hyphenate the maiden name and the husband's name. And some just keep their own names."

"Then we can do what we want?" Sam asks.

"Yes, as long as the name does not violate the rules."

"Does 'Hope' violate the rules?" Sarah asks.

"No, it does not."

"Great, I'll use it," she says. "What about you?"

"You sure you want to make this permanent? We've never really talked about it," Sam says.

"Really?" Channing blurts out.

Sarah and Sam look at her, and then back at each other. "Do we need to talk about it?" Sarah asks.

"I don't, but I didn't want to assume you did."

"I think we crossed that bridge a long time ago. Especially after two kids," Sarah informs him.

"Good," Channing says, "then it is settled. You and your children will all have the surname 'Hope.' That certainly simplifies matters." She turns to the laptop, typing in the name on Sam's form. "And what about a middle name?" she asks him.

"Geeeez, is that required?" he says, exasperated.

"No, but it is helpful."

Sam looks at Sarah, lost.

"How about stubborn?" she suggests, smiling broadly.

"No, I am afraid that will not do at all," Channing says in a deadpan voice.

"Just kidding," Sarah assures her, eliciting a knowing smile from the other woman.

"How about…" Sam starts to say.

"Francis," Sarah tells him.

"Francis?"

"Yes. We'll make that his first name, your middle name. We'll make Judy's first name Judith and that can be my middle name. Will that work?" she says, turning to Channing.

"Brilliant. What about the children's middle names?"

Sarah looks at Sam, seeking help, but he's too busy laughing to provide any. She smacks him on the arm. "This isn't funny."

"Yes, it is," he says, getting his mirth under control. "We've never had to deal with paperwork, we don't remember anything, and now we have to invent everything."

"Okay, funny man, I got us first, middle and last names. You come up with the kids' middle names. And they better be good!"

"Are these required?" Sam asks Channing, hoping they're not.

"It helps," she says again.

"Rats. Okay. Let me think," he says, sitting back in his chair and gazing at the ceiling. "How about … no, not that…. How …" he trails off again. "How about Rebecca? Judith Rebecca Hope. Do you like that?"

Sarah thinks about it for a moment. "Hmmm, I'm not sure." Frank is done eating and fallen back to sleep. She gently puts him into the makeshift bassinet by her chair, then puts herself back together. "You know," she says, sitting up, "it will do nicely. I think I like it. But why Rebecca?"

"It sounds right?" Sam responds, not sure why he chose the name.

"Be sure, please," Channing says. "Once it is part of the official record it will play the devil to alter it."

"No, go ahead and use that," Sarah tells her. "And Frank's?" she asks Sam.

"Mud? No, I'm just kidding," he quickly tells Channing before she can object. "How about 'Walker'?"

"Why that?" Sarah challenges him.

"Because we walked a hell of a long way."

"But you didn't use that for Judy?"

"Of course not, she deserves a beautiful name."

"And Frank doesn't?"

He looks at his wife for a long moment. "It's a reminder of what we went through so he could live. It's a rugged name."

"Right," Channing says before Sarah can object, "Francis Walker Hope, it is. And yours," she says to Sam, "is now Samuel Francis Hope."

"What? 'Samuel'? Where did that come from?" Sam says, taken aback.

"I assume that since your wife and your children have proper first names, you would want one as well."

"I ..."

"He'll take it," Sarah butts in.

"I will?"

"Yes, you will."

"Then that's settled," Channing says turning back to her computer, typing quickly. "I have most of the forms filled out. We obviously don't have birth dates or places for you two, so we will use 'unknown.' We do know Francis' birth date and place. What about your daughter, Judith?"

"Sorry," Sarah says, "she was born before we sailed, and all we know for sure is that it was the spring."

"Right. We can put down America as her birthplace and birth date unknown, but we do have a year?" The last comes as a question. Sam and Sarah look at each other, do some quick math, and give her the year.

Channing then hits a button and a portable printer comes to life. She gets the documents and places them on the table in front of the couple. "Now, these are your identification documents for the four of you, including birth certificates for the two children. Protect them because you will need them to get jobs, medical care, and the like. Do you need a marriage license?"

"Ummm," Sam says, "we haven't gone through any ceremony, so will it be legal?"

"Let me tell you a little secret," Channing says, conspiratorially, "if you have the document, no one will inquire if you had a ceremony. And, if they do, just tell them it was in America."

"Sounds good to me," Sarah says, looking at Sam who nods approval.

"Brilliant," Channing says, calling up the certificate and quickly filling it out. She then hands them three copies of the printed document. "Now you are official and legal."

"We're done?" Sam asks.

"Not quite. We still have the matter of your skills to work out so you can find the proper employment."

"She's an engineer," Sam says, putting his hand on Sarah's shoulder.

"Brilliant. What kind?"

"Civil. I think," Sarah says.

"You are not sure?"

"I'm not sure about anything before …" she says, her voice trailing off.

"Then how do you know you are an engineer?"

"She knows stuff," Sam says. "When we were building the ship, she designed a crane and pulley system that allowed us to put the mast up, among other things."

"Very good. Would you be willing to take an examination to test your knowledge?" Channing asks Sarah.

"I guess," Sarah says, uncertainty in her voice.

"If you pass, you will be issued a certificate that will allow you to work. If you fall short but show promise, you will be provided the training you need. Is that agreeable?"

"I guess," she says, tentatively. "But what about us? Our family?" she asks Sam.

"She'll do it," Sam says, looking at Sarah. "We'll work it out. I'll pick up garbage if I have to."

"I guess I'll do it," Sarah says with a shrug.

"Brilliant."

"Where do I take the test?"

"You will be sent to either Cambridge or Oxford. That will be up to the ministry. In the interim, you will be moved to London. That's our capital," she adds as an aside. "And your skills?" she asks, turning to Sam.

"I'm a Marine."

"Ah, a soldier,"

"No, ma'am," Sam says, offended. "A Marine."

"Is there a difference?" she asks, confused. "Your friend, Lynne Sherman, informed me he was a soldier."

"Sherman?"

"That is the name he picked. He said that it sounded right."

"Okay."

"And you object to being called a soldier, why?"

"Marines are better trained and more aggressive."

"I see. Were you an officer or in the ranks?"

"I don't know."

"Alright," she says, filling out his form. "You also will go to London, where the military will contact you, if you are willing to serve. And I would encourage you to do so. We need experienced soldiers, and Marines," she adds hurriedly.

"I guess I can talk to them," he says. "Will I get a shot at The Enemy?"

"Is that what you want?"

"Look, lady, I'm not anxious to get shot at again, but I've got a score to settle with those bastards. Besides, I want to protect my family, and if that means fighting for your country, then count me in."

"I would point out that this is now your country as well," Channing says.

"Good point."

"Now, over the next couple of days, you will be provided with train tickets, some money and food vouchers, and a furnished flat in the London area."

"A flat?" Sarah asks.

"An apartment," Channing says after hesitating for a moment to find the right word. "Once you are settled in, you will each be contacted by the proper authorities about what to do next. Since you both have skills of which we are in need, you should have a short wait. Any questions?"

"No, I guess not," Sam says, looking at Sarah.

"If you do, here is my card. You may call me, but please not at night or on weekends."

"Sure thing," Sam says. "What day is this anyway?"

"Thursday."

"Thanks," Sarah says.

After Channing leaves, Sarah and Sam decide to get together with the others to find out where they will be going and what they will be doing. They push together some tables in the restaurant. George is in and out with them because he is now overseeing a kitchen with eight employees. He's staying with the restaurant, and he looks happier and more confident than anyone has ever seen him.

Jessica is going to take a test as a primary school teacher, and either start teaching or get training. She's planning to stay with George, so it will be in this area.

Mary apparently can run an office, so she's waiting to find out where she will be sent as an office manager. It seems they are in short supply in government offices.

Becky is being sent to London to take a test of her medical skills. She is on the road to becoming either a doctor or a nurse, depending on the results. Josh is going with her, although he's not sure what he'll be doing. His skills as a carpenter will probably land him a job.

As for Lynne, he is also being sent to London to interview with the Royal Army. He's satisfied to join as long as they don't try to make him an officer. His comment was "I ain't no fuckin' officer." Debbie is going with him, her future somewhat uncertain, although she'd like to be involved with agriculture. Besides, she's now pregnant. They also have a marriage license.

They all linger over dinner, late into the night. The children fall asleep in their parents' arms. They eventually break up, going to their rooms and their separate ways.

In the morning, Sarah and Sam are the first to go. A messenger brings them their train tickets, one thousand, five hundred pounds—five hundred pounds for each adult, and two hundred fifty for each child—meal vouchers good at train stations and some restaurants, and the address and keys to their flat, as well as directions from the train station in London.

W.R. Blocher

The directions include bus routes, but the messenger tells them that they may want to take a taxi since they have two small children.

Three hours later, after final goodbyes, they are on the noon train to London.

CHAPTER TWENTY-SIX

S o, this is home," Sarah comments after they walk into their apartment. They drop what few possessions they have in the small foyer and go exploring. Sarah's carrying Frank, while Judy is holding her father's hand.

Riding in on the train, they had examined the directions and map of London they were given. They quickly realized the apartment was too far to walk, especially with a toddler who is just learning to walk, and an infant. On the positive side, they didn't have much in the way of personal belongings to haul around. They debated taking a bus or a taxi, finally settling on a bus since it would be cheaper. At least they assumed it would be.

The bus dropped them off a block from the apartment, and the driver pointed them in the right direction. When they reached the building, they discovered the apartment was on flight up.

"Why are we always on the second floor?" Sam groused as they stood just inside the building entrance.

"It's the first floor," Sarah reminded him.

"What? Then what floor is this?"

"The ground floor. Just like in the hotel. Now come on," she says, leading the way up, carrying the infant and a bit of their baggage. Sam lifts Judy onto his shoulders, telling her to hold on tight, which she does by grabbing his hair with both hands. He carefully picks up the rest of their belongings and follows Sarah up.

They don't need a lot of time to look around their new home. "Stop calling it an apartment," Sarah tells Sam. "It's a flat."

He just gives her an irritated look.

"It's just two bedrooms," Sarah says. "The kitchen is tiny. The bathroom is even smaller. The furniture looks kind of cheap."

"Yeah, but we have hot water, flushing toilets, beds, and, best of all, no one is chasing us, shooting at us, and this place isn't trying to drown us."

"Always the optimist," she says. "We don't have a crib, and Judy is too young to sleep in a bed by herself."

"Well," Sam says, thinking, "we have this makeshift cradle Frank can sleep in, and Judy can sleep between us for now."

"I suppose that will have to do," Sarah says sighing. "We do have a telephone, a TV, and a radio."

"And a clock," Sam says, pointing to the time piece on the wall.

"I guess the first order of business is to get some food. I wonder where we go for that?"

"Here," Sam says handing her a list of area stores he found on the table. The list includes what they sell, along with their addresses. Perusing it together, they find the list also has some restaurants which take the food vouchers they were given.

"Great. Let's check out the kitchen," she says. They find a gas stove and oven, a variety of pots and pans, spatulas, serving forks and knives, plates, bowls, tableware, and glasses.

"Can you cook?" Sam asks.

"I don't know. Can you cook?"

"I don't know," he says with a shrug. "We are really going to miss George."

"That's for sure. But there is nothing we can do about it now. Let's go get something to eat."

They head out and find a restaurant, and after eating, find a grocery store. The next few days are spent settling into their new home, learning the neighborhood, and buying clothes for themselves and the kids. Overruling Sam's objection about spending the money, Sarah insists on buying a real cradle for Frank and a mattress for Judy, so they can have the queen-size bed to themselves. If Judy rolls off the mattress, she will only drop eight centimeters. She does exactly that the first night. In the morning, they find her contentedly sleeping on the carpet, wrapped tightly in her blanket.

On the fifth morning in their new home, they are just finishing breakfast when someone knocks on the door.

"Who could that be?" Sarah asks.

"There's one way to find out," Sam says as he heads to the door. When he opens it, he finds a tall man in a business suit looking back at him.

"Good morning," the man says. "Samuel Hope?"

"Sam, yes."

"Yes, I'm John Schwartz from the Home Office. Lady Channing has asked me to be the liaison for you and your wife. May I come in?"

"Yes, of course," Sam says, standing aside. After Schwartz limps past him, he closes the door.

"Who is it?" Sarah asks coming out of the kitchen.

"Good morning," comes the cheerful reply. "John Schwartz here. I am your liaison from the Home Office. I am here to help you settle in and get on track for your futures. I have some paperwork for you. Not to fill out," he assures them as Sam ushers him into the living room, "but information on appointments, and things like childcare, which I presume you will be needing if you both plan to work."

"We do, and please sit down," Sarah says, indicating a chair next to the coffee table. Judy comes up and climbs into her father's lap as the family occupies the couch, which is at a ninety-degree angle from the chair.

"Brilliant," Schwartz says, as he opens his briefcase, pulling out three folders. "This one is for you," he says, handing it to Sarah. "It contains information about the office you need to contact, and the time and place for your civil engineering examination. We made the appointment here in London so you don't have to schlep to Oxford or Cambridge."

"Schlep?" she asks.

"Sorry. Travel," he says, picking up another folder. "And this is for you, sir. It also contains information about the office you need to contact. In your case, it is the Ministry of Defense. If the appointment times are inconvenient for either of you, you have the proper phone numbers to call to make other arrangements." He looks up from the checklist from which he's been reading to make sure they are following him and understanding. They both nod.

"Here are mobile phones," he says, pulling two from his briefcase. Each phone has one of their names on it. "You have one year's free service, after which you will be expected to assume the cost. If you look in the directories, you will discover that we have taken the liberty of programing in each of your numbers into the other's phone, along with the numbers of the relevant offices you will need to contact, and the numbers of your fellow refugees, should you want to stay in contact. My office and mobile number are also there."

"Thanks," Sarah says.

"Yes, thanks," Sam adds.

"Our pleasure. Now, you may live here for up to one year. Once you have found employment, you will be expected to make your own living arrangements. You may contact a local rental agent, or, if you wish, ask the Home Office for guidance. Now, any questions?"

Sam and Sarah exchange looks. "I don't think so," Sam finally says. "You?" he asks Sarah.

"None that I can think of right now."

"Very good," Schwartz says. "We have opened a bank account for you, which contains a balance of two thousand pounds. Here is the documentation for that," he says as he lays the bank book on the coffee table between them.

"Thanks," Sam says, picking it up.

"That's very generous of you," Sarah adds.

"Yes, well, apparently you two have skills that are in high demand, and the government wants to make sure you are well taken care off."

"We do?" Sam and Sarah say simultaneously.

"Yes. Now, if that is all?" Schwartz says, looking at them expectantly. Not receiving any indication to the contrary, he gathers his material, and stands to go. They also stand, each taking his extended hand. "Good luck to the both of you."

"Thanks," Sam says. "May I ask how you injured your leg?"

"My leg?" Schwartz says, taking a moment to realize what he is being asked about. "Oh, that. It's actually a prothesis. I lost the real one on the Continent, oh say, five years ago. My unit got into a bloody awful fight with those people," he says, waving toward the east.

"Sorry," Sam says. "I didn't mean to pry."

"No worries. I received a medical retirement and this cushy job," Schwartz replies. "My wife is ecstatic. I'm home every night and can spend plenty of time with our children. It has its upside, you know."

Sam just nods.

"Thank you," Sarah adds as they walk Schwartz to the door.

Once he's gone, they look at each other, both excited about finally having something to do. They each read their material, look over the childcare information that was in the third folder, along with general information about the greater London area, the country, and a brief history of Britain. They also find maps of Britain, the Atlantic basin, and the world. Looking at the map of the Atlantic, they realize what they crossed to get here, even if they didn't intend to do it. They also play with their new phones, calling the others to check in on how they're doing.

Sarah's first appointment is in two days, but Sam's is the next day. He walks the three kilometers to the Ministry of Defense, arriving at seven a.m. At the reception desk, he is directed to an office where he is given a complete physical. Then he is sent to another office, where he takes a battery of tests. He starts at ten in the morning, taking one exam after another until seven that evening with a short break for lunch, which involves a cheese sandwich in a box and some vegetables, along with coffee and water.

A Royal Marine officer sits at a desk in the front of the room, monitoring and changing tests as he completes each one. The first officer is relieved by another one when he is about halfway through. When Sam's done with the tests, he is shown into an office with some wooden chairs along the walls. What looks to be an enlisted man—he has three chevrons with a crown over them on his sleeve—is sitting at a desk in front of another office door. Some kind of Sergeant, Sam decides. The Color Sergeant glances at him when he comes in, waves him into a chair, and then goes back to doing some work on a computer.

After what seems like hours to Sam, but is only about forty minutes, the Color Sergeant pushes a flashing button on the speaker phone. "Color Sergeant, you may bring Mr. Hope in."

"Yes, sir," the Color Sergeant says, rising quickly from his chair. Sam gets up as well. The Sergeant ushers him through a door and then closes it behind him.

Sam finds himself in a spacious, wood-paneled office with what appears to be an officer who is reading while sitting behind a large, polished desk in front of a bank of windows. Sam automatically stands at attention in front of the desk, ignoring the chairs on either side of him.

The officer looks at him for a moment. "You may stand easy."

Sam goes to parade rest.

"I am Major General FitzRoy. I understand you want to be a Royal Marine officer." She waits for a moment. "Well, man, speak up. You may speak freely."

"Yes, ma'am," Sam replies. "I am a Marine already. I don't know about being an officer."

"Weren't you one already in America?"

"I don't remember, ma'am."

The Major General sits back in her chair, looking Sam up and down. "Right. Take a seat," she says.

"Yes, ma'am. Thank you, ma'am," Sam says, sitting down.

"We have done background checks on you already…"

"Ma'am?" Sam asks, not sure how they can check his background when even he doesn't know it.

"As well as we could," FitzRoy says. "We have talked to your fellow refugees, and the civilian officials who have already interviewed you. It seems you were the leader of this group that made its way out of America, and you managed to keep much larger forces at bay by picking the proper locations for your actions."

"Not the last one, ma'am. They would have caught and killed us if it hadn't been for Debbie and Josh McFarland."

"Yes, yes. I know all about that. We have strict requirements for the Royal Marines. You do not have the records to show if you meet them. However," she hurries on, "the tests you took today show an extremely high aptitude, and knowledge equivalent to a first in a university…"

"A first, ma'am?"

"A degree." Sam nods in understanding. "In any case, we are willing to waive the requirements, and since you are now a British subject, I would like to offer you a training slot as a Royal Marine officer cadet. Are you interested?"

The question stumps Sam. He had never thought about being an officer. He just wanted to get at The Enemy, to defend his family and now his new homeland.

"Well, man, speak up!"

"Ma'am, I am, provided it's in the infantry."

"So, you want to fight."

"Not really, ma'am. What I want is to make sure those bastards, pardon the language, never threaten us again. I've seen what they do. I don't want them doing it here. And I don't want some job sitting on my ass waiting for them to come, ma'am."

"I think we can accommodate you. Provided you pass training."

"I will, ma'am."

"Very good. You will be contacted in a few days about when to report for training."

"May I ask where the training is, ma'am?"

"Lympston in Devine. It's down on the southeast Channel coast. That's the English Channel, across from France, or what used to be France. Our administrative offices, such as this one, are in London near the Ministry of Defense, which we commonly refer to as the MOD. The operational units are all on the Channel coast."

"How far is Lympston from here, ma'am?"

"Approximately two hundred eighty kilometers. You'll train there for sixty weeks. When you graduate, you'll be commissioned a Second Leftenant and posted to a unit."

"Ma'am, I'm married with two small children."

"I know all that. You'll have to work that out with your wife. I understand she'll be standing the civil engineer examination."

"Yes, ma'am."

"We don't want to break up your family. When you're posted, we will do our best to find her work nearby. The Royal Marines use civilian engineers, as well as civilian job opportunities that will be available for her. So, are we set?"

"Ma'am, I need to talk to my wife. If she's on board with this, then yes, ma'am, we're set."

"Very good. I expect to hear from you by the morrow."

"Yes, ma'am."

"If the response is positive, plan to start training in a fortnight."

"Ma'am?" Sam asks, confused.

"What? Oh, two weeks," the Major General tells him. "You really must learn the language, Cadet Hope."

"Yes, ma'am," Sam says.

"I look forward to hearing from you," FitzRoy says. "A moment more, Cadet."

"Ma'am?" Sam says, who had made a move to leave, thinking the interview was done.

"I think you need to know the situation. I forgot to mention it."

"Ma'am."

"About thirty years ago," she says, "something happened on the Continent. We have never been able to determine exactly what, but what we do know is that hordes of some kind of military force started to sweep west from somewhere on the other side of the Urals. That's a mountain chain in Russia," the Major General says when she sees the questioning look on Sam's face. "You must acquaint yourself with the geography."

"Ma'am."

"Anyway, this horde slaughtered everything in its path, human and animal. We sent forces to help the Europeans defend themselves, but it was quite hopeless. There were just too many of them. They would just launch human wave attacks overrunning our blokes regardless of the massive casualties they suffered. That is something you seem to be familiar with, according to the statement you gave when you landed."

"Yes, ma'am."

FitzRoy nods. "We suggested using tactical nukes against them, but our European allies wouldn't agree at first, afraid of what it would do to their countries. By the time they were willing, most of the countries were already gone and the few on the coast were rapidly being overrun. We finally gave it up as a bad job and pulled back across the channel with as many people as we could evacuate."

She stops to collect her thoughts, as she stares out the window for a moment. "We saved thousands. Millions were lost." She swallows hard and turns back to Sam. "We destroyed the Chunnel to keep the foe from attacking us through that, depending on the Royal Navy to prevent a seaborne invasion."

"Chunnel, ma'am?"

"Yes, right. It was a tunnel under the Channel linking us to France."

"Ma'am," he says, nodding he understands.

"We were ready to use nukes to destroy any attempt to invade before it could start, but we soon discovered that whoever those people are they couldn't seem to, or didn't want to, mount a seaborne invasion.

"By the way," she says. "you are fortunate to come when you did. When this thing started, you would have been sunk out of hand. You must understand we didn't know what we were dealing with at first. In fact, a number of small boats filled with people were sunk trying to cross the Channel, killing everyone aboard."

"What changed?"

"Some of those people landed on the Channel islands. Since we did not know what we were dealing with, we quarantined them and sent over doctors with full biological protective equipment. We discovered that it wasn't a virus or some other kind of disease that was causing the problem. To this day, we do not know how or why this happened. Just that it did.

"In any case, with this increased population and our continental food sources cut off, we had to become self-sufficient. We have turned every available piece of land into a garden to produce food. And we ration food to make sure everyone has enough to eat. But the early years were beastly. Many people starved until we got things in hand. We have managed to keep up our industry, barely, mainly to support our defense. Personal cars are a thing of the past.

"On the positive side, as I already noted, those people," FitzRoy continued, waving a hand toward the east, "haven't been able to do anything with the naval ships they captured, nor with the military or civilian aircraft. We keep watch on them through satellites. We would fly planes over, but if any suffered mechanical failure, the pilot would be lost. We have hit a few Troop concentrations and places we have identified as command centers with tactical nukes, but that didn't seem to make any real progress."

"The rest of the world, ma'am?"

"Ah, yes. Well, Australia, New Zealand, Iceland, Japan, the Philippines, and Indonesia, the island nations, have survived. There may be communities surviving in the mountains around the world. We had contact with them for a time, but not for years, so we don't know. There was an area around the Isthmus of Panama in your former neck of the woods where the people managed to build defenses. But, again, we lost communication with them decades ago. We have managed to re-establish limited trade with the island nations, but it is spotty and dangerous because if anything goes wrong, a ship has no safe harbor to go to and no place to refuel. Hence, they travel in convoys." The Major General shrugs, looking down at his desk.

"Well," she says, looking up at Sam, "I guess you best be on your way and have that talk with your wife."

"Ma'am." Sam stands, turns smartly and leaves the office.

He spends the walk home thinking about what just happened. He's so deep in thought that he's a block past the apartment building before he realizes it and has to retrace his steps.

"What's up?" Sarah asks when Sam walks into the flat.

"They want me to be an officer in the Royal Marines," he says, sounding perplexed.

"You? I didn't think you liked officers."

"Where are the kids?" he asks, trying to change the subject.

"Sleeping. Well? You giving orders?"

"I said I didn't like taking orders. I never said I minded giving them."

"I sort of noticed that."

"You did?"

"How could I miss it," she replies, smiling. "What are you going to do?"

Sam shrugs. "I have to let them know tomorrow."

"What do you want to do?"

"I want to go after those bastards. I want to make sure you and the kids are safe. I'm tired of running. I want to hit back. I want to knock those assholes all the way back to the hell they came from."

"And if you get killed?" she says, worry creeping into her voice. "What happens to us then?"

Sam just looks at her. "That is a risk I'm willing to take," he says finally.

"You're willing to take? You'd be dead," she says sharply. "What do I do then? There are others who can go fight them. You've already done enough!"

"I'm not built that way, and you know it. Besides, what would you do if those assholes get here? We'd all be dead then. I want to make sure that doesn't happen. I am thinking of you and the kids."

Sarah sits down heavily in a chair, just as Judy comes wandering out of the bedroom, and crawls into her mother's lap, snuggling down. "Okay," she says, hugging her daughter. "But if you don't come back, I will hunt you down and kill you myself. Understand?"

"Yes, dear," he says, a bit sarcastically, which provokes a withering look. He explains to her where he will be training and that he was told she would be found a job nearby.

"I hope you're right," she says, gently stroking Judy's hair.

Sam nods and goes into the kitchen, where he calls the night duty officer to accept the appointment. He is told he will receive his orders in two days.

CHAPTER TWENTY-SEVEN

The next morning, Sarah sets out for her appointment at the Home Office. She catches a bus since the office is across the city. She arrives at nine in the morning, finds the office—and spends the next six hours taking test after test, with a half-hour break for lunch, which she gets in the department's cafeteria.

When she is finally finished, she is ushered into a waiting room, where she sits for another two hours. And where she starts getting hungry for dinner, and thinking about her husband and children. Sam hasn't been alone with them as much as she has, and she worries about him getting overwhelmed with a small child and an infant.

Finally, she is ushered into a large office with a woman sitting behind a big desk. She's invited to sit down. After an hour-and-half interview, she is on her way home, her head swimming, a new briefcase containing papers in her hand.

As soon as she is out of the building, she calls Sam, first to find out how the kids are—they have both been fed, bathed, and put to bed—and to let him know she's starving. She is going to stop for dinner, does he want any? Since he does, she decides to get some takeaway at their favorite fish-and-chip shop.

She refuses to tell him what happened, until she gets home. She catches the bus, sitting quietly, staring out a window, wondering about the day, and what just happened.

Forty-five minutes later, she walks through the door to their home, briefcase in one hand, and fish and chips in the other. The apartment is silent. Sam is dozing on the couch, Frank asleep on his chest.

The closing door rouses him. He gets up carefully so as not to wake Frank, carrying the sleeping boy into the bedroom. When he comes out, he asks, "So, what happened?"

"Food first," she announces, dropping her brief case on the floor. Sam disappears into the kitchen, coming out with plates, napkins, and tableware. He goes back for two beers and glasses, while Sarah plates the fish and chips at the dining table. When they sit down, she starts eating hungrily. Sam nibbles at his food, smiling at her.

"Hungry, huh?" he says.

She nods as she chews another bite. Finally, her hunger sated, she asks, "How did the kids do today?"

"They were fine."

"Did you have enough milk?" she asks.

"Plenty. There's still a bottle left."

"Good. I have to pump right after dinner. I'm about to burst."

"At the pace you're downing that food, it won't take you long," he observes.

"Funny man. You didn't spend all day taking tests, and then sitting on your ass, waiting for some bureaucrat."

"That was yesterday," he quips. "And the result of all that for you? When do you start training?"

"I don't," she says between bites.

"What!" Sam says outraged. "How can they not give you training! You're brilliant! Better than anyone they have now! I'll stake my life on it!"

"Don't do that!" Sarah says, holding up a hand to cut him off.

"But …"

"Stop! I'm not getting training because I don't need it."

"You don't?" he asks, calming down and now perplexed.

"Nope. I passed all the exams with flying colors. In fact, I did better than ninety-five percent of the applicants."

"Just ninety-five percent?" Sam asks mischievously.

"That's the highest statistic they keep, you ass."

"Fair enough. What happens now?" he asks.

"I took six hours of tests, mainly in civil engineering, but also electrical and mechanical. You are now looking at someone who is certified in civil and mechanical engineering. I didn't do well enough for electrical, which I'm kind of happy about. I was never that interested in it."

"And a job?"

Sarah looks at him, her head tilted a bit to one side. "I was offered a job—they call it a posting—as chief civil engineer in a little town in southeast England called Lympstone."

"Lympstone!" he says, perking up.

"Yup. It seems they knew you would be training near there. Go figure."

"The Major General told me they would take care of us," he says. "That's great. We'll be able to stay together."

"Okay, in the interest of full disclosure, they offered me a commission in the Royal Engineers."

"The Army? You didn't take it, did you?" Sam asks, concern rising in his voice.

"It's okay for you to put your life on the line, but not me?" She fires the accusation at him.

"I didn't mean that," he responds defensively.

Sarah looks at him for a long moment, deciding not to torment him anymore. "No. I didn't take it. One of us has to be able to be with the kids. Besides, I want one or two more."

"You do?" Sam looks bewildered. "You enjoy being pregnant?"

"Well, no. I don't enjoy that whole labor thing. But I love being a mother. Don't you love being a father?"

"Yes, but I'm not the one who gets pregnant and gives birth."

"Good," she says triumphantly. "Then we're in agreement."

"You don't want to start trying right now, do you?"

"Hell no! Next year will do just fine."

"Good," Sam says, sitting back relieved.

"There is one more thing," Sarah says, slowly, watching Sam for his reaction.

"What?" he says suspiciously.

"I did accept a reserve commission in the Royal Engineers."

"You did? That's the Army!"

"Yes, but I'm not supposed to go for training until after you're done."

"What happens if we are both deployed at the same time?" he asks.

"They have what they call certified care. They have people, mostly women, who are paid to take care of children when both parents are deployed."

"And we get to pick the one we want?" Sam asks, suspicious of the process.

"Of course," Sarah assures him. "You don't think I would agree to turn our children over to just anybody, do you?"

"Just wanted to make sure," he says, relieved.

"Your Major General only told part of the story," Sarah says after Sam tells her what he learned. "The guy who gave me my credentials told me there was mass starvation at first when the Continental food imports stopped and before agriculture production was increased here. Many people died. Now the country is trading on a barter basis with the other surviving island nations. We're getting raw materials and sending back manufactured goods," she says, already seeing Britain as her nation.

"We are importing food and raw materials from such places as Australia and Hawaii in the Pacific, as well as Indonesia and the Philippines, and Greenland, Iceland, Prince Edward Island, and Nova Scotia, across the Atlantic. I'll show you where they are on a map later," she says when she notices that Sam is clueless about where those places are.

They sit in silence for a time, side by side on the couch, digesting what has happened the last two days. And wondering where their future will take their family in their new country.

"You know what I don't understand," Sam says, "is how can we remember nothing of our past but still I pass tests saying I have a college degree and you know all about civil engineering. The others as well, such as George and Jessica."

"That, my love," Sarah replies, "is a mystery we will probably never have an answer to. Crap, Frank is crying."

"I'll get him," Sam says, getting off the couch and heading into the nursery.

CHAPTER TWENTY-EIGHT

A week later, Sam and Sarah find themselves standing in front of the cottage they have been assigned in Lympstone. Judy is exploring the fenced yard, or garden, as they are learning to call it. The driver of the van that brought them from London is busily unloading their clothes and such things as the crib they have bought for Frank.

"Shall we see where we've landed?" Sam asks.

"Why do they call this a cottage?" Sarah wonders, as she cradles her squirming son. "It's two stories. It looks huge."

"Let's not complain," Sam says, leaning toward her.

"Sir, madam," the van driver says, "do you need help moving your property inside?"

"Yes, if you don't mind," Sam replies, somewhat distractedly. The two men quickly have all the family's belongings inside the front door. Sarah thanks the man for his help; he then heads back to London.

"No car," Sam says. "It's nice we're right outside the village."

"Hmmm, yes, I suppose," Sarah replies as she wanders through the downstairs with Sam trailing behind her, and Judy following. The furniture looks old, but in good shape. The rooms all have hardwood floors and off-white walls. The kitchen is well equipped and has an island and a small breakfast table by the windows.

Upstairs, they find four bedrooms and two bathrooms. The closets are small and the ceilings low.

"Good thing we're not over two meters tall," Sam observers as he ducks through one door into the bedroom they decide will be the nursery.

"Do you think we should buy this place?" Sarah asks as she looks out the lone window in the nursery onto the unkept garden below.

"Let's live here for a while before we decide. Just pay rent," Sam responds. They were told they had six months to decide whether to buy the house from the government, keep renting it, or move.

They spend the next week before Sam has to report for training settling into their new lives, and meeting their neighbors, who help them find the best places to shop for food and necessities. The village also has a variety of recreational activities, none of which Sam can take part in once he heads off for training at the nearby base. Sarah also has little time for such things as she settles into her new job, arranges for childcare while she works, and learns how to become the wife of a Royal Marine officer, effectively a single parent for long stretches of time.

Sam heads off for his sixty weeks of training for Royal Marine officer candidates. During the first half of the training, he is only able to get home once to see Sarah and the kids. His next leave comes halfway through training when he is given a week at home. He doesn't see them again until he graduates as a Second Lieutenant. What no one can explain to him is why that word is pronounced "Leftenant." He's told that's just the way it is.

In the meantime, Sarah has started work on a number of projects for the village and the surrounding areas, including upgrades in water and sewer service, and strengthening bridges. Because of the pressures of work and taking care of the children, she is unable to attend Sam's graduation.

Wearing his new dress uniform, he gets dropped off at his front door.

"Hi, I'm home," he calls as he sets down his kit and takes off his hat.

Judy comes running, yelling, "Daddy, Daddy, Daddy!" and throws herself at him. Sam scoops her up as they exchange kisses and hugs. The little girl is clinging to him as Sarah comes downstairs carrying Frank. With his left arm holding Judy, Sam wraps his other around his wife, who wraps her free left arm around him, exchanging a deep, long kiss. Frank squirms a bit, but the one-year-old reaches up to touch his father's face.

"You finally got here," Sarah says as they disentangle and Sam takes Frank in his right arm, kissing his son on his head, while he holds Judy tightly in his left. "We've missed you."

"I have three weeks to make up for lost time. I have missed you all so much. We have never been apart this long," he says.

Sarah steps back from him a bit, surveying her husband. "I guess we better get used to it now that you are a Royal Marine officer," she says touching the pip on his left shoulder.

Sam smiles, then steps back, looking at Sarah up and down. "You look different. Glowing. What have you changed?"

Sarah smiles broadly at him. "You know I said I wanted more children."

Sam, raising his eyebrows, looks at her middle, and notices the small bulge.

"In case you haven't figured it out," she says, laughing a bit. "Remember when you were last home?"

"But, but, you didn't tell me," he protests.

"You know I couldn't call."

"You could have written," he complains. "The letter would have reached me."

Sarah just shrugs. "I didn't want to distract you." Then she turns serious, "Are you happy about another child?"

"Happy? I couldn't be happier," he says, putting Judy down and wrapping his arm around his wife, pulling her close and exchanging a passionate kiss with her. "But what happened to a year?"

Sarah shrugs. "Biology. Of the passionate kind."

Sam smiles and shakes his head.

All four of them go to the parents' bedroom, where Sam puts away his clothing with Judy's help, while Sarah keeps watch on Frank who is crawling around the bed.

"You know," Sam says as he finishes, "I could eat."

"You could, could you?" Sarah says. "It's only five o'clock," she says looking at her watch. "But we can get started. Will you help?" she says looking at Sam.

"Help? Love to," he says, following her downstairs.

In the kitchen, Sarah pulls out some chicken, carrots, potatoes, and peas, along with a variety of spices. With her directing, and Judy trying to help, they cook dinner over the next forty-five minutes. Sarah pulls some pureed carrots and chicken from the refrigerator and warms them for Frank.

With the meal ready, Judy in a booster seat and Frank in a highchair, they gather around the rectangular dining room table. Sarah is feeding herself with one hand and helping Frank eat with the other. Sam helps Judy get food on her plate and makes sure it is in small enough pieces she can eat it safely. Sarah has produced beer for her and Sam, while the children have milk.

While they eat, the parents chit chat, with Sarah bringing Sam up to speed about the children, and Sam telling her about his training, which was tough both mentally and physically.

"Daddy, you okay?" Judy asks, who has become worried listening to her father describe the training regimen he just went through, which included how to keep themselves and their Marines alive in the worst of conditions.

"I'm fine, sweetie," he says. "The training was actually fun," he tells his daughter, provoking a bit of a laugh from Sarah.

"You know," he says, returning his attention to his wife, "I think with this group we can take the fight to The Enemy and do real damage."

"You didn't say win," Sarah observes.

Sam shakes his head. "Not right now. Things have to change. We have to get stronger if we can, and The Enemy has to get weaker. That, by the way," he hurries on, forestalling the comment Sarah's about to make, "is apparently happening. There are indications The Enemy's forces are declining, that they can't supply enough food for all their troops."

"What, exactly, does that mean?"

"I'm not sure," Sam says, sitting back with a crooked grin on his face. "But it can't be bad."

"Let's hope not," Sarah says.

The conversation lags as they concentrate on their dinner and helping their children eat.

"By the way," Sam says, "Judy seems to be picking up the local accent really well."

"Yes, she is," Sarah says.

"What's accent?" Judy asks, looking back and forth at her parents.

"It's just how people say the words," Sam says.

"You know how I say words a little differently than your friends and Mrs. Collier?" Sarah asks. "That's her pre-school teacher," she adds as an aside to Sam. "Well, you are starting to say words the way they do," she says, turning her attention back to Judy. "And that's a good thing," Sarah hurries to add when she sees the look of concern on her daughter's face.

"Why?" Judy asks.

"Because," she replies, "it means that they will be able to understand you better."

Judy thinks about that for a moment. "Okay," she says as she picks up a carrot to eat.

Sam and Sarah just exchange glances.

"By the by," Sarah says, a mischievous tone in her voice, "I outrank you, you know."

"You what?" Sam says, his fork stopping halfway to his mouth.

"I outrank you," comes the saucy reply.

Sam looks confused. "Why? Because you're my wife?"

"No," Sarah says, a bit slowly, "because I am a full Leftenant and you're just a Second Leftenant."

"Okay," Sam says, sitting back in his chair and putting his fork down, "you're going to have to explain that."

"Well, about a week after your leave," she says, unable to suppress a grin, "I got called for training."

"What about the kids?"

"I found care for them. A beautiful older woman who did a wonderful job caring for them. In fact, she now takes care of them when I'm at work."

"Go on," Sam says, somewhat suspiciously.

"The training lasted two months, but I got to come home every weekend. And we didn't do much survival training, so it was easy."

"But you're pregnant!" Sam protests.

"That," she says with a bit of a laugh, "is how I found out I was pregnant, when they did the medical tests when I was inducted. They said at that stage the training would not endanger the baby. And they were right."

"Good," Sam says, relieved. "But how did you jump to full Leftenant?"

"When I graduated, I was commissioned Leftenant in the Royal Army Engineers. Apparently, with my level of skill, they decided to let me skip that first step. You know what this means?"

"What?" Sam answers, his level of suspicion increasing.

"When we are both in uniform, you'll have to salute me," Sarah replies, a grin stretching across her face.

"Great," Sam says as they both dissolve into laughter.

CHAPTER TWENTY-NINE

Wearing his dress uniform, Sam gets off the bus next to the car park in front of Royal Marine Brigade Headquarters on Friday morning after his leave expired. The small car park is filled with military vehicles and staff cars. Private cars are mostly a thing of the past, with just a few antiques still on the road.

When he enters the building, the Corporal manning the information desk directs him down the central hallway to Brigadier Stanley Cooper's office. The walls are painted a drab gray with brown doors leading to offices on either side. Most of the doors are closed as Sam walks the twenty meters to the door at the end, which bears a large metal plate stating Brigadier's Office. Sam stops himself just before he knocks when he remembers this door just leads into a reception room. He opens the door and walks in.

Across the large room is a desk manned by a Color Sergeant. Sam quickly glances around, seeing five of his classmates already there, seated in chairs along the wall. Six more are still to come. He's relieved that he's not the last to arrive.

He strides to the desk and stands patiently in front of the Color Sergeant who is busy typing on a computer. Finally, he clears his throat.

The Color Sergeant jerks her head up and looks up at him in surprise. "Sorry, sir, I didn't notice you were there."

"Not a problem, Colors," Sam replies. "Second Leftenant Samuel Hope reporting."

"Very good, sir," she replies. "Please have a seat. The Brigadier will see you all when the others arrive."

"Thank you," Sam says, then turns smartly about-face and walks to where the others are sitting, exchanging greetings with them. All of them are nervous about meeting the Royal Marines' top field commander. A few make a try at starting conversation, but no one is really in the mood for small talk, or speculation about what lies before them now they have completed their training and received their commissions.

A few minutes after Sam arrived, the last six come in, having caught the bus together from the Bachelor Officers' Quarters. After they report to the Color Sergeant, they are also told to sit down and wait for the Brigadier to call them.

Five minutes later, the Color Sergeant puts down the phone and stands up. "Leftenants, the Brigadier will see you now," she announces.

The twelve newly minted officers all stand in unison and march toward the door, which the Color Sergeant opens and then stands out of the way. The dozen men and women march into the large wood-paneled office, splitting to the right and left in front of the Brigadier's large mahogany desk. Cooper is sitting back in his large plush chair watching them. Behind him is a large picture window looking out over the nearby forest.

As the group comes to rigid attention about a meter in front of the desk, all of them locking their eyes straight ahead, Cooper slowly sits up, looking at each one intently, starting from his left. When he reaches the end of the line, he slowly gets up from his chair, walks around the desk and goes behind the line, inspecting each one.

"Stand easy," he finally says as he walks back to his desk and sits down. In silence, he looks at each one in turn again, a few return his gaze while the others keep their eyes straight forward.

"First off," Cooper finally says, "you probably think your training has ended." He pauses for effect. "It hasn't," a commanding tone entering his voice as many of the Second Lieutenants shuffle a bit uncomfortably. "Training is what keeps you sharp and," he says, emphasizing his words, "keeps you alive." He pauses for a moment to let what he just said sink in. "Starting on the morrow, you will all be posted to Troops, even those who are destined for noncombat roles." Another pause. "You will train with experienced officers and with the ranks. You will learn everything you can about what being on an actual battlefield is like." Another pause. "Pay close attention to your senior NCOs. You can learn a lot from them which will help you lead effectively and keep you and your Marines alive. Any questions?"

"Sir," Second Lieutenant Jason Whitebread says, his voice sounding tentative, "how long will this phase of our training last?"

Cooper gives him a withering look. He then thumbs through the files on his desk, pulling one out and opening it. "Ah, yes, Second Leftenant Whitebread. Destined for the Intelligence Section," the Brigadier says, then looks up at his victim as he closes the file. "I'll tell you a dirty little secret, Second Leftenant Whitebread," Cooper says, pronouncing each word in the name distinctly, "intelligence officers, especially junior ones, are frequently on the front lines. That is where the intelligence is to be found. I suggest you don't worry about how long this phase of your training will last and focus on learning well enough to stay alive."

"Yes, sir," the clearly chastised Whitebread replies.

"Very good, then," the Brigadier says. "You all have your assignments. Report by zero six hundred Monday. Dismissed. Except for you, Hope," he quickly adds.

The other eleven come to attention, do an about-face and head for the door, some casting curious glances at Sam, a few giving him looks of pity.

When the room is clear, Cooper looks up at Sam who is standing at attention again. "Oh, for God's sake, man, stand easy." As Sam comes to parade rest, he adds, "Take a seat." Cooper indicates one of the two padded chairs before his desk.

"Yes, sir," Sam says, wondering what this is about as he sits down.

"Colors," the Brigadier says as he pushes a button on his phone, activating a speaker, "two teas."

"Sir," Sam hears over the speaker.

Cooper studies Sam for a moment. "You are probably wondering why I asked you to stay behind."

"Yes, sir."

"I have a special assignment for you," he says as a Corporal comes in with a tray bearing a tea pot, two cups, sugar, and milk. The Brigadier motions for a filled cup to be put in front of Sam, then the other is put near him on the desk, with the milk and sugar between them. "Privilege of rank," he says when he notices Sam staring at the sugar. "And, I suppose, it doesn't hurt to have a brother-in-law in the import-export business."

"No, sir," Sam says, picking up his cup after deciding to forego the sugar and milk, neither of which he normally uses.

"As I was saying," Cooper says as he puts a small spoonful of sugar and a splash of milk into his tea, "I have a special assignment for you."

"Yes, sir?"

"I am breveting you Leftenant and giving you command of a Troop in Four Two Commando," Cooper says, pushing a box with Lieutenant's insignia pips across the desk to Sam, along with a copy of the orders with his temporary promotion.

"Sir?" Sam says, picking up the box and looking into it.

"Look, Hope, you come with some extraordinary qualifications. You graduated second in your class, you have glowing fitness reports from all your superiors, but what really makes you stand out is that you have actual combat experience with those people," Cooper says, waving his left hand toward France while taking a sip of tea. "And I've been informed that you think well on your feet and know how to interpret orders."

"Sir, my combat experience was more than a year ago, and on another continent," Sam responds, deciding to ignore the last comment.

"True, but from the intelligence reports we have and from what has been reported, the situation is pretty much the same. By the by, I will make your advancement permanent as soon as I can."

"Yes, sir. What is it you want me to do?"

"I want you to train your Troop intensely so your lot can be sent across the Channel on raiding and intelligence missions. I understand," Cooper says, holding up a hand to forestall any objection, "that is Thirty Commando's job. But they are stretched thin. They send small observation parties to points all along the coast, from Norway into the Baltic and down to Spain."

"What would my Troop's role exactly be, sir?"

"You will scout their defenses and bring back prisoners we can interrogate. In other words, you and your Marines will probably be going into combat. You are unique among my officers in that you have fought these people. On top of that, you managed to withdraw successfully."

"I lost a man in one fight, and we only survived ultimately because of help from the McFarlands," Sam protests.

"I don't need to remind you," Cooper says sternly, "that combat always carries the risk of casualties. As for the other, you were hampered by a pregnant woman you had to care for."

"And we could easily be hampered by casualties in the future," Sam points out.

"Yes, yes, of course. But I have faith that you will sort that when the time comes. You have shown the ability to think on your feet. Hope, I need you for this assignment."

"Yes, sir," Sam replies, putting his cup down as he finishes the tea. "How long do I have to train my Troop?"

"Five months. I think that should give you ample time since you will have a well-trained Troop to start with."

"Yes, sir."

"Brilliant. Report to Leftenant Colonel St. Anthony Monday morning."

"Sir?" Sam says, leaning forward in the chair. "Permission to speak freely?"

The Brigadier studies him for a moment. "By all means, Leftenant. And I think I know what is on you mind."

"Sir?"

"It is true that Four Two is not up to the same standards as the others," Cooper says, leaning forward to rest his elbows on his desk as he stares intently at Sam. "And St. Anthony is the weakest of the commanders. Is that about right?"

"That is what I've heard, sir," Sam replies, sitting back in his chair.

"Very good," Cooper says, also sitting back. "So, why you? Why am I, in a sense, putting you in what could be a no-win situation. Is that correct?"

"Partly, sir," Sam says. "I would also like to know how much latitude I have in dealing with the Leftenant Colonel. And if he is so weak, why is he still in command?"

"Good questions," Cooper says matter-of-factly. "As for the first one, you can't kill him. And you must obey orders, obviously."

"Obviously, sir," Sam agrees.

"But I am not throwing you to the wolves, either. You will be in command of Six Troop of B Company. Your Company commander will be Captain Marsha Banning. She is as good and as tough as they come. She will run as much interference for you as she can."

"Yes, sir. Thank you, sir."

Cooper dismisses the thanks with a wave of his hand. "As for the second question. Well, let us just say there are, umm, political considerations at play. But as soon as a suitable billet opens, I plan to resolve the issue."

"Yes, sir."

"What I want from you," the Brigadier says, leaning forward again, "what I need from you is to train your Troop to such a high level that it will set the standard for the entire Brigade. I need your Marines to be as tough and resourceful as it is possible to make them."

"Yes, sir. I understand," Sam says, wondering in the back of his mind if he can accomplish that feat.

"Now, Hope, you must understand that I have told you this in the strictest confidence. You are not to repeat any of this to anyone," he says, looking hard at Sam. "And that includes your wife. Is that clear?"

"Yes, sir," Sam says, swallowing hard.

"Very well. I suggest you head home and get ready to report Monday morning. It will be quite a journey to your new command."

"Sir," Sam says, rising from the chair and coming smartly to attention, saluting, then executing an about-face.

"By the way," Cooper says, before Sam can move toward the door, prompting him to turn back around, "check with Colors on your way out. You are being assigned a staff car."

"Sir?" he says, turning back around.

"For your commute," he says, smiling. "We need to keep our valued officers happy."

"Yes, sir. Thank you, sir."

"Dismissed, Leftenant. And good luck."

"Sir," Sam says, doing an about-face.

He stops at the Color Sergeant's desk, who hands him keys to a car, tells him where it is parked and that he can get fuel on base.

As Sam heads into the car park, he has two things on his mind. The first is telling Sarah that he'll be on long commutes and often gone for days at a time. The second is starting to develop a training plan for the forty Marines he will be responsible for.

CHAPTER THIRTY

Just before zero six hundred hours Monday, Sam walks into the headquarters of Four Two Commando. He looks around the grey-painted square room furnished with three desks and some hard chairs against the outside wall. He spots what he assumes is the Commando's Color Sergeant who inhabits a desk in front of a door labeled COMMANDER. He walks past the other two desks, one on each side of the room, drawing faint interest from the two ranks working at them.

He stands in front of the Color Sergeant's desk waiting to be recognized.

After a few minutes, the Color Sergeant looks up at him. "Yes? What do you want?"

"Is it acceptable for even a Color Sergeant to address a superior officer in that manner?" Sam spits out in the most withering tone he can muster, assuming St. Anthony's poor attitude has infected his staff.

The Color Sergeant stands quickly at attention. "Sorry, sir. My mind was on my work. I didn't notice your rank, Leftenant. It won't happen again."

Sam just nods in reply. "Please let Leftenant Colonel St. Anthony know Leftenant Hope is reporting for duty," he says in a formal tone, handing the Color Sergeant his paperwork.

"Yes, sir. Right away, sir," the Colors says, taking the folder with his left hand while picking up the telephone receiver with the other. He pushes a button, and in a moment relays the message to St. Anthony and listens to the reply. "Yes, sir," he says, then puts down the receiver. "Leftenant Hope, if you kindly will have a seat the Leftenant Colonel will be with you directly."

"Very good," Sam says, then retreats to the chairs and sits down, drawing renewed interest from the Sergeant and Corporal at the other two desks. He glances at those two ranks, who quickly go back to their work.

Sam looks at the wall clock: zero six ten.

He starts thinking about Sarah's response to his new posting. While they both knew he would have to be away a lot, it came too quickly for either of them, especially since she is pregnant. 'Oh, well,' he thinks, 'it can't be helped.' He then forces his mind onto the problem confronting him: How to train his Troop up to a razor-sharp edge in five months, without destroying morale. His Bootnecks will face challenges much greater than they have before, lessons they will have to learn well if any of them are to survive the missions they will be going on.

Lost in thought, Sam looks at the wall clock again: zero seven twenty-seven. Obviously, he thinks, St. Anthony is proving a point about who is in charge. Childish. St. Anthony is a Lieutenant Colonel. Sam is a Lieutenant. It was obvious who's in charge. Besides, making him sit around wasting time irritates him. He watches as the Color Sergeant picks up his papers and goes into the office, then returns and resumes his post at his desk.

At 0818 by the wall clock, the Color Sergeant gets a call and then calls to Sam, "Leftenant Hope, Leftenant Colonel St. Anthony will see you now."

"Very good," Sam says, rising from the chair and striding the five meters across the room. The Color Sergeant holds the door open for him, closing it after he has gone in. Sam strides across the dark wood-paneled room, lit by a single overhead light and small windows across the back wall. St. Anthony is reading some papers in front of him by the light of the desk lamp.

Coming to attention in front of the desk, Sam says, "Leftenant Samuel Hope reporting for duty as ordered, sir."

After about five minutes, St. Anthony puts the papers down and looks at Sam. "It's Brevet Leftenant, if I am not mistaken."

"No, sir, you are not," Sam responds.

"Good. From now on, let's be accurate about your rank. Or the lack of it."

"Yes, sir."

"Brevet Leftenant, it goes without saying, I am opposed to this whole situation. You do not have enough active service to lead a Troop. And I do not appreciate having such an inexperienced officer, especially one with no pedigree, being foisted on me."

Sam just stands at attention, looking straight forward over St. Anthony's head.

"Well, man," St. Anthony finally says, "what do you have to say for yourself?"

"I'm following orders, sir."

"You expect this to be a big boost for your career, do you?"

"Sir," Sam says, still at stiff attention, "I just want to do my duty. Nothing more, sir."

"And do your duty you will," St. Anthony says sharply, slapping the desk. Sam saw the move coming out of the corner of his eye, so he did not react to the noise. St. Anthony looks disappointed by the lack of response. "Do not expect any favorable treatment here. You will be watched closely and any mistakes, and I do mean any, will be noted and go against you in your fitness report."

"Yes, sir," Sam responds impassively.

"Dismissed, Brevet Leftenant," St. Anthony says peevishly.

"Sir," Sam says, putting on his cover, saluting, performing an about-face and marching smartly out of the office. He stops at the Color Sergeant's desk to get directions to B Company's headquarters. Then he leaves the building to make the half-kilometer walk.

As Sam walks into the small building housing B Company HQ, the Sergeant at the desk at the far wall looks up and then stands at attention.

"Sir!" he barks out.

"Stand easy," Sam says as he reaches the desk.

"Yes, sir."

"I'm Brevet Leftenant Hope reporting for duty."

"Yes, sir. Let me alert the Captain," the Sergeant says as he reaches for the phone.

Sam nods in acknowledgement.

"Ma'am," the Sergeant says into the receiver, "Brevet Leftenant Hope is reporting for duty." He listens a moment, a small smile crossing his face. "Ma'am." Putting down the phone, he looks at Sam, "Leftenant, this way please, sir."

"Lead on," Sam says, gesturing with his right hand.

The Sergeant turns and opens the door to the inner office, then steps out of the way, allowing Sam to enter, then closes the door behind him.

Sam strides into the small office with a lone window on each of three plywood walls that have been painted Royal Marine blue and covered with maps and photos of Marines training. He takes this all in as he crosses the three meters to the desk, behind which Captain Marsha Banning stands up, smiling at him.

He comes to attention in front of the desk. "Brevet Leftenant ..."

"Oh, knock it off, Leftenant Hope. That 'Brevet' crap is something our peerless leader might insist on, but here you are Leftenant. Understood?" Banning says, extending a hand across the desk.

"Yes, ma'am," Sam says as he relaxes and reaches out to shake her hand.

"Have a seat, Hope," she says, waving him to one of the three metal chairs in front of the desk.

"Thank you, ma'am."

"Want something to drink?"

"Yes, ma'am."

"Good, so do I. And you can drop the 'ma'am' business."

"Yes, ma' ..." Sam says, catching himself.

Banning smiles at him as she goes to a cooler. "Porter or lager?" she asks over her shoulder.

"Porter would be nice."

"Brilliant," she says, bringing a bottle of lager for herself and a porter for him. She hands him his beer and then retreats behind the desk, sitting down and taking a swallow. "Now, I understand you are here to provide intensive training to Six Troop."

"That's what I'm told," Sam says.

"By the way, I expected you several hours earlier," she says, raising her eyebrows.

"I was, shall we say, delayed at Commando HQ."

"Kept you cooling your heels waiting, did our Leftenant Colonel?"

"Yes, ma'am, he did."

She nods in acknowledgement. "Have you developed a training plan?"

"Not exactly," Sam says. "This was all dumped on me Friday by the Brigadier. I have ideas and I have an outline, but nothing more than that at the moment. Besides, I would like to take the next week evaluating my Troop."

"Lovely," Banning replies. "I will run interference for you with St. Anthony."

"Interference?" Sam asks, concern in his voice.

"Yes, our lovely leader has a strict training regime and expects us all to follow it with no deviations. Should he notice you are deviating, he will become, shall we say, somewhat upset."

"Look, I'm not here to create problems for you."

"No worries. I can trump our Leftenant Colonel with a full Colonel," she says with a big smile.

"Ma'am?"

"Colonel Flemming, our Brigade executive officer," Banning announces.

"Yes, I know who she is," Sam says.

Banning looks at him questioningly for a moment. "What apparently you don't know is this is all her idea."

"It is?" he responds in surprise. "No one mentioned her to me."

"Well, it is. She pulled your file and sold the idea to the Brigadier. She then decided our lovely St. Anthony needed some shaking up, and you and I were the two to do it. Or so she said when she called me Thursday to make sure I was alright with it. So here you are, or should I say, here we are, about to embark on an interesting adventure." Banning pauses for a moment to let that sink in. "Sort of like tiptoeing through a mine field."

"Great," Sam says with some exasperation. "Something I always wanted to do."

"We'll sort it." Banning looks at her watch. "Just about time for lunch. Come along to the Officers' Mess and I'll introduce to the rest of B Company's officers."

"Right," Sam says getting up from the chair. "What happened to the former Six Troop leader?"

"She was transferred to operations. The Colonel thought she would have bigger impact on staff."

"I see," Sam says.

"By the way, I'll have your kit collected and delivered to your tent," Banning says as they walk to the Officer's Mess. "Your Troop HQ is in your tent. And you have, in Color Sergeant Annetta Jones, arguably the best NCO in the Brigade. At least I think so. She was my Colors when I had a Troop."

"Thank you. My kit is in the boot of the staff car the Brigadier gave me to use."

"Indeed. And one other thing," she says as she stops, turning to face him, "I hope you won't mind if I observe your training methods. I won't interfere. What I am hoping for is to learn from what you come up with. After all, you are the only one of us who has actually been in combat with our enemy."

"I'll do my best."

"Do better than that," Banning says as she resumes heading for the mess. As she enters, most of the rest of the Company's officers are already there. "Ladies and gentlemen," Banning announces in clear, loud voice, "I have the honor to present our newest Troop leader, Leftenant Samuel Hope. He's newly minted from Lympstone, and he has had extensive experience battling our Enemy before joining the Corps. He brings valuable knowledge and experience to this Company." She then turns to Sam and motions him to go meet the other officers.

"Yes, ma'am," Sam says formally and heads off to exchange names and shake hands.

"Shall I accompany you to your Troop?" Banning asks as she and Sam walk out of the mess with the other officers after lunch.

"No, no thanks, ma'am," Sam says, thoughtfully. "I think I want to walk in on them cold. But you could point me in the right direction and tell me how I can spot Jones right off."

"Brilliant," she replies. "Six Troop is that way, just on the other side of Five Troop. The larger tent is yours that you share with your Colors. As for Jones, you'll know her when you see her: She is 1.6 meters tall."

"Isn't that below regulation height?" Sam asks.

"Just a bit," Banning says with a laugh. "I don't know how she did it, but she got in. And never make the mistake of underestimating her. I've known a lot of blokes who have come to regret doing that. And don't say anything about her height. She is sensitive about that."

"Thanks. I'll keep that in mind," Sam replies with a bit of a laugh of his own.

"Very good. Well, off with you, Leftenant."

"Yes, ma'am," Sam says, unable to resist saluting his new commander. She returns the salute and they go their separate ways.

CHAPTER THIRTY-ONE

Sam walks through the Five Troop area, which consists of a grass street with tents with vertical sides and slopped tops on either side. He then crosses a three-meter space as he enters into another group of six tents of Six Troop arranged in the same fashion. The area is deserted. He studies each tent carefully as he walks along the street.

Halfway down, he comes to one tent larger than the others. He stops in front of it, studying the inside. He sees two tables, both with laptops on them. Halfway back is a tent wall with openings on either side. He walks in to take a look. The tent is set up on a wood floor. A radio is on the right side, with papers neatly stacked in two piles. On the other is a phone on an empty desk. Walking to the back, he lifts the flap on the left side. Inside is a cot, a table and a dresser. He sees his kit has been put on the cot. A canvas wall separates the two living quarters. He is tempted to look into the other side, but decides he would probably be invading his Color Sergeant's privacy.

However, he has no problem invading the privacy of the other ranks. He tours each of the other five tents. They are all identical: four cots on either side, with foot lockers at the end of each. All the tents are clean and the kit properly stowed.

As Sam walks out of the last one, a column of twos comes marching into the area, with a tiny woman on the left counting cadence. The Marines are dressed in shorts, t-shirts, and tennis shoes, and despite the cool September weather, they are all sweating.

"Troop! Halt!" the small woman commands. The Marines come to a smart stop, all standing at attention.

The small woman marches to Sam and stands at attention and salutes. "Color Sergeant Annetta Jones reporting, sir."

"Stand easy," Sam says, returning the salute. "I'm Leftenant Sam Hope, your new Troop leader."

"Yes, sir. We've been expecting you."

"Brilliant," he replies. "Dismiss the Troop. You and I need to have a chat."

"Boss," she says smartly. She turns around and calls, "Troop. Dismissed."

The Marines immediately break ranks, most of them casting glances at Sam. A few study him.

"Let's go into the tent," Sam says to Jones.

"Yes, sir," she says, following him in.

"I assume that's your side," Sam says motioning to the right, "and that's mine," waving to the left.

"Yes, sir."

"Anything to drink around here?"

Jones raises her right hand with a lifted index finger to indicate 'just a moment.' She disappears to her sleeping area and quickly returns with two beers.

"I'm afraid they're both lagers," she apologizes.

"So long as they're not hot," Sam responds.

"No, Boss, that they are not," she says, handing him one of the bottles.

"Please sit down," he says motioning to a chair, "and you can drop the 'sir' and 'Boss' when we're alone. And always speak freely. You're no good to me, this Troop, or the Corps if you keep things to yourself."

"Very good."

They study each other for a moment. "I understand," Sam finally says, breaking the silence, "you're the best Color Sergeant in the Brigade."

"And I've been told you have combat experience with our Enemy and are here to train us up to attack them," she responds.

"I've been told the same thing," Sam says with a smile. "I need to evaluate the Troop. So for the rest of the week, we are going to be doing things differently. I need to know what each Bootkneck is capable of and what their weaknesses are."

"We have a strict training schedule the Leftenant Colonel insists we follow without deviation."

"I'm aware. Colonel Flemming has given permission to deviate from the schedule and Captain Banning promises to run interference."

"This should be interesting," Jones says, a sly smile on her face. "Boss, I need to tell you two things. First, you have my full support in this, and I believe the entire Troop will gladly come along, especially when they find out they will be getting a shot at the enemy."

"And the second?" Sam asks.

"If you ever make a comment about my size, I will hurt you," she says in a very serious voice.

"Well," Sam says, sitting back and smiling, "I certainly don't want to court destruction. No worries there."

"Thank you," she says.

"Okay," Sam says, switching to an official voice, "muster the Troop. I want to let them know what they are looking at. I," he pauses for a moment, "apologize for not giving you specifics first but I never like repeating myself."

"Not a problem," Jones says, getting up and going outside. She returns in about five minutes. "Sir, the Troop is mustered."

"Very good," Sam replies. He had taken the break to change from a formal uniform into fatigues. Putting on his beret, he goes outside to find the Troop in a three-sided formation in front of the tent with Jones standing in the center.

"Troop! Attention!" she calls, prompting all the Marines to move from parade rest.

Sam looks at them for a moment, his eyes traveling around the square. "Stand easy," he finally says. "Oh, hell, take a knee or sit down. We're going to be here awhile."

A ripple of laughter flows through the ranks as the Marines either kneel or sit on the grass. Jones comes to stand behind and to the left of Sam, watching her Troop carefully.

"I've been detailed to train this Troop to be raiders. We will have five months of intensive training. And I mean intensive. After that, we will be making raids onto the Continent to gather intelligence and grab prisoners." A ripple of approval runs through the Marines. "If you want to stay alive, you have to train harder than you've ever trained before. We will train all day every day, weekends included. You will be exhausted. You have to learn to keep going when you are so tired you don't think you can take another step." Sam looks them over.

"Your enemy does not want to capture you. He wants to kill you. And he doesn't care how many of his Soldiers die doing it. I know, I've been there. You have to learn to kill without mercy because they will show you no mercy. Our advantage is our training and morale. Enemy soldiers are driven by fear of the Sergeants, driven like cattle. They know only human-wave attacks. We also have an advantage in weapons. The enemy has few, if any, heavy weapons. Usually, machine guns at the most."

Sam walks around the formation looking at each Marine, letting his message sink in. He goes back to standing in the center. "We will train so that everyone knows everyone else's job. Make no mistake: If we get into a fight, we will take casualties. Each one of us has to know what to do when someone gets hit. Otherwise, we'll fall apart and none of us will survive. But we will leave no one behind. Everyone comes home." He pauses again. "It's alright to be afraid. Fear is normal. Fear will help you stay sharp. We will train hard so that when fear strikes it won't matter. Our bodies and minds will know what to do and will keep on doing it. All we'll have out there is each other. So train hard. Train as a team. Your life depends on it. Any questions?"

The Troop members look at each other and at Jones, who has a grim expression, but nods at them. Silence. Most look nervous, a few excited, a few worried.

"If anyone does not feel capable of this job," Sam says slowly, "then please request a transfer. No blame will attach. You can see Colors in private."

Sam studies the circle again. "Very good. We start at zero six hundred tomorrow. Uniform of the day will be fatigues and boots."

Turning to Jones, he says, "Dismiss the Troop, Colors."

"Sir," she says, saluting. She then calls the Troop to attention and dismisses them.

Sam goes into the tent and sits in his desk chair for a moment. Then he picks up his mobile phone to call Sarah. It will be at least a month, maybe more, before he goes home. It's not a call he is looking forward to making.

When Jones comes into the tent, she finds Sam staring at the top of the tent, his eyes not focused on anything.

"Boss?" she asks as a way of breaking into his thoughts.

Sam comes back to the room. "Sorry. I was thinking. I won't see my wife and kids for at least a month. That's not a pleasant thought. But that is the life I signed up for. Are you married?"

"Yes, sir. Two children. I had them before I joined the Corps. They are eleven and twelve now. Their father takes care of them when I can't get home. My mum also helps."

Sam nods his head. "Mine are a lot younger and we're expecting our third. Anyway, about tomorrow. I want the Troop to fall in for a long march. We'll leave before breakfast. They are to bring two rations with them, along with a full combat load."

"Live ammunition?" Jones asks.

"Yes. We won't be using it tomorrow, but I want them to get used to carrying it. How are your feet?" Sam asks, a small smile crossing his face as he looks at Jones.

"My bloody feet are just fine, thank you very much," she replies, a bit indignantly.

"Good. We are going to take it easy tomorrow. We'll go probably no more than twenty kilometers. We'll alternate between quick march and running with a ten-minute break about every hour. Here, I've laid out a possible route on the map, if you would like to see," he says, motioning Jones over to his desk and swiveling the map around so she can see it.

After studying it for a moment, tracing the route with a finger, she says, "Looks good to me. If you want to really challenge these blokes, though, we could take them this way." Jones traces a slightly different route starting two-thirds of the way into the circuit Sam has planned. "The terrain is hillier here."

"Yes," Sam says, looking at her route. "Good idea. But can we save it for a later march? I wanted to keep this one easy to get them into it."

"Now, don't spoil them," Jones says with a big smile, looking up from the map.

"Colors, I would never think of that," Sam says, smiling back. "Shit!" he says as he notices the time on his watch. "I've got to run, literally, or I'll be late for the Captain."

"Don't want that, now would we."

"No, we don't," Sam says, grabbing his beret and running out of the tent.

Being in formation at zero six hundred hours meant waking up at zero five thirty. Jones rousts the Troop's members and then turns the rest of the job over to the various Sergeants and Corporals whom she had briefed the night before.

When Sam walks out of his tent, with his full kit including his sidearm and a rifle– the rifle draws an interested glance from Jones who has never seen an officer carrying one before–the Troop is formed up in column of twos.

"Very good," Sam says. "Colors, move them out."

"Sir," she says smartly. Turning to the Troop, she barks, "Troop, quick march. March!"

As an entity, the Marines step off together on what turns out to be a grueling day for them since marches never exceeded ten kilometers before and were always in exercise uniforms with sneakers and no kit. And usually they ate before starting. Today, they had rations on the first ten-minute break.

The following days are filled with longer and harder marches, long spells at the shooting range perfecting their marksmanship, and working on tactics both for attack and retreat. He drums into them that, because they will be simply raiding, pulling back safely is just as important as attacking effectively. Through it all, Sam keeps emphasizing they are never to give up, there is always something they can do no matter how bad the situation may seem. Quitting is not an option.

Sam has his Troop working seven days a week, at least sixteen hours a day, even in downpours. His Marines are worn out, sometimes so exhausted they can barely keep moving. They accept it because he pushes himself just as hard—and explains to them that when they are on an operation, they may not get any rest, any breaks. If they want to survive, they have to get used to functioning at a high level even when exhausted.

Mid-way through the second week of training, Sam is watching members of his Troop practicing withdrawing while other members take the part of the enemy.

"Brevet Leftenant Hope!" Sam hears St. Anthony yelling. He turns around to see the Lieutenant Colonel striding toward him. "What the bloody hell is going on here?" he hollers as he comes up to Sam. "Who gave you the authority to deviate from my training schedule? I will have you court-martialed for this! You will be cashiered right out of the Corps!" St. Anthony stops a few centimeters from Sam, his face contorted with rage, his mouth still working but no words coming out.

"With all due respect, sir," Sam says quietly, "Colonel Flemming ordered me to train this Troop in the most effective way possible to fulfill our mission."

"The Colonel did, did she?" St. Anthony says, his rage working up to a higher level. "I never received a copy of such orders! I would have if she has issued such an order! And what is your mission? I was never informed of any mission?"

"Sir," Sam says, enjoying the situation but keeping that out of his quiet response, "I don't know why you weren't informed. That is, after all, above my pay grade."

"You received these orders directly from the Colonel?" St. Anthony just about spits the words out.

"Yes, sir," Sam says, silently thankful for the call Banning arranged. "She called me a few days after I took command of the Troop."

"We will see about that! Have no doubt! We will see about that!" St. Anthony says, his body stiff as he rises on his toes, turns around, and stalks off without another word.

Sam watches him go for a moment, then shakes his head. When he turns around, he finds everything has stopped in the field exercise. Everyone is looking at him. He suppresses a laugh, then calls out, "I don't recall telling you Cabbage Heads to take a break!"

Everyone immediately goes back to training.

CHAPTER THIRTY-TWO

Sam and Jones are standing on a slight rise watching the four-member fire teams maneuver across an open field with half the teams providing cover for the other half. Each team is now armed with an automatic weapon while the other three Marines carry standard issue semi-automatic rifles. They have had the cannister-fed machine guns for a bit more than a month, requiring each fire team to change how it operates within itself and with the other teams.

While the two Troop leaders talk quietly about adjustments that need to be made, Brigadier Cooper, with St. Anthony and Banning in tow, comes up quietly behind them. The Brigadier stands quietly waiting to be noticed.

Jones catches movement out of the corner of her right eye. She wheels around and freezes at attention with a salute. "Sir!" she says sharply.

Her movement wrenches Sam's attention around. He wheels, comes to attention, and salutes as well. "Sir. We were not expecting you."

"Exactly," Cooper says, smiling. "Stand easy. I came unannounced because I did not want to disrupt your training schedule with any unnecessary distractions. Banning here tells me you two have been doing a brilliant job with this lot."

"Thank you, sir," Sam answers.

"I also wanted to see what you are doing with all those machine guns. They are quite an innovation."

"Sir," St. Anthony says, jumping into the conversation, "if I may. I really do believe that is much more firepower than a Troop needs. It is a waste of resources."

"Yes, yes," Cooper says, "so the Colonel informed me of your opinion. What do you think about this, Banning?" he says turning to the Captain.

"Sir, Leftenant Hope sold the idea to me and the Colonel, so I will let him explain."

"Quite," Cooper says. "By the by, Hope, you are now a fully appointed Leftenant."

"Thank you, sir," Hope says, glancing over the Brigadier's shoulder to see the sour look on St. Anthony's face. "Sir, if, or rather when, we get into a fight, the enemy will use human-wave attacks. To defeat such an attack, we need all the firepower we can bring to bear. By equipping each fire team with a high-capacity automatic weapon, we stand the best chance of defeating such an attack."

"But, sir," St. Anthony interjects, "we will be able to bring artillery and mortars to bear, which should be more than enough to break up any attack."

Cooper, who turned to look at the Lieutenant Colonel, now turns back to Sam. "What say you about that, Leftenant?"

"We are dealing with an enemy who has no regards for casualties. It is likely that they will just push through any artillery fire. If that happens, my Marines will need all the fire power they can lay down if they are to have a chance to stop the attack."

"Sir," St. Anthony objects again, "each Commando has a heavy weapons section that is more than capable of laying a heavy volume of fire."

"With all due respect to the Leftenant Colonel," Sam says, "that would not be enough to stop a large-scale attack on a broad front. Besides, my Troop is going in without any support. We need all the fire power we can muster."

"So, Leftenant," Cooper says, "are you suggesting that all our fire teams be so equipped?"

"Yes, sir. I believe that will save a lot of lives and help us win."

"Very good," Cooper says, holding up a hand to halt whatever St. Anthony was about to say. "I thank both of you gentlemen for your thoughts. I will take this under advisement and discuss it with the Colonel and the other Commandos. Now, Leftenant Hope," Cooper says, turning to Sam, "you are nearing the end of your fifth month of training. Will you be ready for deployment?"

"Yes, sir, we will."

"Brilliant," he says, turning back to St. Anthony and Banning. "Colonel Flemming will be sending orders in about a week. Understood?"

"Yes, sir," both respond, Banning sharply while St. Anthony looks glum.

"Very good," Cooper says. "Well, you carry on. I must be getting back."

Sam and Jones come to attention and salute. Cooper returns the salute, then turns and walks off, followed by the other two officers. As she leaves, Banning flashes a smile and a wink at Sam and Jones.

"Well, bloody hell, Boss," Jones says as they watch the trio walking away. "It fills my heart with confidence when our Commando leader doesn't think shit-all of us."

"I guess," Sam says, "we'll just have to make do with the Brigadier's support." He smiles at Jones, who just looks sour. "And watch our backs," he adds. Then they both turn back to watching their Marines.

A week later, Sam is in his tent during lunch. He gets a call, listens for a moment. "Yes, sir. Right away, sir." He puts down the receiver and thinks about the call for a moment.

"Lance Corporal Nettles," he calls to the duty runner, "find Colors and tell her I need to see her immediately."

"Right, Boss," Nettles says and runs off.

As he watches Nettles leave, he picks up his phone and rings Banning. "Captain," he says when she answers, "Hope here. In case you haven't heard, the Leftenant Colonel has summoned me. It seems our orders are in."

"Thank you for the heads up," she says. "I wasn't informed. Do you wish me to accompany you?"

"Ma'am, that is your call. I just wanted to keep you apprised about what is happening," he says, his tone implying he can handle it alone.

"Right," she says. There is a pause for a moment. "I believe I will not attend since I wasn't invited. Just keep me informed."

"Yes, ma'am. I certainly will," he says, hanging up as they say their goodbyes.

Sam sits back, thinking again about how to handle this meeting with a superior officer who doesn't like him and opposes his mission.

"Boss, you wanted to see me?" Sam looks up to see Jones standing in front of him.

"Colors, our orders have arrived and we've been summoned to Commando HQ."

"Boss?" Jones responds, perplexed because such meetings are for commissioned officers only.

"Look," Sam says as he gets up, retrieving his jacket and beret, "you will be second in command on this little outing. If anything happens to me, you will have to see the mission through. The only way you can do that is if you know the details. You are coming along."

"Yes, sir," she says, emphasizing the 'sir,' falling in half a step behind and to the left of Sam as they march to Commando HQ.

When they arrive, Sam enters first and strides across to the Color Sergeant's desk in front of St. Anthony's office door.

"Leftenant Hope reporting as ordered," he says sharply.

"Yes, sir," the Color Sergeant responds, getting awkwardly to his feet, remembering their first meeting. "Please have a seat, sir, and I will let the Leftenant Colonel know you are here."

"Very good," Sam says formally. Turning he gives a knowing look to Jones, who tries to hide a smile, as they retreat to the back of the room to where the chairs are.

Fifteen minutes later, the Color Sergeant puts down the phone and stands at his desk, "Sir, Leftenant Colonel St. Anthony will see you now."

"Thank you, Color Sergeant," Sam responds as he stands, motioning Jones to come with him.

"Sir," the Color Sergeant says, "I was not aware of any of the ranks joining this meeting."

"And you are aware of everything that goes on?"

"No, sir," he responds a bit sheepishly.

"Then stand aside," Sam says as he opens the door, leading Jones inside. They come to attention before St. Anthony's desk, who is reading some papers. He ignores them for nearly five minutes. When he looks up, he is startled to see Jones standing next to Sam.

"What the devil is she doing here?" St. Anthony says, irritation and exasperation mingle in his voice.

"Sir, I have asked Color Sergeant Jones to participate in this briefing. She is second in command of the Troop, and should anything happen to me, will have to know all the details of the mission if she is to carry it out."

"Can't you brief her yourself later?" St. Anthony says.

"Sir, it is more efficient if she is here. I might forget to mention something otherwise."

"Oh, very well," he says, resignation and disgust in his voice. "Your orders," he says, picking up some papers, "are to stage on Guernsey. From there you are to land on the shore of Brittany or Normandy. Here," he says, nearly throwing the two-page order at Sam, "take them and follow them to the letter. And do try not to get your entire Troop killed."

"Yes, sir," Sam replies formally, still at attention.

St. Anthony looks up at him sharply. "This is a fool's errand led by a fool. You should not be in command of a Troop. Your methods are unorthodox and I do not approve of them. You should be a Second Leftenant tracking supplies. That is what you are good for. For God's sake, you're not even English. What the Brigadier and the Colonel see in you is beyond me, but orders are orders. Dismissed." St. Anthony waves at him with the back of his left hand.

"Sir," both Sam and Jones say, both saluting

St. Anthony glares at Sam for a moment, ignoring Jones, then returns the salute, again waving a hand dismissively at the pair. They both do a smart about-face and leave.

"A nice sendoff," Jones says wryly as they leave the building.

"Quite," Sam mutters. He suddenly stops in his tracks. "That son of a bitch! That bloody son of a bitch!"

"Boss?" Jones says.

"I don't trust him. I am afraid he will do everything he can to sabotage our mission, or at least not help us. Except for the Captain, we'll be on our own. Let's hope she can work miracles if we need it." Sam pauses for a moment, then explodes. "That bloody son of a bitch sod."

"Yes, sir," Jones says, trying to hide a smile. "When do we shove off?"

"Tuesday. Zero five hundred hours," Sam says, calming down. "I'm going to see the Captain to fill her in. You go back and start getting everyone prepared. Today is Wednesday," he says almost to himself. "Everyone gets liberty from zero six hundred Friday to twenty-four hundred Sunday."

"Yes, Boss. Shall we draw stores tomorrow?"

"Yes, all the stores and ammunition we can get, along with medical supplies. Oh, why am I telling you this?" he says with a shake of his head. "You know the drill as well as I do, if not better."

"Yes, I probably do," she replies with a grin.

"Oh, crack on," he says, waving her off as they both head their separate paths. "Oh, here," he says, turning back to her and handing her the orders, "you'll need to read this. When you get the boats, I think it best that we also have electric motors so we can go into the coast as quietly as possible."

"Yes, Boss," Jones says, taking the orders and heading off.

Sam catches Banning just as she is leaving Company HQ. "Ma'am," he calls, "may I have a moment?"

"Of course, Leftenant," she says, changing course and walking toward him.

"We are to shove off for Guernsey at zero five hundred Tuesday," he says as they meet. "From there we are to land on either Brittany or Normandy, our choice, and conduct up to a five-day recon, bringing back prisoners for interrogation if the opportunity arrives."

"Very good. Draw up your plans and bring them by tomorrow morning."

"Yes, ma'am. I am also authorizing, with your approval, weekend liberty from zero six hundred Friday for the entire Troop, including myself."

"Everyone?"

"It will be the first time for any of these guys to be in a combat situation. I think having the weekend will help keep their minds off what is coming and help them relax."

Banning looks at him at moment. "Very good, Leftenant," she says. "See you in the morning, say ten hundred."

"Ma'am," he replies and walks off.

CHAPTER THIRTY-THREE

Sam walks into his tent. It's nineteen hundred hours Sunday. He hated to leave Sarah and the children early, especially on a deployment that could take a month or even a bit longer, but he thought he should be back in camp first to set an example and make sure everything is in order.

As he tours the Six Troop area, he discovers he wasn't the first back. Some of the single people have already returned. And from the looks of them, most of them are sleeping off the effects of a weekend of partying. He smiles to himself as he greets the ones who are conscious, telling them to relax and be ready for a busy day Monday.

When he gets back to his tent, he sits down, staring at the canvas wall on the other side, lost in thought. Part of his mind is on the mission, but most of it is on pregnant Sarah and their two children.

"Boss," Jones says as she enters the tent. "Good to see you."

"And you," Sam replies, breaking off his thoughts. "How's the family?"

"They're all good, thanks, though my husband, Farleigh, is a bit worried about our deployment."

"A bit?" Sam asks, skeptically.

"Actually, more than bit. How about your wife?" she asks, throwing her bag through the flap onto her cot.

"Sarah is not thrilled. And I am not happy about being that far away while she's about to have our third child. But there is not much either of us can do."

Sam and Jones spend the rest of the evening finalizing plans and checking to ensure everything and everyone is ready. The next day is spent making sure the Troop has all the supplies they can gather and loaded onto trucks. Sam and Jones then gather everyone together for a final predeparture briefing.

At zero four hundred Tuesday, the members of the Troop are up and having breakfast. By zero five hundred, they are on the trucks and heading out for Plymouth where their kit and supplies will be loaded on board the ship that will take them to the Isle of Guernsey.

It takes hours to load all their supplies and kit onto the freighter. The Royal Marines have hover landing craft which could have taken the Troop and everything they need straight to the landing site. But Sam rejected that option because those craft make a lot of noise, and as he told the Brigadier, Colonel, St. Anthony, and Banning, this is a raid, not an invasion, so the less noise they make going in, the better. Instead, he opts for ten rubberized boats with power outboard motors and quiet electric motors for the final run into Brittany. Each boat will hold four Marines and their kit, with plenty of room left for any prisoners they may capture.

The ship only needs a few hours to reach Guernsey. Once docked, the Marines, with the help of locals hired for the job, unload the ship, putting everything in a large warehouse that hasn't been used in years. The boats are left upside down on the pier.

"Greetings, Leftenant Hope, I believe?" a little round old man dressed in a suit, wearing a fedora and walking with a cane says as he approaches Sam, his hand held out.

"Yes, sir," Sam says turning around and taking the hand. "And you are, sir?"

"I am Pierre Duprise, mayor of our little island. We are happy to have you. We occasionally receive visits from the Navy, but this is the first anyone can remember from the Army," he says, pumping Sam's hand. "I hope you plan to stay a time?"

"Well, sir," Sam says, suppressing a laugh, "you still haven't received a visit from the Army. We are Royal Marines."

"Oh, so sorry. I do hope you'll forgive me."

"Of course," Sam says with a chuckle. "As for the length of our stay, I am afraid that will not be overly long. We are just planning to visit France for a few days. But," he hurries on when he sees the disappointment on the mayor's face, "I do we believe we will be making return visits."

"Oh, splendid," Duprise says.

"As for right now," Sam says as the two start to walk along the stone wharf to distance themselves from the noise of the unloading, "we will be here a few days to get organized and await the right conditions for our visit. At the moment, the seas are a bit too rough for our purposes. And when we are done in France, we will come back here."

"Brilliant," the mayor says again. "You and your men and women should feel free to visit our pubs and restaurants. What are your sleeping arrangements?"

"We are setting up in the warehouse. There is plenty of room for us to establish berthing quarters that meet our needs."

"Yes, yes, of course," the mayor replies, visibly disappointed. "But if you wish for some more comfortable quarters as befits one of His Majesty's officers, we have a splendid hotel just down that street," he says, pointing with his cane toward a broad avenue running from the pier.

"Well, thank you, sir. I will take that under advisement," Sam says. "Now, if you'll excuse me, I have to see to the unloading and storing of our kit and supplies."

"Yes, yes, of course," the mayor says, holding out his hand again. "Well, goodbye."

"And to you, sir," Sam replies giving the mayor's hand a quick shake, then turning around and walking briskly back to the where the Marines and locals are working.

Jones gives him a questioning look when he returns.

"Nice mayor," Sam says, returning her look. "How's it going?"

"Oh, splendid," she answers, a small smile on her face.

"Knock it off, Colors," he says laughing.

Everything is inside and the berthing area is set up by twenty-one hundred. Sam retires to his private spot, and calls Sarah. Their conversation falls into its normal pattern of talking about the children, how her job is doing, how his work is coming along. What they don't talk about is where he is going, and what might happen.

The next morning, reveille is sounded at zero six hundred. The day is spent organizing the supplies based on what boat each will be loaded with.

Once they are done, Sam gives everyone liberty to wander the town and the island, admonishing them to be on their best behavior.

Now, all they can do is wait for the weather to improve so the surf will drop enough for them to land.

"Boss," Sergeant Brady Ollershaw says as he comes into the makeshift office Sam and Jones share, "the weather is clearing. We should have mostly clear skies by later today with morning fog on the morrow. Seas are expected to be half to one meter. The high is expected to be 19, pleasantly warm weather."

"Finally," Sam says. "Sergeant, gather the team and squad leaders. We need to get cracking. Colors, we're on."

"Yes, Boss," she says enthusiastically. "My arse is getting sore sitting on it so much."

"That, my friend, is over," he says.

As they walk outside the office, the squad leaders are gathering in front of them. A crowd of lower ranks is hanging on the perimeter, the word having spread of the clearing weather and pleasant temperatures.

"Stand easy, ladies and gentlemen," Sam tells the Sergeants and Corporals leading the various fire teams and squads standing before him. "The weather is clearing and the temperatures will be perfect for our little outing." The announcement brings nervous smiles to the faces of the non-commissioned officers in front of him, and a ripple of sound from the others gathered behind them. "We will shove off at eighteen hundred hours. We should be able to cover the first ninety kilometers in about two-and-half hours. We will then switch to electric motors for the final ten kilometers. That should put us ashore about twenty-two hundred, well after sunset."

Sam looks around the semi-circle. "Any questions so far?" No one responds. "Brilliant. You all know the drill. I expect everyone to carry out our mission as flawlessly as possible. Make sure all radio equipment is working properly, especially the three long-range transceivers. Our very lives may depend on them. Make sure everyone has their night-vision gear and rifle suppressors in working order. Remind everyone our mission is to observe and gather intelligence. We are not there to fight. Not this time. If we do get into a shooting situation, I want everyone to know immediately so we can react properly. Understood?"

"Yes, Boss," comes the chorus of replies.

"Right. It's zero nine seventeen. We have less than nine hours to get underway. Let's get cracking. Dismissed."

The non-commissioned officers all come briefly to attention and then spread out. The rest of the Troop members, having heard what Sam said, scatter as well. The boats are put in the water. The motors tested. Communication gear is checked. Supplies are loaded. Each Marine carries five days' rations, two water bottles, a first aid kit, and two hundred rounds of ammunition. Sam carries the same gear, plus a sidearm. It's a heavy load, but his Troop has been training with heavier ones for weeks. Extra ammunition, food, water, and medical supplies will be left with the boats.

"Boss," Jones says as she comes into the office tent where Sam is studying a map.

"Hmmm, yes, Annetta," Sam replies distractedly using her first name for the first time. He finally looks at her.

"We are loaded and set to go. It's only 1600, if you want to leave early."

"Hmmm, no," he replies, straightening up, "no. I don't want to be anywhere near the shore before sunset, which won't be until after 2100."

"Understood."

"I just got a call from our Navy brethren," Sam says. "Seems we are going to have a naval escort. Three destroyers will shadow us going in and coming out, just in case. They will be able to provide fire support should we need it."

"Brilliant," Jones replies.

"Yes," Sam says, "come look at this. It's a map showing their firing grids." She walks over and looks down at the table to see the map. "This is your copy," Sam says, sliding the map over to her, "and these are the radio frequencies we are to use." He hands her a copy of them. "See that those are preset in all three transceivers."

"Will do," she says, folding the map up and taking the list of frequencies. "Do you want Belman to have a map?"

"Yes, I do. Unfortunately, the Navy only sent us two copies. I sent mine off with Day to have a copy made at a print shop in town. That's not kosher, I suppose."

"We are Marines," Jones says, laughing. "Adapt and overcome."

"Right," Sam says, laughing in his turn. "Make sure everyone is fed and they have their beer ration. That may be the last they get in a while. And let them relax, if they are capable of doing that."

"I'm not sure. I think several of them have organized a football game of sorts."

"Well, whatever keeps them occupied and out of trouble," Sam says, going back to studying a topographical map of Brittainy, especially the coast and the area just behind it, as Jones leaves.

"Boss, your maps," a breathless Lance Corporal Sean Day says as he comes running into the tent.

"Thank you, Lance Corporal. Any change?" Sam asks, raising his eyebrows.

"Yes, Boss," Day says, handing him the balance of the twenty pounds Sam had given him. "It was just six pounds twenty."

"Thanks, now go get your beer ration before someone drinks it for you," he says, putting the money away.

"Sir, Boss, sir," Day says enthusiastically as he salutes, and then sprints out of the tent.

Sam chuckles to himself, then heads out to find Sergeant Penny Belman, who will be in charge of securing the boats during the operation, to give her a map and to make sure she is clear on what to do if they need naval gun support.

Sam then walks around, checking with various members of his Troop. Half an hour before they are to shove off, Sam orders everyone to get their kit and make final checks. The Marines start loading onto the boats ten minutes before departure. At eighteen hundred, Sam leads the procession out of the harbor and into the channel at high speed.

CHAPTER THIRTY-FOUR

As the boats pull quietly up to the shore about an hour after sunset, the Marines ease out into the knee-deep surf, with sixteen quickly climbing the cliff behind the beach to establish a security perimeter. The rest pull the crafts onto the beach and quickly unload them, putting all the kit, extra food, water, and ammunition above the high-tide mark and then pulling the boats up near the cliff. Camouflage netting is then spread over the lot as the Marines make the boats and supplies look as much like the landscape as possible.

"Sergeant Belman," Sam says quietly as he, Colors, and the section leaders huddle together, "deploy your security detail and keep your radio operator close."

"Boss," she says, going off to get things organized.

"Right," Sam says, looking around at the others. "You all have your orders. Get your guys organized and ready to go. We move out in fifteen."

"Boss," they all say quietly and disperse.

"Well, Colors, this is it. We'll put all that training to the test."

"That we will, Boss. The blokes will do just fine," she replies, her voice betraying some skepticism.

"Hmmm, keep an eye on Crisp. She's probably the shakiest of your lot."

"I'll do that. And you keep watch on Ross."

"Oh, I think he'll be fine, providing he doesn't trip over himself."

"There is that," Jones says with a quiet laugh.

"Well, let's shove off. Stay in touch and stay safe," he says as they stand.

"You as well."

Sam nods as they walk off in their separate directions. Sam has picked a landing spot between two inlets. His plan calls for leaving ten Marines to guard their boats, their only means of escape. The rest he split into two groups of fifteen ranks, with him leading the patrol that will head into the interior while Jones takes an equal number just inland from the inlet on their left. He realizes he is taking a risk by splitting his Troop this way, but he rationalizes that by the fact they are to avoid combat. Should that happen, he knows thirty won't do much better than fifteen. Besides, this way they can cover more ground.

"Alright, you lot," Sam says quietly to his patrol, glancing at his watch: twenty-three forty-five. "Let's get cracking. Keep it quiet. Wainwright, you have point."

"Boss," Lance Corporal David Wainwright says, and sets off, followed by two more Marines, then Sam, then the rest. Simultaneously, Jones moves off in the same manner with her patrol. All the Marines are wearing camouflage face paint and radio headsets with an earpiece in one ear. Left behind is anything shiny or that could make noise, such as metal hitting metal.

The dark on this moonless night is intense. The night-vision goggles are the only thing allowing the patrols to make progress quietly and to stay together. Sam's patrol follows an old road that is overgrown with grass for the most part with only a bit of the pavement remaining.

"They need better road repair," Sam hears someone whisper behind him.

"Silence!" he says sharply but in a quiet whisper.

After they've walked just more than a kilometer, Wainwright holds up his hand and goes down on one knee. Everyone follows suit, except Sam who goes up to him in a crouch.

"What?" he asks in a whisper.

"There, Boss," the Lance Corporal says, pointing off to their left. "Do you see that faint glow? It could be a fire."

Sam exchanges his night goggles for the night binoculars he carries. He studies the glow for a moment. As he puts down the binoculars, he says, "Good job, Wainwright." Then he turns back toward the others. "You're with me," he tells Private Edmund Leavey, who responds with a nod. "Sergeant Percival!"

"Boss," Joe Percival says as he moves next to Sam.

"Move the patrol off the road and under cover until we return. Do not engage unless you have no other option."

"Boss," he says and starts to leave.

"If you hear gunfire, Sergeant, you will not come for us. Do you understand?"

"Yes, Boss," he replies, reluctance in his voice.

"Joe, I'm depending on you to keep your mates safe. If something happens to me, you have to complete the mission. Understood?"

"Yes, Boss."

"Right, Leavey, let's take a walk," he says as he moves off the road in the direction of the glow, followed by the Marine. The pair walk as quietly as they can for just more than a kilometer, both scanning the area around them for any hint of movement. As they approach a line of trees, Sam goes to ground, followed by Leavey. After studying the tree line, he crawls cautiously forward until he can see the other side.

What he sees is a large encampment with various fires burning among the tents and what he assumes are Sergeants patrolling the grounds. "B1 to B4," he says quietly into his microphone.

"B4," Percival replies.

"Large encampment. We are pulling back."

"Understood."

Sam takes a circuitous route back to his patrol, making a wide sweep to check for any surprises. What he finds are fields that are being plowed. But with no animals or tractors, he doesn't understand how they are doing that. By the time he gets back to the patrol, he has formulated a plan.

"Sergeant," Sam says as he kneels next to the prone Percival.

"Boss?"

"There is a gully about one hundred and fifty meters that way," he says, pointing to his right. "Take eight guys and conceal yourselves along there. About seventy-five meters on the other side is a field that appears to be in the midst of plowing. I want to know how they do it and how many are involved. The sun will be up in about thirty minutes, so you'll have to hurry. This is the rally point after full dark."

"Boss," the Sergeant says, then quietly gathers eight Marines and heads out.

Sam watches the Sergeant and his party move out. Then he motions the remaining six to follow him. He leads them to a clump of tall trees with thick foliage. He looks up at the thick branches that rise to at least ten meters up.

"Well, guys," he says turning to his group. "Pick a tree and go as high as you are comfortable with. Be sure that you are not visible from the ground. The mission is observation. We have to watch what these people are doing. This one," he says, indicating the tree he is next to, "is mine."

They all nod, then scatter, five swarming up the trees. The exception is Ross who can't seem to figure out how to get started.

Sam watches him for a moment and then walks over to him. "Need some help, Marine?" he asks.

"No, Boss, I can figure this out."

"Look," Sam says, shaking his head, "do this." Sam puts a foot in the Y formed by two branches and pulls himself up. Letting himself back down, he turns to Ross, "that is how you get started and then it is a simple matter of climbing a ladder."

"Yes, Boss," Ross says, uncertainty in his voice.

"Go on, lad, give it a try. Besides, you don't want to be on the ground when the sun is up." It's too dark for Sam to see Ross's face, but he can almost sense the panic on it. The Marine is soon swarming up the tree with relative ease, if not grace.

Sam, shaking his head, first makes sure all his Marines can't be seen from the ground and then returns to his tree and climbs up about six meters, positioning branches to make it hard to see him from the ground but allowing him to peer through the leaves. "B1 to B2," he says quietly, calling Jones.

"B2," comes the reply after a brief pause.

"Settled in for the day?"

"Affirmative."

"B1 out." Sam then watches as the light slowly filters over the horizon, slowly bringing color back to the world. He scans the area with hooded binoculars but as yet sees no movement, although he can see more smoke coming from the Enemy encampment. He also sees half a dozen stone houses with their roofs caved in and windows gone clumped together in what must have been a small village. He settles back, taking a sip of water from a bottle and then breaking out an energy bar, making sure to secure the wrapper.

About an hour after sunrise, Sam sees Soldiers marching out of the trees from the direction of the camp. They are in column of fours with Sergeants supervising them—screaming and threatening.

"Okay, guys," Sam says quietly into his mic, "here they come. Stay sharp. Stay quiet. Stay hidden." He studies the columns, relieved to see only the Sergeants are armed.

One group of about forty breaks off and heads toward the field beyond Percival. Another group, Sam estimates at about twenty-five, heads east, away from them, while a third group of about the same size heads in his direction. As Sam watches the group approaching him intently, he hears a faint noise coming from behind him. Then it grows louder before falling off again.

"Shit," he says to himself. Then he keys his mic. "Ross!" he says sharply but quietly. "Ross! Wake the bloody fuck up!" He hears a rustling of branches behind him. He's tempted to turn around to see if Ross is about to fall out of the tree but realizes he can't turn—the approaching soldiers might see the movement.

"I'm awake, boss," Ross says quietly—Sam says a prayer of thanks for that—"I wasn't asleep, I promise."

"You better stay that way, Enemy coming this way. Go silent," Sam says as he watches the column come within twenty meters of his position. As they pass under his tree, he slowly turns his head to track them. They move through the grove, carrying hoes and other gardening implements, and keep going. Sam realizes he's been holding his breath and lets out a long exhale. Tracking that group will be the responsibility of the Marines behind him. He plans to try to track the group that headed east.

He quickly finds them as they spread out in a field with tall grass or grain. Sam watches through his binoculars as the Soldiers start cutting the stalks—it's grain of some kind—with scythes. 'That must be backbreaking work,' Sam thinks to himself. After one harvester has cut a bundle, some stalks are tied around it and it's set down. The group works until early afternoon when they take a short break, eat something and drink water. Then they go back to work until near sunset. They collect the grain they've cut and head back to camp carrying it. As they leave, the group that passed through the grove comes back. They are not carrying anything, neither is the group who had gone to the field Percival was watching.

After it's been full dark for at least an hour, Sam signals for everyone to meet at the rally point. When they are together, they head back to the beach. When they get there, Sam checks in with Belman and hears the report he wanted to hear—no one came near them. He then gathers his patrol together to hear what each of them saw. Then he goes to the top of the cliff and lays down near the sentries and starts scanning with his night binoculars.

"Boss," Corporal Bert Kinsey says quietly, as he eases over near Sam.

"Yes, Corporal," Sam responds.

"Shouldn't Colors and her blokes be back by now?" The worry is clear in Kinsey's voice.

"Yes, they should. They must have run into some kind of problem," he says, lowering the binoculars, "but we haven't had a call for help or heard any gunfire. Whatever it is, it's nothing Colors and her mates can't handle."

"Yes, Boss," Kinsey replies as he moves a bit away, sounding relieved. Sam just wishes he was as confident as he sounded. "Where the devil is she?" he asks himself as his worry grows.

"Boss," Lance Corporal Rolly Kapica says, coming up from behind him, "you've got a call from HQ."

"A what?" Sam irritated reply comes out a bit more forcefully than he had intended.

"Colonel Flemming, boss."

"Yes. Right. Brilliant," Sam says, exasperated as he slides quietly down the cliff. The conversation is short with the Colonel asking how things are going. Sam tells her that all is going to plan—in the back of his mind he hopes he is telling the truth—and he plans to come out before dawn on the fifth day. With that conversation finished, Sam goes back up to the top of the cliff to resume his watch. Shortly after midnight, a rustling in the tall grass framing the top of the cliff is heard.

"Cabbage," a woman's voice calls quietly from the dark.

"Head," Kinsey replies.

"We're coming in," another voice, this one belonging to Jones, says. Soon, Colors and her patrol are back on the beach.

"What happened?" Sam asks her as she opens some rations.

"Foragers. They were all over the place. And they didn't go back to the big camp we saw at sunset. They bedded down in the fields. They must have been there when we arrived. It's a miracle we didn't step on them. We waited until I thought they were asleep, and then we pulled out carefully and quietly. In the dark, they must have thought we were other Soldiers."

"What were they foraging for?"

"It looked like food," she says, taking a drink of water to wash down her meal. "They were digging up what looked like vegetables and eating them right there. They all looked hungry. The Sergeants looked decently fed but no one else."

"Interesting," Sam says, thoughtfully. "We tracked three groups. One group was harvesting some kind of grain by hand. Another group apparently was working in a vegetable garden. A third group was plowing a field."

"Plowing?" Jones asks, her hand stopping as she was about to take a bite.

"Yes. Percival says they hooked eight guys up to a plow. They pulled it while another guided. A Sergeant walked beside each plow with a whip in case they weren't pulling hard enough. Apparently, the whips were used a lot."

"Bastards!" Jones spits out.

"Quite right. Anyway, let's get the guys settled in. We'll go out again tomorrow night in different directions."

"Mind if I finish eating first?" Jones asks a bit sarcastically.

"Why Colors, I wouldn't have it any other way," Sam says with a bit of a laugh.

Shortly before sunset, Sam and Jones form up their patrols, taking the Marines who had guarded the landing area, replacing them with Marines who had been on the previous day's patrol. Sam's goal is to give everyone experience with the operation, although in the back of his mind he is a feeling of relief not to have to worry about Ross.

Tonight's mission is a mirror-image of the previous one, with Jones leading her patrol near the right inlet's shore while Sam takes his group on a parallel course further inland. In the deep darkness of the new moon night, they walk cautiously through the silent landscape, staying in formation in case unwelcome eyes see them so they will look like a marching formation. They pass derelict houses and farm buildings but see no sign of life.

Coming through a stand of trees, Sam's patrol sees a small village in front of them with one road through it and trees all around it. Sam studies it through his binoculars for a time but sees no movement.

"Alright, guys, gather round," he says in a whisper. "We can't assume the town is deserted. It is not the kind of place the Enemy puts an encampment and we have seen no signs of activity. Right?" He looks around at the others, who all nod or murmur assent. "But that's no guarantee. So, here's what will we do. Sergeant Neal," he says, looking at Ed Neal, who is the senior NCO on the patrol, "will take half the patrol down the left side." He points to the Marines who will be go with Neal. "I'll take the rest down the right. If anyone is watching, they'll be looking at the road, so we'll come in from the sides, and meet in the middle. From there, we'll clear the town. Be careful and be quiet. Any questions?"

No one says anything.

"Let's get cracking," Sam says.

The two groups move out, staying inside the tree line and moving cautiously. When Sam's patrol reaches the side of the town, they stop, listening for any sounds. Hearing nothing, Sam motions them to continue. They carefully move toward the backs of the buildings in front of them. When they get close, Sam motions them to stop and crouch down. They study the windows but see nothing. They listen intently but hear nothing. Sam indicates for half of his guys to go down one side of the building, which appears to have been a store, while he leads the others down the other side. When they reach the front, they can see where the store's windows and door used to be. The roof, like most on most of the structures in the village, has fallen in.

A few minutes after Sam's group arrives, Neal's patrol comes in. Sam sends them to the north while his patrol takes the south end of the village. They are just about at the end when Sam gets a call.

"Boss," a whispered voice comes through his headset, "fifty meters to your north. We've got six, maybe seven sleeping."

"Stand fast," Sam replies. "Sergeant McArthur," he says quietly, "finish clearing this end. If you find nothing, come join the party on the north."

"Yes, Boss," Audrey McArthur replies.

Sam heads north, walking quietly and staying alert.

"Boss," Neal says when he reaches that group, "we have confirmed eight people sleeping in there." He motions toward what appears to have been a two-story building. The roof has caved in completely, while the upper story's walls have partially collapsed. But what seems to have been the floor of that level is still holding for the most part. As Sam cautiously peers inside, his night-vision goggles allow him to pick out eight sleeping figures. What he can't tell is if they have weapons.

"Weapons?" he whispers to Neal when he steps back.

"Sorry, Boss, we can't tell."

"Okay," Sam says, thinking for a moment. "Have you cleared the rest of the buildings?"

"Three left."

"Right," Sam says, pausing for a moment. "Leave two of your guys with me and finish the job."

"Boss," he says, then details two Marines to stay with Sam and leads the others off.

Sam puts a Marine at either end of the building, then starts thinking about how to handle the situation. Does he assume they are armed and hostile and go in shooting? That would protect his guys but they probably would not come away with any prisoners. And what if they are not armed? It's not like the enemy to let what may be a squad just leave a camp. And if there is a Sergeant among them, he would love to capture one of those.

Before he can make up his mind, McArthur comes along. "Boss, all buildings clear," she says in a low voice.

"Right. We have at least eight sleepers in this building. Weapons status unknown. Neal is finishing clearing this end. Deploy your guys around the sides and back of the building," Sam says, having decided on the course he wants to follow. "I don't want anyone firing except in self-defense or if one of them tries to escapee."

"Boss," she says, then quietly deploys her Marines. Just after she leaves, Neal returns.

"All clear," he tells Sam.

"Right. McArthur has her patrol around the sides and back. I want you and two others out front here, but in a covered position. The other three will come with me inside. All of them are to use their torches when we enter. It will be dawn in a few minutes. It's time to wake these sleepers. Remind everyone to only fire in self-defense or if someone is trying to escape. We want prisoners. By the way," Sam says, stopping Neal as he's about to head off, "Betz speaks French doesn't she?"

"Better than anyone else here," Neal says.

"That will have to do. Send her along."

"Boss," Neal says, then heads off to get things organized.

A few minutes later, a Corporal and two Marines report to Sam. "Fix your torches onto your rifles. When we go in, I want to intimidate these people just in case they're armed. Betz," Sam says.

"Boss," Lance Corporal Polly Betz says.

"How's your French?"

"Passable."

"Well, that's better than mine," he says with a snort. "When we go in, I want you to keep calling out as loud as you can that they will not be hurt if they surrender peacefully. Can you do that?"

"Yes, Boss," Betz replies confidently.

"Then let's get cracking!" Sam says raising his voice and charging into the building, followed by Betz yelling at the top of her voice. The other two Marines follow, their rifles at the ready.

The eight Soldiers inside wake up terrified, three scurrying to the far side of the building, the others frozen in place. Sam and his group quickly discover they have no weapons. Their uniforms are nearly rags. Five of them have no boots. The blankets they slept under are in tatters. Sam calls in Neal and his group to help sweep the building and has McArthur establish perimeter security.

"Betz," Sam says, "see what you can find out from these people."

"Yes, Boss."

Sam is a bit worried. In his camp, each squad consisted of eight Soldiers. And no one was allowed outside the camp at night. So, what were these eight people doing out here?

"McArthur!" he calls out, not bothering to keep his voice down now.

"Boss," the Sergeant says as she comes trotting up.

"Send out a two-member patrol that way about half a klick," he says, pointing toward the direction of the camp on the other side of the peninsula. "Tell them to keep a sharp lookout. If they see anything, or hear anything, and I mean anything, they are to get back here as fast as they can run. Understood?"

"Yes, Boss," she replies, an unasked question in her voice.

"We may be getting some unwanted visitors," Sam says, his gaze fixed across the fields as he tries to will himself to see what's going on in that camp. If that one is like his was, they have maybe thirty minutes around dawn before the squad is missed. And then maybe an hour more before a search is launched. Sam goes stalking back into the building.

"Well?" Sam asks as he kneels beside Betz who is sitting on the floor talking to the Soldiers.

"Boss, they're scared. They all deserted after curfew last night after that one," Betz indicates a woman who is sitting partially behind two others, her gaze fixed on the floor, "was beaten nearly to death by some Sergeants because she ate a carrot. A bleeding carrot? They were harvesting carrots and she ate one. They are all starving and need water."

"Right, give them these," he says handing her his three ration packs and then one of his water bottles. "Tell them we will protect them if they come with us now and do as we say. Tell them we have to leave right now if any of us are to survive. Have you told them who we are?" he adds almost as an afterthought.

"Yes, but that confused them. They didn't know we existed."

"They'll get over it. Tell them to eat up and get ready to move."

"Right, Boss," she says, pulling her rations and one water bottle out and handing all six ration packs and two bottles to the Soldiers who attack them hungrily but also share them.

"Woodman!" Sam calls as he emerges from the building.

"Boss," Lance Corporal Bill Woodman says as he comes running up, carrying the long-range radio.

Without a word, Sam turns him around and picks up the handset. "B1 to B2." He waits a second. "B1 to B2." He waits a second more. "B1 to B2."

"B2," Colors responds, much to Sam's relief.

"Mission compromised. Return to rally point immediately."

"Understood. Out."

Sam pauses a moment. "B1 to B3."

"B3," comes the immediate response from Sergeant Bart McConnel, who is in charge of beach security today.

"Mission compromised. Returning to rally point. Stay alert for unwanted visitors."

"Understood. Out," comes the reply.

"Neal! MacArthur!" Sam calls. "Gather everyone here now!"

After the patrol is gathered around him, Sam scans them. "Here's the situation: These eight people are the members of a squad who deserted after one of them was beaten for eating a carrot. The Enemy is going to come fast and hard to find them. They will shoot anyone and everyone they see. We have to get moving fast. Any questions?"

"No, Boss," comes the chorus of replies.

"These eight people are in bad shape, but we have to keep them moving. Share your water with them but keep them moving. Sergeant Neal, I want you to take charge of our guests. See to their needs as well as you can."

"Yes, Boss."

"Sergeant MacArthur, I want three flankers fifty meters on our right when we are in the open. They need to keep a sharp lookout. Take the three fastest runners. They may need all the speed they have."

"Yes, Boss."

"Right, let's get cracking," Sam says. He and the two senior non-coms quickly get things organized and the column moving in just a few minutes. The eight Soldiers have a mixture of fear and hope on their faces. They are placed in the middle of the column with Neal and two other Marines with them.

Sam sets a fast pace, checking over his shoulder to see how their new additions are doing. He slows down when he sees a number of them flagging, but then picks up the speed a bit. They are five kilometers from their base, which means more than two hours at the best speed these beaten down people can make.

As they approach some woods, the flankers come running. "Boss!" one of them calls. "Vehicles coming in fast."

"Can you tell how many?" Sam asks.

"Not for sure, sir," another flanker says. "At least two, maybe three. I don't think there are any more," she says, looking at her partner who nods in agreement.

"Right." Sam looks off in the direction they came from. He can hear the faint sounds of engines, growing louder by the second. "Into the trees!" he orders, pointing toward the woods the road enters about twenty meters in front of them. Everyone immediately complies, even the Soldiers, who first hesitate, then move as fast as they can at Betz's urging.

Once in the woods, Sam has his patrol deploy off the road to the left. The Soldiers are taken far back into the trees with Betz and another Marine to watch them. Sam and the rest of the patrol arrange themselves in concealed positions in the thick underbrush about two meters off the road. The Marines are under strict orders not to fire unless ordered.

As the engine sounds approach, Sam raises up a bit to see what is going on. The three pickups that have been crossing the fields roll onto the road and pause. One truck heads toward the village Sam and his patrol have left while the other two drive slowly into the woods, their mounted machine guns and rifles pointed at both sides.

A scream of terror comes loudly out of the woods behind Sam. It is abruptly cut off, but not before both pickups come to a sudden stop. After a few seconds pause, the machine gun and all the rifles begin firing into the woods. The firing is well above their heads, so Sam waits. He hopes the third pickup will come back into the woods. He wants to take all three out at the same time if that becomes necessary.

He doesn't have long to wait. The volume of fire suddenly increases as that last truck rolls up behind the second one. Then, as the machine guns keep firing, Sergeants and Soldiers pile out of the trucks, preparing to enter the woods.

"Fire. Fire at will!" Sam orders into his headset.

With the sudden explosion of machine gun and rifle fire from just inside the trees, the enemy doesn't react before it's too late. Everyone in the cabs and the beds of the trucks and on the ground in front is killed or wounded. The only ones who escape the initial attack are the ones who bail out on the right side of the trucks.

It's all over in a matter of minutes.

"Hold fire!" Sam orders.

"MacArthur, take four and work your way around the front truck. Be careful. I think some are hiding back there."

"Yes, Boss," she says.

"The rest of you keep a sharp eye out. Be ready to provide cover fire."

As MacArthur rounds the front of the truck, Sam hears firing from his Marines' weapons, followed by shouts in French. Sam sees MacArthur and her squad stand up, one of them holding his weapon on some unseen persons, the others checking the cab and the bed of the first truck.

Sam has everyone come out to check the cabs and beds of the other trucks.

"Boss, what do we do with the wounded?" one of his Marines ask.

"If he's a Sergeant, kill him. Otherwise, we'll have to leave them."

"Yes, Boss."

Sam walks around the trucks to find three enemy soldiers with their hands up and looking terrified. One of them was hit in the arm. Around them are five bodies, one of them a Sergeant.

"Boss," MacArthur says, coming up to him, "they threw down their weapons and raised their hands so we stopped firing."

"You did the right thing," Sam says. "See to that wounded man's arm."

"Yes, Boss."

The engines of two of the trucks are still running. The middle truck's engine is riddled with bullets, killing it as dead as the driver. Sam has the dead and mortally wounded pulled from the trucks. The seriously wounded are laid carefully on the side of the road. Sam stares at them as they lay there, some groaning. Some squirming a bit. Some just lying quietly. He doesn't hold out much hope for them, but he has no way to take them with him or provide any care for them. He has to get his Marines and the others to safety.

The two trucks are big enough to squeeze everyone on board, changing the two hours to get back to the rally point to ten minutes.

"B1 to B3."

"B3."

"We're coming in with two trucks."

"Understood."

When they roll up at the cliff above the beach, Sam has everyone quickly off the trucks and down on the beach, except for the two drivers and two others. They take the trucks to a spot where the cliff drops directly into the water and push the trucks over.

Sam and the four Marines then hurry back to the beach where the boats are already being loaded with their supplies and kit. The three POWs are under guard and looking terrified. The eight deserters are being fed and given water.

"MacArthur," Sam says as reaches the Sergeant, "send out a patrol about half a klick out. Same orders as before."

"Yes, Boss," she says and heads off to get the patrol out.

First, Sam contacts the destroyers to let them know they are coming out. Then he goes to the top of the cliff and stares to his right, wondering where Jones and her patrol are. He doesn't have long to wait. She and the others come trotting over a slight rise.

"Glad you made it, Colors," Sam says as she comes up.

"Right, Boss. What happened?"

"We picked up eight deserters and then got into a firefight with the group sent to find them. None of our guys was hurt," he says before she has a chance to ask.

"Brilliant. What now?"

"What now? We are pulling out as fast as we can. Those bloody sods will come heavy when they discover what happened. We don't have the firepower to stop them, even with the Navy's help."

"It's still light."

"Can't be helped. We need to pull out before they find us. With any luck, we should be out of range of small arms before they get here. Speed is the key now, not stealth."

"Right, Boss."

"Let's get these guys cracking." Sam and Jones get down on the beach.

The boats are soon loaded, except for the people. "Neal," Sam calls to the Sergeant, "put all eight of the deserters in the same boat. I want the three POWs separated and none of them in the same boat with the deserters."

"Boss," he says, heading off.

"MacArthur! Get the patrol in!" he calls.

"Yes, Boss!" she calls back.

"Colors! Are we ready?"

"Everyone is loaded except the patrol."

"Brilliant. Start with the electric motors. And give the Navy a heads up. We may need them."

"Yes, Boss," she says, turning to get all but two of the boats underway.

Sam nods, then heads up to the top of the cliff. When he reaches the top, he sees MacArthur and the patrol trotting back.

"Off you go," he says as they reach him, and he waves them down the cliff. He gives another look around, relieved he doesn't hear or see anything. He turns and hurries down the cliff. He helps push the last boat off the shore and jumps in. As soon as they are clear of the surf, Sam orders the outboard motors turned on. All the boats head toward Guernsey as fast as possible through the calm waters.

As they speed away, Sam turns to look back at the shore in time to see a pickup truck pull up to the top of the cliff. Six others soon join it.

"Disperse!" Sam orders over the radio. The boats fan out like spokes on a wheel just as the machine gunner on the pickup opens fire. That pickup is quickly joined by six others, also armed with machine guns.

"Evasive action!" Sam orders even though they are traveling at ninety kilometers per hour and the boats are already at extreme range for the thirty-caliber machine guns firing at them.

Then the sound of two Navy shells screams overhead, both falling long. They are quickly followed by more shells that land along and just behind the ridge obliterating everything on it.

"I guess the Navy was watching," Sam says to himself, turning to look seaward where two destroyers are still firing. He reminds himself to send a bottle of good scotch to the skippers.

CHAPTER THIRTY-FIVE

C olors," Sam says as they disembark from the boats at the wharf on Guernsey, "see to the guys. Make sure they get their beer ration. Put the POWs in a secure place under guard. Keep the deserters together and make sure they're comfortable and fed. If we have enough, let them have a beer ration as well."

"What about clothes?" Jones asks.

"I have to kick that upstairs when I phone this in, which I am going to do right now," he says as he turns to go.

"Boss, can we at least get them footgear, socks, and underwear, especially for the women?"

Sam pauses. "Yes. I will take responsibility for that. But we have to leave them in their uniforms until we have clearance."

"Right."

"Ah, Jones, where do you expect to get that kit?"

"Well, sir, we have spare boots, socks, and under garments we brought with us. If we need different sizes, I suppose we'll have to buy them."

Sam nods, "Right, let me know if it comes to that," and he heads off for his HQ office. There he calls Captain Banning to report what his Troop has been doing.

"You have eleven POWs?" Banning asks.

"Not exactly. I'm treating the three we captured after the firefight as prisoners. I have them under guard. But I'm treating the eight deserters more as refugees. They were fleeing their encampment looking for a way out at the risk of their lives. I know what they were going through. I've been there."

"Yes, so you have," the Captain responds. "I'll have to pass your request up the chain. I'll let you know what happens. Get that written report in ASAP."

"Yes, ma'am, by this afternoon," Sam promises.

"Good. And Hope, good job. I'm glad you suffered no casualties."

"Thank you, ma'am. And I need to thank the Navy. Their guns gave us good cover when we withdrew," Sam says as they end the conversation and hang up.

Sam goes back out to see how the work is progressing. The boats are nearly unloaded, and the supplies are being quickly stored in the same order they had been before the raid.

"Boss," Jones says as she comes up to him, "we erected a POW cage out of some chain-link fencing Quinlin found."

"Where is it?"

"In the back of the warehouse, set up against two stone walls."

"Brilliant," Sam says as he turns to inspect it. The stockade, with two guards, consists of two walls of chain-link fencing in a corner with the warehouse walls forming the other two. The fencing goes up to the ceiling, held in place by metal poles that have been driven into the concrete floor and attached to the roof. What he doesn't see is a door.

"Lance Corporal," he says to Bert Quinlin, "I understand this is your creation."

"Yes, Boss," Quinlin says, obviously proud of his work.

"Just one question: Where is the door?"

"Ah that. Boss, we couldn't find a proper door so we rigged one. Here, I'll show you," he says, leading Sam to the corner where the fencing makes a ninety-degree turn. "We used some chain locks we found to keep these two sides together. When we want to go in or out, we just unlock the chains and roll the fence back."

"Brilliant job," Sam says as he turns to leave.

"Thanks, Boss," a grinning Lance Corporal says.

Sam then goes to the area in the warehouse where the deserters are being housed. Eight cots have been set up with one group of five for the women and another group of three for the men, both surrounded by canvas for privacy. The fronts are open now, and the group is all sitting on cots eating and drinking beer and water.

"How's it going?" Sam asks Jones when he comes up to her as she is finishing supervising the storage of their supplies and gear.

"Nearly done," she says. "Next order of business is to get these guests in the showers. As soon as they are done eating and rested, and sober up ..."

"Sober up?" Sam asks, a bit taken aback.

"It seems this is the first beer those blokes have ever had. It hit some of them pretty hard."

"Oh, it did, did it."

"Yep," she says, grinning. "Anyway, I want to get them in the showers as well. They need it."

"How's their health?"

"The town doctor is coming to look at them, so we'll get an official verdict then. But if I had to guess, I would say food and rest will cure most of what's wrong with them. As nearly as Betz can tell, they've been on three-quarter and half rations for months and working twelve to fourteen hours a day with no breaks."

"Typical," Sam says, shaking his head.

"Oh," Jones says, almost as an afterthought, "we are short two bras, three sets of panties and one pair of men's boots."

"Right," Sam says, pulling out his wallet, "here's sixty pounds—my last sixty pounds—send someone into the village to get what they need. And, Colors, I want the change."

"Yes, Boss," she says smiling.

"I also want a watch kept on those eight. I don't expect trouble, but I want to be safe. Keep the watch discreet, I don't want them to feel like they're prisoners."

"That's already been taken care of," she says in a matter-of-fact tone, pointing to the two Marines who seem to be deep in conversation but are facing the deserters with their rifles close at hand. And Betz keeps going back to them to make sure they are alright."

"Colors, you're the best."

"I know, Boss," she says, grinning again.

Sam looks at her, shakes his head and goes back to his office to write his report, snagging a beer and some rations on the way. As he writes, the phone rings.

"Hope," he says after picking up the receiver.

"Your request to reclothe the eight deserters has been denied," Banning says. "Command wants to interrogate them before deciding what to do."

"Understood, ma'am," Sam says.

"Your transportation will be there in the morning. Same ship. You can leave the boats, supplies and ammunition. It's been decided to use Guernsey as a staging area. Load everything else up and come home," the Captain says.

"With pleasure," Sam responds as they say their goodbyes and hang up.

The freighter arrives at zero ten hundred the next morning. Sam and his Troop have everything on the dock, including the prisoners, ready to board. Since they are leaving so much behind, loading is done in a fraction of the time it took to unload. The three POWs are put in one room with two guards in the passageway by the door. The eight deserters are allowed to stay on deck and eat the hot meal that has been sent on the ship. The POWs also get hot food.

Four hours later, they dock in Portsmouth. Sam tells Jones to have the Troop just bring their kit and weapons. Dock workers will unload the rest. The deserters debark with the Troop, as do the prisoners. The difference is the POWs are under guard. All eleven are met by intelligence officers and MPs, then loaded into vans for the trip to Brigade HQ.

The Troop members load onto three trucks with canvas covering the seats in the bed. Sam is in the cab of the first and Jones in the second's cab. When they reach the Four Two Commando's bivouac area, Sam heads for Banning's HQ to report.

As soon as he walks in, she turns him around and they head for Commando HQ.

"The Leftenant Colonel wants a debriefing," Banning says.

"Really," Sam says, the skepticism clear in his voice.

"Really," Banning replies, with humor. "By the way, we have started to train the rest of the Company with your methods."

"St. Anthony good with that?"

"No, not in the least. But after the Brigadier ordered it and the Colonel keeps visiting to check on progress, he had no choice," she says, with a mixture of satisfaction and resignation.

They walk the rest of the way in silence. When they reach Commando HQ and go in, Banning tells the duty Color Sergeant they are there to see St. Anthony. They are then kept waiting.

"Fifteen minutes," an exasperated Sam says. "You think he would have some consideration for someone just returned from an op."

"Oh, come on," Banning says, with a bit of a laugh, "you can't deprive him of his little power plays, can you?"

Sam just gives her a disgusted look.

"Captain, Leftenant," the duty Color Sergeant says six minutes later, standing up, "the Leftenant Colonel will see you now."

Banning and Sam walk through the office door the Color Sergeant holds open and come to attention in front of St. Anthony, who is looking busy studying some papers. After a couple of minutes, he looks at them.

"Stand easy," he says, pointedly not inviting them to use the two padded chairs in front of his desk.

"Well, Leftenant, what do you have to say for yourself?" he demands.

"Sir," Sam says, looking straight ahead, "we conducted the operation within the parameters of the orders and withdrew successfully with three POWs and eight deserters who are now with Brigade Intelligence, we …"

"How can you claim the op was successful," St. Anthony shouts, outrage in his voice. "You were not there as long as planned, and you revealed your presence to the enemy. As far I'm concerned, you and your leadership are complete failures. It is a miracle that you did not suffer any casualties in that ill-conceived battle you fought. I have sent a recommendation to Brigade that you be relieved of command forthwith. If it was up to me, you would already have been cashiered from the Corps. Now get out!"

"Sir," Sam says, coming to attention and holding a salute.

"I said get out!" St. Anthony screams, jumping to his feet with such force his chair flies back against the wall behind his desk.

Sam drops the salute, does an about-face and marches out. He goes back to the chairs along the back wall and sits, waiting for Banning to emerge. A few minutes later, she comes out and motions Sam to follow her out.

"That was pleasant," she says, glancing sideways at Sam who is seething, his jaw locked shut. "By the by, he sent that recommendation to Brigade yesterday as soon as he saw your preliminary report."

"He what?" Sam nearly yells, coming to a stop.

"I guess he didn't want to waste any time. But all that accomplished was to provoke a visit from the Colonel, who told him it wasn't going to happen, and that if he kept up this resistance, it could harm his career," the Captain says, motioning Sam to keep walking. "You are staying put and all he can do is scream about it."

"You let me walk into an ambush?" Sam asks, somewhat offended.

"No, I wouldn't do that. I did not think he would react that way. I guess he's even more petty than I thought," she says in an apologetic tone.

"Thanks," Sam says, calming down. "May I ask what was said after I left?"

"You may," she says in a lighter tone, "but I'm not going to tell you. For one thing, your blood pressure is high enough already. And for another, it isn't anything that will ever impact you. Just let it go."

"Yes, ma'am," Sam says, resigned to never knowing.

"After you and your guys have been debriefed, I want all of you to take a week's liberty."

"That will go down well with my guys," Sam says. "Not to mention my wife and kids."

"And you?"

"Especially me," he says, grinning broadly.

"When you get back, be ready for intensive training. I want you and your NCOs working with the other Troops. We need to get the company in shape for broader deployments. And while that is going on, your Troop is going to make periodic forays along the coast."

"Yes, ma'am," Sam says. "Thank you."

"Don't thank me yet," she says. "You and your guys are going into harm's way again."

"Yes, but we'll be keeping those people," he says waving to the east, "away from our families."

"Right," Banning says. "I'll see you in a week."

"That you will," Sam says, saluting he and walking off quickly.

A day after Sam gets home, Sarah goes into labor, two days past her due date. She tells him their new daughter wanted to wait until her father could be there.

In the hospital after delivery, they start talking about girl's names.

"I want to name her Emily," Sarah says, holding her new daughter as she lies in the hospital bed, Judy and Frank sitting next to her, staring at their new sister.

"Why?" Sam, who is sitting in a chair next to her.

"Because," she replies, "I happen to like it."

Sam thinks about that for a moment. "Okay. A middle name." He thinks for a moment. "How about Sarah? I happen to love that name."

Sarah looks at her daughter, "Welcome to the world Emily Sarah Hope." Then looking at Sam, she says, "I'll have to tell Mary the next time I talk to her."

"I want a brother!" Frank protests.

"Maybe next time, sweet boy," Sarah tells him, provoking a smile from her son.

"You know," Sam says, "he'll hold you to that."

"Not me," Sarah says with a big smile. "It will be your fault."

"Gee, thanks," Sam says, looking sour, as Frank crawls into his arms.

When Sam returns two weeks later—he was given an extra week for paternity leave–he immediately falls into a routine of training the other Troops in the company. First, he and Jones work with the Company's other officers, including Banning, and senior non-coms, bringing them up to speed on the more rigorous training, and in the new organization, that includes an automatic weapon in each four-member fire team.

After a week of that, he and Jones split up, working with the other Troops, using their own Troop's Marines in joint exercises, ensuring their training is maintained while providing a group who are now veterans to help those who have never been in combat. Banning is constantly around, watching, encouraging, admonishing, and taking part.

They see little of St. Anthony. When their commander does come around, he looks disapproving but says nothing, leaving after a few minutes.

After a month of training, Sam leads his Troop on a series of reconnaissance missions along the coast, working their way north from Brittany. They run into little trouble, grabbing a few prisoners, mapping the locations of camps, and gathering information about the size and organization of the Enemy, and the state of supply. A good deal of time seems to be spent growing and gathering food. And Sam and his Marines can't determine where the weapons or ammunition are coming from.

After five months of the new training, the other Troops begin two-Troop raids, the Company's other three combat Troops rotating through with Sam's. At first, Banning goes along as an observer, but after three such outings over the next six months, she leads a three-Troop raid on the Dutch coast.

The next raid, this one into Germany, also involves three Troops, but does not include Six Troop. Sam and most of the rest of the Troop are resentful about being left out, but at the same time, are happy with the break, and a chance to spend time with their families.

The first full Company raid comes more than a year later, along the Norwegian coast. At first, they find nothing along the rugged coast, except for deserted villages with buildings in varying states of collapse.

The surprise comes when they land in Rorvick. The Marines find a fully functional town with friendly people. At least, they're friendly after they find out the Marines are British and not there to kill them. The initial landing was tense, with neither side knowing what to expect. Communication was difficult since none of the Marines spoke Norwegian and none of the Norwegians spoke anything but.

It took some time, but the Marine officers finally determined that these people had beaten back initial attacks by the enemy using Norwegian army weapons and knowledge of the terrain. An early, extremely cold winter also helped. Since then, the enemy has made only occasional attacks, which the town and others further north have defeated. A close watch is kept on the passes into the valleys. Any sign of trouble brings an immediate response.

When the town's leaders ask for military help in pushing the enemy back, Banning has to tell them she will pass the request on. Her Company is not strong enough to do the job. She also says she will pass along a request to help these communities get out of the nineteenth century. Since the attacks began, these Norwegians have been cut off from sources of fuel to generate electricity, heat, or power vehicles and boats. They survive by fishing from boats powered by sail and oars, small farming plots, and keeping sheep, goats, pigs, chickens, and cows, as well as some ducks. Transportation is by boat, horse, or walking.

In return for pledging to help clear the Scandinavian peninsula when the time comes and providing fish, the British government sends an Army Brigade and a company of tanks, along with artillery and attack helicopters, as well as modern arms, to help the Norwegians push south and to train them.

After six months, the Brigade is withdrawn, but all the equipment, except the helicopters, is left. The British provide enough fuel for military uses and fishing. The Norwegians not only push south, but east as well into Sweden.

"Hope," Banning says, poking her head into his office tent, "you awake?"

"You know, Captain," he responds, smiling, and standing up from his desk, "that question would make a whole lot more sense if this was my sleeping quarters."

"Oh, you never know," she replies, returning his smile. "With the pace you've been keeping, it wouldn't surprise me if you were sleeping at your desk. How's the family?" she asks.

"They are all fine. Our latest edition, Emily, is doing fine as is her mother. Yours?" he asks.

"They are all doing beautifully. And now for business. We have a new mission," Banning says, sitting in one of the two chairs in front of the table that serves as Sam's desk and waving for him to sit down.

"Would you like tea or coffee? Or something stronger?" Sam asks.

"How about coffee with a kick?"

"Brilliant," he says, calling his orderly to get two coffees, black. Then he turns back to Banning with a questioning look.

"Yes, the op," she says. "I just came from a meeting with St. Anthony and the other Company commanders. The whole Four Two is going into the Pas-de-Calais on a reconnaissance in force."

"The whole Commando?" Sam asks, perplexed. "The other Companies haven't trained for this."

"No, well, St. Anthony has convinced Brigade that only one of what he calls a 'special company' is needed."

"That stupid bloody sod," Sam spits out, cutting himself off as the orderly comes in with the coffee. Sam has him put it on the table and then pulls a bottle out of a filing cabinet drawer.

"What is that?" Banning asks. "I don't recognize the label."

Sam hands her the bottle as he says, "It's Irish whiskey. A friend makes frequent trips there and brings back the occasional bottle for me." He takes the bottle back and pours some in each cup, putting one in front of the Captain, who takes sip. "For my money, I think Irish goes better with coffee than scotch or anything else."

"I see what you mean," she says, appreciating the flavor. "Do you think you can get me a bottle?"

"I most certainly will," Sam says. "Now, about this op," he says, spitting out the word. "A reconnaissance in force? Does that mean we provoke combat?"

"Exactly."

"With one Commando, three-quarters of which haven't been trained nor equipped for this kind of mission?"

"Those are the orders," Banning says. "And your Troop will take the lead. The Leftenant Colonel says Six Troop has the most experience, and therefore, is to be in the lead."

Sam looks at her with a sour expression. "The bloody sod has no clue what he's talking about. He's going to get us all killed."

"Oh," she replies while sipping her coffee, "I don't think it will come to that. Besides, we will have Navy support, and not just destroyers. They're sending along a couple of cruisers."

"Any attack choppers or armor?" he asks, hope in his voice.

"Not for this party," she replies. "We go in on hovercraft. We'll have some sixty-millimeter mortars, but that's it."

"And if we run into trouble?" Sam asks, not happy with this plan.

"We figure a way to get out of it. We can call on the Navy for gunnery support, but outside of that, we're on our own."

"Whose bloody brilliant plan was this?" Sam asks, sarcasm dripping from his voice, as he puts some more whiskey in his now empty cup, offering some to Banning, who accepts.

"St. Anthony's," she says, flatly. "He has insisted our Commando can handle this on its own and that it will be a good test case for this new approach."

"And Brigade bought that?" Sam asks, incredulously.

"I think they felt they had no choice. He is the Four Two's commanding officer, and he has the responsibility to plan the op."

"Even if it's bollocks?" Sam challenges her.

"Even if it's bollocks," Banning says, resignation in her voice. "Either that or relieve him."

"That," Sam says, sitting up in his chair, "is an excellent solution."

"Won't happen," Banning says, shaking her head. "He's too well connected just to fire him without cause. It did occur to me that Brigade may be setting him up. If the op doesn't go well, then he can be fired."

"And the price will be our blood," Sam says, disgust in his voice.

"I don't think it will come to that. The Brigadier and the Colonel may be letting him plan the op, but as I understand it, they have him on a short leash. He has to have all the contingencies worked out before we go."

"And when is that?" Sam asks, resigned to his fate.

"A fortnight," comes the flat reply.

Sam nods. "I would like to give everyone extended liberty. I'll rotate through the Troop so at least half the guys will be here at all times to prepare. We can do final briefing and table-top exercises the two days before we go."

"Sounds like a plan," she says. "I'll suggest it to the other Troops, too. And we'll have a table top exercise with all Company and Troop commanders."

With that, she drains her cup, puts it down, and gets up to leave. She hands him a folder, "Here are the formal orders and list of supplies you'll take."

"Yes, ma'am," Sam says, standing as well.

"Let's get cracking," Banning says as she leaves.

Sam sits down heavily as he picks up the papers and reads through them.

"Bollocks," he mutters as he reads.

CHAPTER THIRTY-SIX

S am sits in the cabin of the hover landing craft carrying his Troop and their equipment. He keeps going over the briefings he and Jones had with the Troop—details of the terrain, the suspected size of the enemy's camp and its location, and the goal to provoke a fight to test their capabilities. There are also plans for the rest of the Company to come up in support as Six Troop falls back with the whole Four Two Commando close at hand to back them up, and the Navy's heavy guns on standby.

Did he leave anything out? Is there anything else he could have done or said to better prepare his guys? He can't think of anything, but he is plagued by the possibility there is something he hasn't thought of.

To distract himself, he looks around the craft as it roars toward the Pas-de-Calais. 'It's making enough noise to wake the dead,' he thinks to himself. He also can't escape the realization that this craft is capable of carrying a tank along with his Troop and all their equipment. A tank would be nice to have along, but St. Anthony doesn't think it will be needed, since, as the Lieutenant Colonel so pleasantly put it, he's trained his Troop so well.

"The bloody son of a bitch," Sam mutters.

"Excuse me, Boss?" the Marine sitting next to him asks.

"Hmmm?" Sam says, drawn back into the here and now.

"You said something, Boss?" the Marine asks.

"Oh, sorry. Talking to myself," he says, feeling mortified.

"Yes, Boss," the Marine says, giving him a funny look.

Sam quickly falls back into his own thoughts. The only good thing about the start of this operation is they are landing at 0400, well before dawn.

"Leftenant," a hover craft crewman says as he comes up to Sam. "We'll be on the beach in fifteen."

"Brilliant," Sam says. "Give me a five-minute warning."

"Will do, sir," the crewman says as he heads back to the pilot's cabin.

Sam sighs and gets to his feet. "Alright, you Bootys, time to kit up," he yells so he can be heard above the roar of the engines. "We land in less than fifteen mikes."

The few Marines who have fallen asleep are awakened by their mates. Everyone puts on their helmets, web gear, and backpacks, and then double-checks weapons as well as the radio gear they all wear with a headset and mic, and their night-vision goggles. The carry-all drivers check their electric motors for a full charge and make sure extra batteries, ammunition, food, water, and medical supplies are secured. Jones oversees the Sergeants making their final checks of their Marines. Sam keeps a close watch on the proceedings and circulates around, encouraging and reassuring his Marines.

"Five minutes to landing," a calm voice announces over the loudspeaker.

Sam places himself at the front of the Troop so he will be the first on the beach. They feel the craft leave the water and climb the slight incline onto the sand. As soon as it stops, the rear ramp drops. Sam runs out as quickly as his gear will allow and heads up the beach. The members of his Troop fan out behind him. When they reach the top of the beach's incline, they go to ground. Sam studies the nearly flat terrain in front of them. Nothing.

"Forward in skirmish line. One hundred meters. Go."

The Troop advances cautiously. The six carry-alls stay on the beach. At one hundred meters, the Troop takes another pause.

"Go," Sam says quietly after nothing is spotted in front of them.

The Troop goes another hundred meters. This time, the carry-alls move forward, the electric motors making nearly no sound, and stop fifteen meters behind the skirmish line. Sam had decided to add fifty-caliber machine guns to the carry-alls. Those weapons are not standard equipment, and he's sure St. Anthony would not have allowed it, which is why he didn't ask permission. Sam wants all the fire power he can get if they are to provoke a fight. Some of his Marines are adept at requisitioning out of channels anything the Troop needs. And two of his Marines, who are excellent at welding, were able to create mounts and shields for the heavy machine guns.

Each carry-all has a two-member crew and at least one of them has experience with a fifty-caliber. Fortunately, St. Anthony wasn't around when the carry-alls were loaded onto the hover craft. Sam knows Banning saw them but pretended she didn't.

"B6 to BigB, clear at two hundred meters. Moving forward," Sam says on the company circuit that also goes to Commando HQ.

"BigB to B6, Right," Banning replies. "Landing."

The plans call for the rest of the Company to come ashore when Six Troop reaches this point. The rest of Four Two is to land after Bravo Company has moved two hundred meters inland. According to the latest intelligence, a large Enemy camp—estimated to hold at least five thousand—is six kilometers inland, slightly to Six Troop's northeast. The land is mostly flat with slight rises here and there. The only real cover are the ruins of buildings and some small woods scattered around the area.

The rest of the Company is to stay at least a kilometer and a half back. Once Six Troop has kicked the hornets' nest, the rest of the Company, which has the mortars, will either hold its position until the Troop reaches it or come up in support if needed. The rest of Four Two is to form a defensive perimeter no more than one kilometer inland but is available to move up in support as needed. The big guns of the Royal Navy are also available.

As Sam cautiously leads his Troop toward the camp, he starts to shorten his line to increase their concentrated firepower. The downside is that it leaves his flanks more vulnerable. He tries to assure himself that once contact is made, they will quickly fall back on the support of the rest of the Company and the Commando.

Sam orders the carry-alls to stop when they are within two hundred meters of the camp. The crew members know now is the time to prepare the machine guns for combat.

"Okay, guys, nix the night-vision," Sam says quietly into his mic as dawn breaks, "forward carefully. Let's take them by surprise."

Sam leads the Troop forward at a crouch. The sun has just broken the horizon to their right, throwing the whole area into stark contrast. Sentries are patrolling the perimeter but have not seen the Marines yet. When the Troop is twenty meters from the camp's edge, a couple of Sergeants come out to check the lines. One of the Sergeants glances in the Marines' direction. He looks away and then his head whips back. He leans forward staring at what he can't quite figure out.

The Marines have gone to ground in the tall grass and frozen in position, no one moving a muscle. Sam realizes, even if the Sergeant doesn't see the Troop, he will soon see the carry-alls. 'Might as well get started,' he thinks as he rises up a bit and fires a short burst, bringing the Sergeant down. The other Sergeant and the sentries are not only taken by surprise but are confused by the lack of a clear gun sound because of the noise suppressor on Sam's rifle.

"Go, go, go!" Sam orders, leading his Troop up and firing as they bring down the second Sergeant and the sentries. The camp is just beginning to stir as the Marines break in. Sam takes a moment to let Banning know the fight has started.

The Troop advances in a line, firing into the camp when targets present themselves. Sam stops them at the camp's edge. The idea is to provoke a fight to determine their strengths and weaknesses, not to launch an all-out attack. It takes some minutes for the Sergeants to realize what is happening and to organize some return fire.

At that point, Sam pulls the Troop back to carry-alls. The Marines all reload their web belts with more magazines and get into firing positions. The volume of fire begins to increase from the camp, at which point Sam has the heavy machine guns open fire.

Scanning the camp through binoculars, Sam sees attack lines being formed behind the firing line at the edge of camp.

"Time to go," he announces through their headsets, and he lets Banning know. That sets in motion the staged withdrawal they have trained to do with half holding the line while the other half pull back twenty meters. Sam is in charge of the first group holding the line with three carry-alls, while Colors manages the other group, with the other three carry-alls, falling back.

"BigB to B6," Banning says over the company net.

"B6," Sam replies.

"We've received peremptory orders to fall back to the beach immediately."

"We are heavily engaged," Sam says, his voice sounding calm and professional although he is seething with anger.

"Understood. Falling back as slowly as possible."

"Right. Out." Sam stands still for a moment as the sounds of small arms fire surround him. He becomes aware of the sound of bullets zipping past as The Enemy launches a mass wave attack. His attention is yanked back into the present by the cries of Marines, his Marines, who have been hit. They are put on the carry-alls so their wounds can be attended to by the medic as the Troop continues its retreat. The fifty-caliber machine guns rip attackers apart while the light machine guns and semi-automatic weapons bring down scores of others.

As the attack slackens, Sam orders his section to pull back. They leapfrog the second group, falling back twenty meters behind them. As soon as their fire ceases with their withdrawal, a new attack is launched against the second section.

As the attack persists, and Colors' section starts taking casualties, Sam tells Jones to start withdrawing slowly through his lines. As her section moves past, Sam's resumes firing. They leapfrog that way several times before the attacks finally break off, the last of The Enemy casualties no more than five meters in front of Jones's line. They load up their four dead and twelve wounded, and start to fall back as rapidly as possible.

"BigB to B6."

"B6."

"Report."

"Pulling back. Four KIA. Five critical. Seven walking. Under heavy pressure," Sam says as he watches the enemy reforming about four hundred meters away.

"Understood. Under peremptory orders to withdraw from beach. Will delay as long as possible," Banning says.

Sam is thunderstruck. 'We're being sacrificed for no bloody good reason.'

"B6 to BigB."

"BigB."

"Request Navy fire support. Request direct com link to coordinate fire," Sam says as the attack resumes and his section readies to open fire, the Marines having replenished their ammunition from the carry-alls.

"Understood. Stand by."

"Fire," Sam orders as the enemy soldiers reach two hundred meters away, firing as they come. Sam feels a sharp pain in his upper left arm. He looks down to see his uniform torn and blood flowing from a flesh wound. He shrugs it off and goes back to directing his Marines, two more of whom are down.

"BigB to B6."

"B6," Sam replies, raising his voice above the noise of battle.

"Both requests denied," Banning says, her anger and frustration boiling through the radio net. "Sam, get back here as fast you can. I'm getting a lot of pressure to get off this beach. The rest of Four Two never landed."

"Understood. I'll get these guys back as fast as possible if it's the last thing I do," Sam says in disgust.

His Troop beats off that attack, despite a new wrinkle—as the frontal attack nears their line, the Soldiers on either flank start curling in. That attack is met by fire from Jones' section which is behind his, but which slows down the Troop's withdrawal.

"BigB to B6."

"B6," Sam yells to be heard above the noise of battle.

"I have orders to be underway in ten. I'll wait as long as I can."

"Understood," Sam says. His Troop, now carrying seven dead and fifteen wounded, eight seriously, will not make it in time, he realizes. The fifty-cals are overheating. Ammunition is running low. Unless he does something drastic, they're all dead. They're in a lull right now, just more than a kilometer from the beach and have just crossed a slight rise. Sam is lying down watching the enemy reforming again, bringing up reinforcements.

"Forgive me, Sarah," he says quietly to himself. Then on the Troop net, "Colors."

"Right, Boss," Jones replies, realizing he wants to talk to her in person. "Yes, Boss," she says as she drops beside him.

"They," he says, indicating the enemy, "will be coming again in a few. Leave two machine guns and three extra canisters with me. Then get the Troop to the beach. They are shoving off in less than ten. You can make it if you go on the double-quick."

"That's bloody suicidal," she says sharply. "I won't let you do that."

"This is not a fucking bloody debate," Sam replies even more sharply. "I am ordering you to get our guys to safety. I promised to get them all home. Now get cracking!"

"Boss …" Jones starts to say, but Sam's expression stops her. "Yes, Sam, I'll get them home."

Sam just nods and goes back to studying the attack that is forming in front of him.

"Here, Boss. Colors says you want these," a Marine says as she and another Marine put two light machine guns next to him, along with three canisters. "All the canisters are full."

"Brilliant," Sam says without looking at them. "Now get your asses out of here."

"Boss …"

"I said get cracking!" Sam says sharply, glaring up at them. "Now!"

"Yes, Boss," they both say and run back to the Troop.

Sam glances over his shoulder to see his Marines moving off at nearly a trot with some of the walking wounded finding places on the carry-alls. But with many of the walking wounded hobbling along as fast as they can, the column is still not moving fast enough to outpace a charge by the enemy.

Sam's attention returns to the forming attack. Their lines are just more than two hundred meters away. Not an ideal range but manageable for the machine guns in this open landscape. Sam glances once more over this shoulder watching his Marines head toward the beach, some of the walking wounded being helped by their mates.

Sam makes sure the machine guns are both primed and then opens fire with one, sweeping across the lines of The Enemy. He watches as Soldiers collapse and others recoil, but then, under pressure from the Sergeants, break into first a halting run and then a full out attack.

When they have closed to one hundred meters, Sam has exhausted one canister. He quickly grabs a second machine gun and keeps firing. At that range, the carnage he inflicts is horrific. The attacking lines waver and begin to recoil. Many of the attackers go to ground. When he empties that one, he grabs a canister, slaps it in, keeping the fire as continuous as possible, sweeping up and down the lines. The continuous fire keeps the enemy in check.

Every time a Sergeant raises up to get the soldiers moving, Sam shoots him. When groups stand, Sam knocks them down, killing some, wounding others, and forcing the rest to drop down.

But ultimately, the machine gun's canister empties.

He puts in a new canister as quickly as possible, but the few seconds delay is long enough for the Sergeants to get the mass attack moving again. As Sam begins to fire, he glances to his left and right—and sees soldiers curling in towards him. He swings his machine gun to his left where the attack is nearest.

As he swivels into his new firing position, he raises up a bit.

His world goes black.

CHAPTER THIRTY-SEVEN

Pain.

Sam lies as still as possible. His head hasn't hurt like this since he went on liberty with the other officer candidates. That was when he discovered just how much the British like to drink. And when he experienced his first hangover. He had vowed never to do that again. He begins to wonder if he had violated that vow when he licks his lips—and tastes grass.

He forces his eyes open despite the pain. It's dark, but he can see the grass he is lying in. Then the stench of death invades his nostrils. The memory of what happened comes flooding back. He lies still, listening intently for any sound. The silence is pervasive, except...except for low moaning. Battle injuries.

His Marines?

Sam can no longer lie still. He forces himself to rise up enough to look around. In the pale moonlight, he sees bodies in front of him and to his left. He swivels around. No bodies behind him. Is that a good sign? He pushes himself into a sitting position and reaches to key his radio, only to realize he is no longer wearing the headset or his helmet. He feels the left side of his face. His hand comes back sticky with nearly dried blood.

When he swiveled to his left, he must have been grazed by a bullet coming from the attackers on the right. All the blood from that wound apparently convinced them he was dead. Which is probably the only reason why he is still alive.

His rifle is still slung over his back and he has half a dozen magazines for it. He checks his water bottles. Undamaged. One is full and the other about half. He has nearly three days of rations. He picks up the machine gun he was last firing and the spare canister, and heads for the beach. He doesn't expect to find anyone waiting for him there, but he needs to make sure that his Troop made it to safety.

If they didn't, he will find evidence of that.

As he nears the beach, he sees bodies ahead of them. His heart stops for a moment. Then he forces himself to go on. The dead are all The Enemy. And some are just badly wounded. As he stops to check whether they are Marines, a man reaches up to him pleading for help. Sam looks at the gaping hole in his stomach and realizes that he doesn't have long to live. He gives the doomed man some water and then moves on. Another solider, a woman, reaches out and grabs his ankle as he passes.

"Aide-moi s'il te plait," she begs.

In response to her plea for help, Sam, who has taken time to learn French since his Troop started to raid, looks down at her and then kneels to examine her wound. He has seen enough battle injuries to realize her wound need not be fatal, if the bleeding is stopped. The question is whether he should take the risk to help her. He is in a dangerous spot, cut off from safety by the English Channel, surrounded by The Enemy who wants him dead. He stands up on the verge of leaving.

"Ne me laisse pas mourir," she begs.

It takes a moment for Sam to realize she is asking him not to leave her to die. About fifty meters away, Sam sees the ruins of a stone house. "Bloody stupid idiot," Sam mutters to himself. He kneels back down, and pulling out his medical kit, he finds tape and gauze which he uses to slow the flow of blood nearly to a half. "I'll be back. Je reviendrai a nouveau," he assures the woman, hoping that is what he actually said in French, then quickly gets up to head toward the beach, her soft cries fading behind him.

"Soldat! Donne-moi un coup de main!" a voice orders him as he nears the beach.

Sam freezes, then walks to the man who issued the orders. He looks down at the Sergeant. "You want help?" he asks. As Sam kneels beside the Sergeant, he pulls his combat knife. He stares down at the object of his hatred and then plunges the knife into his heart, watching the man die. He pulls the knife out, wipes it on the Sergeant's shirt, then puts it back in his sheath as he stands up and returns to his quest.

He sweeps the beach and the area behind it but finds only enemy who are dead or dying. No sign of his Marines or their equipment. He breathes a sigh of relief as he stares out to sea, an empty sea.

As he turns around, he sees the sky in the east beginning to lighten. He doesn't have long to find cover. Remembering the ruined house, he starts to head there, but then stops. "Bloody fool," he says to himself as he turns back to where he left the wounded woman.

When he gets there, he stares down at her for moment. She reaches up to him. He kneels, gives her some water, and then lifts her in cradled arms, eliciting a cry of pain. She is small, but carrying her and the machine gun is awkward.

As he enters the door in the center of the front wall, he turns to his right into what he hopes is a bedroom. It is. He puts her on an old bed with a moldy mattress in what was once the one bedroom on this floor. He assumes more bedrooms were on the second floor but since the stairs are gone, he can't check it out. The roof has mostly caved in anyway, but the second-story floor is still intact, which makes it a roof of sorts.

He finds a couple of blankets that have been stored in a cabinet; they look to be in reasonably good shape. He puts one folded under her head and the other over her. He still needs to stop the bleeding, but he is out of bandages. He decides the clothes of the dead will have to do. As he walks into what had once been a combination living room and kitchen, he confronts two men in the doorway of the house. One with a wounded left shoulder is supporting the other who has leg and belly wounds. Sam quickly pulls his sidearm.

"Pouvez-vous nous aider?" the one with the shoulder wound asks.

Sam keeps his weapon pointed at them as he considers whether to help them as The Enemy Soldier has asked.

"Vous estes," the one with the shoulder wound says as he lowers the other to the ground, "l'un des envahisseurs. Emmenez-nous avec vous. Nous voulons jeste sortir d'ici."

Sam thinks he understands what the man is saying, but to make sure, he asks the man to speak slowly. The result is a funny look, but the man repeats himself, slowly. Sam translates in his mind as the man speaks: "You are one of the invaders. Take us with you. We just want out of here."

Sam lowers his weapon and motions with his head for the men to come inside. As they settle themselves along a wall, Sam cautiously looks outside as the light quickly brightens. All he sees is some movement among the wounded, all of whom will die without aid, which he can't give and he doubts the Sergeants will.

He steps slowly outside as he sweeps the area. Not seeing any sign of the enemy, he moves quickly to several of the dead, ripping off parts of the shirts of each. He hopes he has not taken enough to alert anyone coming along. He comes across a dead Sergeant who is carrying a mostly full water bottle and a pouch with some bread. He takes both. He checks other Sergeants, finding most of them also carrying water bottles and food. Despite the risks, he decides to take them.

As he returns to the house, he pulls his sidearm and cautiously enters. When he sees the two men collapsed against the wall, he puts the pistol away. He hands them some bread, which they greedily gobble down, and a water bottle, which they quickly drain. Sam heads to the woman who is looking pale. He checks her bandages which are seeping blood. He pulls up her shirt enough to get a good view of the through-and-through wound. Then, using strips of torn shirt and tape, tightly binds the wound which is on her right side. He manages to stop the bleeding. Then he gives her a sip of water.

"Now it's up to you whether you live," he says quietly as he stands up. Then he goes to the two men. He bandages the one with the shoulder wound. The bullet didn't strike any bone as it went through. "Just be happy you didn't get hit with a fifty-cal," he says as he works, drawing a quizzical look from the man. When he looks at the other, he realizes that without surgery the man will die.

"Aide mon ami," the man with the shoulder wound pleads.

Sam just shakes his head. "Sorry. Nothing I can do. Desole," he says in his halting French. "Rien que je puisse faire."

The man just nods in acknowledgement as he cradles his dying friend.

Sam stands in the doorway looking at the battlefield. Unless someone comes soon, anyone still alive won't be. Sam doesn't want to go out there and face more requests for help because he just isn't equipped to do it. He already has two people he will have to take with him, assuming he can find a way to cross the Channel. Any more would make it impossible, and he can't stay here.

He might be able to survive, but he wants, needs, to get back to Sarah and the children. He looks in at the wounded woman. She won't be able to travel for at least two weeks, maybe longer. His eyes sweep the room. The two rooms take up the ground floor of the two-story house. It is bare except for the old bed, a fireplace, a broken-down table, and a number of chairs in various states of disrepair. The front door and all the windows are gone. Everything is covered with a layer of dust and dirt.

His problem is they need food and water. He scans the area again, this time with his binoculars. Then he checks all around the house, looking through the few windows cut into the stone walls. The back door is solid wood. It doesn't look like it is in good shape, so he doesn't chance opening it. He decides to wait until evening to venture out. His head still hurts, and he could use some sleep. He goes to the wall opposite from the two men, but close to the woman so he can hear her if she cries out. He sits down heavily, his pistol in his hand. Almost immediately, he falls into a sleep of exhaustion.

Sam snaps awake. Something is happening. He looks around quickly, raising his sidearm. He doesn't see the man with the wounded shoulder. The other man has died. Scrambling to his feet, he looks out over the field to see if he can see the man leaving. Nothing is moving. Then he hears a sound in the bedroom. Going in, he finds the man kneeling next to the woman.

"Elle est dans mon equipe," he says, glancing at Sam before returning a worried gaze to her. "She is in my squad," Sam translates in his head.

"What is her name? Comment s'appelez-t-elle?" Sam asks, trying to make conversation and get her name.

"Chloe," he answers simply, carefully brushing her hair back from her face. She sighs contentedly.

"And yours? Et le tien?" Sam asks the man, wanting to have a name to put with the face.

"Gabriel."

Sam nods. "Sam." Then he looks at the other man.

"Benoit est mort," Gabriel says simply.

"Benoit is dead," Sam says quietly to himself, nodding. He decides they will have to carry the body out to the battlefield when it is fully dark. Then he can check the other bodies for water and food. If he can find some, that will at least give him some time to figure out how to get more.

"Pouvons-nous l'enterrer?" Gabriel asks.

"You want to bury him?" Sam says, a bit shocked. "No," he says, "that could give us away. Non. Cette pourrait reveler notre presence."

Gabriel just nods and turns his attention back to Chloe.

Sam goes back to the door, watching as the light begins to fade in the west. "Gabriel, j'ai besoin de ton aide," he says, asking for his help to move Benoit. Then realizing Gabriel won't be able to do much because of his injured shoulder, Sam says, "Never mind. Peu importe." Gabriel, who had started to get up, sits back down and turns his attention back to Chloe.

Sam goes to Benoit. He looks down at what had once been a human being. Taking him by the arms, he drags the corpse out of the house and well into the battlefield, arranging the body to conform to how those around him are lying. He finds an odd sense of relief that everyone around him appears dead.

He then goes to where he had fought. He finds his helmet in good shape, with the night-vision gear still attached. He puts on the helmet as the sun sets and flips down the night-vision. Scanning the area again for signs of life, he finds none. He then starts a search of the bodies but finds no water or bread. When he comes across a Sergeant carrying six loaves and two full water bottles, he starts concentrating on the other dead Sergeants. In an hour, he collects enough food and water to last more than a week.

When he returns to the house, he carefully peers inside. To his relief, he sees Gabriel asleep on the floor next to Chloe. He steps quietly inside, puts down his load next to the door, then heads back out.

Six hours later, he has swept the field in the immediate vicinity of the house, collecting enough bread for more than two weeks and water for just less than that, if they are careful. But Chloe will need plenty of fluids to recover. He also has torn enough material off the dead for more bandages. And he brought in the other machine gun. He doesn't know yet if he can trust Gabriel, but if they are discovered, they're going to need all the fire power they can muster to survive.

Sam turns his night-vision off to conserve the batteries, then settles down for some sleep as far away from the two French people as he can get.

"Sam! Sam!"

The urgency in Gabriel's quiet voice brings Sam to full awake all at once.

"Here. I'm here," he says, quickly getting up and going to the window where Gabriel is carefully peering out.

Silently Gabrielle gestures out the window.

Sam edges next to the window and peeks out to where Gabrielle indicates. A detail of about one hundred sixty Soldiers with twenty Sergeants in charge are going through the field, checking the bodies, and collecting weapons and boots. As far as he can tell, only the Sergeants are armed. A sign they are neither looking for or expecting trouble.

"Bloody hell," Sam says under his breathe. "Get away from the window. Eloignez-vous de la fenetre," Sam whispers as he backs away, handing Gabriel his sidearm, and hoping he is right to trust him. Gabriel retreats to the bedroom. Sam retrieves the loaded machine gun, then sits in the darkest area he can find that can't be easily seen from a window but still gives him a clear view of the door.

In the bedroom, Gabriel covers Chloe completely with the blanket and makes himself as small as possible against the wall at the foot of the bed, intently watching the door from the living room and the windows.

Sam can hear the Sergeants yelling and cursing but he can't quite make out what they're saying because they're speaking so fast. What he does know is they are coming closer. As they near the house, Sam tenses up, readying to fight. Do they realize he is no longer where they had left him for dead? If so, they could come looking in here.

A Sergeant's voice is nearby. Sam can hear him clearly. He shifts a little to get into a better position. Then, to his relief, the Sergeant's voice moves off. Sam cautiously goes to the window. Peering out, he sees them going toward the beach as the soldiers collect the weapons and boots, not bothering to check for signs of life. A short time later, he hears them return. Peeking out the window, he sees them marching in formation, the soldiers burdened by the weapons and boots they have recovered.

When they are gone, Sam gives Gabriel food and water for him and Chloe, along with fresh material for bandages. He's decided to let Gabriel care for her, while he patrols the area, looking for water and more food.

"Give Chloe plenty of water. Donnez-lui beaucoup d'eau a Chloe," he tells Gabriel.

"Oui," he answers, taking the water bottles and bread, and shaking his head at Sam's fractured French.

Sam watches him return to Chloe, then heads out the door.

About half a kilometer away, he finds a small stream of what looks like clear, clean water. He tastes a little and is not disappointed. That problem solved, he now has to find a source of food, one the Sergeants won't notice if he pilfers some. What worries him is the sources are probably tightly controlled and monitored. That could make resupply problematic.

He crosses the stream. After another kilometer, he comes across a wheat field. The grain looks nearly ripe. He decides he can return in a week or so and collect some ripe grain without cutting any stalks. If he does it right, no one should notice. Parched grain may not be the ideal meal, but it will keep them alive. He heads back toward the house, taking a different route in the hopes of coming across another food source.

He doesn't.

When he reaches the house, he just walks in, no longer worrying about Garbriel's intentions. What he does wonder about now is whether he can survive the nearly overwhelming stench emanating from the dead littering the area, corpses the Sergeants seem to have no interest in burying.

He gathers the twelve empty water bottles and heads back to the stream. As he walks, he realizes he dodged another bullet—the Sergeants were so interested in retrieving the weapons that they apparently didn't notice the missing water bottles. He just hopes that remains the case. When he returns, he puts the water bottles next to a sleeping Gabriel and goes off to the other side of the house to bed down for the night.

Sam's eyes flutter open in the dim grey light of morning. He hears the rain pounding down outside, a cool wet mist coming in through the door and windows to blanket everything. Including him. He looks around to find the source of dripping he can hear. Most of it is coming from where the stairs used to rise to the upper floor.

He rolls onto his back, then looks around at the ceiling, finding a few other places water is dripping from. Happily, none of it is hitting him. He hopes the other two are staying dry.

He closes his eyes, comfortable in the realization that they have plenty of food and water for today, and that this heavy rain is washing away the stench of death, at least temporarily.

Sam sits up suddenly as he jolts awake. Looking out the windows and door at the downpour, he wonders how long he's been asleep. Looking at his watch, he discovers three hours have passed.

Sam gets up and walks into the bedroom where he finds Gabriel giving Chloe a little water. "How's our patient? Comment va notre patient?"

Gabriel looks up from where he is helping her sip water. "Elle s'est un peu amelioree."

Sam nods, "Good. Bien," he says, happy to hear she is improving, if only a bit. He goes and sits by the doorway, munching on some bread and sipping water, happy to have this enforced inactivity. He can use the rest. He dozes off and on, the rain playing a lullaby. The downpour also washes away the stench of decomposing bodies from the air. Sam enjoys the clean smell.

The rain slows and then stops toward evening, bringing Sam to full alert. He scans the area for any sign of movement. What he sees startles him: Rats are chewing on the dead. Rats. He hasn't seen any sign of animal life except in Norway. So where did the rats come from? And if they survived, did other animals as well?

Sam walks out of the house, surveying the field. He realizes that there must be hundreds of rats scurrying around. And flies. He sees flies swarming some of the bodies.

"Rats." Gabriel's voice right behind him makes Sam jump. He looks over his shoulder, wondering why the French use the same word as in English but make it sound different.

"Oui," he replies. "Do you see them often? Les voyez-vous souvent?"

"Oui. Les ravageurs continuent d'entrer de manger notre nourriture."

Sam just nods, translating in his head that the pests keep eating their food, and turns his attention back to the rats. "Guess they found a new food source."

"Qu'est-ce qui?"

"What?" Sam says in his turn, suddenly realizing that he's been saying everything in English before he can say it in French. "Desole," he apologizes. "J'e suppose qu'ils ont trouve une nouvelle source de nourriture."

"Bien cuits, ils peuvent faire un bon repas," Gabriel comments, obviously remembering something tasty.

"Leave it to the French," Sam says under his breath, "to find a way to cook up a tasty meal of rat." Then it occurs to him that rat may be the only meat these people get.

"Je vais cuisiner un repas savoureux," Gabriel says, volunteering to cook a rat dinner. "Et je sais ou trouver des legumes et des herbes."

That last about knowing where to get vegetables and herbs catches Sam's attention. He gives Gabriel a quizzical look. "Is it dangerous? Est-ce dangereux?"

"Non," Gabriel says with a big grin. Sam realizes he has gotten over his fear of the Sergeants.

"Okay," Sam says, "let's go. Allons-y."

"Oui," Gabriel responds, excited to go on an outing.

As they walk out the door, Sam motions toward the pistol in Gabriel's belt. "Don't use that unless you have no choice. Ne l'utilisez pas a moins que vous n'ayez pas d'autre choix."

"Oui, oui," Gabriel says as he leads the way across the fields toward the camp.

The night is pitch dark with clouds covering the moon. The ground is soft from all the rain. The only sounds are the trees and tall grass blowing in the light breeze from the sea as the weather front finishes passing and the rats scurrying to get out of their way. Sam is wearing his night-vision goggles but follows Gabriel's lead who seems to know exactly where to go.

After about two kilometers, Gabriel takes a sharp turn to the right. He approaches an extensive vegetable garden surrounded by a wire-mesh fence. Gabriel crouches low. Turning to Sam, who has followed his example, he holds a finger across his lips. Sam nods in response. Gabriel motions Sam to stay put as he creeps forward.

Looking around, Sam sees the reason for the caution: Several guards are patrolling the perimeter. They don't appear to be armed, so Sam assumes they are there to keep the rats out.

Time drags on. Sam begins to worry when Gabriel doesn't return. Finally, he shows up with two large sacks full of vegetables. He gives one to Sam and indicates for him to follow as he cautiously moves away from the garden. Sam smiles to himself and follows, both of them moving silently.

"C'etait amusant," Gabriel says when they are far enough away to walk upright and talk softly.

"Fun?" Sam says. "You do realize what would happen if you were caught? Vous realisez ce qui se passeerait si vous etiez pris?"

"Oui," comes the light-hearted reply. "Mais je susi libre maintenant."

Sam just shakes his head at Gabriel's declaration, "But I am free now," realizing the world has taken on a new look for him.

"Maintenant, nous avons besoin d'herbes," Gabriel says, wanting to get herbs.

"Okay," Sam replies following him as they make a number of stops where Gabriel knows to get the herbs he needs for cooking his dish. Sam wonders if he has run into another George.

When they return to the house, Gabriel first checks on Chloe, then gathers some string and small pieces of wood he found and heads toward the door. "Je vais chercher de la viande pour notre petite fete."

Sam just watches him go, amused by Gabriel's announcement that he is going to get meat for their little feast. "I guess that is one way to describe a rat roast."

Sam checks on Chloe, who is sleeping peacefully, her breathing deep and regular. He then goes to the door to keep watch.

Four hours later, his attention is drawn by movement coming toward him. He flips on his night-vision goggles and recognizes Gabriel returning, both hands full of dead rats.

"Maintenant, je vais les cuisine," he proclaims, announcing his attention to start cooking as he walks in.

"No. Non," Sam says sharply. "It will be light soon. The smoke will be visible. Il fera bientot jour. La fumee sera visible."

"D'accord," Gabriel says. "Ce soir, je vais cuisiner."

"Tonight is good," Sam says as he watches Gabriel pull a large knife out of his belt. "Where did that come from? D'ou vient ca?"

Gabriel looks at the knife, then at Sam with a big grin. "Je pensais que le sergent n'en aurait plus besoin."

"No, I guess you're right," Sam says, shaking his head. "The Sergeant won't be needing it anymore."

Gabriel retreats to a corner to start skinning the rats while Sam takes the first watch. Sam has set up a four-hour watch rotation for the two men so someone is always awake in case of trouble.

That night, Gabriel produces an old pot he scrounged from somewhere in the house. He lights a small fire in the fireplace, and with the cut-up rat meat, vegetables, and herbs, produces a stew that Sam finds tastes good when Gabriel offers him a sample, although he still has to force himself to eat rat no matter how good it tastes.

The only problem is that they have no plates, bowls, or tableware. Just the spoons Chloe and Gabriel carry and a third one he took from a body. After feeding Chloe, Gabriel brings the pot to Sam and the two men share the meal.

The following days fall into a pattern. An occasional working party passes near the house, but no one shows any interest in it. At first, Sam and Gabriel go out after sunset for water and to scrounge for food, making weekly visits to the garden. Then just Gabriel goes out twice a week.

After one visit, he tells Sam some guards have been executed, tortured to death, and left on crosses. He thinks the Sergeants suspected them of stealing food. And while his thefts are responsible for their deaths, Garbriel says he will continue to raid the garden. Because the guards are now on alert, and a Sergeant is patrolling with them, Gabriel has some close calls, but he manages to avoid detection and always returns with a sack of food.

Sam sets intelligence missions for himself. He goes out a few hours before dawn, slowly expanding the diameter of his searches, then finds a place of concealment and watches what the enemy is doing, returning after dark when the camps are quiet.

He discovers the large camp Gabriel and Chloe were in is the main one, with five smaller satellite camps radiating out from it likes spokes on a wheel. The smaller camps seem to emphasize military training, while the main camp does some training but spends a good deal of time growing food. Sam brings back wheat grains he gathers from the fields, which they parch, and some wild growing vegetables and berries to add to their diet.

With the hot food and Gabriel's attentive care, Chloe makes rapid improvement. Watching them, Sam recognizes the special bond between the two as they laugh and joke together. After three weeks, Chloe is able to get out of bed and walk around the house. Soon, she is taking nighttime strolls outside with Gabriel.

Sam takes to exploring closer to the coast, looking for some way to get back home. With no radio and the Marines not returning to the same place twice, Sam knows he will have to be inventive to cross the Channel.

One night, he finds a derelict barn just off the beach about two kilometers north of where he came ashore. The roof has caved in and wood has been scavenged from one side, opening the interior to the elements. He enters through that hole to find fourteen barrels sitting off to one side among a series of stalls in various stages of decay. The barrels are empty and ten of them have lids. Eight of them have no holes, although all of them have at least some rust. He also finds meters and meters of rope made out of some plastic material.

"They're right," he says, shaking his head, "this stuff never rots." The front of the barn faces the sea. One of the double doors is hanging loosely on its hinges. The barrels' discovery gives him an idea—build a raft. But where will he find the wood for it? Sam looks around but doesn't see any candidates.

It's getting toward morning, so he heads back to the house. As he walks out of the barn, he pushes the door open. And stops. He looks closely at it. The wood is weathered and in places rotten, but the door is two and a half meters wide and nearly three meters high. It should work.

Smiling, he almost runs back to the house, getting there just as dawn is breaking. He finds Chloe and Gabriel curled up in bed together. He shakes his head, smiling, deciding his news can wait.

He goes to the door to assume the watch.

Sam is sitting near the door in the early dawn, munching on some parched wheat, when Gabriel comes over and sits beside him, his back against the wall. Sam just nods at him as he puts another small hand-full of grain in his mouth.

"Bonjour," Gabriel says.

Sam, sharing some of the wheat with Gabriel, glances toward the bedroom. "Can she travel? Peut-elle voyager?"

"Ton francais pue," Chloe says, who has quietly walked out of the bedroom. "Et je t'entends."

Sam looks down in embarrassment, then back up at Chloe. "Yeah, my French does stink, and obviously you can hear me. So are you fit to travel? Etes-vous apte a voyager?"

"Je ne peux pas courir un marathon, mais je peux marcher partout ou tu veux que j'aille," she responds, a big smile on her face.

Sam returns the smile. "A comedian. Un comedien." He shakes his head, thinking this woman is a lot like Sarah. "So, we won't run a marathon, but you can walk to the beach."

Chloe looks at him questioningly.

"Quoi?" Gabriel asks.

Sam realizes he didn't say it in French. He waves that off, motions Chloe to sit on the grass. "Join us. Rejoignez-nous." Then Sam launches into a detailed explanation of his plan to cross the Channel.

"C'est fou!" Chloe says.

"C'est suicidaire!" Gabriel says almost simultaneously.

"Yes, oui," Sam says. "It's crazy," he says nodding to Chloe. "But it's only suicidal if it doesn't work. Mais ce n'est suicidaire que si cela ne fonctionne pas," he says looking at Gabriel, a crooked grin on his face. He tells them the plan may be crazy but it's the only way he knows to get back to his family. He's going to do it, and they can come along or not. It's up to them.

Chloe and Gabriel look at each other for a long moment. Finally, she shrugs in resignation and acceptance.

"D'accord, nous irons," Gabriel tells Sam. "Nous ne pouvons pas' rester ici."

Sam nods in response, knowing they had no real option other than to go with him. They could no more stay here than he, Sarah, and the others could stay in America. They spend the rest of the day and evening preparing food to take with them. That night, the three of them go to the stream to fill every water bottle they have.

Then, leaving Chloe behind, Gabriel and Sam make a last raid on the vegetable garden.

"Qui est la?" a guard challenges as the two raiders are picking vegetables. Both lay flat and freeze. It is not the first time a guard has heard something that aroused suspicion, but discovery, which they have evaded so far, means probable death. Another guard comes and then a third.

"Rats?" one asks.

Sam can't hear what is said, but the three soon move off, either not interested in chasing rats or thinking it is a waste of time. After a while, Gabriel taps Sam's foot and the two make their way quietly out of the garden, moving slowly and cautiously. Once they are far enough away to feel safe, they rise to a crouch to scurry off. They don't stand up until they are nearly a kilometer away and confident that no one is following them.

The following night, the three move to the barn Sam found.

"Cet endroit est un gachis!" Chloe says as she walks in to see the dirt and dust encrusted interior that is even visible in the moonlight filtering in through where the roof used to be.

"Oui, a mess it is," Sam says. "But it's home for now. Mais c'est chez moi pour l'instant."

"Merveilleux," she says, the disgust and sarcasm clear in her voice.

"Marvelous it is," Sam agrees grinning.

The trio settle in. Sam and Gabriel pull down the door Sam has marked to use for the raft. He wants it done now in case anyone comes along in the morning. The missing door would probably be written off to the advancing decay of the building. They then bed down for the night, although Chloe keeps complaining about the dirt and the dust, which, Sam must admit, is much worse than in the house.

In the morning, after they eat, Sam patrols around the area to see if anyone else is around. The land is reasonably flat and trees are scarce, so anyone approaching should be seen from quite a distance.

Setting Chloe to keep watch, Sam and Gabriel find six barrels that look reasonably sound. They array them on their sides in two rows, then put the barn door on top of them. Finally, they spend the rest of the morning and well into the afternoon using up most of the rope to lash the barrels onto the long sides of the door.

They are just about finished when Chloe comes rushing over. "Ils arrivent!"

"Who's coming? Qui vient?" Sam asks.

"Eux!" she says, panic in her voice.

"Them," Sam says a bit disgusted. "Not helpful."

He brushes past her and goes to the back of the barn where she has been standing watch. Walking toward them are eight armed Soldiers, and a Sergeant. "Shit."

Sam looks around at the raft. He realizes, if it is spotted, they will know something is up. Sam and the other two arrange the remaining eight barrels to shield the raft from a casual glance. He hopes the back wall is enough to shield the raft from that direction, and since the door was taken from the front, the side toward the beach, he is counting on them just walking by.

The fact that the soldiers are armed worries him. If it was just a work party, they shouldn't be. He then motions the other two to hide, giving Gabriel one of the machine guns. They take refuge in a dark corner, in what used to be a stall.

Sam takes a position in the remains of another stall. He lies prone near its front, where he has a good line of sight on the entrance, where the other half of the door is still standing and on the hole on the side. He readies his sound-suppressed semi-automatic rifle—if he has to fire he wants to keep the sound as low as possible. He can't see what the party coming toward them is doing, so he concentrates on trying to hear them.

What he hears frightens him: It is a work detail and the Sergeant is having them tear wood from the back wall. "Bloody sod," Sam mutters, wondering why the Soldiers are armed. He crawls to the edge of the raft. When he can see them, they will be able to see the raft. He readies the machine gun, just in case. Then settles in with his rifle, taking aim at the small but growing hole.

The light is beginning to fade, giving Sam hope the raft won't be seen, despite the gaping hole that now has been opened in the back wall—the east-facing wall. Then he sees one of the Soldiers stop working and peer inside. He can't hear what is being said, but he knows it's trouble by the gestures the woman is making. The Sergeant supervising the work comes over and looks inside. Sam can see the surprise followed quickly by anger on the man's face.

Sam shoots him in the head.

Blood spurts from the wound as the Sergeant falls backward, the look of anger frozen on his face. The members of the working party freeze for a moment, then five turn to run. Sam jumps to his feet and races to the hole, firing as he goes. The first down is the woman who found the hole. Then the two standing next to her. Sam takes careful aim at the runners, bringing all five down in quick succession. He steps through the hole and checks each one. He kills the two who aren't dead yet.

When he returns, Gabriel and Chloe are standing at the hole, staring at him in horror.

"I had to do it. If they lived, we would die. Je devais le fairee. S'ils vivaient, nous mourrions," he tells them. When he steps through the hole, he confronts both of them: "We have to leave. Now. Nous devons partir. En ce moment." Sam had wanted to wait until the Channel was calm. Waves of any size could wash them right off the raft. But now it was leave or die.

Chloe and Gabriel are just staring past him at the bodies lying in the grass.

"Move! Mouvement!" he orders, taking their arms and not too gently pulling them toward the raft. He and Gabriel manhandle the raft the forty-plus meters to the surf, while Chloe carries some of their food to load onto it. They don't need a lot of time to finish loading the raft. Sam then brings down some boards they can use for paddles. Not ideal but the only source of movement they have, outside of the tides and currents.

What he is counting on is being found by a patrol boat or a fishing trawler or washing up onto an island. Their chances are slim, but better than if they stay in France.

Chloe and Gabriel haven't said a word since the shooting, just silently doing what they are told. The three of them push the raft into the surf until they are waist deep. Then all three jump on board. Sam gives Gabriel a board and the two men start paddling away from shore. Sam hopes they can put enough distance between themselves and the beach before the bodies are found. Darkness, which is coming soon, and the outgoing tide are their allies.

CHAPTER THIRTY-EIGHT

You fucking bloody sod of an idiot," Sam mutters to himself as they madly paddle away from shore in the half-meter waves, not high enough to wash over the floor of the raft, but he has no confidence the sea will remain that way. He also doesn't know which way the currents will carry them or whether they can actually paddle across the Channel before being swept out into the Atlantic or back to the Continent.

This could easily be the suicide mission Gabriel fears.

"Keep going! Continuez!" Sam yells at Gabriel as the raft starts veering toward the right, the side where Gabriel is paddling. It's hard work with both men on their knees. Sam is tired but Gabriel is fading. The shout spurs him into renewed effort. Sam looks over his shoulder at the fading coast. He estimates they are just more than a kilometer away. And the tide or current, he is not sure which, is carrying them further. He tells Gabriel to take a break from paddling.

Then Sam scrambles to the middle, where Chloe sits. He gives her some rope, telling her to tie herself and the food and water bottles to the ropes holding the barrels to the raft. In answer to her quizzical look, he explains what could happen if the waves grow bigger. Then he takes some rope to Gabriel, telling him to tie himself to the raft. When he gets back to his side, he ties himself down.

Looking back at the shore, he can see they are still moving away.

Sam lies on his back, dozing in and out, listening to Gabriel and Chloe chatting quietly enough that he doesn't understand what they're saying. He has spent enough time watching the night sky that he has a good idea of which way they are going. They are drifting west, toward Sarah and the children.

For right now, that's enough.

The cold channel water washing over him wakes Sam with a start. He sits up to find the sea is running at one-meter waves, with occasionally bigger ones. The wind has picked up considerably. A bigger wave washes over the raft, pushing him toward the center, where Chloe and Gabriel are clinging to each other. There's no use trying to paddle. All they can do is hope the seas don't become rougher. The stars are gone, covered by clouds and a light cold rain starts falling, as if the cold sea water washing over the raft is not bad enough.

As he shivers, Sam wishes he had the ponchos they had on The Hope. He scoots over from the side of the raft closer to Gabriel and Chloe, who are holding tightly to each other. Sam has lost all sense of direction. For all he knows, they could be heading back to France or out into the Atlantic.

Looking up at the sky, he says, "Would it be too much to ask for to wash up in Britain?"

Fortunately, the storm isn't big or long lasting. As the winds and the sea die down, Sam can see the sky getting lighter in the east. So, at least now he has a general idea of which direction they need to go. He had secured the small boards they were using as paddles to the ropes binding the raft to the barrels.

After checking to make sure the raft is staying together, he gets Gabriel and Chloe paddling on one side while he takes the other. He doesn't really expect them to be able to make much if any headway, but the physical exercise will help them warm up. It would also help if they could get out of their soaked clothing, but they have nothing else to put on.

The sunlight bursts through and under the cloud cover, casting multicolored light all around them. Sam appreciates the beauty, but he would appreciate it more if they were in sight of Britain or rescue. He takes out the compass he always carries in his left pants pocket. It has a metal cover, so it is still dry, and therefore still works. In the growing light, he puts it on the raft's deck. As nearly as he can determine they are drifting generally to the southeast, which means they could miss England.

Chloe comes over, and looking down at him, asks what he is doing.

Sam looks up at her, "Getting depressed."

She looks quizzically at him, since he didn't say it in French.

Thinking better of what he said, he tells her, "It's a compass my wife gave me. C'est une boussole que ma femme m'a donnee." He pauses as he puts it away, "She said I would always find my way back to her with it. Elle a dit que je retrouverais toujours mon chemin vers elle avec."

"D'accord," Chloe says, nodding and smiling, a look of hope on her face.

Sam looks back at the compass. "I hope she's right."

The day passes with the three of them alternating between paddling and resting. The wind high up is pushing the cloud cover from the north. Their food is soggy from the storm, but it is all they have to eat. Chloe observes that a little salt water never hurt anyone. That night they all get as much rest as possible, still cold. Sam envies the other two who are cuddling for warmth, just like he and Sarah have done.

The third day and night pass much as the second one did, except the north wind picks up a bit, pushing the waves high enough to wash onto but not over the raft and sending clouds racing across the sky.

Day four dawns bright and clear. The clouds are gone. The sea is calm. Sam is losing hope. No sign of land. He has a growing fear that they will drift out into the Atlantic, lost forever.

"De quoi s'agit-il?" Chloe calls out, pointing to the southeast.

"What is what?" Sam answers as he stands up to look where she is pointing. Gabriel is also standing now.

In the distance is what appears to Sam to be a fishing trawler. The ship is steaming to the northwest and on its present course will not come nearer than about two kilometers. Not close enough to be seen easily. Sam takes off his shirt and starts to wave it. Seeing what he is doing, Gabriel and Chloe take off their shirts, waving them as well. To no effect that they can see. The ship passes without changing course or acknowledging their existence.

"C'est la vie," Chloe comments, almost sounding cheerful.

"Such is life, my ass," Sam mutters under his breath as he puts his shirt back on and sits dejectedly down. He sighs heavily.

"Peut-etre la prochaine fois," Gabriel says.

"I hope there is a next time. J'espere qu'il y aura une prochaine fois," Sam replies. Then he picks up the paddle and starts to work again. He refuses to give up. Seeing him working, Gabriel goes back to paddling. Chloe is standing in the middle of the raft, scanning the horizon.

The morning passes without them sighting another ship.

"Ecoute!" shouts Chloe, who has maintained her watch.

Sam immediately stops paddling and concentrates on finding the sound she has heard. There, off in the distance, is what sounds like a single-engine prop plane. It is coming in from the northwest. Sam opines that it must be flying low because the sound is growing but they still can't see it. Suddenly the plane with the wing over the body roars right above them, no more than 150 meters high. As it passes it starts to turn, making another pass. Then it climbs to about one thousand meters and begins to circle.

"We're going to be rescued! Nous allons etre secourus!" Sam shouts with joy.

Gabriel and Chloe grab each other and start dancing around, nearly tipping the raft over in their excitement.

About an hour and a half later, a fast patrol boat comes into view. It slows to a stop about ten meters from the raft, the fifty-caliber deck gun is pointed at them. Armed sailors stand ready with their weapons.

"Identify yourselves!" comes the order from someone using a bullhorn.

Cupping his hands, Sam yells back, "Leftenant Samuel Hope of the Royal Marines and two refugees!"

"Did you say Leftenant Samuel Hope?" comes the perplexed sounding reply.

"Yes. Leftenant Samuel Hope."

"Bloody hell," comes the comment from the man holding the bullhorn down but keying the mic. The other reaction is the boat slowly coming alongside, with weapons being put down. As it does, the small plane heads back east.

"Leftenant, everyone thought you were dead," says the Navy Lieutenant who holds out a hand to help pull him aboard.

"Not yet," Sam says as he goes aboard. "I'm still bloody alive and more than glad to see you lot."

"That took a lot of nerve to go to sea on that," the Lieutenant says as the sailors help Gabriel and Chloe aboard.

"They don't speak English," Sam says loudly enough for everyone to hear, before returning his attention to the Navy officer. "It wasn't nerve. It was desperation."

"I see," the Lieutenant says, holding out a hand. "By the by, I'm Leftenant Jack Balding."

"Leftenant Balding, it is a pleasure to meet you. Please thank whoever is flying that plane and whoever on the trawler called in our position."

"You can do that yourself after we land. In the meantime, why don't you and your companions go below. The quarters are cramped, but you can have some hot tea and biscuits. I regret I don't have a new uniform for you," he says, looking at the tatters Sam is wearing. Sam looks down at his clothes and shrugs. "In any case, I have to phone this in," Balding says.

Sam nods. "Thank you."

He motions to Gabriel and Chloe to follow him below. Once in the warmth of the cabin, which is four meters long and about two meters wide with padded benches running down each side with a narrow table in the middle, Sam sits on one side and the other two across from him while a crew member hands each one a blanket to help warm them. They feel the boat quickly gain speed, heel sharply to starboard, before straightening out and heading off at high speed.

They are soon sipping tea and munching contentedly on biscuits—and have become the object of curiosity as various crew members find reasons to look into or go into the cabin.

"Leftenant Hope!" Balding calls down into the cabin. "We'll be landing in about fifteen minutes."

Sam jerks awake at the call. He hadn't realized he had fallen asleep. He looks across the cabin to see Gabriel asleep sitting up with Chloe stretched out with her head on his lap, both wrapped in blankets.

"Hope!" Balding calls down again.

"Right," Sam responds as he stretches, pulling the blanket off. He crosses the cabin and gently shakes Gabriel's outstretched leg. When Gabriel looks at him sleepily, Sam tells him it's time to go. Gabriel nods, and as Sam heads for the weather deck, he hears him waking Chloe.

Sam blinks in the bright sunshine.

"A greeting party is waiting on the dock," Balding says.

"Do you know who?" Sam asks.

"Apparently medical for you and Army Intelligence for your friends," Balding replies. "Don't worry," he says, forestalling the objection Sam is about to make, "they will get proper medical care as well."

"Brilliant," Sam says.

When Chloe and Gabriel come on deck, he explains what is going on. They nod, but both look worried, despite his assurances.

As the port side of the patrol boat pulls up to the dock, a gangplank is quickly slid onto the deck. Sam leads his companions up onto the dock, where they are greeted by several Army officers.

"Leftenant Hope?" says the senior officer. "I am Major Mallory Bay-Mitchel of His Majesty's Royal Army Intelligence Corps. We will take charge of your companions. The Royal Marines will fetch you after you've been medically checked. Your family is being notified of your return."

"Major," Sam replies, relieved and excited Sarah knows he's alive, "this is Gabriel and Chloe. They do not know their surnames nor do they remember anything before the time they were caught up by The Enemy army they were forced to join."

"I see," Bay-Mitchel says, skepticism in his voice.

"Look, Major," Sam tells him, "I've been with these two for a month surviving in hostile territory. At any time, they could have alerted The Enemy to my presence. They risked their lives getting on a raft we built to cross the Channel."

"I see," the Major says, a bit less skeptical. "And how did you meet these two?"

Sam knows what he is about to say won't go over well but he won't lie. "They survived the battle we fought against them as my Troop withdrew to the coast. They were both injured and left for dead by The Enemy."

"And you trusted them?" incredulity in the Major's voice.

"Not at first, not completely, but years ago, I came out of the same kind of situation they were in. And I know most of those Soldiers don't want to be there. They are motivated by fear and brutality. Those are not exactly morale or loyalty builders."

"Yes, I see," the Major responds. "Well, we will take them in hand and see what we can make of it all. Goodbye and good luck, Leftenant."

"Thank you, sir," Sam says. "May I have a word with them?"

"Yes, of course," the Major says.

Sam goes to the pair and explains what is going on. He tells them to be honest and open with the people who will question them, and they will be alright. They thank him, then a French-speaking Army officer leads them off to two ambulances where medics are waiting for them.

"Leftenant Hope?" says a Royal Navy medical assistant who comes up to Sam as he watches the two leave.

"Yes?" Sam says, turning to the sound of the voice.

"If you'll come this way, please, sir," the medic says, leading Sam to another ambulance, where he is given a quick check and then asked to climb aboard. He sits on the stretcher comfortably as the medic climbs in, shuts the doors, then uses the intercom to let the driver know to go.

It's a short drive to the naval hospital where Sam is taken to an exam room. He exchanges his tattered uniform for a hospital gown and receives a complete physical. The doctor's verdict: He's undernourished and dehydrated but otherwise fit for service.

He thinks ruefully that he could have told them that as he dresses in the new uniform and boots he is provided. He looks around for his old uniform to get his rank pips but can't find it anywhere. He shrugs and decides his identification card will have to suffice for now.

As he walks out of the exam room looking for a ride home to Sarah and the children, he runs into Brigadier Cooper and Colonel Flemming. Sam quickly comes to attention.

"Sir. Ma'am," he says, coming to attention.

"At rest, Hope," Cooper says. "Oh, hell, man, let's go into this office," he says, indicating an office off the corridor with a sign "Dr. Haverly." "I've asked the good doctor to take a long lunch," Cooper says conspiratorially as he leads the other two into the office.

"Take a seat, Hope," he says as he walks around the desk in the small office with off-white walls, small filing cabinets, and medical degrees and family pictures adorning the wall, taking that chair. The Colonel takes one of the two chairs in front of the desk.

Sam remains standing. He comes to attention. "Sir," he says, "may I speak freely?"

"Of course," Cooper says, "but if it's about St. Anthony don't bother."

"But sir …" Sam starts to say but is cut off when the Brigadier holds up a hand.

"The Leftenant Colonel is no longer a member of this Corps," Cooper says, a harshness in his voice.

"Sir?" Sam asks, somewhat bewildered.

"He resigned in disgrace rather than face a court of inquiry," Flemming says, drawing Sam's attention. "We listened to the recorded radio transmissions, then read Banning's report and interviewed Navy officers who were present."

"It was all pretty damning," the Brigadier says. "St. Anthony very obviously left you and your Troop to die. We can't have officers who do that. If it weren't for your Company commander disobeying her orders, he would have succeeded."

"Yes, sir," Sam says, bitterly. "But he got off easy. He is responsible for the deaths of my Marines. I would like to dump the bloody sod into France and see how long he survives."

"Speaking of dying," Flemming says, ignoring Sam's outburst.

"Do sit down, Hope," Cooper interjects.

"Sir," Sam says, finally sitting down.

"Anyway," the Colonel goes on. "We were all convinced you were dead. None of us could see how you could survive."

"Well, not all of us," the Brigadier says.

Sam looks at him quizzically.

"We sent two officers to your home," Flemming says, laughing a little, "to inform your wife that you were presumed dead. They barely escaped with their lives."

"She let us know in no uncertain terms you were not dead and you would turn up eventually," Cooper adds. "Facing that certainty, we thought the better part of valor would be to, um, humor her and hold off any formal findings."

"It seems she was correct," Flemming says.

"Yes, ma'am," Sam says, looking down and smiling broadly. When he looks up, he says, "I would like to get to her as soon as possible."

"She is on her way here," Coopers says. "We sent a chopper to fetch her."

"Thank you, sir."

"Now, about your future," Cooper says.

"Sir?"

"The one thing we couldn't do was to leave your Troop without a leader. We found a good candidate whom your Colors is whipping into shape as we speak."

"Yes, ma'am. Exactly, how many of my Troop made it back?" Sam asks, tensing up and not being able to withhold the question any longer.

"Rest easy on that account," Flemming says. "You trained them well. Everyone made it back, including the dead. No one was left behind."

"Brilliant," Sam says, relaxing. "Thank you, ma'am."

"Don't thank me," she says. "Thank your Colors and the Marines you trained. They are outstanding."

"Thank you," Sam says, a bit sheepishly. "As for Colors Jones, she deserves recognition for her bravery and resourcefulness in facing overwhelming numbers of Enemy and getting her Marines to safety."

"Already taken care of," Flemming says. "She has been nominated for the Victoria Cross."

"She deserves it," Sam says.

"So have you," Flemming adds, a sly smile on her face.

Sam just looks embarrassed.

"And a number of your Marines have also been nominated for various lesser honors," she says.

"That's good, ma'am," Sam replies.

"Colors Jones and all of Six Troop wanted to be here," Flemming says, "but we denied that request on the grounds you needed time with your family."

"Yes, ma'am," Sam says.

"That nearly started a mutiny," Flemming says, smiling, "'til we promised them you would pay a visit when you returned from leave."

"That I will," Sam says, his voice revealing a certain pride.

"Now, as I was saying about your future," Cooper says, drawing Sam's attention. "On the way here, the Colonel and I had a discussion about what to do with you." The Brigadier smiles a bit at the worried look on Sam's face.

"By the by, Hope, you are out of uniform," the Colonel says.

"Ma'am?" he replies, his head jerking around to look at her, confused about what she is talking about.

"Here," she says handing him a small box.

"Ma'am," Sam says as he takes it. When he opens it, he sees Major's insignia inside. He looks at the two senior officers in confusion.

"We need officers who can get all of Four Two up to the level of Six Troop. The solution we came up with was to do something that is never done: We bumped Banning up to Leftenant Colonel. The current Executive Officer is good, but mostly good at paperwork. When we discovered you were still alive, we decided to transfer him to supply, where he will do an outstanding job. And since we bumped Banning two ranks, we decided to do the same with you, to Major. I am assuming you will have no problem working with her."

"No, sir," Sam says, still perplexed by what is going on. "I will happily serve with her."

"Excellent," Cooper says. "Now, take a month's leave. Get reacquainted with your family. The only interruption will be some intelligence types who will come around to debrief you."

"Yes, sir. Thank you, sir," Sam says, putting the Major's crowns insignia on.

"Your wife's helicopter should be landing anytime now," Flemming says, looking at her watch. "I think," she says looking at Cooper, "we should escort the Major to the helipad and then leave him for his reunion."

"Excellent idea," the Brigadier says. "The chopper will take you both back to base, where you will be driven home by a staff car. But before that, we have arranged a special steak dinner with an excellent bottle of wine for you in the officer's mess."

"Thank you, sir. That is very kind."

"No, Major, thank you. You have brought this Corps to the next level," he says. "For that, we owe you a debt of gratitude. Besides," he adds, a gleam in his eye, "a man who can survive what you did is a lucky charm the Corps has to hold onto."

"Shall we go?" Flemming asks before Sam has a chance to say anything else.

The trio leaves the room with Sam holding the door. They walk down the long hospital corridor, and out the doors that lead to the helipad.

"That wife of yours," the Colonel says as they come to a covered walkway where they wait for Sarah's helicopter, "is a force to be reckoned with. I understand she is in the Royal Engineers."

"Reserve," Sam says.

"We are lucky to have her on our side," she says, as both her and the Brigadier smile at Sam's correction.

"You don't know the half of it, ma'am," Sam says.

Before anyone can say anything else, the sound of a helicopter breaks in.

"I think we'll take our leave now," Cooper says. "Again, welcome back, Major," he says, holding out a hand which Sam shakes.

"Major," the Colonel says, "we look forward to your return to duty in a month."

"Yes, ma'am, I do, too," he says as he shakes the offered hand. The two senior officers then stroll off toward a second helipad where their helicopter waits, the Colonel half a step behind the Brigadier.

Sam watches them for a second before returning his attention to the approaching helicopter. As it lands, he trots toward it. Before the sliding door completely opens, Sarah comes flying out. She stops for a moment to orient herself. When she sees Sam coming toward her, she rushes to him without saying a word, flying into his arms, nearly knocking him over. They kiss passionately for several minutes.

Then she pushes herself away from him.

And slaps him hard across the face.

"What the bloody hell?" he says, taken by surprise, his hand going automatically to his left cheek. "What was that for?"

"Don't you ever scare me like that again! They told me you were dead!"

"Here I am," he says, stretching his arms out.

"You were gone for a month! A bloody, fucking month! Not a word about you! Your bloody Marines wanted to declare you dead! I was worried sick! The kids have been scarred for life!"

Sam reaches out and pulls her into his arms, holding tightly as she starts to cry. "I love you," he says gently, kissing the top of her head.

"I love you, too. But if you ever, ever do anything that bloody stupid again, I will kill you. Do you understand?" she says, pushing herself back but not out of his arms.

"I love you," he says. "How are the kids?"

Sarah just looks at him. Then kisses him. "They miss their father. Judy and Frank are planning a surprise for you."

"What kind of surprise?" he asks.

"You'll just have to wait to find out," she declares.

"Shall we go?" Sam says. "I could use a good meal. They have one waiting for us at base."

"I bet you could. You've lost a lot of weight," she says, moving to his side as they start to walk toward the helicopter, their arms wrapped around each other.

"I made Captain," Sarah says.

"That's nice," Sam replies, grinning. "I made Major."

"You what!?" she says, stopping and squaring off at him.

"See?" He points to the crown insignia.

"Is this your reward for almost getting killed and driving me to near insanity with worry?"

"Not exactly," he says. "You're beautiful, you know that?"

"Are you trying to change the subject?" Sarah demands.

"Guilty as charged. But you are beautiful. What do you say we go have dinner?"

"As long as I don't have to salute you."

"I would never dream of it," Sam says as they board the helicopter to go home.

Printed in the United States
by Baker & Taylor Publisher Services